PLC 10 author

BLACK FRIDAYS

BLACK FRIDAYS

MICHAEL SEARS

G. P. PUTNAM'S SONS   New York

G. P. PUTNAM'S SONS
Publishers Since 1838
Published by the Penguin Group
Penguin Group (USA) Inc., 375 Hudson Street, New York, New York 10014, USA • Penguin Group (Canada), 90 Eglinton Avenue East, Suite 700, Toronto, Ontario M4P 2Y3, Canada (a division of Pearson Penguin Canada Inc.) • Penguin Books Ltd, 80 Strand, London WC2R 0RL, England • Penguin Ireland, 25 St Stephen's Green, Dublin 2, Ireland (a division of Penguin Books Ltd) • Penguin Group (Australia), 250 Camberwell Road, Camberwell, Victoria 3124, Australia (a division of Pearson Australia Group Pty Ltd) • Penguin Books India Pvt Ltd, 11 Community Centre, Panchsheel Park, New Delhi–110 017, India • Penguin Group (NZ), 67 Apollo Drive, Rosedale, North Shore 0632, New Zealand (a division of Pearson New Zealand Ltd) • Penguin Books (South Africa) (Pty) Ltd, 24 Sturdee Avenue, Rosebank, Johannesburg 2196, South Africa

Penguin Books Ltd, Registered Offices: 80 Strand, London WC2R 0RL, England

Library of Congress Cataloging-in-Publication Data

Sears, Michael.
  Black Fridays / Michael Sears.
     p.   cm.
  ISBN 978-0-399-15866-7
  1. Finance—Corrupt practices—Fiction.   2. Ex-convicts—Fiction.   3. Self-actualization (Psychology)—Fiction.   4. Parents of autistic children—Fiction.
5. Wall Street (New York, N.Y.)—Fiction.   I. Title.
  PS3619.E2565B57   2012   2012011085
  813'.6—dc23

Printed in the United States of America
1 3 5 7 9 10 8 6 4 2

BOOK DESIGN BY NICOLE LAROCHE

This is a work of fiction. Names, characters, places, and incidents either are the product of the author's imagination or are used fictitiously, and any resemblance to actual persons, living or dead, businesses, companies, events, or locales is entirely coincidental.

While the author has made every effort to provide accurate telephone numbers and Internet addresses at the time of publication, neither the publisher nor the author assumes any responsibility for errors, or for changes that occur after publication. Further, the publisher does not have any control over and does not assume any responsibility for author or third-party websites or their content.

9/12

As ever, to Ruby

BLACK FRIDAYS

THE WOMAN SCREAMED for the first three seconds. Three seconds took her down only fourteen stories—she still had twenty-four to go. She fainted. Her arms and legs stopped flailing, her body went limp.

The few pedestrians on Maiden Lane, forced by circumstance to brave the baking midafternoon sidewalk on the hottest first day of summer in New York City history, all froze at the sound, like grown-up children playing a game of Statues.

The bicycle messenger, a recent veteran of two tours of duty in Afghanistan, was busy chaining his vehicle to the NO PARKING sign. When he heard the scream, he dove clear across the sidewalk, landing behind a large concrete planter.

Wind resistance on the woman's skirt, combined with the relative effects of gravity upon the denser mass of her head, spun her so that when she struck the roof of the idling Town Car at more than one hundred miles per hour, she hit headfirst—like a bullet. Her heart, unaware that the woman was now legally dead, continued to pump for another few seconds, spewing streams and geysers of blood out of various wounds and orifices.

Despite some doubts, the investigating team from NYPD found no reason not to treat the situation as a straightforward successful suicide—thereby both clearing a case and, with the same stroke of the pen, keeping the murder rate down below the previous year's, a measure of great importance to the mayor's Office of Tourism.

No one paid much attention to the shaky veteran who told anyone who would listen, "When you want to die, you don't scream like that."

**1**

I WAS THE FIRST alumnus from my MBA class to make managing director. I was also the first, as far as I know, to go to prison.

They make you skip breakfast the day they release you. It's not the final indignity, and far from the worst, but it's such a small thing, so petty, so unnecessary, that it just hammers home one last time, as though you needed another reminder, that in prison you are nothing. Nothing.

I followed the guards down a short corridor, through a final electrically controlled gate, and into a small room with a metal door, two molded plastic chairs, and a three-inch-thick plexiglass window on the far wall. Through the window I could see my father in the next room, showing his ID and signing his name with a pen that was chained to a clipboard. They probably had to throw the whole thing away whenever they ran out of ink.

He saw me staring at him and gave a short wave. He had been to visit only a month before, but he looked years older—grayer, paler, shorter. I imagined there were more pleasant things to do on a late-summer morning than pick up your only son from prison.

My sentence had ended at midnight; that's the way they do it. For two years, time had been marked by lights on, meals, lights off, with random violence the only relief from boredom. The guards—polite, almost respectful for the first time—had arrived a few minutes early. It didn't matter—I hadn't slept.

"Good luck, Jason." My cellmate was awake as well. He had another four months to go on a two-year stint. He was a car wash owner turned tax protester, who had believed some Internet nonsense about income taxes being unconstitutional. So for a pissy hundred grand or so, he had become a guest of the state, learning the hard realities behind constitutional law.

"Take care, Myron. Give me a call sometime."

I doubted he would. Neither of us would want to remember where we had met.

There were a few murmured good-byes from the darkened cells as the two guards walked me off the block. Otisville harbored a more congenial, less confrontational clientele than Ray Brook, where I had served the first eighteen months of my sentence. At Otisville, it was possible to play a game of cards that did not lead to getting jumped in the yard the next day. I hadn't exactly made friends there, just acknowledged fellow travelers.

Two years. Two years earlier, in the midst of a plea bargain meeting, I thought I had misheard. "Two years." For an accounting shuffle? Ridiculous. You pay a fine and move on. Time served. That's how these things end up. But the Feds wanted my scalp. It was a half-billion-dollar accounting shuffle, which had come close to bringing down a major investment bank. The stock had plummeted. Investors were outraged. The president's mother-in-law lost almost ten thousand dollars! The Feds needed someone to put in the stocks and get pelted with stones and rotten fruit. I was their man.

My first stop was Ray Brook. It's about a long home run from the Canadian border, high in the Adirondacks. It's the real deal. Somehow, when you do time for a white-collar crime, you think you're going to spend the days passing around *Barron's* and discussing your portfolio with like-minded individuals. Work out, grow a beard, and catch up on your reading. It wasn't like that.

Most of the habitués were there on drug charges, racketeering, or both. It was an eye-opening master class in Diverse Patterns of Confrontation in Modern Gang Culture. I barely passed. The macho posturing of Wall Street does nothing to prepare you for the moment when a three-hundred-pound Latino man with a dark purple scar running across his throat looks up at you from across the chow hall table and rasps out the words, "Hey, *baboso*. Give me your lunch."

I rapped twice on the table and offered him the bread and mashed potatoes. Truce.

In comparison, Otisville was cake. It's no country club, no matter what the *Wall Street Journal* implied when I was moved there, but the prisoners are all short-timers and less prone to violent solutions to minor disagreements; no one wants to risk getting his sentence extended when he's marking off the last days till he goes home. And the food was better.

"Mr. Stafford?"

I hadn't heard him come in. He was a clerk, not a guard. A little pudgy—baby-faced. Happy to have a ten-dollar-an-hour clerical job with full benefits—even if it was the night shift at the federal prison camp. I had a sudden flash of panic—they weren't going to let me leave. There was a mistake and this unlikely boob had been assigned the job of letting me know.

"I'm your release expediter. I have some forms to go over with you."

I sucked in a breath, let it out slowly, then did it again. My pulse rate slowed.

"Will this take long?" As though I had an appointment.

"I'll do what I can." His voice went up at the end of every sentence, making it a question. I didn't know how much of it I could take. "I know you have someone here to pick you up." He nodded toward the window. A guard was steering my father into an office and out of view. "I hope to get you out in no time at all."

He wanted to be nice. He wanted me to be nice, too. I thought of some of the other detainees he must have mustered out. It was a high-stress job. I decided to try to make it easy on him.

"What do you need from me?"

Forms. He explained them in bureaucratic detail. I signed them. He handed me a big padded envelope that held my clothes from the first day I entered the system. Underwear, jeans, and a polo shirt. I signed for them. I signed a release form that said I had been advised of the necessary procedures I would have to take in the event that I wished to protest any violations of my civil rights I may have suffered during my incarceration. I signed a separate form that absolved the Federal Government of all responsibility for any such violations committed by employees and a third form that said there hadn't been any such violations anyway. For such a brutal, stone-cold bureaucracy, the powers in charge were pretty sensitive about covering their asses.

"That's it, then. You can get changed now. I'll be back to get you in a while."

The clothes didn't fit. My waist and hips were slimmer, my chest and shoulders broader. At the ancient age of forty-four, for the first time in my life I had pecs.

"In a while" was still on prison time. No one was rushing to speed my way home. My father was still hidden in the office. I sat down, propped my feet on the other chair, and tried to imagine life on the outside.

No man ever admits to having been asleep, but I had dreamed. Dreams of pain and torture. My body was on a rack, and each click of the wheel shot sharp spasms along my spine.

"Fuck!" I staggered upright and stretched. I had felt much younger going into prison than I did coming out. Outside, two years is an episode—inside, an eternity.

My stomach was telling me it was six, maybe seven. I thought about the hamburger at the 21 Club. Actually, any hamburger would do. And a cold beer.

The door slammed back against the wall.

"Stafford!" It wasn't the clerk; it was a dull-eyed dayshift guard. That meant it was already after eight. "This way." He stepped back and waved me out ahead of him, looking me over as though he expected to find I'd stolen a chair and hidden it down my pants.

He swung the final door open and I felt like I was taking my first full breath in two years.

My father wrapped his arms around me and while I wanted to pull away, it just felt too good. I let him go on hugging me until he pulled away in damp-eyed embarrassment.

"Hey, son."

I looked him in the eye; I owed him that. "Hey, Pop." There was too much to say—regrets, recriminations, disappointments—so we did what we always did. We said none of it.

It was raining and windy. The tail end of summer was giving way to fall all too quickly. The chill came right through the light nylon jacket he had brought for me. The collar smelled of his Viceroy cigarettes, though he hadn't smoked in years—not since my mother died. The coat must have come from far back in his closet. We climbed into his near-classic Olds 88 and headed home.

"I thought you might want to spend a night or two with me. Until you can get the apartment together."

It was a bad jolt. Prison shrinks your brain. I had thought about food and sex and taking my son to a Yankees game and the smell of the ocean and what it would be like to sleep in a room with an unlocked door. But I'd managed to hide from all the big questions.

My marriage. Work. The nuts and bolts of basic survival. A future. All the things I hadn't thought about began screaming for attention. I felt a surge of claustrophobia.

"Thanks, Pop, but no," I finally managed. "Give me a day or two. I'll come over for dinner some night." I wasn't up to explaining that after two years of no privacy whatsoever, I just wanted to be alone. For at least one night.

"I've been aging a nice pair of prime steaks. Some fresh asparagus. A Caesar salad."

"Great. Sounds great. Friday night?" The prison stench was still in my nostrils, turning my stomach every time I inhaled. I tried breathing in through my mouth, out the nose. The smell faded.

He held back a sigh. "Friday night it is, then."

"Thanks for understanding," I said, though I knew he didn't.

"I brought you a black-and-white." He handed me a white paper bag. "From Carla's."

Carla's black-and-white cookies had been my unfailing cure for the blues. When I was ten. "Thanks, Pop. Maybe later." I was hungry enough, but I was afraid I'd start bawling if I ate it.

"So, I thought we'd take 84 over to Milford and then 206/15 down to 80. It's a pretty drive."

"Nyah. You want 17 to 87 and over the Tappan Zee," I said.

"I hate the Tappan Zee. How about the other way on 84—all the way to Brewster and then down the Hutch."

He was comforting me with his own obsessions. My father could debate four different ways of going down to the 7-Eleven for a pint of half-and-half on a Sunday morning. Around the time I started growing pubic hair, it started making me crazy. Then in college I found myself doing it. Later, I found it made my wife nuts. That's not fair. My wife was more than a bit nuts when I met her.

"You know what I want? I want to see New York from the GW Bridge."

"It's your day."

We rode in silence for a while.

"You want to play something on the radio? You go ahead." This was a hugely magnanimous gesture. Not only was he tone-deaf—he loved to repeat the old line "I only know two songs. One of them's 'Happy Birthday.' The other isn't"—but he also had, what I considered to be, an unhealthy addiction to sports talk radio.

"Thanks, Pop. I'm enjoying the quiet."

The quiet didn't last long.

"Have you heard from Angie at all?"

Angie was my wife. Ex-wife. We met at a Bear Stearns party at the Metropolitan Museum of Art. She and two hundred other models had been hired to circulate at the party and "add color." I'm sure that it was the first time she had ever been there. I was an adult version of a nerd, a Wall Street trader, and a multimillionaire. Angie was an underwear model with a charming, bubbling ditziness—think Myrna Loy in a D-cup—that disguised all clues to her dark side. She was also a monumental narcissist, a street fighter, and—I discovered later—a lush. But she was never boring. We were both asked to leave that party after Angie convinced me to go wading with her in the fountain at the Temple of Dendur. For the first time in eight years, I called in sick the next day. And I stayed in bed all day—her bed. We were married eight weeks later. I thought I knew what I was doing.

"Idiot!" Pop said, as an SUV swerved into our lane without signaling. The car behind us flashed its brights in protest.

I let him ask the question again.

"So, I was saying . . . heard from Angie?"

"Nothing," I finally answered. "Not since they left."

It had been almost eight months. At first she made regular once-a-month trips up to Ray Brook. I grew to resent how dependent I became upon those visits. They brought no pleasure—divorced men get no conjugal visits—only desire, pain, frustration, and anger.

But they were all I had. I never thought they must have been tough for her as well.

She sent me a card announcing the move. Gilt lettering on heavy linen stock, like a wedding invitation. "Angie and Jason Jr. are leaving New York and heading home. Y'all come see us sometime." Underneath was her mother's address in Beauville, Louisiana. There was no signature. I suppose I should have been gratified that I was on the distribution list.

"I'll go see her," I said. "We can straighten this all out." I might have believed it, too.

My father made that little noncommittal grunt that manages to express nonbelief in the most nonconfrontational manner and we lapsed back into silence.

The traffic was starting to get to me. They all drove too fast. The trucks and SUVs all looked impossibly large and the way everyone careened from lane to lane with only limited regard for human life—their own or anyone else's—gave me a headache. I put my head back and closed my eyes.

A few minutes later, I felt my father's hand cover mine. He gave a gentle squeeze.

"Keep the faith, bud. Fresh start. It's all going to work out."

I didn't tell him about the big trucks and the headache. I just squeezed his hand back. Maybe he was right.

"Thanks, Pop." I nodded off for a bit.

The rain tapered off, leaving a thick fog. I couldn't see shit from the GW Bridge. If New York City was throwing a party for my return, it was well hidden.

THE FIRST STEP had been just a mistake. An error. I put the wrong date on a trade ticket and the computer, rather than catching it and spitting it back to our clerk, assigned the trade to the following year.

In this case, changing the settlement date gave a huge boost to the plus column for the day's trading. The group had already had a very good day—we were up almost five million according to the computer. The fact that we should have been up only four and a quarter mil got lost in the euphoria.

Two days later, my clerk came to me with a report showing our unsettled trades. It was immediately apparent to me what had happened, and under normal conditions, I would have told him to make the corrections and shrugged off the restatement of our earnings.

But it was not a normal day. I had just had a major antler-crashing session with a bureaucrat from the risk management department who didn't understand why my group kept going over their intra-day risk limits. I tried to explain that it was an inevitable function of our business. Customers often ganged up, all leaning in the same direction at the same time. We waited for our moment and then struck—sometimes we made out, more often lately we had not. But forcing already stressed traders to keep watch over their shoulder while in the middle of the fray was a sure way to get them all to sit on their hands. They would manage themselves toward the risk goals rather than the profit goals. The bureaucrat thought that this was a good thing.

I took the report from the clerk and ran my eye down the page. The mistake stood out like a pink elephant in Antarctica. Why hadn't anyone else caught it?

I checked the computer—the trading desk was having a bad day. A brutal day. They were down close to three mil. If I authorized a correction on the trade, we would be down almost four. I made a second mistake.

"Why are you sticking this in my face, Joseph?" I only called him Joseph when I was pissed at him, otherwise he was Joe, or Joey if he had done something of special note.

He almost flinched. "It just needs your initials, Jason."

"Is there a question? Do you think there's something here I should see?"

He hesitated. "No, sir."

"Fine." I signed off with a scrawl and dismissed him.

I walked off the trading floor and hid in my office for the next hour, watching the red numbers accumulate on my monitor. The desk was getting crushed.

At that moment, I still had every intention of correcting that one trade just as soon as we had one good day. We had had many more good days than bad in the previous years. This was just a dry spell. A batting slump. The market had changed abruptly after the introduction of the euro. We would find a way to get our groove back. When we did, I would put through the correction.

That was the plan.

The next time was not a mistake. Once again, I had just walked out of a meeting. The little fucking bulldog from risk had taken his problem up the chain of command. I had to "explain" the "discrepancies" to a bunch of suits from the risk committee. The senior guys were all graybeards who hadn't traded anything since Nixon let the dollar float. They did not understand. Markets had moved on. They should all have been out playing golf rather than wasting my time.

The truly fucked-up thing was that they were not asking me about a three-quarter-million-dollar mistake—that I had signed off on twice—but about limits of risk exposure that my twelve traders collectively violated each and every day—and always had—but for only brief moments. An hour at most. Not a big deal. To me.

The seat-of-the-pants approach for risk had always worked well enough for me. You take on what your gut tells you is right. If it smells bad, get out. And don't risk more than you can make back in a day. So, if a young trader's best day ever was up a hundred grand, you don't let him take positions that might move against him by more than that in a day. This approach can sometimes be hard to quantify and the manager needs to keep an eye on what the troops are doing. Sometimes you have to cut somebody some slack, sometimes you have to rein a guy in, or even shut him down. Those are judgment calls. It used to be called managing.

But Wall Street fell in love with models. Not like Angie, these were black-box models that took in numbers, mashed and mangled them through t-statistics and standard deviations, and spit out other numbers. And since really smart guys were making the boxes—and, I must admit, sometimes creating huge profits with them—the rest of the world fell in step. This created a bureaucracy of monitors—typically not traders, but programmers and mathematicians—to watch over the rest of us and make sure we didn't do anything to upset their black boxes.

I had never agreed to those limits when they were introduced—they were forced on me by this same group of old mother hens, who imagined they were appeasing the regulators by strangling my ability to get business done. My boss understood. He knew what the game was about. But in that meeting he just kept his head down and let me take the flack.

They let us leave only when I had agreed to abide by another meaningless set of even stricter guidelines. Another victory for form over substance.

I buttonholed my boss in the elevator.

"Why did you leave me hanging out there, David? I kept waiting for you to come charging to the rescue, flags flying and bugles blaring."

He spoke quietly and urgently. "You just dodged a bullet, Jason. When the firm is doing well, producers run the show—you know that. But we're not. The suits are taking over. We've had a couple of tough quarters and the board is looking for someone to take the fall."

"Come on, man. You know it's just the cycle. We've been through it before. We'll be knocking 'em out of the park again soon enough."

"Right now, the board would be thrilled with some consistent singles. You run a good team, Jason. Everybody knows it. If you keep your head down and your group starts making a little money on a regular basis, you should be fine."

That stopped me. "And if not?"

"Those old farts will serve you up to the board as the sacrificial lamb, and there won't be a thing I can do about it."

I had just bought Angie another new toy—a sixty-thousand-dollar Cadillac Escalade. She wanted it to ferry her fashion-world friends out to the Montauk house. But Angie hated to drive. So did I. She would lose all interest in that huge machine by midsummer. Ironically, it was a belt-tightening gesture on her part; she would not have to hire a limo each time she wanted to show off the beach house. But buying her expensive presents—on a whim, to feed her acquisitive and mercurial spirit—was part of how I saw myself then. It was important to my self-image that I could go on being that guy for her. And for that I needed a job—a big job. With a big bonus.

"I hear you, David." I wasn't going to let a bunch of empty suits stop me. "Thanks for the heads-up. Don't worry. I'll make it work."

I checked in with the trading desk. We were down just under a mil for the day. That meant we were only up two for the month. It was a meager showing for a dozen experienced traders. I checked the trade blotter. They hadn't really been doing so badly, most of the trades were reasonably profitable. And one was not. It was a big trade with a Middle Eastern monetary authority. My trader had been caught wrong-footed and had dropped two mil before he could get right way round. I couldn't undo the trade, or the trades he had done to offset the mini-disaster, but I could shift the settlement date. Instead of settling three days in the future, it would settle 368 days in the future. The desk would be up a mil on the day—four for the month—and today's problem would become next year's problem. I could reverse it again the next time the desk had a big day. It would only be for a few days. Or a week. If anyone caught it in the meantime, I could bluff it out. If a junior clerk caught it, I'd tell him I was right and he was wrong. If anyone more senior asked, I would call it a mistake. Just like the previous one.

From the vantage point of a prison cell, it was ridiculously easy to see the flaws in my logic. By the time the markets became more favorable, and my group was hitting homers on a regular basis, I owed the future over fifty mil. There never seemed to be a right time to go back and make the corrections. A year later, it was two hundred and fifty. Every time I rolled out a settlement date, our profits ballooned. The board was thrilled. Dave made sure I was very well compensated. The graybeards and the suits backed off—reluctantly and only temporarily.

The day—five years ago—when Angie brought the Kid home from the hospital, I had three grand worth of flowers delivered to the apartment, and I stayed in the office until almost midnight. I was scrambling to offset a pair of trades that were finally due to settle. I waited until the Tokyo markets opened, executed enough large trades to offset the problem—baffling the Japanese traders—and plugged in the long settlements. Then I went home to meet my son.

Jason Jr. was not an easy baby. He never giggled or cooed; he screamed when he was held; he resisted making eye contact unless caught nose to nose, in which case he became almost feral, clawing and biting. Angie, having sacrificed her normal pillar of vodka, for the sake of this child, was a wreck. She cried whenever she was awake. Maybe not every woman should be a mother, but not every mother had to deal with a child like mine. Vodka bottles began showing up in the recycling bin. I started sleeping on the couch.

I was busy. I had to keep trading so that I could keep rolling settlement dates into the future and keep posting the phony profits. On the Kid's first birthday, I gave Angie a teardrop sapphire pendant the size of a robin's egg. That was the day that the hole I had dug hit five hundred million. Half a yard.

I stayed late every night reviewing old trades to watch for upcoming settlement dates. I gave up vacations because I was afraid of being found out if I were out of the office for more than a day or two at a time. I rarely had a pleasant word for anyone. I was sure a couple of my traders were starting to suspect me, which I ascribed to paranoia until the day I found one of them had "mistakenly" dated a trade 368 days in the future, generating a large, and false, profit of one million dollars. I told Joe to correct it and barricaded myself in my office for the rest of the day. That night, I found myself arguing with myself as I walked home—out loud. Very loud. I frightened a homeless man who scurried out of my way when he heard my two-sided tirade.

The only thing that made the grinding machine in my head stop for even a brief moment was sex. Angie provided. She was where I went for oblivion. We were barely even speaking by then. She was dealing with her own feelings of inadequacy and rejection by her own child and living on 80-proof fruit drinks. But most nights, before I headed for the couch, we met on Frette sheets for a brief and savage encounter—that left us further apart and more alone, but at least exhausted and able to sleep.

By the time David called me into his office for our last chat, I had been running the scam for three years. I knew it was over. The group had run up profits of over a billion dollars during that time—more than half of it was legit. I had even started reversing some of my "mistakes," covering the losses with our legitimate gains. David had been showing me off at board meetings; my traders were being treated like rock stars by the sales force; I made it onto the CEO's Christmas card list.

But the graybeards had, quite sensibly, determined that it was statistically impossible for our group to have performed that well, given our mandated risk parameters. They started the investigation— not because they had any inkling that I had been fudging the books to create profits, but because they thought I was cheating on their stupid risk levels. They called in the accountants to check. The green eyeshade guys found the fiddle, panicked, and notified the SEC.

Things began to get weird. I started getting requests for clarification of trades that had happened years ago. My clerk got "transferred" to the accounting department, though he seemed to spend all of his time in the eighth-floor conference room with a lot of guys in ill-fitting gray suits. It wasn't hard to read the smoke signals—I was surrounded.

I hired a lawyer and gave him a huge retainer. I put the Montauk house on the market. I set up the trust fund for the Kid. Angie and I set up the divorce scam to keep some of our assets from the Feds. Then I waited.

David finally called me in, late one Friday morning.

"I won't insult your intelligence by pretending you don't know why you're here. It's over, Jason."

There are times when a trader gets stuck in a losing trade and hangs on way too long waiting for it to get better. He loses all perspective. That trade is all he can focus on. It becomes an obsession. His whole body becomes involved. He finds himself walking stiffly, as though his nerves had turned to glass. Cramps and flatulence are typical symptoms. So are headaches, blurred vision, and sleeplessness.

At that point there is only one thing to do—take your lumps. Sell out the position causing you pain. Take the loss and move on. The first loss is always the easiest. A bad position never gets better, it just gets older.

Traders call this "puking" because the feelings before and after are just the same. For all the pain and discomfort in the moment before puking, there is as much relief, release, and resignation immediately after. Puking is always better than fighting it.

I felt the cold sweat on my back, the hot, green flush on my cheeks. I choked back the acid rising in my throat.

David was still talking. "The firm has agreed to provide you with legal counsel, but only insofar as our interests coincide."

In other words, "Get a lawyer."

"Thank you. That won't be necessary. I've already taken care of that." My head was clearing. The angry knot in my stomach that had me drinking Pepto-Bismol for lunch every day was loosening. The hundred-pound anvils that had been sitting on each shoulder for the past three years metamorphosed into butterflies and flew away. This was far from over, and the ulcer- and angina-inducing symptoms would return many times over the next year, as the Feds threatened and my legal team negotiated, but at that one moment I felt the elation of finally being caught.

"Jason, it's been a good run. We have all benefited from your group's performance. This is a tragedy. I'm sorry it has to end this way."

What was he saying? Of course everyone benefited. He had benefited even more than I, that being the reality of the Wall Street compensation pyramid. The chairman and CEO benefited. The bank had weathered the recent credit crisis by jettisoning the mortgage portfolio early, but it had been a close thing. Now they would have to restate earnings to the tune of half a billion dollars—the stock would take a hit. A big hit.

"I just wish you had come to me with this, Jason. I am sure we could have worked something out. A quiet resignation with an acceptable severance package. The restatement of earnings could have been spread over the next few years. We all thought there were avenues we could have pursued. We were prepared to work with you."

They knew. They fucking knew! I was sure my usual stony expression was shot, but I managed not to gasp like a fifth grader finding out about sex for the first time.

"How long?"

"Almost since the beginning." He shrugged and smiled. "It was a trying time here. It suited all of us to have one department that seemed to be doing well."

"I don't know whether to shit or go blind."

He stood up. The meeting was over.

"Everything we have discussed here is deniable, of course. I really am sorry, Jason. I enjoyed working with you."

I shook the proffered hand without thinking about it. I was shattered. I knew the poker warning: if you look around the table and can't identify the mark, then you're it.

The Feds knew. They offered me a six-month sentence at a low-security country club with views of the Allegheny foothills if I agreed to give up all I knew about the "conspiracy." I had nothing to give them. I went to Ray Brook for two years instead.

The press figured it out. Floyd Norris at the *Times* kept hammering away that upper management had to have known what was going on. The *Journal* and the *Financial Times* followed suit. The pressure built.

David was allowed to retire. They vested all of his deferred compensation and gave him a twenty-million-dollar check—in return for signing a stack of documents that prevented him from being able to testify about his years of working there. He and his second wife moved to the south of France. Last I heard, he was learning to windsurf.

Just before they transferred me from Ray Brook to the downstate facility, I saw an item on the news that the chairman of Case Securities was stepping down to spend more time with his family. In a surprise move, the board elected not to name the CEO to take his place. His resignation was expected as soon as a new chairman was announced. Each of their severance packages was rumored to be enough to buy a small country.

**2**

MY FATHER DROPPED ME OFF on Seventy-second Street and handed me the apartment keys.

"Oh, and don't forget this." He reached into the backseat and brought out my Valextra briefcase.

I had left it at his apartment in Queens the last night before entering the system.

The case contained the last remains of my previous life. My passport, the Breitling watch I had given to myself when I first made managing director, my platinum wedding band, now too loose to wear comfortably. And a half-dozen stacks of fifty-dollar bills, still in the bank wrappers. Enough to keep the wolves away until I could straighten things out with Angie.

"Thanks, Pop," I said, raising the bag in a nonchalant salute. "See you Friday."

He pulled away. I took a deep breath and began an inventory of the neighborhood.

Change is the constant of New York City geography. The mark of a true New Yorker is how many evolutionary generations of storefronts on your block you can remember.

The Papaya King was still there, but there was a big hole in the ground on the far corner where the fruit market had been. I looked up Amsterdam. The weird little store that sold perpetual motion machines and maps of the universe was gone, but somehow P&G's, the local dive bar, had survived. Over the park loomed the Apple

Bank, looking more like a prison than any of the institutions I had visited. And just beyond it, looking like some Austrian wedding cake on growth hormones, stood the Ansonia Hotel. Home.

I bought the apartment in 1999—the year of the euro. My group of traders had cleared over $200 million on the conversion and I took home my first ten-million-dollar bonus. I got used to that quickly. I loved everything about that apartment—the neighborhood, the history of the place, the architecture, the way it was a condo but still run like a residential hotel, the commute (twelve minutes to the office on the express train across the street), and the tax benefits.

Angie hated it. We met a few years after I moved in.

"But why? I just don't get the Upper West Side. Isn't it all gay?"

"Not really." No more than the Village or Gramercy Park or most of the rest of Manhattan below Ninety-sixth Street.

"But there's nothing up there. What is there to do?"

"There's the Beacon Theatre," where I'd been to see the Allman Brothers every March. And RatDog. And Phil Lesh and Friends. And the Dylan–Patti Smith show.

Angie raised one eyebrow. I wished I could do that back.

"All right," I tried. *"Lincoln Center." I didn't go there as often, but I had found it rarely failed to impress.*

"Oh, please." Angie managed to squeeze five syllables out of those two words. "And there's nowhere to eat."

"We just went to Cafe Luxembourg a month ago. It was your choice."

"That was years ago. I remember because Brooke Shields was at the next table and I thought she looked really young for being so old."

"That's because it was Liv Tyler—who is almost your age. And we weren't dating years ago."

"Really? You were so mean that night. You wouldn't let me order champers."

"I didn't let you order champagne because you were already sliding out of your chair from the martinis at the Monkey Bar."

Angie picked out our apartment downtown. I was too besotted to care. I would have bought her a planet just to hear her laugh.

I never sold the apartment uptown. After the move, I sublet it. But a few years later, when the tenants moved out, my mind was on other problems. The place had been empty ever since.

Room 811 was a one-bedroom—with alcove—in the southeast turret. It got tons of sunlight. And it was the only prime-numbered apartment on the floor. Some traders believe in luck, some in value, and some attach magical importance to various mathematical progressions. If a trader made money, I didn't care if he read chicken entrails at Santeria gatherings. I wasn't superstitious. Patterns of numbers revealed themselves to me without my bidding. I didn't *do* it; I couldn't help it.

The lock opened too smoothly. Someone had been in recently. Probably my father, airing the rooms for me. He would have driven in from Queens and taken care of it, never mentioning it or expecting thanks.

The apartment was smaller than I remembered and still palatial. I was used to sharing an eight-by-twelve space with bars in place of a fourth wall and nothing beyond a toothbrush to call my own. This space—where I could walk more than five paces in any direction without running into a wall—was all mine.

The three tall living room windows looked down on Broadway. New York—or my little slice of it, at least—was laid out below me. Not at some distance where all the human beings on the street were reduced to ants, but immediate, as though I could become just another man on the street, going about his business, never having been to prison. Never having had my fifteen minutes of infamy.

I turned back to the room and began an inventory.

The furnishings were all mine, but nothing felt right. It was like walking through a diorama of someplace I had once lived.

Dust covered everything. I would need to have the place cleaned.

Then I realized I couldn't afford to think that way anymore. I would need to buy a vacuum. A broom. A mop. I had no idea where to shop for those things, but that's one of the things I love about New York. You can always find anything you might ever want at any time of day. And have it delivered.

Three large cardboard boxes blocked the entrance to the bedroom. I opened the first, and recognized the faint scent of Bolt of Lightning. Angie. The box held linens, blankets, pillows, all still wrapped in Bloomingdale's bags. The sheets were Ralph Lauren—600-thread count—and all in various shades of lavender. Angie was incapable of giving a present that wasn't something she would rather have bought for herself. I would have bet she got herself a set as well.

The second box was full of clothes—suits, shirts, socks, etc.—all custom-fitted for a different man. A man two years younger. A man with the concave shoulders and nascent paunch of a desk-bound Wall Street executive. I doubted that I would ever fit that model again.

The last box touched me. It was my music. Hundreds of CDs—jazz, rock, funk, fusion, and a smattering of classical all mixed together in a plastic soup. It would take hours—days—to sort through and arrange my collection, but the fact that Angie had even thought to save it all for me was enough to generate a single shaft of hope.

She'd called four days after the party at the Met.

"Hey, cher. Are you busy?"

It was the middle of the trading day.

"Not at all," I said, all thoughts of the euro's two-cent plummet driven immediately from my mind. "Where are you? I thought you were working this week."

She had flown to the British Virgin Islands on Sunday.

"We're done. Paolo finished shooting this morning. Everyone is going home."

"That's great. Can I pick you up at the airport?"

"Well," she said, with a sly smile in her voice, "I have this huge room with a private pool outside where I can lie out all day with nothing on but my sunglasses."

"I see." Crashing disappointment met full-color mental images of her basking while she was talking to me. At that moment I wouldn't have known a British pound from a Thai baht.

"And it's all paid for through Friday and I was thinking it would be a shame to just up and leave!"

The magazine had booked Richard Branson's Necker Island resort for five days for the shoot. The annual swimsuit issue.

"Everyone else is leaving?"

"Almost. I'll be all alone on this whole island with no one to rub lotion on my back. There's this one little spot I just can't reach."

I was on a flight three hours later.

The dust and the memories were starting to get to me. It was hard to breathe. I needed to get out. I went for a beer.

I grew up living over a neighborhood bar. My father owned what he affectionately referred to as a "gin joint" in College Point. It was the kind of place that can be a gold mine or an albatross, depending on how much time and energy the boss puts into keeping an eye on things. We had a six-room railroad flat on the third floor, and my father's commute, seven days a week, fifty-two weeks a year, was up and down those stairs. I did my homework most nights, sitting on a barstool, sipping my Coke or ginger ale and listening to the locals tell each other tall tales. To me, that joint was just another room in our home.

The P&G wasn't exactly like that, but it may have been a close second. I hadn't been there since moving downtown.

The afternoon crowd hadn't changed. Vinny the Gambler nodded from his corner by the window, his *Racing Form* folded and cushioning his forearm, his short snifter of Rémy and his pack of Camels on the bar within reach. The two Johns, Ma and Pa, a respectable gay couple who had been holding up the far end of the bar for three or four decades, gave a polite "Hello" and went back to their crossword. There was a new bartender, Rollie, but otherwise the place was just the same. The bucolic, medieval-themed mural that covered the wall over the single bathroom in back was still there, permanently nicotine-stained to an old master's sepia finish. A third television had been added, but as all three showed the same horse race, it didn't affect the overall decor. The jukebox had not been updated—a mixed blessing, as it held, in my opinion, way too much mid-career Neil Diamond. I put a foot on the rail and sipped my Bud Light.

There was a copy of the *Post*—every New Yorker's guilty pleasure—lying on the bar. When I first started working on Wall Street, the head foreign exchange trader had a framed copy over his desk of the *Post*'s then most famous front page. "Headless Body in Topless Bar." The editors had worked hard to maintain that level of journalism.

The headline I was now looking at read "He Sleeps with the Fishes." There was a picture of a bloated corpse—facedown and therefore not in such bad taste as to cause lawsuits—wearing a torn and faded life jacket. Without the picture, the story would have been nothing more than a follow-up buried on page 12. A few weeks earlier, a junior trader from a Wall Street firm had fallen overboard in a storm on the Long Island Sound. His body had just been discovered thirty miles away by a pair of sport fishermen out for striped bass. I followed the story to page 3. There was a picture of a dismasted yacht, broken and leaning at an impossible angle, high on the rocks in a bay near Greenwich. The captain of the yacht had no comment. The guy's employer had no comment. His parents had no comment. Even his roommate had no comment. The Coast Guard had ruled it accidental and had no further comment. Still, the paper managed to instill the story with intrigue, cover-up, and the hint of scandal.

Two men walked in, arguing agreeably about something about the Grateful Dead. I eavesdropped until I found a way to insinuate myself into the conversation. I mentioned that I, too, had been to some of their shows. Immediate acceptance.

"So, you gonna buy me a drink or what?"

I looked around. The saddest-faced little man in the world stood at my side. Despite his age—somewhere well past Medicare eligibility—he looked like he was made out of rubber, like you could stretch him in any direction and when you let go he would zap back into the same compact form.

"How are you, Roger? Long time."

He was a late-afternoon regular. When the cocktail hour crowd began to arrive, he tended to take his glass of brandy and retire to one of the back booths. I had joined him there many a night before I met Angie.

We had met on the corner of Seventy-second Street. I was running late and just wanted to get to the subway. Blocking the sidewalk was a clown. A happy clown. With a big, cockeyed smile, like the letter J. He was trying to raise a wheeled trunk up over the curb. The trunk was as big as he was. It wasn't going too well.

"Give me a hand here, willya?"

I acted as though he must be speaking to someone else.

"Come on, big fella, don't be a hump. It's gonna hurt you to do a good deed?"

I stopped. I was in a hurry, but he was right. Besides, it would make a good story for the guys on the desk. I helped a clown.

Together we wrestled the trunk up onto the sidewalk.

"You're all right. Hey, I seen you. Over to the bar. Am I right or what?"

Was he one of the sad-eyed regulars who could be found propping up the bar at P&G's any hour of the day or night?

"I've never seen any clowns in there," I said.

He laughed. "Sure you have. The joint is full of 'em." He reached into a pocket. "Here, take my card. You never know, you might need a clown someday."

"JACQUES-EMO and WANDA the WANDAFUL—From Birthday Parties to Corporate Retreats—We'll make you smile."

"What does Wanda do?"

"It's my act," he said. "She's just there for color, know what I mean? I do some magic and she keeps the rubes from watching too closely."

I pocketed the card. "Nice to meet you, Jacques. I've got to run."

"It's Roger. Jacques is the name of the clown."

"I'll remember," I said.

I ordered us a round.

"So how ya been?" He did a little hop that got his butt up onto the barstool.

It could have been a loaded question—my picture had been plastered all over the news two years earlier—but maybe I was being paranoid. I didn't want to talk about where I had been the day before or the two years prior. But I trusted Roger. We'd been friends—bar friends. We didn't vacation together or even send cards at Christmas, but we had spent hours together talking about everything and nothing once upon a time.

"I've been away, Roger," I said, hoping he would hear my reluctance.

"I ain't talkin' about that," he said. "You moved downtown, what? Five years ago? Six? And you never once come uptown to see your old friend? You should be ashamed."

Something else to be ashamed of. Pile it on.

"I got married. Had a kid. Things got a little crazy with work for a while."

He was shaking his head. "I coulda read all that in the paper. I'm asking, how you been?"

I had no prospects of a career. Few friends. An ex-wife, who I may still have loved, but maybe not, and maybe I didn't really know what that meant anyway. And a son. Sick and a thousand miles away and being cared for by the alcoholic ex. It was all rather complicated.

"I've been better."

"I hear ya."

"And worse," I said.

"Ain't it always the way."

And something went click and I felt like I was home. The wolves were still outside, there was a hurricane brewing, and madmen ruled the world. But for the moment, a cold beer in a comfortable bar was pure bliss.

FRIDAY MORNING I MET with my parole officer. He had bad hair plugs and breath that stank of cigarettes and coffee. The man who would have absolute control over my life for the next three years didn't bother to hide his boredom. He rattled off all the restrictions I would have to live with—including no travel outside the five boroughs without his written permission and don't expect it anytime soon—then he gave me a list of ten employers who would hire ex-cons. I ran my eyes down the page. Terrific, I could become a bicycle messenger or a dishwasher. He saved his inspirational speech for last.

"Listen up." For the first time, he made eye contact. They were not kind eyes. "I wish you the best of luck and I hope you make it. Nobody wants to go back, but it happens. It happens often. I've got a good record with my clients and I'd like to keep it that way. But have no doubt—you screw up, you start missing meetings, you get caught hanging with the wrong people—I will file a request for an arrest warrant and never give it a second thought. Are we clear on that?"

For a moment, I felt the walls closing in and thought I smelled the stench of prison. "Understood," I managed to say.

Still, the interview marked my first official act as a free man. No one was coming to take me back today. I headed home. When I walked through the door of the Ansonia, a smiling man in uniform held it open for me. A second greeted me by name and held the elevator. I had gone from a prison to a palace, and I could luxuriate in the differences.

There was a broken spring in the seat of my leather easy chair, so that I had to shift my butt over sideways, but it was the best seat in the house. Looking out on the city, I had not a touch of the claustrophobia that had been haunting me since my release. The weather had turned again. It was stunningly hot, a late-September surprise, and the women on Broadway had responded with shorter skirts and skimpier tops. I considered investing in a pair of binoculars.

I pulled out my cell phone—my lifeline to this new world of freedom—and started picking up the pieces. My first call was to my father—to check in, give him the number, and assure him I would see him that night.

Then I made a flurry of calls to old colleagues. Though I was barred by court order from contacting anyone from my old firm, there were plenty of other acquaintances to be renewed. Networking, my parole officer had assured me, was the key to finding some kind of employment.

Some people would not take my call. I respected that. Others took it and shined me on. Cowards. But a few sounded genuinely glad to hear from me, wished me luck, and promised to keep an ear open for anything that might fit.

I was going to be a tough fit. Anything but advisory or consulting work in the securities industry was out of the question. I was also specifically prohibited from any position where I would be handling money—a basic requirement for just about any job on Wall Street.

I was avoiding making the one call that mattered.

A **LESSON LEARNED EARLY** in my trading career was "Always do the hard thing first." Once you get whatever it is out of the way, the rest feels easy and your brain functions better without the distraction. I was having a difficult time applying that discipline to my life.

I was afraid to make that call. Whatever Angie might have to say, the odds were good that it was going to hurt.

I finally dialed the number anyway.

Her mother answered on the third ring—not enough of a delay for me to chicken out and hang up—and as soon as she realized who was calling, her voice went into that shrill effusion that is often mistaken for southern charm. She was so pleased to hear from me. She had missed me. She was so sure that I was good for Angie and it was all so sad about my legal problems, but she was sure it would all be sorted out someday and those men who had hounded me—hounded me, she repeated—would have to accept that they were wrong. She was sure of it. And then she asked after my dear father. All of it came out without a pause, almost without a breath. It was like being smothered in butterflies and molasses.

"I was hoping to get to talk with Angie," I said.

That brought on another tornado of words. She was thrilled to have her little girl around, though she didn't get to see her as much as she wanted because her Evangeline was so busy, reconnecting with all of her old friends and such, and she could not understand why that girl had felt the need to rent herself a house down to Morgan City while there was plenty of room right there.

I fought my way through. "Could you give me her number down there?"

She couldn't. She would not give out Angie's number, or her address, without checking with her first.

"After you-all's difficulties, it just would not be right, I don't think," she whispered, as though speaking of our divorce in a normal tone of voice might have been offensive. "But I will pass on your good wishes and I'm sure she will get right back to you. I will be seeing her this weekend, of course, when she comes up to visit the boy. She comes up every weekend. Without fail. She is such a good mother to that boy."

Once a week.

"How is my son?"

"Well, he is a trial. A trial. But I believe the Lord has a plan for that boy, Jason."

That made me nervous.

I let her ring off with her usual "Bye-bye, now."

Sometimes doing the hard thing first turns out to be ripping the top off Pandora's box.

The last time Angie came to visit up at Ray Brook, she was drunk. Not falling down. Not even sloppy. Just a little louder than absolutely necessary. Louder and a lot more Bayou.

It was eleven o'clock in the morning and she was telling me about our son's latest round of doctors' examinations. Four years old and barely able to speak. He communicated in grunts, growls, and snatches of ads he picked up from the television. Angie made it sound like he wasn't trying. I lost it. I yelled at her. Told her to clean up her act. She owed it to the boy. Implicit, of course, was the accusation that all of the Kid's problems were in some way her fault.

She cried. Then she screamed. Then she called me a maggot and I laughed. I thought it was funny that in the midst of her histrionics she would think of the word "maggot." And that's when she hit me with the BIG news.

Autism. Our son had been slow to walk, slower to talk. He never goo-gooed or giggled like other babies. He practically flinched when anyone tried to look into his eyes. If I hadn't had my head screwed on backwards all that time, I might even have noticed.

When I first accepted that my illegal accounting scheme wasn't going to go on forever—and before I had felt the SEC closing in—I had set up the divorce scam. I signed over the Tribeca loft and half the assets to Angie and set up a small trust fund for the Kid. It worked. The Feds let me keep my old apartment uptown, but they took everything else. They left Angie alone. They never even looked her way.

The plan was that we would hook up again as soon as I got out. We'd move to some tax haven and live off the interest. Of course, the whole fantasy depended upon Angie coming through—being there when I came home. Like building a mansion on a cliff, the view may be great but the foundation is the key.

I made the assumption that my chances of getting my P.O. to approve me taking a trip to Louisiana were exactly zero. Therefore, he must never find out. I called and made my travel arrangements.

I was due at my father's house for dinner at six. There was nothing to do until then but drink coffee, stare out at Broadway, and write the script for what I was going to say to Angie.

My cell phone rang, giving me a sudden shock. It was the first time. So far every conversation I had had on the little device was one I had initiated.

"Jason Stafford."

"Mr. Stafford? This is Gwendolyn in Mr. Stockman's office. Are you available to speak with him?"

My mind was racing, trying to place the name. "I'm sorry. You're with . . . ?"

"Weld Securities." A medium-sized boutique firm, I remembered, with a middle-market focus. "Mr. Stockman is our Chief Financial Officer."

I remembered him. We had been introduced at a Federal Reserve meeting years ago. An accountant, not a trader. A lightweight, I thought, a bit out of his depth and working too hard to impress. He dressed too well and wore cologne to a business meeting. He was also on the short side, which I didn't hold against him, but judging by the lifts on his custom-made shoes, I had guessed it was an issue for him.

"Certainly. Do you have any idea why he wants to talk to me?"

"I'm sorry, sir. Mr. Stockman does not always confide in me. Will you hold, please?"

I held. I vowed to project confidence, aggressiveness, and strength. I felt desperate, unsure, and needy. Minutes dragged by, draining my strength.

Finally. "Jason? Thanks so much for waiting. I'm glad I could get you. How are you? How you holding up?"

So he knew my history. Now we could comfortably talk around it.

"I'm doing well. Glad to be enjoying this weather. Looking forward to being productive again, in some way."

"Excellent. Excellent. This might dovetail nicely for both of us. I was talking to an old friend of yours today—Al Pierce, over at your old shop."

Al Pierce had never been my friend. He had been CFO at Case Securities when I was there and it was discovered that the billion dollars in profits my group had run up over three years was, in fact, only a half-billion dollars, the rest being a function of my imagination and faking a few hundred trade tickets. Al hadn't caught it and was gobsmacked when the Feds showed up with the evidence. It was a mystery to me how he'd held on to his job. He had no reason to be doing me any favors.

"He suggested I should give you a call. We have a situation here and he thought you might be able to pilot us through these troubled waters."

"Listen, Mr. Stockman . . ."

"Bill, please."

"Okay. Bill. It's nice to be thought of, but I'm not sure what I can do for you. I am permanently barred from my old job, and I don't know whether Al mentioned it or not, but I'm under court order not to even speak to him."

There it was—as out in the open as I could make it. If he was still interested, that told me something. It told me he was scared.

"Yes, he made that clear. But this is an unusual situation, Jay . . ."

I hated it when people called me Jay. They always wanted something.

". . . and we would not be asking you to do anything that would jeopardize your legal standing."

There was a tell in Stockman's voice. He was smooth—a Wall Street senior bureaucrat, and they're the worst kind—but he didn't sound smooth. He sounded like somebody had his balls in a vise, but hadn't started squeezing. Yet. I wanted to hear more. But I didn't want him to know I wanted it.

"Bill, I'm sorry. I just got home. I have personal things I need to sort out. What's your timing on this?"

"We are prepared to make this worth your while."

"You have my full attention."

"A young trader at the firm was in an unfortunate accident this summer. There was no question at the time that it was an accident. A boating accident . . ."

"Is this the story that was in the news this week?" I interrupted.

"Ahh, you saw it." He sighed, as though the world would be a much better place if William Stockman controlled the flow of all information. "Yes, well, what was not mentioned by the press was that the SEC has indicated an interest in his trading reports. They have asked us to turn over all of his trade blotters, tickets, reports, notebooks, and market diary."

"What are they looking for?"

"I don't know. I have had our internal auditors and compliance officers go over everything and they've come up with nothing that would interest the regulators."

"But you're not comfortable with that?"

"The markets are in turmoil every day. I am focused on doing whatever it takes to guarantee the survival of this firm . . ."

I wondered if I was supposed to salute.

". . . and if there is anything there that could jeopardize my work, I want to know about it. Before I hand it over to the SEC."

I was interested. My parole officer would be happy. My bank account would be happy. And I wouldn't mind beating the Feds at their own game. A little bit of payback.

"I can clear up my issues and start a week Monday. Does that work for you?"

"I was hoping to get you started next week. There are bigger considerations. I doubt this will take more than a week or two, but I need it cleared up well before the SEC deadline."

My return ticket from New Orleans was for Wednesday, which would get me back a full two days before my next P.O. meeting.

"I might be able to swing it by Thursday."

"I'm prepared to offer you five thousand a day, plus expenses, if you can start this Monday."

Two weeks' work at five thousand a day. I was willing to bend for that kind of money.

"Make it Tuesday and you're done." I could find a late flight back on Monday.

"Done. Come to my office. I'll expect you at nine-thirty Tuesday morning. And thank you."

I did the Dirty Bird touchdown dance around the living room.

There was money coming in. I was on top of the world. Persuading Angie to return seemed possible. Anything was possible.

I went across the street and stopped at the oldest wine store in America to pick up something a little special to take to dinner at my Pop's. I ogled the Bordeaux—the seven-hundred-dollar Mouton Rothschild, the three-hundred-dollar Cos. I almost bought a ninety-dollar Barolo—it was on sale and I was sure it would be worth twice that in a year or two. Finally, I settled on a twenty-dollar California merlot. Times had changed.

**3**

STOCKMAN KEPT ME waiting outside his office for over an hour. I didn't sweat it. It was his dime and it felt like the first time I had sat down in days. Maybe he thought he was punishing me—I had kept him waiting a full week after my trip to Louisiana. The meeting with Angie had not gone as well as I'd hoped. I read through both the *Journal* and the *Financial Times* to reacclimatize myself to the world I was about to reenter. But my mind was elsewhere—on the rotting carcass of my marriage. I must have been scowling fiercely.

"Mr. Stafford?" Stockman's secretary was standing over me. "Are you all right?"

I looked up at her kind face. Gwendolyn could have been forty or sixty—it was impossible to tell. She radiated calm, patience, and sympathy. And efficiency. "Thank you. I'm fine. It's been an unusual week."

She smiled and I felt blessed. "We all have them." She cleared her throat. "Mr. Stockman will see you now," she said.

"Thanks." I stood up, shook off the memories, and prepared to go to work.

She ushered me into the great man's presence.

"Jay! Sorry to keep you waiting. Forgive me, it won't happen again. I had Volcker on the phone."

Paul Volcker. The most respected lion ever to have presided over the Federal Reserve. MISTER Volcker, to you, chump, I thought.

"We go back, you know."

I wouldn't know. I had never spoken to Paul Volcker in my life, but I doubted he and Stockman had any history more intimate than maybe having shared an elevator one day.

Bill Stockman still dressed too well. His hair was combed, blow-dried, and brushed into a mini-pompadour that added an inch to his height. His desk sat on a three-inch riser—it helped a little, but when he stood up he still knew he was short.

The view behind him was as good as it gets in New York. The harbor and the lower bay were laid out forty floors below. The Statue of Liberty. Ellis Island. The Verrazano Bridge. The rusting remains of the Brooklyn Navy Yard. To the east were Brooklyn, Queens, and the rest of Long Island, so flat that it was possible to imagine the curvature of the earth. To the west was New Jersey. Enough said.

"You've got a great view."

He looked over his shoulder, as though surprised that there was anything worth looking at there. "I'm afraid I never have much time for it."

He turned on a practiced, Broadway smile. "You're looking good, Jason."

I wasn't. I was older, grayer, my jacket was a size too small for my current build, and I was red-eyed from lack of sleep for the past week.

He looked good. Unchanged. He was probably waiting for me to say so. I didn't.

"So? Your affairs in order? Are you ready to get started?"

It was a pointed question—pointed, hooked, and barbed. I was a week late. He wanted no confidential explanations, he just wanted to remind me that I now owed him one.

I ceded the point. "Thank you for the extra time. I'm here. I'm ready to go."

"May you live in interesting times. Isn't that what the Chinese say? Let's hope this next tax package puts some sense back into the markets." The line sounded well practiced.

I didn't think it was the Chinese who had said that. I thought it was one of those made-up proverbs, too dependent upon irony to be real. But everyone on Wall Street trotted it out whenever the markets misbehaved. I'd used it myself, but not in the last decade or so.

"Thank you for coming in on this. Forgive me if I come right to the point. This project has the potential to derail some very high-level negotiations. This cannot be allowed to happen. I need to know that there is nothing to this investigation. And I need it yesterday."

If that was another slap for taking more than a week to get started, he was going to have to hit a lot harder before I took any notice.

"I'm here," I said again.

There were pictures on top of the cabinets in front of the window—Stockman with his wife and children. The wife was pretty, in that wholesome, blond, middle-American way. The two daughters looked like her clones—two or three years apart. But in every picture, the camera had been focused on Stockman. Either he was the center of the grouping, or the other three were staring at him in adoration. And all the shots were upper torso only, with Stockman's head showing just a millimeter or so higher than his wife's. He must have been standing on a box.

"Brian Sanders," he said, as though announcing the first slide at a PowerPoint presentation. "The Coast Guard has officially closed their investigation of the young man's death. It was an accident. Unfortunate."

I wasn't there to investigate a boating accident.

"Would I have known the guy?"

"I can't imagine. Sanders came to us from B-school. His family is from the Midwest somewhere. Kansas City?" He said it like I might not have heard of it. "Obviously, the family is still reeling. As are we. All of us. He was a good trader. Popular. Well liked. He would have had a long and prosperous career here."

"So you knew him?" I asked.

Stockman's eyebrows shot up. "Me? No. I'm just repeating what his cohorts have said. It seems he was an unusual young man."

If he was both well liked and a good trader, he must have been unusual. Most young traders had to start their careers with enough arrogance to last multiple lifetimes. The market burned it out of them quickly. If they learned to roll with it, they stuck around. What they lost in arrogance, they made up for in skepticism. I don't know that the trade-off made them any more attractive as human beings, but it did make them better at the job. What doesn't kill us makes us stronger. Nietzsche would have made a good trader.

"Why now? I mean with all that's going on in the markets, all the fallout from the mortgage mess—here we are four or five years down the road and they haven't come up with more than a handful of indictments—they've got insider trading running rampant, there's all this going on, so why has the SEC chosen this month to investigate some junior trader? Have they asked about any other traders?"

"No. Their letter of intent mentions no other traders."

He was hedging.

"But you suspect something," I said.

"My contact there—a friend, looking out for me—mentioned that this little fishing expedition of theirs could be expanded."

One rogue trader is rarely capable of bringing down a bank—Barings being a notable exception—but a conspiracy of traders could easily be a huge problem.

"On the phone you mentioned that compliance had already been over this. Why bring me in?"

"Our people found nothing that the SEC might care about. Sanders' managers were shocked to hear he's being investigated. But I need an outsider's eyes for confirmation."

Shocked? I doubted that. Traders whip around millions of dollars a day—sometimes billions—trying to make a minuscule profit on 60 percent of their trades. It is never a "shock" to find that someone cut some corners. Traders front-run customers—buying for their own book and running up the price before filling a customer order—though it's illegal. They fade their bids—backing away, dropping their price when the customer wants to sell—when they know the market hasn't moved. They often mismark their book—falsely pricing the securities they own—to smooth out the bad days. And a few brazenly trade on insider information. Sometimes it is surprising when they get caught, but never "shocking." Mostly it's just sad. But unless it was really egregious, these things were all handled internally. They don't usually draw the regulators' attention unless there is a lot more to it. I was interested to see what had the sharks homing in on this guy.

"You've got me. I'm hooked. Let's get to it. What currencies did this guy trade?"

"Ahhh," Stockman said in a long exhale. He raised one finger and shook it like he was doing the hokey pokey. "Mr. Sanders was in fixed income. Bonds. Eugene Barilla runs that department for us. You may have run into him at some point. He can fill you in on the details."

"Hold up. I don't know squat about bonds. I don't want to talk my way out of a paycheck here, but I don't know what I'll be able to do for you."

"It is not your product knowledge that will be of help to us. There are any number of ex–bond traders who could do that. It is your expertise in other matters that we want."

"Because I'm a crook." I wanted to see if he would squirm in the face of directness.

He did. "Uh, well. Many top IT security people began as teenage hackers."

It sounded like he must have rehearsed that line, too.

"That's a flattering comparison," I said. It wasn't, but I figured Stockman was much too full of himself to recognize irony.

"I have drawn up a check for the first week." He handed me a slim envelope. "Speak with Gwendolyn about getting yourself some space to work. She can set up your interviews as well."

I tried to appear casual about taking a twenty-five-thousand-dollar check and sliding it into my jacket pocket. It would appease my parole officer and replenish some of my rapidly disappearing funds. I planned on making sure the job lasted the full two weeks. I wanted that second check.

Stockman stood up, wiped his palm on the seam of his pants, and shook my hand. The three-inch riser under his desk helped, but he still had to look up to me.

GWEN PUNCHED IN the code on the security pad and the door swung open. The familiar hum of a trading floor in full mid-morning operation rolled over us. I became instantly hyper-aware— every sense heightened, sharpened. I felt smarter, younger, and fearless. Once upon a time, I had started every working day feeling like that.

She walked me along the football-field-length floor to the row of executive offices at the far end. The smell of money hung in the air. Money to be made or lost. It was not the slightly rancid odor of consumption or the hallucinogenic aroma of a casino; it was the clean, pure, fresh scent of money for its own sake, trading hands in the blink of an eye.

The air sizzled with the undercurrent of barely controlled panic. Blood in the water.

Voices called out.

"I've got a 29 bid for your size."

"We're firm at 30. We're working an order. He's not going to move."

"Listen up, people. We are a seller of dollars. At the market. Get me some bids."

"What kind of size?"

"Surprise me."

"Hey! Fannie Mae on the tape!"

"Fuck! What now?"

The New York Stock Exchange, the futures exchanges in Chicago, New York, and Singapore, every trading floor in every major bank in every money center in the world—they all spoke one language. They all had the same buzz. Money moving quickly. A drug that, once ingested, doesn't ever leave your system. I was hooked for life, and at that moment I was as close to it as I was ever going to be again in this lifetime.

Gwen knocked once on the door to a glass-enclosed office and ushered me in. She spoke both our names and retreated.

Eugene Barilla had been global sales manager for Fixed Income when I was back at Case. We had crossed paths occasionally. He was direct, sometimes brusque, but very much a team player. A facilitator. I had liked him.

He didn't like me. I found this out when he told me so.

"Jason Stafford? I don't like you." He stood up, looked me in the eye, and ignored my outstretched hand. "I don't like what you did. I think you got off easy. And right now I really don't like your getting paid for looking over my shoulder. Sanders was a good kid. I liked him. But if he was up to something ugly, I'll find it. I don't need you."

He had a big, square jaw that he jutted forward for emphasis when he spoke. It made a tempting target. I breathed out slowly and spoke softly.

"Nobody died."

"That's not the point."

"I did real time, Gene. I did it and got through it whole. I'm not proud of what I did, but I paid for it. Slate's clean."

"Do you have any idea how many people lost their jobs after that mess? The bank made major cutbacks—across the board—thanks to you. And how about the ones who lost their life savings when the stock took an eighty percent hit that week? Guys like you pretend it's some victimless crime, but it's not. You caused a lot of pain. Do you ever spend any time thinking about that?"

I had, but I wasn't going to share it with him. "And I lost everything and spent two years in federal prison. I try very hard not to look back. It's not always easy, but I try. Now, can we get down to business?"

"I told you. I don't have shit to say to you."

"Great. In the meantime, I'll be sitting in some conference room, surrounded by stacks of computer printouts of trades that I don't understand. It's not prison, but it still sucks. But I will still be collecting five grand a day and I will milk that teat as long as I can. Or, you can give me some help and get me out of here by the end of next week. Your call."

We glared at each other across the desk. He was a big, broad-shouldered man in his mid-fifties, more salt than pepper on top, but slim-hipped and still in good shape. I pegged him for an after-hours basketball player. He blinked first.

"Sit down."

I took it as an invitation rather than an order.

His office was almost homey. The furnishings were all a dark cherry, offset by a rich Middle Eastern carpet. On the wall behind his desk hung framed pieces from his collection of bonds that had never paid off: Confederate States of America bonds; Patagonia Economic Development Bonds from the late 1800's—backed by gold that was presumably still in the ground; and a Chinese Railway zero-coupon bond from the 1920's that was denominated in guilders. Financial innovation is as much recycling as it is invention.

"What do I need to do to get you out of my life soonest?" he asked.

"I need someone—maybe a junior trader, or a sharp trading assistant—to sit with me and go over the trading records. To tell me what I'm looking at. A translator. Next, I will want to talk with some of this guy's buddies. Other traders? Salesmen? Sometimes people see things they don't know they saw."

"And sometimes there was nothing to see."

I nodded. "I've got no axe on this. If there's nothing there, I will be happy to say so."

"All right. No problem. I'll set it up. What else?"

I had him cooperating. I leaned back in the chair and made myself comfortable.

"Tell me about Sanders."

Barilla let out a long breath. "I meant it. He was a good kid. I thought he was a straight arrow."

"Where'd you find him? He have a rabbi?" Wall Street had become much more inclusive over the twenty-some years I had been in the business, but nepotism was still the most common way to get a start.

"No. He came in through the training program. Usually, I don't have much use for MBAs unless they have some great quant credits—MIT or Chicago. They're all too eager to please. They do all right in sales. But Sanders stood out. He had balls and a bit of flash. And he could crunch numbers."

"What did he trade?"

"Bond basis. He was part of the proprietary trading group. There's a small group of senior traders who report directly to me. They trade whatever they want as long as they make money. They take a lot of risk, but they're the guys you want handling it. There's a few junior traders who sit with them. They get the experience of working with some real hitters, and every once in a while, maybe, generate an idea for something new."

"Sanders was one of them?"

He nodded. "It's a good team. Rich Wheeler heads it. You might remember Neil Wilkinson. He was also at Case—back in the Dark Ages."

I did remember Cornelius Wilkinson. He was a genius and a gentleman—a rare combination anywhere, but especially so on Wall Street.

"Back to the top," I said. "Bond basis?" I had a vague idea of what he was talking about.

"The short version? He traded U.S. Treasury notes and bonds and arbitraged them versus the futures market. You did something similar in currencies, right?"

"In foreign exchange, we call it trading to the date."

"Sharpies can buy in one market and sell in the other, for future delivery, and lock in some small profit. It's a relatively low-risk, low-return strategy that demands quick reflexes and extraordinary attention to detail."

"But all this is computer-generated these days, right? You don't need a trader—you want someone who's good at video games."

He laughed. "Maybe so, but there's enough moving parts that you're always trying to hit a moving target. So there's some art to it as well. Not everybody is suited to it."

I wouldn't have been. "Was Sanders?"

Barilla leaned back and looked at the ceiling for a minute before answering. "For two years, he was thoroughly adequate. He kept his risk levels low—spent his time learning the product cold. Then this winter he took off. The senior guys on the desk must have let him off the leash a bit. He went from racking up two or three mil a year to being up eighteen mil by end of second quarter. I'd say he figured it out."

"So where was he screwing up?"

He gave me another hard look. "I don't think he was screwing up. Remember? The Feds have it wrong, or they've got the wrong guy. Christ, years down the road and the whole mortgage market is still in disaster mode. So why is the SEC suddenly concerned over some junior guy who never made more than chump change?"

Exactly what I had said to Stockman.

"So why is Stockman so concerned?"

"Stockman is basically an empty suit with ambition—and he's up to something. There are so many rumors going around, you could write a book."

"It sounds like I'm going to have an easy few days. I'll be gone before you know I've been here."

"I already know you're here, and I don't like it."

KEN TOLAND WAS a sales manager. Not all sales managers are bottom-feeding lowlifes. It's a tough job—they are constantly putting out fires, stroking huge yet fragile egos, and adjudicating disputes. Salesmen ostensibly report to a sales manager, but that doesn't mean they listen to or respect him—or, in rare cases, her. Some are fair and hardworking—mentoring junior salespeople, keeping older war-horses productive, and willing to take a stand on what's right. Those guys burn out fast. The politicians are the ones who last—the two-fisted hand-shakers, the ass-kissers, the promise-breakers, the glory hounds, the self-promoters. The markets are tough, and the clueless get ground up and spit out—or they manage to keep dancing and become sales managers. A sure sign that Toland was coasting was that he was the only person available to take me to lunch in the middle of the trading day.

We rode uptown in a Town Car. Toland gave me nothing but platitudes. Sanders had been "the star of his training class" and "every department wanted him." As a trader, he was "very customer-friendly" and "kept the sales force happy." A Boy Scout.

Ben, the maître d' at Le Bernardin, didn't recognize me, or was too polite to let it show. That was fine with me. Anonymity suited me. Toland made a show of speaking French and requested a table "out of the traffic."

"May you live in interesting times," he said, raising his glass of Sancerre.

I grunted.

Toland didn't notice. He was busy playing with his wine, slurping and gargling like he'd learned to do in some expensive wine course he'd once taken.

It wasn't until we were done with the first courses—grilled bacalao salad for me and the marinated Kumamoto oysters for him—that I got any relevant information.

"Most of Sanders' business was done with only a handful of accounts—hedge funds and money managers. The salesmen generally let the clients speak directly to the traders on that kind of business. There's not much value-added from the sales side."

He had already finished the bottle of Sancerre. I was still nursing my first glass. He gestured for another.

Salespeople are the point men and women for the firm, and are responsible to their clients for the firm's best efforts on their behalf. Traders are responsible for the firm's interest. They set price and manage risk. Together they act as a counterbalance, like two kids on a seesaw. But Wall Street is a zero-sum game—there are always winners and losers—and the moments when the best interests of firm and client coincide are rare. Keeping the sales and trading functions separate allows human beings to concentrate on their own primary goals. Of course, everyone's primary goal is to make as much money in as short a period of time as possible, so the system is far from perfect. Some kid is always jumping off the bottom end of the seesaw.

"You don't run into compliance problems that way? Who resolves trade discrepancies? Who's responsible for suitability? All the 'He said, he said' issues."

"That is ultimately the salesman's responsibility, of course, but these are all big boys. Sophisticated, savvy, institutional accounts."

"So the client and the trader do some business and then they report it to the salesperson?"

"Essentially."

"What do they do when there's a fuckup?"

"As I said, these are all big boys. They resolve these issues themselves. Every once in a very long while, I am called in to settle a squabble."

Not too often, I thought, if you're out to three-hour lunches on a regular basis.

It sounded like a lot of trust and responsibility to be laid on a fairly junior trader. It also sounded like a breeding ground for shortcuts.

The main courses arrived and, for the next few minutes, my prison-starved senses were overwhelmed by the pan-roasted monkfish in red-wine brandy sauce. Toland was swilling his way through the second bottle of wine.

"If you like, we could set up a call with some of those clients. They might give you some insight on the kind of trading he was doing."

I gave a polite cough. "Sorry, that won't work. Direct contact with clients could get me in some serious trouble. I'll have to get what I can from your salespeople."

Toland seemed embarrassed at the gaffe—Stockman must have filled him in on my situation. He took another long swallow.

I kept eating.

"Yes, well," he finally mumbled. "I'll set that up for you first thing in the morning."

"No chance of getting started today?"

"Afraid not. I have a client meeting here uptown after lunch. You take the car. The driver will get you back to the office."

I thought he was going to have a tough time with a client meeting. The second bottle was down below the label. His face was flushed and his eyes a bit watery. In his condition, I would have been headed home to sleep it off.

We shook hands outside the restaurant like the best of friends.

I climbed into the back of the Town Car while he weaved off toward Broadway.

"This a regular thing with him?" I asked the driver.

"I'm his regular driver, sir," he said, which answered the question.

As we made the turn onto Broadway, I caught sight of Toland, head down and shoulders hunched, ducking into a doorway in the next block. Flash Dancers—one of New York's many gentlemen's clubs. Basically a titty bar with pretensions. I supposed he could have been meeting a client—business gets done over cocktails more often than over the phone—or he could just have been another bottom-feeding lowlife.

IT WAS AFTER THREE by the time I got back to Weld. Gwendolyn had arranged a tiny conference room for me to use as an office. It was smaller than my cell at Ray Brook. There was a small, round conference table, four chairs, and a credenza with a phone and a computer terminal. No window, no art on the walls, and no clock, though there was an overactive air-conditioning vent overhead that seemed to find me wherever I went in the room. I kept the door open, but the cold gray walls started squeezing in on me the minute I sat down. I kept my jacket on.

I wasn't there long enough to start screaming before a serious-looking young man arrived bearing two boxes of reports.

"Did Stockman's office send you?"

"No. Mr. Barilla said to help you."

I could tell he wasn't a trader—his tie was pulled up and tied, his sleeves were rolled down, and he neglected to swagger when he came in the room. "Are you the trading assistant? You worked for Brian Sanders?"

"Sometimes. They rotate us through the group."

"Who do you work for now?"

"I'm still unassigned. I cover for whoever is out." He projected eagerness rather than efficiency. He was young—just out of school, I judged. His dark brown hair was still a little too gelled for Wall Street, his shoes more fashionable than expensive.

"Perfect. You are now assigned to me. Sit down. Do you know who I am?"

"No. I guess you work for Mr. Stockman."

"Jason Stafford," I said. The name meant nothing to him. When I had last been famous, he was probably too busy beer-ponging to have seen my name in the press. "He's hired me to look into Sanders' trades. I report only to him."

"Okay." He seemed neither pleased nor displeased. Nor suspicious.

"What do you think about that?" I found that if I kept focused on him and the task, the walls tended to behave better and keep their distance.

He hesitated. "About what?"

"About somebody looking into Sanders' trades."

He shrugged. "He could be pretty secretive. I don't know. I guess we'll see."

"We will," I said. "What kind of secrets?"

He thought for a moment. There was an answer on the tip of his tongue, but he held on to it. When he finally spoke, I felt like I was getting the story he thought I wanted.

"Well, a lot of the traders like talking about what they're doing in the market. Like bragging, but not really. Brian never explained. Even if I asked him something straight out, he would give me half an answer at best."

"Anything else?" He was holding something back. "It's all going to come out. Sooner is a lot better than later."

"I guess it wasn't that much of a secret."

"What's that?"

"Brian was a serious hound. Always in pursuit mode. It got weird sometimes when he was trying to keep all the different girls straight."

Ah. That kind of hound. "A player."

"Exactly."

I had been a virgin when I graduated from high school—having been skipped ahead two years in elementary school and never quite recovered socially. My introduction into the mysteries of the flesh by Meagan Albright occurred during my second year at Cornell. She and I had several brief entanglements, the main purpose of which, as far as I could tell from her monologues on the subject, was to evoke jealousy in the heart of a fellow math major who had spurned her advances. And though I was far from celibate in the intervening years, before I was swept up into a state of slavering, perpetual concupiscence by Angie, I had never been a player.

The active pursuit of not just one woman at a time but many, with all the schedule and emotional juggling required, seemed more stressful than the job. I had the necessary calculating, predatory reserve, but I channeled it into my work, rather than sexual conquest. There was no jealousy on my part toward those who chose to live that way, no moral outrage, no need to defend the honor of womankind; it was more a sense of disbelief that anyone would devote themselves so single-mindedly to the pursuit of something so ephemeral.

Angie opened my eyes.

I looked at the young trading assistant. He seemed more than a bit in awe of Sanders and the games he played. I didn't hold it against him, but I wanted information.

"What kind of women? Co-workers? Clients?"

He shook his head. "Well, not co-workers anyway. But he would get maybe a dozen calls a day from girls. Girls he met at clubs or out at the beach or wherever." He must have interpreted my interest as shared esteem because he continued. "There were these two

Hilton-wannabes at Morgan who kept calling him and he managed to talk them into a three-way one weekend out at his share in Quogue."

This was getting me no closer to understanding Sanders' business or what he may have been up to, and the underlying air of hero worship was pissing me off.

"Save it. Let's get back to his trading. What's in the boxes?"

"Trade reports. P&L. Notebooks."

I nodded. "By tomorrow morning, I need to understand it all, *capisce*? I'm not a bond guy, so you are going to have to interpret for me."

"No problem," he said.

I wasn't sure. The SEC would bring a dozen accountants to wade through that much paper, and a time budget of "as long as it takes." I had an inexperienced trading assistant and two weeks.

"I want a list of all the clients Sanders did business with—and the salesmen assigned to them. Then go through every trade and flag anything that looks unusual—for any reason. Really big trades, different products, new accounts, you follow?"

"No problem. I can get most of it off the computer. I can match it up with the paper trail." He looked up at the blasting AC vent and tried shifting his chair a bit. It didn't help.

"Great. I can use a computer, but there's a lot I don't know or don't have time for. I'm going to be leaning on you a lot. Next, see if you can find any trades that look off the market. Let me see those as well."

"That's going to be trickier. I know what you want—trades where the price doesn't really line up with where the market was trading at the time, right? I just don't think I really know his product well enough."

"I thought you knew about bonds." Did I need somebody else?

"I do. But matching up prices that way could be a problem."

"Then leave it for now. We'll deal with it down the road." The walls were playing tricks on me, inching in on my peripheral vision, but moving back when I looked right at them. It was time for me to go. I was beginning to shiver—from the cold or my claustrophobia or both. I stood up. "I've got someone waiting for me. You and I will get started in the morning around eight-thirty. By tomorrow night I need to know everything you know—and more."

"No problem."

"And see what you can do about that goddamn vent."

"Will do, Mr. Stafford."

That made me realize. "By the way, what's your name?"

"Frederick Krebs. But everybody pretty much calls me Spud."

"As in potato?"

"It was a fraternity thing . . ." he began.

"Please," I stopped him. "Say no more."

I WENT HOME to meet my son. It was his first day of school and the nine hours I had spent at Weld was the longest time we had been apart all week. He was why I had kept Stockman waiting—getting him settled in New York had been a bigger priority for me than saving Weld Securities from zealous regulators.

Not that it had been easy.

A week before, I was dripping sweat outside the Louis Armstrong Airport in New Orleans, waiting for Enterprise to bring me my Dodge Charger—I had splurged the extra two dollars for the full-sized car. It was high hurricane season, with both temperature and humidity hovering around one hundred, yet the Saturday-morning flight had been almost sold out. *Laissez les bons temps rouler.*

Three hours later, I made the turn onto Hoptree Lane and pulled up into the white oyster-shell driveway of Mamma Oubre. The house sat back from the road with a single, ancient live oak dominating the front yard. Spanish moss hung motionless in the still, humid air. I had stopped for a quick lunch and the shrimp and Tabasco were grinding away in my gut—or maybe it was just my system telling me I was afraid of what I was going to find.

When I opened the car door, the humidity swept in, coating the windows with fog and nearly suffocating me. It was like trying to breathe soup. I wiped off my sunglasses and got out of the car. Mamma came out the front door and stood on the porch. I felt like she had been watching and waiting for me. She looked like she was having a hard time deciding whether to welcome me or warn me off.

The welcome won. In her part of the world, it almost always wins.

"Well, isn't this a nice surprise? Young Jason, all the way from New York City." Mamma was only five years older than I, but she had become a grandmother at forty-seven. I guessed I would be "Young Jason" for another twenty or thirty years.

"Is Angie here?"

Mamma made a slight frown—directness in approach was one step away from rudeness. But she must have forgiven me, either because she was still fond of me or because she recognized that most northerners suffered from the same affliction and it was sinful to think badly of the disabled.

"Come up here and give me a decent hello. I want a hug and a chaste kiss on the cheek before I let you interrogate me."

I did as I was told. We sat under a gently turning overhead fan, on a pair of very tired white wicker chairs, and drank sweet tea—a concoction that seems to lose all of its flavor north of the Mason-Dixon line. On Mamma's porch that day, it became an elixir. She asked after my father's health and made me promise to give him her best regards. She renewed her vow to visit New York one day—a vow I had long since learned to ignore. She reminded me that despite her minister's admonitions about the theater being sinful, she had a much more modern view and would one day dearly love to see a Broadway play.

"Maybe *Hairspray*. I did so love the movie."

I did my best to be charming—it was really all she wanted of me, as though a bit of pleasant conversation could keep reality at bay. I liked her, despite myself, and I was content to let the antediluvian moment play out. She had married in high school—to a bum whose sole contribution to family harmony was his departure. A year later, as his daughter began kindergarten, he had died in an oil-rig accident.

Insurance refused to pay because of the flask in his back pocket, and a blood alcohol level well over the state maximum for operating heavy machinery. Mamma raised two children—Angie and her brother, Tino—on a school cafeteria cook's salary. Her church, her children, and her spirit kept her going.

"I know you haven't come all this way just to keep me company. You may ask me about Angie now, but I really don't know how much I can tell you. She comes by on most weekends, and takes Jason for an hour or so, but she doesn't really stay to visit. She has some friends down to Morgan City, I know."

Amid this whirl of hints, misdirection, and polite stonewalling, one fact leaped out at me. I couldn't believe I hadn't realized it earlier.

"The Kid is here? Where? I want to see him."

The Kid. My son had resisted almost every other name we had called him. "Jason" was my name, it seemed, and it confused and angered him when we tried to call him that. "Junior" was worse. Angie had called him "Boo," but she called almost everyone that at one time or another. "Kid" stuck.

Mamma made a show of looking at her watch. "He's napping now, but I expect him to be up sometime soon. It's no good waking him. What they say about sleeping dogs? You know. The boy can be a terror when he gets woked."

"I want to see him. I won't wake him up, but I really need to see my boy." I had tried to keep the desperation out of my voice, but I was begging.

Mamma gave a sigh. "All right. But if you wake that boy, let it be on your head. You don't know what you are asking, young man."

The last room on the front of the house had a hook and eye holding the door shut. Mamma quietly flicked it open. I felt a flash of sudden fury. I wanted to know why my son was being locked in like some nasty pet, but Mamma raised a finger to her lips and shook her head. She pushed the door open slowly and I looked into the darkened room.

Despite the dark curtains and the lack of air-conditioning, the temperature in the room was almost pleasant. A fan hummed in one corner. The furniture was a bevy of hulking shapes in the dark, but the faint light from the hallway fell on the single bed against the far wall. On a wrinkled *Star Wars* sheet, the top sheet kicked off and bunched around his ankles, lay my son. Angie's son, because there was no denying her genetic influence. The Kid looked like a miniature replica of his mother. He was beautiful. The round baby face and wispy few strands of platinum hair that I remembered had been transmuted into a delicate, elfin-featured oval, framed by waves of strawberry blond. I wanted to rush in and wrap him in my arms and beg him to forgive me for ever being away from him. Mamma felt my urgency and laid a hand on my arm. She shook her head and pulled the door closed. I swallowed hard and nodded. I could wait.

I followed her back to the porch.

"Sit. Sit."

"Mamma, why in hell do you keep the boy locked in? What is that about?"

She winced at my profanity, but not the question. She took my hand. "Oh, Young Jason. Your boy hurts himself. He leaps, he jumps. He thinks he's flying. If I don't watch him every minute, he will break an arm, a leg, or his back."

Which all sounded to me like things every five-year-old boy tried. I gritted my teeth.

"And right now," she continued, "you're thinking it's normal. It's normal for little boys to do things like that, and I won't say you're wrong. Only you don't know your boy. What he does is not normal, and if I don't keep one hand on him all day, he will find some way to put himself in the hospital."

She sat holding my hand and staring into my eyes. The years

between us shrank. She wasn't just my mother-in-law, ex or not. She wanted me to know she was my friend and she understood. I took a breath and a sob escaped, surprising us both.

"All right, I'm okay. Thank you. You're right, I don't know. I've read some things—books and articles when I could get them, while I was away. But you're right. I don't know." I had read enough, knew enough, to know that I really didn't know anything. But I was sure I knew better than some. I would have to bide my time, watch, and decide what to do later.

"I say prayers for that boy every day," she said.

While I don't believe in the same deity, I recognize that prayers can perform miracles. Sometimes the only miracle is the comfort it gives to the one doing the praying—but that can be enough.

"I know. Thank you for that, Mamma."

"I pray for you and my daughter, too. I thought you could be so good for her. She can be wild, I know. She has some of her father in her that way. But I thought she could find some peace with you. You were so solid."

"It was a good front."

"I don't believe that. I don't know anything about money and all what you do, but I know you are not a bad man, Jason. And I still pray for you."

"Thank you." I didn't think I was a bad man either, but it was nice to hear someone else say so.

"But I don't hold with divorce. It is a sin. I never divorced my husband. What God has joined? Hmmhmm? I don't believe it was right. And it hurt Angie. She wouldn't let you see, but it hurt her bad. I could tell."

Angie and I had talked it over too many times for her not to have heard what I was saying. Maybe I hadn't heard what she had to say.

"I never meant to leave her—or have her leave me. The divorce was just a way of hanging on to some of our money. The Feds took almost everything that wasn't in her name. The plan was for her to wait and we could start again fresh. If she hadn't bolted, we would be up in New York waiting on a new marriage license right now."

"And so this divorce was just about the money?"

She understood. "Exactly. The court left me enough to pay my lawyers and I was lucky to get that."

She was shaking her head. "Young man, I don't know why you don't see. Money only makes it worse. The sin of greed does not excuse the sin of divorce."

I felt another sudden rush of anger. It was like trying to talk politics with a Libertarian. Practicality always falls to ideology.

"Mamma, can we agree on this? I am here and I want to make things right. I want me and Angie to be one again. I want us to have a life together and to try and raise our son—whatever his problems—together."

For the first time, she would not meet my eyes.

"I know how my little girl made money. She posed for those underwear ads wearing nothing but a spot of lace. I can tell you I was most pleased when she found you and stopped all that. And I know she loved living in the big city and playing at being a sophisticate. But that is not all she is. She is still just an upland Cajun girl who had the looks and got lucky. And when her man divorced her—over money, mind you—she took it very hard. My girl is hurting, Jason."

There was something else she wasn't saying, but at that point I still believed there was some way of rescuing the situation.

"I need to see her. I need to talk to her. I can't change what's past, but I can try to arrange things a bit better for the future."

Mamma looked off over the front yard with its sparse, burnt-brown grass and the line of white-painted rocks along the road. She was looking for something that left a long time ago.

"All right. I will call her. Tell her you're here. I will even, for all it's worth, tell her I think she should come here and talk with you."

"Thank you." There wasn't anything else to say.

"I'll fix up a room for you." She stood up heavily, looking twenty years older than her years. "The boy'll be up soon."

I decided to go for a short run to work out the kinks from traveling all day. I changed in the spare bedroom and briefly stuck my head in the door of the Kid's room. He had flipped to his other side, facing the wall. His skin was so fair that in that dark room he looked unreal—a ghost of a boy. I closed the door and stood there debating whether to replace the latch. Screw it, I decided. He was my kid and I wouldn't have him locked up in the dark, like in some nineteenth-century gothic novel. I left it undone and tiptoed down the stairs.

The late-afternoon heat and humidity were still deadly. I did one eight-minute mile and one twenty-minute stroll back toward the house, staying in the shadows of the live oaks and cedar elms.

Coming in the front door, I could hear Mamma in the kitchen, softly singing along with some preacher's choir on the radio. I started up the stairs.

There was a sudden scurry of footsteps from the landing above and I looked up in time to see the Kid at the top of the stairs. He was humming loudly, a single note, and hopping from one foot to the other, his arms outstretched.

"EeeeeeeeeEEEEEE." He got louder and louder. The scream was undoubtedly coming from a little five-year-old cherub, but it had a remarkably mechanical sound. It took a moment before I recognized it. It was a near-perfect rendition of the sound of a jet engine revving for takeoff.

And then he took off. The Kid threw himself off the landing and out into space, arms wide, like airplane wings. He didn't hang in the air. There was no magical moment when his belief in his ability to fly outdid the laws of physics. Time did not slow to an agonizing, portentous crawl. The Kid just fell. Like a rock.

I raised my hands and caught him, staggering back down a step or two with the sudden weight. The Kid laughed and wriggled, flapping his arms and occasionally kicking his feet, as though to go higher.

I backed carefully down the stairs, holding him as high as I could. Mamma appeared behind me and began yelling something about putting him down "right this minute," but I ignored her. I was busy remembering. Remembering holding this same boy as a baby, high overhead, just as I was doing now, and watching his often stony features break into a wild grin. We were doing it again. He was years older, and many pounds heavier, and his wriggling kicks were already tiring my upraised arms, but we were both in momentary heaven.

We traveled back through the front room, with me swooping him down over the couch and the armchair. He squealed and giggled. This was what two years away had robbed me of; this was what my mistake had cost me.

My arms were beginning to quiver and I brought the Kid down and landed him gently on the couch. He lay there for a moment, gasping and giggling. I collapsed beside him, shaking a cramp out of my arm. For an instant, I was happier than I had been in years.

And in that instant he looked into my eyes. They were his mother's eyes—the same ice-blue, pale and startling. I felt my throat choking up.

He looked away, leaped to his feet, and began dancing in front of me, arms uplifted as though demonstrating exactly what he wanted.

"No way, Kid. You almost did me in. I'm going to need a good long rest after that."

He danced faster and the look of happy expectation began to morph into a mask of anxiety. He began the keening "Eeee" of the jet.

"Nope. Not now. No, Kid. I'd love to, but if I tried right now I'd drop you." I stood up and reached for one of his flapping hands.

His distress increased exponentially. The noise from his throat was an ugly, angry growl. The color of his face went from pink to red to purple. His eyes lost their focus and began wandering erratically, seemingly disconnected from each other and the rest of his face.

I bent down and reached out to hold him. "Come on, Kid. It's okay. We can do this again later."

He turned and raced for the stairs. I raced after him. He was fast and had moves that Curtis Martin would have envied. We passed Mamma in the hallway—her arms were folded across her chest and her face glowered with suppressed anger. She didn't even try to stop him.

I got to the bottom of the stairs just as he reached the top. He turned and began the dance again.

"No! Kid, no!" I advanced up two steps. He was weeping and drooling, but there was still some crazed, desperate hope in his eyes. "No! Not now! Later!"

"Wanna get away!" he cried, and threw himself off a second time.

I got my hands up in time, but I wasn't centered to take the sudden weight. My arms still felt shaky. We both went down. I fell to the landing, the Kid cushioned by me, but still shaken. I was hurt. Nothing broken, I could tell, but I wasn't going to be out running for the next day or two.

The Kid sat up, wrapped his arms around my neck, and began pulling at me. "Jason, up! Jason, up!"

Mamma intervened before he pulled my head off.

"No! Stop that, boy! Jason is hurt. Now you leave him be."

"Sorry. Sorry. Sorry. Sorry." He couldn't stop. The word kept coming in a mechanical singsong, guaranteed to make any injured party want to wallop him.

"Enough." I pulled myself up. "Listen, Kid. I will take you flying again tomorrow. No more until tomorrow. Now, let me go."

He listened.

"Promise buttery spread?"

The question was clear. "Yes. I promise."

He stared at me as though trying to read the depth of my commitment. I let him. He came to a decision and nodded once. Then he jumped up and ran back up the stairs to his room.

I stood slowly, checking for cracks and bruises. Mamma glared at me.

"Are you going to be there to catch him every time?"

I thought about it. "I'm going to try."

She turned and walked back to the kitchen.

ANGIE FAILED TO SHOW that day or the next. I spent the time sitting on the front porch, watching my son place his collection of cars in perfect rows along the floor planks. The only breaks in the line were where a plank ended—no car was allowed to bridge the space between boards. I let him fly off the front steps a few times, until I realized that each successive repetition only increased his need for the next. More tantrums. More promises.

It wasn't until late Monday morning that she showed.

Angie's brother was cutting my hair. Tino had a high-end salon in Lafayette, which is not the same as a high-end salon in New York, but he managed to do well enough to vacation twice a year in San Francisco, Provincetown, London, or Berlin. He was called a "bachelor" by his family and clientele. We had always got on well despite our different backgrounds and proclivities.

"Do you have a plan yet for what you're going to do up here?" He gently tapped the top of my head with the scissors.

"No comb-overs, okay? I'm not going bald, I'm just letting a little more light in."

"You could wear it all a bit longer. With your height, it would be years before anyone would notice."

"I like to keep it simple."

He gave an exaggerated sigh and kept clipping.

The Kid had his cars. From inside, Mamma's kitchen radio was giving off the baritone sounds of one of her preachers—her Cajun Catholicism was ecumenical when it came to listening to the radio. The sermon was broken intermittently by commercials for local businesses and brands of products I had never seen offered at Zabar's: Zatarain's Wonderful Fish-Fri; Mello Joy brand coffee; and Boudreaux's Butt Paste.

It had rained briefly that morning, taking the humidity out of the air for a bit, and there was a slight breeze rattling the canebrake hedge. For the moment, the peaceful, slow pace of southern Louisiana wasn't making me nuts.

A brand-new metallic-silver Chevy Silverado Platinum pickup pulled into the driveway and rolled to a stop. It was tricked out with fog lamps, spotlights, roll bars, custom wheels, Yosemite Sam mud flaps, and a Confederate battle flag decal. Tino stopped cutting.

"Well, there goes the neighborhood," he said.

The sun was reflecting off the windshield and I couldn't see more than two vague shapes in the cab.

"That's Angie?"

"And her friend. You won't like him much."

"No?"

"No one does."

The passenger door opened and my heart stopped. I tried a brave smile and dismissed it. I couldn't carry it off. I let my face relax in my normal scowl.

She was wearing jeans, cowboy boots—Lucchese, if I knew my Angie—and a lavender tank top. I was draped in an old sheet and covered with hair clippings.

I was primordial putty. She was perfect. Wild and unpredictable, childish, willful, irresponsible. Perfect. She strode across the yard like it was the main runway at Fashion Week. She was a leopard—graceful, powerful, and very dangerous. She was a fawn—delicate, insecure, and exquisite. She was the devil's daughter for whom I would have sold my soul a thousand times over.

She stopped at the foot of the porch steps and looked up at me.

"Hey, *cher*. I heard you were here."

I had a hundred well-rehearsed opening lines. They all flew out of my head.

"You look great, Angie."

She shrugged. Looking good came a lot easier to her than anything else. She noticed the Kid for the first time.

"Antoine! Why'd you let my boy out of his room? He gets hurt real easy. You know that."

Tino didn't answer.

"I brought him down, Angie," I said. "I thought he needed some air. I've been enjoying his company."

She gave me a hard stare. When it didn't cause me to cringe in fear, she gave it up and shrugged.

"Thanks for the CDs. My music. That was kind of you."

For a moment she went completely blank. She had no idea what I was talking about. Then she shook her head. "I didn't know what else to do with them. The auction man said they weren't worth much." She took a long pull from her Evian bottle.

I had a co-dependent's flash—it wasn't water in that bottle.

Maybe this was going to be harder than I'd imagined.

She flashed one of her well-practiced smiles at her brother. "Tino? Be a dear, will you? Take my boy inside, so I can talk with Jason?"

Tino put the scissors and comb down on the table next to me and walked over to the Kid. He got down on his haunches and looked out into the yard.

"I was thinking of having some ice cream. You want some with me?"

"Mouthwatering French vanilla?" The Kid sounded exactly like the ad reader on Mamma's radio. He gave Tino a suspicious look from beneath furrowed brows. Vanilla was the only flavor he would eat.

"It's what we got."

The Kid got up and walked into the house. Tino followed.

Angie ignored the exchange, though she made it quite clear with attitude alone that she was just waiting for it to finish. The door had barely closed when she began her attack.

"You have no goddamn idea, Jason, what in hell I have been through while you've been gone."

"I wasn't 'gone,' Angie. I was 'away.' There's a difference."

"That boy is strange, Jason. You don't know. I can't hug him. He won't look at me. He cries or screams or throws a goddamn fit if I look at him."

"He's sick, Angie. We knew that."

"Well, I didn't know that. I didn't know what it meant. You weren't there, you sonofabitch." She leaned in to me and I could feel flecks of her saliva hit my cheeks as she spoke. I wanted more.

"Angie. I couldn't be there. I wanted to, but I couldn't. I'm sorry. We talked about this. We talked about how it was going to be. What happened?"

"That boy, Jason. That's what happened. You have no idea, no goddamn idea, what it is like to live with that boy day after god-damn day."

I leaned forward. I wanted her to know that I knew. That I cared.

"Angie, listen to me. I read every book I could find on autism while I was up there. I had Pop send me books, magazines, anything that would help me understand what you were going through. You're right, I don't know what it means every day, day after day, but I tried, Angie. I have tried to understand."

She slumped into the other chair. She looked soft. I wanted to stroke her hair and tell her I could fix everything. I had read the books. I could do this. All she had to do was come along with me.

But Angie was rarely soft when she looked it. Vulnerable was just another pose.

"You think you know because you read a book?" She made the last words sound particularly vile. "So you know what HFA means, or maybe you think your boy is some genius savant with Asperger's? Well, what's your opinion on chelation therapy? Did we do this to our baby by getting him inoculated against measles? Are you going to tell him he can't have his ice cream because he has to cut back on caseins? Have you ever tasted gluten-free bread? How many times have you sat in some doctor's office, waiting and praying, while they did their tests and then they come when it's all over and the boy is all quiet and frozen and shrunk down and you wonder just what the fuck they were doing to your child in there? And you listen to another Harvard graduate tell you he doesn't know what it is. He doesn't know! Could be Asperger's. Autism. Pidnose. That's my favorite. Do you know what Pidnose is, Jason?"

I shook my head, as much in answer as in response to the whole assault.

"PDD. It means Pervasive Developmental Disorder. That right there tells me nothing. Zip! And the 'nose' part? NOS. It stands for Not Otherwise Specified. In plain English that even a currency trader or a model could understand, it means DUH! As in 'Duh, I don't know'!"

I tried to take her hand as I spoke.

"Angie, I just want the chance to try to understand. I can do this."

She pulled away and folded her arms. She spoke to the floor. "And you weren't there the night I found him gushing blood from banging his head on the coffee table—again—because, despite the fact that he was almost three years old, he hadn't quite learned how to walk yet. And I rushed him up to Saint Vincent's—the boy humming away like there was nothing the matter at all, like he didn't even feel it—and while they're stitching him, the nurse calls me into another room. And you know what happened then?"

I could imagine, but I didn't think I was supposed to answer.

"There's two detectives. NYPD. Goddamn Briscoe and Green have nothing better to do than grill me about hitting my boy. And there's this fatass bitch from Social Services in the corner smiling like she can't wait to pounce. They made me take a breathalyzer!" She took another swig from the Evian bottle.

At another time, it might have been funny.

"I'm sorry," I said. "It must have been embarrassing."

Angie burst out laughing, but there was still nothing funny.

"Embarrassed? No. Maybe I was embarrassed when I had to call the pediatrician in the middle of the night and ask him to explain to the police that my boy falls down a lot. That's a tough one to explain to the answering service. Police and pediatrician aren't supposed to go together. No, Jason, I wasn't embarrassed. I was pissed. I was really, really mad because you weren't there to help me. You weren't there to help our son."

I wasn't there because I was in prison. That fact was going to stick in my craw for quite some time.

"I'm here, Angie. And I'm ready to do my part. We can do this. We can't just dump the Kid on your mother. It's not right."

"Oh, please, Jason." She looked at me as though I was trying to sell her a bridge. "There's nothing right. It is all wrong, and the rest is just us tryin' to make our way."

I tried again. My castle on the cliff was sliding down into the ocean. "Angie. Come with me. We can make it right. There's money enough for the three of us to be just fine. We'll get help for the Kid."

"What in hell is the matter with you, Jason? Did prison make you stupid? You left me, you sonofabitch. You left me with that boy and he goddamn well hates his mother. Do you know that? What little boy hates his mamma? Like I'm some kind of monster. The boy doesn't care whether I am alive or dead."

"So you leave him locked in a closet?"

"That's his bedroom. And Mamma takes care of him."

"Screw that, Angie! I'll take him. I'll take care of him." The words came flying out of their own volition. I would swear I had never had that thought before in my life.

She gave me the look again. "Bullshit, mister. I'm not buying that. The boy will stay with Mamma."

"No chance. I'll fight you, Angie." I wasn't thinking, but something in my gut drove me on.

We were both standing, glaring at each other.

"Fine. Take the boy. Let's see how long it takes you to dump him on your father."

The door of the pickup truck slammed. I looked over. One of the bad guys from a *Walking Tall* movie was headed in our direction.

"Who's your chauffeur?"

Angie didn't answer for a second. Then she hit me with it.

"That's my husband. We got married this morning."

The pain shot through my head like a cold steel spike—it continued down and split my heart.

"Aw, shit, Angie. This is all fucked up. What are you telling me?"

"What am I telling you? What the fuck am I telling you?" She was screaming. "I am telling you that you ran out on me, Jason. Me and that boy. And I did what I needed to do."

"Angie." I tried reason. "We had a plan."

"*Your* plan! All about the money. If the bills are all getting paid, then everything else can just go hang, right?" The tears started flowing, but she was still spitting venom. "Well, I have the money now and I am moving on. I'm taking care of Angie."

There I was, listening to the end of my marriage being forced down my throat, and all I could think about was that being this close to the woman after years apart was giving me a woody that would soon need attention. Our best fucks always followed our best fights.

I looked up. There was a Cajun cowboy standing over me. He was ten years younger, a good four inches taller, with a body sculpted by hard work and immense vanity—and he had all his hair. He was wearing a skintight white T-shirt, black jeans, and boots. Black cowboy boots with little shiny metal stars across the arch and up the sides. I couldn't see his face because the sun was casting a rainbow aura around his head. I could see his belt buckle. It read BORN TO KICK ASS.

"Whaddup, dawg?" I tried a bit of my prison-learned Ebonics on him. At that point I was so full of anger and hormones, it would have taken a dozen of him for me to back down.

He slapped me. I fell back into the chair. I still had the damn sheet wrapped around my neck and couldn't even get my hands up to defend myself.

"Get up, old man. Get up, so I can knock your ass back down." He leaned in and spoke right in my ear. "You made Angie cry, so I will fuckin' hurt you. You will beg me to kill you before I'm done. You got that, old man?"

He put one very large hand on my throat, squeezing just enough to hold me steady, and began backhand slapping me. I was gasping like a landed trout. I tasted blood.

One of the first lessons I learned while in the care of our government was this: real hard guys don't tell you all about it first—only the bullies do that. But if you don't take the bullies down right away, they can hurt you almost as much as the quiet psychos.

I reached out from underneath the sheet and grabbed Tino's scissors. Then I stabbed them into Bubba's leg. Straight in. I was careful. I didn't want to hit an artery.

He took two deep breaths like he was sucking his soul back into his body, then his eyes rolled back and went white and he fell back off the porch. He landed in the front yard like a sack of feed.

Angie dropped her Evian and started screaming. No words, just sounds, but I wasn't paying attention. The cowboy came to and looked up at me with surprise. I would have bet it was the first time he had ever felt real pain.

"You better get that looked at," I told him.

"You killed him!" Angie had found her voice again, but she was two steps behind.

"He goddamn fainted, Angie. Get him a band-aid or something." I looked around. Tino and Mamma had run out onto the porch. "Sorry about your scissors, Tino."

He looked over the situation and gave me a small smile. "No problem, Jason. They'll clean up just fine. It was a good cause."

I looked for the Kid. He was still inside. I realized a bit belatedly that I should have been thinking of him all along.

Tino bent down and helped Angie get her Galahad to his feet. "Come on, sister. This boy needs a doctor." They hobbled off to the Silverado and seconds later peeled out of the driveway, Tino at the wheel.

"I'm sorry about this, Mamma." I pulled off the sheet and shook out the remaining hairs. "I should go."

"Blood is blood, Jason. I got to stand by my girl, you know that."

"I know. I understand." I did. I was somewhere way out in Wonderland or Oz or Middle Earth for all I knew, but rules still applied. It was time for me to get back to New York City. "I'll pack and be gone in no time. I'm sorry."

The Kid walked out to the porch working on a mini vanilla ice cream cone. He sat down and began driving his cars into a tightly packed square. Mamma stood watching him, her shoulders stooped with too many years of fighting too many demons. I have never seen eyes so sad, so pained.

I made a decision. I have reconsidered it many times, but I always come up with the same conclusion. I have never regretted it.

"He'll come with me, Mamma. I'm taking my son. Back to New York. I'll get him help." I didn't know why I was saying all those things. Part of me didn't know it was me talking. But part did.

She looked at me for a long time.

"You don't know what you're saying, son. Angie is right. You don't know."

"Maybe I'm ready to start learning, Mamma. Angie can't do it, we both know that. I don't know if I can, but I want to try. That's the best shot he's going to get right now."

And maybe I just couldn't leave without taking a piece of Angie with me.

I packed my things quickly, put together a bag for the Kid, and was back down on the porch in minutes.

"Hey, Kid. Let's pack up your cars. You and me are going on a trip."

"Can't." He wasn't angry or stubborn, he was just making it clear to me that he couldn't go.

I gave a big sigh of impatience. "All right. Tell me why you can't go."

He gave a big sigh back. "Bath," he explained, as though to an idiot.

It had been years since I had witnessed the Kid in one of his monumental breakdowns—where, in total terror, he would fight like a cornered bobcat, screaming, scratching, and biting to get his way, even if the thing in question seemed as inconsequential as whether or not he got to clean the ice cream off himself before going on a trip.

I bent to pick him up.

"Later for the bath, my man. We have to hit the road."

He howled and gnashed his teeth. It was feral. I pulled back.

Something told me that going back to prison for stabbing a man while violating parole was the easier path. I hoped Tino and Angie would keep the police off my back long enough for a short bath.

"I'll run the bath. You get undressed."

Mamma helped without hovering or taking over. "You'll be doing this yourself tomorrow. Best you find out how right now."

The Kid had a disconcerting trick of sinking below the surface and holding his breath until I was ready to panic, but otherwise he seemed to enjoy himself.

I told him we would be flying for real that day—in an airplane. I had a rental car that would take us there.

"We Try Harder?"

"No, it's from Enterprise."

"Featuring cars from Dodge and Chrysler."

"It's a Charger."

"The Dodge Charger." He didn't smile—he almost never smiled—but I could tell he was pleased and excited. "The Dodge Charger comes equipped with a 2.7-liter V-6 and a four-speed automatic transmission."

That was the first full sentence I heard from my son—one that was not a quote from some advertising copy.

"I bet you're right," I said. "Now stand up and let me get you dried off."

He sank beneath the surface again.

I waited. Bubbles rose up and burst. The moment my will gave out and I decided to risk hauling him out, he sat up.

"The SRT8 model has the 425 horsepower V-8, the most powerful American-made powerhouse of its time. . . ."

He went on. He described the history of the Dodge Charger and its full specs. I couldn't get him to stop—or get out of the tub. His voice lost its usual harsh bark and became the soft, syrupy sounds of his grandmother.

"Mamma, does anyone know he can talk like this?"

"Boy'll talk your ear off, as long as he's talking about cars." She whisked him out of the tub and wrapped him tightly in a towel before he had a chance to complain. "He doesn't like nappy towels. You got to get him the smooth ones. I put those I got in your bag. And don't brush his hair—he thinks the brush is stealing his hair. Just let it dry on its own. And when its time to get him a haircut, you call Tino and he'll walk you through it. Tino tricks him into it somehow. The boy thinks his hair hurts when it gets cut."

"He was talking." I was still in awe.

She glared. "About cars." She started dressing him in blue shorts and T-shirt—identical to the ones he had been wearing all morning. "Now today is Monday," she said. "He will only wear blue on Monday."

I felt myself beginning to drift. I knew so little. How could someone so small have so many rules?

"Listen, Jason. That's how you'll get by. You listen to him. Let him tell you what he needs and you'll do fine." She hustled us down to the front porch and sat on the bottom step to say her good-byes to the Kid. She loved him. She would miss him. He was always welcome to come back and stay with her if that's what he really wanted.

The Kid responded to all this outpouring of love with a quick, "Okay." He turned and walked down the driveway.

I kissed her cheek and hurried to catch up.

All the way to New Orleans, he chattered about the Dodge Charger. I tried to remind him when he was repeating himself—to no effect. The technical history was lost on me, so I let him rattle on. He was happy talking about it, and I had my own thoughts to conquer.

Arrogance, spite, and anger weren't going to be enough to raise my child. Angie and her mother were right—I didn't know much. And what I knew scared me. Doctors, babysitters, other helpers, special schools, diets, treatments. It was all going to cost a fortune. The Kid's trust fund would help, but I was afraid we could run through that in the first two years. I had work coming at a great daily rate, but it wasn't going to last more than two weeks. And time! How was

I going to be able to work if I was caring for the Kid? I focused on the money so I wouldn't think about the rest of it. A co-dependent's cowardice.

The Kid started crying the minute he realized we were not going to keep the Charger. All the way from the rental lot to the check-in desk he sobbed and hung from my arm like an anchor. I made the mistake of bribing him with the promise of an ice cream, only to find, once we were past security, there was none for sale. I tried picking him up and he screamed like I'd set him on fire. When I put him back down, he wrapped all four limbs around my left leg and sat on my foot. I limped along, swinging the encumbered leg in an exaggerated arc to cover as much ground as possible with each painful step. He cried all the way to the gate, sobbing, "'Nilla, 'nilla."

We finally arrived at the waiting area and I collapsed onto the nearest available seat. The Kid wriggled up into my lap, pulled out one of his car books, and began flipping pages frantically. I tried shifting my weight in an attempt to make us both more comfortable and he snapped his head back and pounded me in the nose. The pain was horrible. I wanted to toss him across the aisle. I didn't. I maintained.

Then the overhead announcements began.

"Will the passengers Everett Unintelligible and Lortel Mumble-Crackle report to Gate B-Four. Your flight is boarded." Or it could have been Gate C, D, or E-Four. And Everett could have been Edward. The booming voice was accompanied by blasts of static and electronic squeals. The Kid threw himself off my lap and onto the floor, hands pinned over his ears, eyes squinted shut, and emitted a hideous, high-pitched shriek. I tried rubbing his back to soothe him, but my touch sent him instantly into an even bigger fit.

"I want you to know, sir, that I have reported you to airport security. I have been watching. The way you treat that boy is shameful." A heavyset, older woman in a floral-patterned summer dress was standing over me. Her fists were clenched. She looked like Barbara

Bush, only meaner. An embarrassed-looking twenty-something man in a seersucker suit and white buck shoes was pulling ineffectually on her arm.

"Come on, Grandma. You've done your good turn. Let the police deal with this."

"I'm going to pray for that boy," she hissed at me. It was a threat.

The garbled announcements came to an abrupt end. The Kid stopped screaming and sat up.

"Looks like it's working," I said.

"Jesus is watching you."

I let her have the last word.

The gate attendants called our flight and we queued up with the other families traveling with children. Out of the corner of my eye, I saw two uniforms approaching the gate—security. They didn't look like they were interested in long explanations.

"Excuse me, sir. Is that your child?"

We were steps away from boarding.

"Would you step out of line, please?"

The Kid shuffled along at my side, head down, shoulders slumped, looking just like what I imagined a battered child would look like.

"What's the problem?" I tried to give them a pleasant smile. It is not what I do best.

"We had a report of a child being physically abused."

"My son is fine. Take a look." I silently cursed all meddling grandmothers.

The cop got down on his haunches and inspected him. The Kid scowled back at him.

"Tell me, boy, are you all right? Has anyone been hurting you? We're here to help."

The Kid's eyes rolled up toward the ceiling and he moaned with the force of a ghoul in an Irish fairy tale, "'Nilla! 'Nilla!" Then he gave a sigh of immense heartbreak. It was a Tony-winning performance.

The cop looked up at me.

"Ice cream," I said. "He wants ice cream."

"Oh." He stood up. "Sorry." His partner was trying not to smile.

"Can we go now?" I said.

They waved me through.

I thought I was in the clear. I was proud of us. We had weathered our first storm together. The Kid and I were struggling, but we were making it work. No problem.

That sense of well-being lasted all the way through the boarding bridge. The step from there to the plane itself involved crossing a half-inch gap. The Kid began shrieking.

In the few seconds it took me to identify the Kid's problem, he managed to terrify all of the other children who were in line with us. He also wet himself, soaking not just his pants and underpants, but his sock and one shoe as well. And he broke out into a slimy sweat all over, so that when I grabbed him and propelled him over the crack and into the plane, it was like wrestling a greased piglet.

I don't think pigs bite as readily as he did, though. He didn't bite the flight attendant who reached forward to help me, which would probably have had us ejected on the spot, if not arrested. He bit me—hard enough to put two holes in my Ralph Lauren blazer. He also bit himself, but that was later.

He fought me as I changed him, pulling clothes out of his carry-on while annoyed passengers pushed by us. At first, he refused to wear the seat belt, but once it was locked in, he kept pulling it tighter until I became afraid he was going to cut himself in two. I was ready for an in-flight vodka on the rocks and we were still at the gate.

The shrieking didn't start up again until we were in the air and the pilot came over the overhead talking about what time we should expect to land and what the weather was going to be like. The Kid looked around wildly for the source of the annoying hum that accompanied the pilot's voice, and then, without warning, started screaming. The man in the seat immediately in front of the Kid reacted as though he had been slapped in the back of the head with a shovel. People wearing earbuds, blasting music into their heads, heard the shriek and turned to look. It was a scream of both pain and terror so powerful that it set off ancillary, less resonant cries from the other toddlers seated near us. Everyone on board under six started crying.

The Kid fought back against the Powers of Chaos. He bit my other arm, giving the jacket matching holes. He attacked the wall of the plane as hard as he could, using his head as his weapon. He managed to do this at least half a dozen times before I was able to get an arm around and restrain him.

For the next hour, the Kid alternated his behavior between hysterical, nausea-inducing, gasping, sobbing tears of helpless rage, and ear-splitting shrieks of rage that didn't need any help. He grunted, barked, and hissed.

Then he bit himself. He latched onto his own hand, shaking his head like a pit bull with a shih tzu. I wrapped one arm around him and pulled him to me as tight as I could, while with the other hand I reached over and pinched his nose. He had to open his mouth to take his next breath, and I got his hand away from him. I held him while he gnashed at me, until with a great sigh he fell back against the seat. He was instantly asleep.

My heartbeat returned to normal. I was exhausted. In prison, I had seen a huge man go berserk in the yard one day. He moved through the crowd, punching, gouging, and kicking. He seemed to pick men up and throw them. I didn't see what had set him off, but found myself staring at him, mesmerized as though watching a distant tornado. Then he suddenly veered in my direction and I was sure I felt Death approaching.

The guards stopped him with repeated charges from a Taser. The relief I felt as he fell at my feet that day was nothing compared to what I was going through as the Kid fell asleep.

I put my head back, and in seconds I was asleep as well.

A half-hour before landing in New York, I awoke to find the Kid slumped next to me, his head pillowed on my arm. It felt good.

THE KID SPENT the week visiting Park Avenue doctors, early-childhood specialists at Columbia and NYU, and school admissions officers—public and private—in three boroughs. I trotted behind, writing checks.

By Saturday afternoon, he was enrolled in school—private and specializing in teaching autistic children—and his trust fund had dropped by an equivalent of more than two full years at Harvard. He had a host of doctors, all of whom gave me variations on the same theme—the Kid might improve, he might not, have hope, not expectations—and all of whom charged as much per fifteen-minute visit as I was going to be earning in an hour. And he had Heather.

Almost as round as she was tall, tattooed and with more facial jewelry than the entire front row of a Marilyn Manson concert, Heather was the Kid's shadow, his minder, his behavioral tutor. A wizard. She was finishing a Ph.D. program at Columbia in early-childhood development and was glad to get firsthand experience working one-on-one with an autistic child. She was so glad, in fact, that she was willing to work twenty hours a week for a mere forty-eight dollars an hour. She was my guide in the wilderness that was my son.

Meanwhile, the Kid and I were discovering each other's boundaries and needs. The days of the week were marked by what was allowed for breakfast, and what color scheme was acceptable for the way he dressed. Blue was reserved for Monday. Yellow never. Beige was best on Wednesday and Saturday, Friday was always black. No plaids. Ever.

Eggs were scrambled, never fried. Pancakes must be served with corn syrup, not maple, and only on Friday and Sunday. Mustard, he had convinced me, was an abomination, never to be allowed anywhere near his food. He called it "Poo," a word he would scream very loudly in any setting, including the coffee shop across Amsterdam. I was beginning to get him to accept food that was not just white or yellow. Green was still in the long-term-planning stage.

I kept a stack of books on the sideboard, which I ran to frequently for advice, solace, or courage. Case histories, personal stories, theories, and practices. Sometimes the books helped. But as Mamma had pointed out, what worked best was simply listening to my near-nonverbal son. He made his likes and dislikes known quite clearly.

Escalators were not allowed under any circumstances. Elevators, on the other hand, held no terrors. He had traveled in them from the womb. He walked in, the doors closed, and when they reopened, the universe had changed. It was a form of magic with which he was quite familiar.

The black and white tiles in the lobby of the Ansonia presented a surprising challenge. There was a wide expanse of large white tiles, interspersed in an irregular pattern with black tiles. They were the problem.

The first time, the elevator doors opened and the Kid froze.

"Come on, Kid. It's no problem." I stepped out, placing a foot on a tile of each color.

"Nggnngnggg." It came out half growl, half cry. It was a sound no child should be able to make.

As I turned to hold the elevator doors for him, I took my foot off the black tile. He relaxed.

"Let's go, bud. Doors are closing."

Elevator rules: you never let the doors close once the adult has stepped out. The Kid carefully stepped out onto a white tile.

"Hole," he shuddered, pointing to the offending black tile.

Whether it was a hole in the floor or the firmament, I never learned. But I had already come to respect his fears—and fight only the battles that mattered. We crossed the floor in an awkward pas de deux, garnering smiles from the staff and neighbors we passed. Two days later, he had Heather avoiding the black tiles as well.

TUESDAY.

Spud was unshaven, wearing the same clothes as the night before, and slumped over the little conference table—fast asleep.

"Rise and shine, Spuddy-boy." It had been a rough night with the Kid, and I had no patience.

Spud jerked erect, startled to find that his bedroom had been transformed into a ten-by-ten gray box.

"You need a minute? Want to get yourself some coffee or something?" I tried to put as much sarcasm into my voice as possible. The Kid had been up twice with night terrors—aptly named events that I was assured were "perfectly normal" and which had left me with a sleepless adrenaline hangover and a very short fuse.

"Whoa. Sorry. I mean, no, I'm fine." He was barely registering my presence, still shaking his head and blinking his eyes.

"Big night?" I drew it out.

He finally heard the edge in my voice.

"Wait. No. Not at all. I've been right here all night. I must have dozed off."

I looked around the room. The trash can in the corner was overflowing with a cardboard pizza box and at least a six-pack's worth of empty Diet Coke cans. He had somehow managed to shut off the damn AC vent. I cut him some slack and softened my tone.

"Sorry. Take your time. Pull yourself together and, when you're ready, give me a report."

"I'm good." He cowboyed up.

"I thought this was going to be cake. No problem, I think you said."

He nodded ruefully. "It started that way. But when I ran the final spreadsheet, I found there were a whole bunch of trades missing."

"Okay. So you didn't pull them all in when you grabbed the data." Garbage in, garbage out.

"First thing I checked. But the system dropped selective trades, not just a column."

That was odd. "So how'd you catch it?"

"Brian did a big trade back in late June. He was psyched about it. It was an unwind of a position he had been working on for over a month. He took me for beers that night to celebrate."

"And that trade didn't show on the computer run?"

"Right. It should have jumped right out on the spreadsheet, just because of the size."

"So, you went back to the paper files . . . ?"

He nodded again. "And started finding other missing trades right away. Dozens."

"Any pattern to them? All big trades?"

"Yes and no. The size was all over the place—no pattern at all. But they were all with the same client—a small hedge fund called Arrowhead."

"What do you know about them?"

"Nothing. Brian did trades with them and told me to write the tickets."

As much as any trading assistant would be expected to know, I thought. I changed tack.

"So, how would these trades just get dropped from the system?"

"They're not! They're all in there. When I do a search for a specific trade, they show up. They only show up missing when I run a request for all trades by Brian Sanders."

I still thought it was just a glitch, but if it was something more, I wasn't ready to discuss it with a trading assistant.

"Are they all back in your spreadsheets now?"

"As of around four-thirty this morning." He paused as though he had more to say.

"What? We have a lot of ground to cover today."

"It's just that no one on the trading or sales side would have the security codes to rig something like this."

It was my experience that people put a lot more faith in things like security codes than was appropriate. I had no doubt that given a few hours with no one looking over my shoulder, I would have been able to engineer something myself. I'd done it before.

"I'll pass it on to Stockman. If he wants to follow up, it's on him. All right?"

Spud seemed satisfied.

"Now show me what we've got."

Nothing else stuck out. Spud was of some help with the technical aspects of the bonds Sanders traded, but he was an admitted neophyte. Most of the trading was done dealer to dealer through a network of intermediary brokers. The few trades with clients—non-Street accounts—were all with the same handful of hedge funds and money managers. An hour later, I had learned a few things about the bond market, but I was still a long way from discovering any misconduct.

"Okay," I sighed. "Just give me the breakdown by salesman. I've got to start meeting with them. We'll see if any of them can shed some light."

I wanted a nap, hours of uninterrupted sleep with no child biting me or screaming like the damned. Instead, I commandeered a broom closet–sized office and began interviewing the salespeople who had worked with Sanders. The room belonged to an IT project manager out with the flu. It was a third the size of the mini conference room, but offered a touch more privacy. The sole decoration on the wall was a monochromatic print of the city skyline, old enough that it still showed the twin towers. It was a beautiful, even majestic view, given a terrible poignancy by those two dark monoliths. I moved my chair so I would not have to look.

Securities salesmen—and women—are no different, as a class, than salespeople in any other industry. There are conniving bastards who would plunder the jewelry off their mother's corpse and smile while they did it, and there are honorable, hardworking professionals who are justly proud of the value-added service they provide their clients. In twenty-some years on Wall Street, I had come to believe the latter were far more numerous, but it was always the other guys who got the press.

The first three interviews were pleasant, unsurprising in any way, and of no help to me whatsoever. All were senior guys who had been around for years and while they were willing to cooperate, they had little to say. And they were all hungry to get back out to the trading floor. Time away from their phones and computers was money out of pocket. I heard what I had already been told—Sanders was a good guy who knew his markets. He was no pushover, but he was flexible and very sales-friendly. They all parted with the same message: it was a shame about the accident, and they were surprised that anyone was asking questions about his trading.

The walls were beginning to get to me—the room was smaller than an upstate cell. If the IT guy worked typical Wall Street hours, he lived more than a third of his life in that room. If I had had to spend much more time there, I would have had to ask Spud to take my belt and shoelaces.

I decided to do one more interview before lunch.

"David Rhys Jones." He announced himself like a television game show host. "Call me Davey. Everyone does."

Mr. Jones was an expat Brit, complete with the loudly striped shirt, with solid cutaway collar and oversized French cuffs, over-the-ankle zippered boots, and a custom-made suit that hadn't been pressed since leaving the tailor's shop. He was carrying a McDonald's bag.

He jerked my hand up and down for a few shakes, as though he was showing off some newly acquired skill, and sat down. He looked around the tiny room as though it were the ballroom at the Waldorf.

"Nice digs. Spared no expense here, mate, what?" He gave a much too hearty laugh.

His accent was an odd mix of the BBC and the East End. I couldn't tell if he was upper class and playing the fool, or working class and reaching higher.

"Brian Sanders," I said. "What can you tell me?"

"Oh, yes. Very sad." He made a long face to demonstrate what sadness was.

"You did a lot of business with him."

"Good lad. Bottle and glass." He opened the fast-food bag and spread his lunch on the desk. Double cheeseburger. Fries. Soda. "You don't mind, I hope. This is my only chance for a bit of tucker."

"Bottle and glass?"

"Class," he said around a large bite of burger.

I found Cockney rhyming slang to be as bewildering as the gangsta Ebonics I had dealt with in jail. My first cellmate had taken offense when I had not responded to his kind offer of "a dime a lala, it be da butta." Luckily, his kindness extended to educating me enough that I understood he had been trying to sell me a small amount of very good marijuana. I declined. Politely.

"What kinds of accounts do you cover?"

"All crooks," he laughed. "Babbling brook, the lot of them. Those that aren't, are pirates."

Like many of his countrymen living in the States, he seemed to enjoy "playing the Brit," based on the shaky supposition that all

American women found British accents sexy, and the even shakier idea that because American men like John Cleese, they're also going to love Hugh Grant. Or Benny Hill.

"The only client of mine that did any business with young Bri' was the one small hedge fund—Arrowhead. I imagine that's who you want to hear about."

I did. The missing Arrowhead trades were the only anomaly I had seen so far.

"Let's start there, then."

Jones stuffed a handful of fries in his mouth and closed his eyes in rapture.

"You Yanks have no idea how well off you are. Food this good for next to nothing on every corner. Bloody amazing."

The smell in the small room was overpowering. I wanted to finish up and get out of there before I got sick.

"Arrowhead?"

"Right. Well. Arrowhead is a British hedge fund. Chartered in Jersey—which tells you there's some tax fiddle involved there, eh?" He grinned as though we were fellow conspirators united against the tax man. "There's rumors—rumors only, mind—that they run money for the artsy set. Damien Hirst and that crowd. I wouldn't know. Another rumor is that it's all American money, growing off-shore, unimpeded by Uncle Sam. The fund is closed, however, so it makes no difference. They take no new subscribers and stay under the reportable limit, so they have to report next to nothing to the regulators."

Arrowhead sounded like a classic FBN account—Fly By Night. And some genius had assigned the account to Davey—a cross-cultural clown with an admiration for larceny.

"They tend to run on a shoestring—at least over here. Geoffrey Hochstadt is their New York trader. He does a fair bit of business, but I don't get the feeling he holds positions very long. More of an in-and-out-and-move-on approach. Does that give you some idea?" He licked a glob of ketchup off of his little finger.

"Just the one trader?" I said.

"As I say, it's a small operation. Geoffrey and an assistant. They have a one-room office across from Grand Central."

"This guy, Hochstadt. Is he a Brit, too?"

"Geoffrey?" he laughed. "Not bloody likely. Born and raised in Darien." He pronounced the word like a native, back in the throat with the teeth almost clenched. "House on a hill. I imagine there are water views, if you can climb a high enough tree."

"How did you two get along?"

He had finished the burger and was using the last of the fries to wipe up the smears of ketchup, cheese, and grease from the waxed paper.

"Brian or Geoffrey?"

"Both."

"Brian had not yet picked up the heated paranoia of the more seasoned traders. Never got all Punch 'n' Judy—except after bonuses. And don't they all? A good loaf."

"And Hochstadt?"

"A wanker. Almost abusive if you're not right on top of your game. We got together once or twice a year. I can't say I knew him in any sense. One day, dear Kenneth stopped by my desk and told me I had a new client, and bob's your uncle. I've been to the man's house. Like all you Yanks, he loves to burn meat alfresco and serve it up ash and all. We had a meal—we weren't mates." He stuck the straw down to the bottom of the cup and began to slurp in earnest.

"Did he and Brian hang out? Were they mates, would you say?"

"Geoffrey liked to entertain the young traders. He was always leading his tribe of Lost Boys out on some evening adventure. As I understand there was a rotating clique of two or three dozen—from every department. Mortgages, corporates, stocks, derivatives."

"He traded in all those products?" I said.

"He traded anything he wanted, didn't he? The more obscure the better, it seemed. Options. Derivatives. CDOs. Commodities. More bonds than anything else, I'd guess."

"Let's run through a trade, then. This Hochstadt would call you up looking for a market in something esoteric—Bolivian government bonds, for instance—and you'd call the trader for a price. Right so far?"

"Well, not always. Most of my business is in corporate bonds and derivatives. I don't have the expertise to talk a good game in many of these other areas."

"So, you would just hook him up with a trader?" Just as Toland had described.

"Right. Let them work the magic together and I'd write a ticket. It all tended to be low margin, if you see my point."

Meaning that the sales commission on those trades had been small—another good reason for Jones to have paid little attention. He had done no real work with the client and had no expectation that more work would be rewarded. "Know Your Customer" is the foundation of Wall Street's ability to self-regulate, as often ignored as practiced. Jones was lazy enough—and mercenary enough—to treat the account like "found money."

"How did you keep track of all those different trades? All those different products?"

"Not by half. Hochstadt's assistant would call at day's end and read them off to me. Then I just confirmed with the trader and wrote a ticket."

"And there was never a problem. Never a discrepancy. Never a buy that should have been a sell, never a disagreement over price?"

It was obvious from Jones' bewildered expression that he had never before considered the question. "Never. Not once. The trader always agreed."

Impossible. It defied the laws of probability—and common sense.

"Let's back up for a minute. Sanders and these other traders would be out with this guy regularly? Once a week? Once a month?"

"Oh, a good bit more than that. Hochstadt was standing them to grilled beef dinners two or three times a week. He would bring along traders from other firms as well. It was a great way for the young turks to meet and mix, wasn't it?"

"You never invited yourself along?"

"Once. It was a bore. All they talked about was their last brilliant trade—or their last trip to AC."

"AC?" I was thinking of the broken air-conditioning vent in the little conference room.

"Sorry. Atlantic City. Hochstadt would take a half-dozen lads gambling most weekends. Usually up to Connecticut or down to the Jersey shore. Once or twice a year out to Las Vegas."

"You didn't go?"

"Missing the necessary gene, I'm afraid. Gambling itself holds no allure—I hate to lose, and if you're going to play games where the odds are stacked against you, you have to accept the fact that you are going to lose more often than you win. Besides, I find casinos in this country to be the nadir of American culture. Loud, crude, and desperate." He finished his soda with a loud, crude, bubbling snort.

In a world of private jets to the Bahamas, ten-thousand-dollar wine bills, and dwarf-tossing parties, a few young traders throwing their money away at Foxwoods sounded like kid stuff. If I had been their manager, I would have been concerned, but not overly so. Entertaining, usually lubricated with alcohol, was a necessary evil.

"Well, Davey, one last question. Did you ever have the feeling that Brian Sanders was up to anything?"

"Bent?" He wadded up the wrappings from his lunch and dropped them into the wastebasket, ensuring that the room would smell of fast food for the rest of the afternoon.

"Anything not quite kosher."

"Bit of a prig, actually."

I let him go. If I had learned anything of value, I didn't know what it was. Stockman would laugh me out of his office if I walked in and announced that a junior trader had been dealing direct with a client who regularly wined and dined him in Atlantic City. It may have been a red flag, but it was no smoking gun.

THERE WAS A VERY different buzz in the air out on the trading floor. Controlled panic had given way to near pandemonium.

"Bid out!"

"I hit you!"

"No way! I told you my bids are out. Everything's subject."

"Fuck that!"

I kept to the edge of the trading floor, staying out of harm's way. There was real fear and menace in the air. I stopped one of the salesmen I had interviewed that morning.

"What's up?"

"Hey." He looked up with a harried air. "It's a shit show. There's rumors of a bank going under—this week. And the way the mortgage traders are acting, it could be us."

"Have you seen Spud? The assistant who was working with me?"

"Oh, yeah. The mortgage guys grabbed him—they need bodies." He pointed across the floor and I saw Spud surrounded by a half-dozen other young assistants, all appearing to be buried under tickets and computer runs. I wasn't going to get him back easily—or soon.

I was at loose ends. Without Spud, the investigation was stuck in neutral. And I was interested to see if the rumors had any basis. I headed for Stockman's office.

Gwendolyn was away from her desk and the door to Stockman's office was closed. There was an angry rumble beyond the door.

I could hear Stockman talking—controlled, reasonable, and pissed—but not the words. A sound like rolling thunder answered him. Stockman said something that cut it off abruptly.

The door flew open and a large, gray-suited man barged out, moving with the ponderous grace of a bulldozer. He saw me, his eyes went wide, and for a split second I felt an irrational fear of bodily harm.

"You! You're the guy." He turned back to face Stockman as he came through the doorway. "I'm right. Aren't I? This is him."

I was stuck between the couch and the coffee table, unable to retreat and any move forward would look like an advance.

"Who am I supposed to be?"

He aimed a thick index finger at the middle of my chest and made stabbing motions as he talked. "I know who you are. You're Stafford. Well, I run compliance at this firm and you don't want to get in my way. I will run right over you and not even feel the bump."

The finger felt dangerously close. Where I had been, if a man touches you, he owns you. Unless he's a guard, in which case he already owns your ass. This guy smelled like a guard.

I swatted the finger away. "Enough. Back off."

Unfortunately, I managed to swat his finger just at the moment of approach. His finger caught against the front of my shirt and a button flew through the air.

I looked down. There was a minuscule tear around the button-hole.

"Jesus, Jack! Stop this playground posturing." Stockman looked so put out, I thought he might stamp his foot.

The big man glanced down at him, and for a moment he may have looked embarrassed. Then he glared back at me. "We're not done," he said, and left, almost colliding with Gwendolyn as she came in from the hall.

I turned to Stockman, my anger and confusion not yet dissipating. "What in hell . . . ?"

He held up one hand and spoke to Gwendolyn. "Hold my calls, would you? Mr. Stafford and I will be in conference. Not to be disturbed." He took my arm and guided me into his inner sanctum. "Sit," he said. "Take a minute."

My blood was still racing, but I took his advice. "Who the hell was that? Please tell me he's worth at least ten mil, so when I sue his fat ass, it will be worth my while."

Stockman smiled politely. "Sorry. Nowhere near it. Jack Avery is our head of compliance."

"I gathered that."

"He is responsible for defending the firm and is party to all of the issues we are dealing with. I imagine the stress of recent events has affected his judgment. He will apologize."

I fingered the torn buttonhole. "He owes me a shirt."

Stockman gave a nod of benediction. I was behaving. "Thank you for your understanding. Give Gwendolyn your size and I'll have a half-dozen delivered."

"What's his problem with me?"

"Jack was with NYPD for twenty years before finishing his law degree and joining the firm. He is very good at his job, but he does tend to see people in terms of 'citizens and perps.' He knows your history, and places you in the latter category, I'm afraid."

"Can you keep him away from me? I just want to do my job and go home and look after my son."

"I can do you one better. I'll have a word with him. Give me a day or so. I can guarantee he will be more reasonable."

Reasonable sounded good. So did an aluminum baseball bat. I made a mental note to bring one to our next meeting.

"How goes your little investigation? Anything for me?"

I was reminded of what an annoying prick he was.

"Nothing yet. But unless I get that assistant back, I'm not going to get much further. Mortgages stole him."

"Ah," he sighed. "They are under the gun today. I will take care of it. What's his name?"

I blanked. I couldn't say Spud, I would have sounded like an idiot. "Fred . . ."

"Young Krebs? I know him. His father ran our high yield department for years. Let the dust settle and I will make sure you have him back first thing in the morning. Take the rest of the day—you won't get much cooperation around here with all of these rumors flying."

I had no argument with that. I went home to my son.

THE KID AND I were celebrating his second day at school. As he refused to drink milk or anything with either pulp or bubbles, the Kid had water. I had a beer.

I set him up on a barstool facing the jukebox and gave him a handful of quarters. He always played the same song—C104, Dire Straits' "Sultans of Swing"— incessantly. But no one complained, if they noticed. As long as the quarters held out, and the lights flashed in front of him, he was content.

The Tuesday-afternoon crowd was just beginning to thin out. Vinny the Gambler was gone, but Ma and Pa were still holding up their end. They always stood, never sat. If they had enough of their respective gin and scotch that they were having trouble standing, they went home. It was their form of self-discipline.

Tommy and Billy, the two Deadheads I had met my first night back in town, were seated at the fifty-yard line, continuing their never-ending debate: of the two hundred thirty-two times the Grateful Dead had performed "Dark Star" in concert, which was the most awesome? I had made the mistake of joining their conversation that night—before I knew better.

The song ended and I checked on the Kid. He was slipping quarters into the slot with the intense focus of a neurosurgeon.

The door opened and Roger came in with an athletic-looking woman. She was at least a full head taller than he—and thirty years younger. They made an odd couple. Roger's eyes scanned the bar and his face jerked briefly into a semblance of a smile when he saw me.

He pushed his way through, gesturing impatiently for the woman to follow.

"So, right about now," he said in place of hello, "you're asking yourself, 'What the fuck is this ugly old clown doing with a classy-looking lady young enough to be his daughter?' Am I right or what?"

The woman snorted. "Granddaughter!"

She had to be only an inch or two shy of six feet, and all of it well put together. Her face was strong and sharp-featured. The kind of mouth that challenged for a kiss, rather than begged. As far as I could tell, she was wearing no makeup, or was very good at applying it. Dark brown, shoulder-length hair. Big green eyes that seemed to offer both a laugh and a challenge.

"Nice to see you again, Roger," I said.

He turned to the woman. "See? I told you he was a nice man. Now, say hello to the nice man."

She looked me over and must have decided I wasn't an ogre.

"Hello, nice man."

She had a nice voice. Low, warm, and so accentless she must once have worked hard at it. "From Rollie's description, I was expecting someone older and . . ."

". . . wiser?" I smiled.

"No. Maybe a bit more 'schlumpy.' Not quite so . . ."

". . . virile," I finished.

"Serious," she said, giving me a passable imitation of what I saw in the mirror each morning.

I laughed. I knew what I looked like. "Takes long years of practice to maintain this."

"I bet you look just fine when you let yourself smile," she said.

Roger pulled himself up onto a barstool. "Rollie! A white wine for the little lady!" For some reason, he found this very funny. "And a gasoline. I am very low on fuel this evening."

"You must be Wanda the Wandaful?" I said.

"Just Wanda." She smiled. It was a great smile. My brain was wiped clean, my throat closed up, and my tongue tied itself into a knot. I wanted to invite her to fly with me to Fiji for a week, or at least come see the view of Broadway from my apartment for an hour, but I couldn't speak. Then she looked away and the spell faded.

"Health," Roger said, raising his snifter. He slurped a third of his cognac like it was soda, then gave a shudder. "Oh, that's much better."

He immediately looked better. His face was still sad, but there was a spot of color in his cheeks. He started flipping through an abandoned copy of the *Post*.

The music started up again. "Sultans of Swing." I was suddenly self-conscious—was the Kid bothering people? Was he bothering Wanda?

"I hope you like Dire Straits," I said to her.

She took a sip of wine, tipped her head to one side, and made a sound somewhere between an assent and a grunt. "Hmmp."

"Hey, Jason! Jason!" Tommy was yelling to me from down the bar. "Tell Billy, will ya? The *Live* album version smokes, right?"

"The *Live* album smokes," I said, hoping that if I gave Tommy what he wanted he would leave me alone.

"What I tell ya?" he yelled at Billy. "He knows. He *knows!*"

"You're a Deadhead?" Wanda said, giving me a look of reappraisal. "Somehow you don't look old enough. Or young enough."

"I went to some shows a long time ago." More than ever, I regretted introducing myself to Tommy.

"How many?"

"No idea."

"But more than a dozen, let's say."

Twenty-six. I tried not to squirm. "Yeah, I guess."

"You're a Deadhead," she laughed. It sounded like wind chimes.

"Are you one?" I asked.

Al Franken and Ann Coulter are both Deadheads. We are everywhere.

"Me?" She laughed again. My toes curled. "The way I was brought up, there were only two kinds of music—country and western. I learned to love 'em both."

Country-western music. Could I ever learn to love a woman whose heartstrings were moved by a pedal steel guitar? But love wasn't strictly necessary for what I had in mind.

Roger gave up studying Page Six and swung around. "Excuse me. Coming through." He hopped off the stool. "My prostate just told me it's gonna let me pee. That's like a big event in my life."

I stood back and let him pass. He walked with a bowlegged, rolling gait, leaning forward, as though his legs were perpetually trying to keep up with the rest of him.

I slid in next to Wanda again. "So where's home?" She didn't sound at all country. Or western.

"I'm an army brat. Athens, Georgia, to Athens, Greece."

I had not been this close to a woman in years, and had never been a brilliant conversationalist before then. I tried to think of something brilliant to say to keep her looking in my direction. I vowed not to ask what she did for a living. She looked away and sipped her wine. I wanted to inhale her.

"So what do you do in the act? Roger claims it's all his show."

She shook her hair down to cover one eye. "It's a secret," she teased.

"You know about my secret life as a Deadhead."

"There must be no secrets between us." She switched from Lauren Bacall to Marlene Dietrich and then back to her own voice. "I'm a student. I'm working on my doctorate."

"So you're not a professional clown," I said. The words poured out of their own accord. I would rather have strangled myself than listen.

"It's a job. I hand him the props and try and stay out of his way. Then I go home and work on my thesis." She had stopped being playful—not quite cold, but definitely not as warm.

She seemed a decade older than your average grad student, but I managed to keep that thought to myself. I took another swig of beer.

When you've already dug a deep hole, you might as well jump in.

"Listen, I'm sorry. Can we start over? I'd just like to have a conversation with a beautiful, intelligent woman. It's been a while." And that was as much information as I was ready to give up on that subject.

She looked me over. "Look, I'm sure you are a nice guy. Roger says so and he hates everybody. But nice guys are married. Or gay. Which are you?"

"Divorced."

She gave a resigned nod. "Nice guy with baggage."

"You're divorced?" I asked.

She cracked a smile. "How can you tell?"

"Guy must have been a piece of work."

"Given the choice of sitting here and talking about (A) my ex, or (B) your ex, I choose (C). Whatever it is."

We sipped in silence. I wasn't prepared to give up, but I needed a new tack.

"I'm not very good at this, I know. Lack of practice. The last time I tried chatting up a girl in a bar, the only thing I could come up with was 'What's your major?'"

She laughed. It wasn't wind chimes this time, it was a big whooping guffaw. She looked me over again. She made a decision.

"So go ahead and ask me," she said.

"Let me guess. Comparative lit. Early twentieth century. American."

She scrunched up her face and shook her head. "Way off. How about Physical Therapy? I'll have my DPT next May."

I hadn't known you could get a doctorate in physical therapy, but I managed to keep that to myself as well.

Roger came rolling back and squeezed between us. "Jesus, you don't know what it's like. You're a young guy. You'll see. I walk around all day feeling like I'm about to let loose like a goddamn race-horse, and when I go, the best I can do is squeeze out a few drops. Take my advice, don't get old."

"Your kidneys are getting too much of a workout," Wanda said.

Roger sighed. "My kidneys. We're talking about my kidneys! Do I talk about your kidneys? Can't I get any privacy?"

"And you should drink more water," she continued.

"You know what W. C. Fields said about water."

She squeezed her face into a moue of distaste. "Something about what fish do there."

Roger shook his head. " 'You can't trust water . . .' " he began.

" '. . . even a straight stick turns crooked in it,' " I finished. "One of my father's favorite lines."

"I like your father," Roger said. "And I look forward to meeting him someday." He turned to Wanda and spoke in a stage whisper. "So, how are you two getting along? Has he offered to buy you a meal yet?"

She stage-whispered back, "I think we were just getting there."

He turned to me. "I think I softened her up for ya, sport. Time to make your move."

I cleared my throat and leaned across. "If I promise not to talk about our exes, can I buy you dinner sometime?"

"I'm very busy," she said.

Roger rolled his eyes.

"Even doctoral students eat," I said.

"I'm thinking about it."

There was a tug at my sleeve. The Kid. "Quarters," he said.

I hadn't heard the music stop.

"Just a sec, Kid." I smiled at Wanda. For once, it didn't feel like my cheeks were breaking.

"This is my son, Jason. I call him Kid. Say hello to Roger and Wanda, Kid."

Roger grunted at him. The Kid grunted back.

"Quarters." He pulled harder on my sleeve.

"My God, what a beautiful little boy," Wanda said. "Hi there, Jason." She put out her hand to shake.

He didn't bite it—a good sign.

"Quarters." It was an unpleasant rasp.

Heather, his shadow and teacher, had instilled in me the idea that setting firm guidelines for the Kid's behavior was of absolute importance. Please. Thank you. May I? These were all meaningless concepts to him. If he did not learn them soon, he would never.

"I think you mean 'Please, Jason, may I have another quarter?' Don't you?"

The Kid was tired. He wasn't having any of it. "Quarters!" He sounded more like a Marine drill sergeant than a five-year-old boy.

I turned back to Wanda. "I've got to run. Please," I said. "Dinner some night?" Heather stayed late on Thursdays. "Thursday would be great."

"Thursday, it is." She gave me that smile again. "But I get to choose. Meet me here."

"Six-thirty?"

She nodded.

"QUARTERS!" It was really loud. Everyone at the bar reached for quarters.

"Kid, we have worn out our welcome." I gestured for everyone to keep their change. "We are out of here. Come on, I'm gonna get you a grilled cheese and some fries."

"Golden brown and extra-crispy," he said, sounding exactly like the actor on the Ore-Ida commercial.

"Don't worry. They know just how you like them."

TWO HOURS LATER, the Kid was fed, bathed, read to, and—blessedly—asleep. Nirvana.

It was a warm night and there were still plenty of people down on Broadway. The ebb and flow of pedestrians and traffic was soothing. I poured a glass of water and sank down into my chair.

I realized that I was more content with my life than at any time in years. Heather had told me that the Kid was bright and responsive and might soon surprise both of us. The school reported that he was both happy and engaged—and had not tried to bite anyone since lunchtime.

There was a date to look forward to, with a woman I could talk to—almost.

And I had work. Something to both occupy my brain and fatten the coffers. The opportunity to use old skills, to get outside the looping track of anger, self-pity, recrimination, and depression that had marked the last few years of my life. The challenge of solving a puzzle. It all combined to give me a healthy shot of serotonin.

The Kid's light snoring stopped. I went to his room to check. The Kid had managed to free one foot from the sheets, his pale skin glowed in the darkness. I considered pulling the sheet back into place, but held off. Peace trumped order. If the Kid was uncomfortable, he would let me know. I was learning.

An hour later, I nodded out over an article purporting to be the final word on mercury toxicity as a causal factor in autism. The one thing I was sure of about anything to do with my son's condition was the final word had yet to be written.

WEDNESDAY—A BEIGE DAY. I dressed the Kid in a pair of khakis and a polo shirt that Angie would have described as ecru. I was glad that neither the Kid nor I was capable of making such distinctions. Wednesday was also an egg day. Scrambled—never fried.

The cab dropped us on the corner and we walked the half-block to school. There were two on the block—the Kid's and a more mainstream private school. The street was solid with cabs, Town Cars, and SUVs, all holding one or two adults and one child—all inching forward one car length per child delivered, and all spewing enough hydrocarbons to make Dick Cheney smile.

"Mr. Stafford? Jason? Hellooooo." I knew that voice. I cringed.

I felt for Helene Wyckoff, but her neediness terrified me. The first day of school, she had identified Jason and me as newbies and latched herself onto us. In five minutes, she had dumped on my unsuspecting shoulders the full story of her and her son's lives.

She had been married to an oral surgeon who left her for a dental hygienist soon after the boy was born. The autism became apparent before the divorce decree, and her settlement mushroomed. But her life had shrunk to encompass only her son and her dog. The boy was a year older than the Kid, but did not yet speak. He carried a notebook with pictures of various foods, clothing, and places—a toilet, his bed—so that he could point and communicate his needs, but he rarely used it. Most of his time was spent sitting, staring, and humming tunelessly. His mother tried to arrange playdates for him with anyone she could buttonhole, in some kind of mad hope that her son might notice another young person and miraculously begin to interact.

"Good morning, Helene," I called, silently wishing the Kid to step faster.

"Hurry up now, Prince." She had the dog in tow—a high-energy, scruffy Jack Russell, inexplicably named for the Broadway producer Hal Prince. Her son came up behind her, eyes on the ground, bounding slightly on the balls of his feet, as though trying to shed some energy too painful to contain. "Now, Jason, I haven't forgotten your promise to get our boys together sometime soon."

I had never even hinted that such a thing was a possibility. Helene might even have admitted this if challenged, but she refused to let reality stand in the way of her dreams for her son.

The Kid saw the dog and dropped down on his haunches for some penetrating, heartfelt eye contact. There were times I would gladly have traded places with a dog.

A Jack Russell is a working dog—bred to hunt fox. They need lots of exercise. They need to run and dig and burrow down tunnels looking for rats and snakes and foxes. They're not great on a leash. People who live in apartments get them because they're small. Those people should think it through a bit longer.

The little terrier was hopping up and down and yipping like a Chihuahua, its head whipping back and forth and its bobbed tail vibrating like a rattlesnake. It was not into making peaceful eye contact with a weird little human.

The Kid was getting frustrated; he wanted to bond with that hyperactive canine and he was getting no cooperation. He began to grunt in frustration.

Helene rattled on about the fall fund-raiser—a silent auction—and how she had no idea what she could contribute, though the year before she had paid thirty dollars for a facial at a salon on Broadway and she had never used it and wondered if she spoke to the store, could she get them to maybe donate a manicure as well. I had no opinion. I didn't need one.

The dog barked. The Kid's grunting was beginning to spook it. Next, it snapped its jaws in his direction—not a bite, barely a threat, but the situation was escalating.

I dropped to one knee and held out the back of my hand. It took a full minute of cha-cha-ing back and forth for the dog to get up the courage to sniff me. The Kid watched fascinated. The little terrier finally sniffed and immediately relaxed.

"That's how you say hello to a dog, Kid. They don't know any better. They have to smell you to be your friend."

The dog squirmed its way under my fingers and I scratched its head and neck.

"Go ahead. Give it a try."

The Kid held out his hand. The dog cautiously advanced, did its sniff, and barked once. The Kid didn't move; he waited.

"That's right, just wait him out."

The dog advanced again. This time it sniffed and did the same squirmy dance under the hand. The Kid scratched. The dog relaxed.

Helene was still holding up her end of the conversation about the fund-raiser. I wasn't needed.

"Nice work, Kid. Now you see? He likes you."

The Kid nodded seriously. The dog scampered back, its claustrophobic hyperactivity taking over again. We stood up.

"So?" Helene finished. "Call me, we'll make a plan." She moved on, her son and dog behind. "Ta-ta." She waved.

The Kid's teacher met us out front. Ms. Wegant was a stern-looking, breastless, hipless woman who managed—without ever saying any more than "Good morning"—to make me feel guilty for abandoning my son to her each day.

"Good morning, Mr. Stafford." It worked again. "Good morning, Jason."

The Kid ignored her.

"Say good morning, Kid," I said quietly.

"Good morning, Ms. Wegant." He didn't quite look at her, but he got the words out perfectly, though I thought he sounded an awful lot like Heather when he spoke. Nevertheless, I felt an absurdly disproportionate rush of parental pride.

I got down on one knee to say my good-byes and the Kid surprised me. He looked directly into my eyes. Then, he slowly raised his arm and held out the back of his hand. I took a second to think. I sniffed his hand, then I held out my own. He sniffed me back. Then he turned and walked into the building with Ms. Wegant.

I walked to the subway on billows of euphoria, taking ten-foot strides with each step. My kid liked me.

SPUD WAS BACK in the conference room—shaved, showered, and rested.

"You didn't think to mention the casino trips?" I said instead of "Good morning."

He shook his head. "It was no big deal. Everybody knew."

"Who else went?"

"I don't know. A bunch of guys. It was something they all did."

I handed him a legal pad. "Give me names."

He shrugged and began to write.

"How about you?" I asked. "Were you ever invited along?"

"Not a chance. Traders only." He pushed the pad back to me. "These are the only guys I know from this firm."

Carmine Nardo—corporate bond trading
Sudhir Patel—mortgage-backed trading
Lowell Barrington—OTC stocks

"I'm going to want to meet with each of them. Who do I talk to about setting it up?"

"I can take care of it. I don't know anyone over in stocks, but I'll find Lowell."

Specialization and compartmentalization start early on Wall Street. No one is a generalist.

"Good. Then, I want you back on the Arrowhead trades. I'm convinced there is something there. I don't know what, but look for any patterns that stick out. The obvious thing is to see if there was any way Brian could have been hiding losses."

Or generating phony profits, the way I had done.

"Meantime, I'll get us coffee."

There was an alcove adjacent to the trading floor, with a pair of coffee machines, a small fridge, and a junk food dispenser. Some bright Ph.D. candidate should do a thesis project plotting bull and bear markets versus traders' consumption of Oreos and Fig Newtons.

The air of panic from the day before was gone, replaced with a dull sense of disassociation. There was no business getting done. Half the people on the floor were on the phone with headhunters and the rest were waiting nervously for a call back.

"Hey. You're Stafford, right?"

The speaker was a dark-browed, good-looking man in his late twenties.

"That's right. And you are . . . ?"

"I know why you're here." He sounded both accusatory and petulant.

"I didn't know it was a secret. Do you mind telling me who you are?"

"Carmine Nardo. Brian Sanders was a good friend."

He had saved me a search.

"Well, this is good news. I was going to look you up today. If you've got a minute, let's talk now. Get it over with, all right?"

"I don't have to talk to you." Now he was angry and petulant. There was a theme here.

"No, you don't, but you started this conversation."

"I don't know what Brian had going on. I know you're supposed to stick something on him. But it's not going to work. Brian didn't do anything." The anger was overtaking the whining.

"Somebody's feeding you bad info, guy. I've got no axe here. If there's nothing to find, I will be happy to report that."

"Yeah, right."

I was fed up. "Look, Carmine. If there's something about Brian Sanders you want to share with me—personal or professional—I want to hear it. But I don't want to fight about it with you."

"There's nothing to say." He looked as though he was thinking of more to say about having nothing to say and decided against it. He turned and stalked off.

"Wait, Carmine. Just one thing, all right? Tell me about the trips to Atlantic City."

He took the bait. He whirled around and came at me, fists clenched.

"There's nothing. I'm telling you to forget about that shit." He took a long breath and tried to pull himself together. "We played craps. Blackjack. Had a few laughs. That was it! Now leave it the fuck alone." His face was angry, his pose adamant, but his eyes were two dark pools of misery. Carmine was not a good liar.

"I'll be sure and include that in my report. Stockman should know how helpful you've been."

For a moment, I thought I had pushed too far. He wanted to hit me. But he decided against it.

This time I let him walk away. My Pop always said I was good with people.

SPUD LOOKED UP as I put the two cups of coffee down on the table.

He counted off with upheld fingers as he reported. "Mortgages are still in a mess, but I got Sudhir's boss to agree to let you have him for an hour on Friday. Eleven-thirty, if that's okay."

"That's fine," I said.

His index finger came up. "Lowell Barrington wants to know what this is all about before he agrees to meet. I'll talk to him again. He wants to buy me a beer tomorrow night."

"The guy's a little paranoid?"

He shrugged. "He sounded distracted. Carmine was off the desk when I called. I'll try again in a few." The middle finger was coincidentally appropriate.

"Don't bother. We just met."

"Oh? How'd it go?"

"Carmine's a lying little shit. And scared. I'll let him stew for a bit before I talk to him again."

Spud added his ring finger. "And."

"Yeah?"

"Gwendolyn called from Mr. Stockman's office. You have a ten-thirty with Jack Avery. In his office."

"Why can't everybody who wants a piece of me just come here? We can give out numbers, like at Zabar's."

"You know they call him 'Iron Man'? He does triathlons. He's done the Around Manhattan Swim a few times. He's not fast, but he's like a hippo. He goes forever."

"Hippos don't really swim," I said.

"Really?"

"They kind of run underwater, I think. I read that somewhere. They're also very aggressive. They kill more humans every year than lions or crocodiles."

There was always a chance that Avery wanted to see me to apologize and offer me whatever help he could. And a chance that I would spot a pig with a six-foot wingspan circling the building. "So, where do I find our Iron Man?"

"Up on thirty-nine."

"Down the hall from Stockman?"

"No. Head of compliance doesn't rate the harbor view. He's on the other side of the floor—all the way back in Legal. Surrounded by lawyers."

My vision of hell.

A HARRIED-LOOKING receptionist was on the phone as I came through the double doors.

"Avery?" I asked softly.

She waved vaguely back over her shoulder.

I thanked her and moved on through a warren of cubicles surrounded by stacks of paper. Cardboard file boxes lined both sides of the narrow hallway, reducing the navigable space to the point that I was practically walking sideways. It was like walking in on a caucus of hoarders.

And everyone was grim. They were doing serious work. Serious typing. Serious talking on the phone. Serious xeroxing. All were dedicated, cult-like, to the care and breeding of documents. I had another one of my brief flashes of claustrophobia.

Jack Avery didn't have a window, but he did have a small room to himself, buffered from the somber surroundings by an uninhabited secretary's desk. He seemed to be the only lawyer on the floor without a gatekeeper. I poked my head around the door and gave a discreet knock. He rose, gave my hand a polite shake, and gestured me to take the only other chair in the tiny room.

The wall behind him held a pastel-colored watercolor of a vaguely rural scene—bland, corporate art, designed to be ignored. The only hint of character in the room was a set of framed photos over the desk. They were all pictures of Jack Avery in competition. Jack Avery charging up the beach, water streaming from him, his massive gut looking in perfect proportion to his outsized shoulders, thighs, and arms. Perched on a bicycle, pedaling up a mountain highway. Red-faced and pouring sweat, as he crossed a finish line beneath a banner reading "Ironman World Championship, Hawaii." My respect for him went up a notch—he wasn't just a big brute, he was a big brute in incredible shape.

"Thank you for coming up. I want to apologize for my behavior yesterday. Like a lot of people here at the firm, I have been under a lot of stress lately. That is not an excuse, merely an explanation."

He paused, reached under the desk, and handed over a Thomas Pink shopping bag. "I understand I inadvertently tore your shirt. Please accept these as replacements."

I didn't know who had done his speechwriting—though it sounded a lot like Stockman—but his delivery was well rehearsed and almost flawless. His eyes betrayed him, though. I could see he still wanted to beat the crap out of me.

He had the cleanest, barest desk in the department. There was a yellow legal pad and two sharpened pencils in front of him. That was it.

He picked up a pencil. "I want to cooperate with your investigation. Please tell me what you need."

Somebody must have jerked very hard on his leash. I looked in the bag. There were a half-dozen white Egyptian cotton pinpoint button-down dress shirts.

"Thank you. You didn't have to do this." I knew he did.

"They make a nice shirt."

I needed to pick his brain, but if he stood up suddenly or got that look in his eyes again, I was going to be out the door and gone.

"Everybody is telling me that Brian Sanders was a great guy and squeaky clean. So, what do you think has the SEC riled up? I'm coming up with nada."

"I was never a fan. I think traders in general have a big chip on their shoulders. He was no different. But I looked. If there was something there, I would have found it."

It sounded like he had his own chip, but I let it pass.

"In your experience, what are they usually looking for?"

"Number one. Insider trading. Doesn't apply, though, 'cause the guy traded government bonds. There's been maybe two cases of that in the last century. Next, fraud. Mishandling funds. That kind of thing. But there's no sign of anything like that. His book was marked to market. There were no trade settlement problems. I've gone back over his trades twice now. Nothing."

"All of his trades?"

He tried not to look startled. "Of course. What do you mean?"

"Come on, Jack. The missing Arrowhead trades? That was you who tried to hide them, wasn't it? You've got the security codes. Give me credit for some brains."

He nodded once, like it hurt.

"I just don't get the 'why' of it. The SEC would have turned them up anyway. Then they'd be sure they were on to something."

He looked deflated, beaten—embarrassed. "That's what Bill was reaming me out about. I thought you heard it all."

I shook my head. "I didn't hear a word. So, what was the point?" Then it hit me. "It was about me, right? You wanted to trip me up."

"I figured if I sent you off on some wild-goose chase with the

Arrowhead bullshit, you'd waste your time and still come up with nothing in the end."

"So I would get the boot and you'd be Stockman's go-to guy again."

"Something like that."

Spud was still back in the conference room up to his earlobes matching Arrowhead trade tickets.

"Well done. It worked."

If the problem wasn't with the Arrowhead trades, it could be anywhere. I'd have to start again from the top.

"Look, thanks for the shirts. And thanks for opening up. Believe me, Jack, I am not your problem. I'm going to be gone in less than two weeks."

"From now on you've got my full cooperation. Anything you need, you let me know." He handed me a business card with both his office and cell-phone numbers. I tucked it into my wallet and left.

I had been reassured. Comforted. Confessed to and cosseted. But I couldn't shake the feeling that I had also been manipulated. Outmaneuvered. Maybe it was a hangover from my time upstate, but I was not comforted by the thought that an ex-cop was now my bosom buddy. Cops were the best liars of all.

I GOT HOME minutes before the Kid and Heather arrived.

The Kid came in the door first, looking borderline meltdown. The eyes were darting, his fingers were beating an odd rhythm on the palms of his hands, and he was doing the one-note hum without ever seeming to take a breath. I went into a near meltdown of my own. I wanted to hold him and comfort him, I was afraid of the coming explosion, and I felt guilty that a moment before I had been happy and not thinking of my son.

Heather followed him in. "He's okay, Mr. Stafford. Really. Actually, he's doing really well. We just ran into Mrs. Montefiore in the elevator."

When the Ansonia converted to condominiums, enough of the opera community that had always called it home stuck around and kept the place interesting. The Kid loved music, but some of the Ansonia's characters were a bit larger than life—operatic—with all the trappings of divadom. Mrs. Montefiore spoke in arias, projecting to the back of the house in any setting. She was also a big woman—in every direction—and dressed to be noticed, in brilliantly colored caftans and hibiscus-print muumuus. She wore too much dangly jewelry and seemed to douse herself in Tabu each morning. For a five-year-old autistic child, being in an elevator with her was like being locked in a closet with Godzilla.

"Maybe I should read to him," I said, looking wildly about for one of his car books.

"He's coping, Mr. Stafford. Let him." She crouched next to him and spoke in his direction, but not directly at him. "He's home now. He's in his safe place." She turned to me. "The finger thing is healthy. Stimming. It helps him focus."

Heather had a tattoo of an ornate butterfly trapped in barbed wire on her arm that made me uncomfortable every time I looked at it. But she had the magic when it came to the Kid.

The Kid took a breath and began pacing. He walked from the front door to the living room window, to the door to his room, and back to the start. He did the circuit three times, his fingers flicking impossibly fast the whole time, keeping exactly to the same course, the same steps, each time. And with each lap, he became less stressed. He stopped next to Heather and turned to me.

"Hello, Jason." He spoke in his little robot voice—no inflection or emphasis. Heather, the school, and I were all coaching him on the basics of social interplay. He had surprised us all by being a quick study.

"Hey, Kid. Rough day?"

"Fine." A quick study, but still as communicative as a teenager.

"How was school?"

He thought about the question for a very long minute. It was too non-specific. I thought of amending it, but he answered first.

"Fine." And he turned and walked into his room. A perfectly normal American child.

SPUD LOOKED EXHAUSTED. I must have looked worse; he at least had youth, natural good looks, and all of his hair.

It was four o'clock on Thursday afternoon and we had been plowing through trades all day, with only short breaks for coffee and bathroom. The mountains of computer printouts had moved from one side of the room to the other.

"We are wasting our time," I announced. My neck muscles were so tight I thought I was developing a hump.

Spud leaned back in his chair. "Maybe we're finding out there's nothing there."

I didn't believe it. "I need a different approach. Context. I need to speak to those other traders."

"You've got a full day with them tomorrow."

I nodded. "Tell me something. Barilla told me that Sanders was not a big producer for his first two years. Then this year he suddenly explodes. He's a power hitter. Six months later, he's dead and the SEC is asking questions. Why didn't someone check up on him earlier?"

Spud shook his head. "No one asks why when you're making money."

"Nyah. It's a natural question. Some junior trader comes along and thinks he discovered the money tree, the first thing you ask is 'How are you making it?'"

"It wasn't anything illegal. Everybody knew what he was doing."

"Spud, lad. Have you been holding out on me?"

"No! Really, there's nothing to tell. He made a few big bets early on this year. The big guys on the desk knew all about it. He checked with them first."

"Tell me."

"Brian thought the market had been too quiet for too long—we were due for a shakeout. When the shit finally hit the fan, he figured two things would happen. First, volatility would explode. So he loaded up on options. It was the cheapest way to get the most leverage out of the trade. He cleared over five mil on that trade alone."

"Wasn't he over his risk limits?"

"Yeah, but the big guys knew. They let him."

Risk limits are internal controls—the SEC wouldn't have cared. "What else?"

"He figured the most vulnerable part of the market was still housing. Mortgages. He wasn't supposed to trade in that stuff, but he made a good case. So they let him go short a few hundred mil or so."

"The guys in risk management weren't all over him?"

"The senior guys on the desk backed him up. I think they had the same trade on."

Again. Nothing illegal. It was fairly typical internal rule-bending but nothing that should have brought in the regulators.

"It was that big options trade that showed me there were missing trades."

"Say again."

"All those trades that were hidden in the system? The Arrowhead trades."

"Yeah, I remember. And this big trade, where he cleared millions, was one of those?"

"The unwind, yeah. Arrowhead took him out of the whole position. Brian was psyched. I thought he left some money on the table, too. Arrowhead probably made a half-mil or so themselves."

"Goddamnit!" If I'd known what questions to ask, I could have saved myself a lot of time and headaches. "Spud, that client keeps coming up. I want you to pull every Arrowhead trade. We're going to look at them all over again."

"Not again."

"Think of it as penance for holding out on me," I said.

"I wasn't holding out." There was no passion in his denial. "I don't know why anybody would care."

"I don't either. But I don't think Barilla had any idea this was going on. Stockman certainly didn't. It may all be quite legal, but it keeps failing the sniff test. I'm not letting go until I know everything about those trades."

He made a show of looking at his watch. "And you want me to start now?"

"Got a date?"

"As a matter of fact. Remember? I'm supposed to meet Lowell Barrington for drinks." Sanders' buddy over on the stock side.

"All right," I sighed. "Soften him up for me. Do what you can on the Arrowhead trades before you leave. We'll pick it up again in the morning."

I stood up and tossed my empty coffee cup into the trash.

"And you're cutting out?" He sounded more teasing than aggrieved.

"Privileges of age and seniority."

"Got a date?"

"As a matter of fact . . ."

I SHAVED, SHOWERED, DEODORIZED, and trimmed my nose hairs. I put on a fresh pair of boxers and one of my new Thomas Pink white dress shirts. I gargled a second time, just to be sure. And I reminded myself of my father's advice: "It's not what you say to a woman, it's how well you listen."

The last time I had gone on a date, I was a multimillionaire Wall Street managing director with a summer house in Montauk that I rarely had time for. And I had all my hair.

Now I was an ex-con and celebrating my first paycheck in years. I looked my age and then some. Though my face had picked up a touch of normal color, the rest of me was still the standard prison hue—pasty white. I gave myself an honest appraisal. I smiled. The mirror didn't break. Wanda was right—I looked better smiling. Still, I was no prize.

Wanda and I had traded voice mail messages all day but had not yet actually had a conversation, so there was a touch of relief in see-ing her striding up Amsterdam from the subway. I was waiting for the light. She saw me, waved, and gestured for me to wait.

She walked like an athlete, long-legged and confident, with a touch of street attitude. Her wraparound dress clung in just the right spots. I liked watching her. So did other guys on the street—she turned heads. I felt more than a bit outclassed.

"Hey. Would you mind if we didn't start the evening in there?" She gestured toward P&G's.

"Not at all. I was going to suggest that myself."

She smiled, acknowledging the lie, but accepting it as a compliment. She put her arm through mine and turned us toward Broadway. With her heels, we were the same height.

"I made reservations at Cafe Luxembourg, but if there's someplace you'd rather?"

She gave a short shake of her head. "Too showy. Too expensive. And they have nothing I like."

"You've been there?"

"Never. Let me ask you. Do you do Greek?"

"Not on a first date."

She laughed lightly. "Come on, make an exception."

"Where to?"

We started up Broadway. There was a Greek restaurant a few blocks up, but Wanda strode past it and continued uptown. I tried to match her pace. It wasn't easy.

"Is it far? Shall I get us a cab?"

"I like to walk."

Maybe conversation could get her to slow the pace a bit.

"So, do I ever get to find out what you do in Roger's act?"

"Ah, yes. My secret." She smiled. It was a great smile. "Very little. I wear a costume like Wonder Woman—that seems to be the most important part—and I hand him props. It also helps if I act a bit clueless."

"I can't imagine you as clueless."

"Thank you. I am, after all, a doctoral candidate. It's all misdirection. Smoke and mirrors."

She stopped in the middle of the sidewalk and struck a pose—one hip forward, back bent to accentuate her tits and ass. Her face was transformed by a smile of pure brilliance—or incipient idiocy—and a gaze of unfocused elation. She had magically lost all signs of higher brain functions, and it didn't matter.

"Scary, huh?" she said, relaxing the stance and turning uptown again.

"No, not at all. Impressive, in fact. I'd say Roger's lucky to have you."

"He acts like a stinker, but he's not so bad. It's easy money and it doesn't interfere with school."

The conversation hadn't slowed her pace at all. I swallowed a huff and kept up.

"How far uptown are we walking? Columbia?"

"My school. Not quite."

We passed the Zabar's empire.

"Why physical therapy?"

"That's a story," she said.

"But not a secret?"

"No," she laughed again. I was already in love with that laugh. "I was a dancer. I spent eight years with the Rockettes, did two national tours—*Fosse* and *42nd Street*—and for three years I did *Cats* in London, Paris, and Frankfurt."

"Wow. That's some résumé. Like I said, Roger's lucky to have you."

"And one day my left hip started to hurt. Like any dancer, I ignored it for six months until both hips hurt so bad I couldn't work. I came back to New York, and saw a bunch of doctors who all told me the same thing. If I wanted to keep walking, I had to give up dancing."

"Your walking is just fine."

We had crossed Eighty-sixth Street and were charging up past Murray's Sturgeon Shop. I was barely maintaining.

"After months of physical therapy. That's when I became a believer. And next May I will take my hard-earned degree and go to work treating other dancers."

"Do you ever dance these days?"

"Are you asking me to go dancing?"

"Please. There's all sorts of ways I can embarrass myself. I don't need to go out on a dance floor to do it."

"Aaah. I bet you're a natural. You've never had a secret passion for salsa? Rumba?"

"Secrets, again." I hop-skipped a quick step to keep up.

"Am I walking too fast for you?" She deliberately slowed.

"You have the longest, most beautiful legs I have ever seen."

"That's a yes, then."

"It is."

"Hmm." She didn't look happy, but she did walk a touch slower.

We were well north of Ninety-sixth Street and still moving uptown. The character of the street had changed incrementally. A tourist would not have noticed. My sensors automatically went on the alert.

"We are heading out of my area of expertise," I said.

"And into mine. Come on, you're more than halfway there."

We walked steadily, if just a hair slower, for the next few blocks.

"I thought all New Yorkers walked fast," she said.

I laughed. "We do, don't mind me. Set your pace. I'll manage."

She threw her head back in victory. "Thanks," she added. We sped up again.

"So you've had me doing all the talking."

"And I've been enjoying it," I said.

"I've got to ask you something, though."

Here it comes, I thought. The "prison" question. She's heard about my past and has to ask. I tried not to cringe.

"Sure. Go ahead."

"Tell me about your son."

The Kid was an even more convoluted subject.

"Ah. He and I are just getting to know each other."

The tension of not talking about it ran head-on into the tension of talking about it. I decided I wanted her to understand. I kept talking.

"His universe is very small, unique, and nothing like the one you and I travel through. And it is my challenge every day, first, to try to see the world through his eyes—and I fail at that all the time—and second, to try to get him to see the world as we see it—and I fail at that, too, but not as badly. I think."

I gave her a quick glance and got an encouraging nod.

"He is autistic. There are all levels of functionality. You have geniuses like Temple Grandin and Daniel Tammet, and you have kids who can't speak and have zero connection to the real world. A couple of weeks ago, my son was living in a locked room because my wife—and her mother—thought he couldn't do any better and he tended to hurt himself if he got out. I took a chance that there was something more there—having no clue about what I was getting into. I'm blown away by how much progress he's made already. But . . ."

I had tried sharing some of these thoughts with my father, but I constantly choked myself off. There was no one else. Once started, I found it impossible to stop.

"I don't care about his becoming a genius. I'd just like to have a conversation with him. That would be huge. Right now he speaks almost exclusively in quotes—mostly from commercials. I'd like him to be able to play a game with other kids—without biting them. But I can't imagine that ever happening. He barely acknowledges the existence of other children. Someday I'd like him to have a girl-friend. It happens. But nobody can tell me yet what's attainable. They don't know. He's two years behind some of the other kids in terms of training. That's a lot. Some kids never make it up. Some do. We'll see."

We had stopped walking. Wanda was staring into my eyes, fol-lowing every word.

"He hates being touched or picked up. Hugs are out. Most of the time he looks right through me, like I'm not there. Unless he's hungry. And sometimes he flies into a rage or screams in terror over nothing and the only thing that quiets him is for me to wrap myself around him and we rock back and forth together until his body just gives out on him and he collapses. And it makes me feel like a brute. Like I'm his jailer. But it feels really good to be able to actually do something for him."

I was beyond trying to make her understand—I was talking for my benefit alone. I looked away and continued.

"Sometimes I go in, after he falls asleep, and I kiss the air over his forehead. I'm afraid that if I touch him, he'll wake up and have a fit—he's got a thing about germs." I gave a short rueful laugh. "At least he's clean. He is the cleanest little five-year-old you can imagine."

I looked back at Wanda. The intensity of her sympathy was hard to face.

"I'm sorry," I said. "Shit. I got carried away. I don't get to talk about this much. God, you just wanted the short answer, right? 'How's your kid?' 'Oh, just fine. Fine.' Really, I am sorry."

"No, no. It's okay. You just caught me off guard." She took my arm, pulled it to her, and turned again uptown. We walked about a dozen steps before she spoke again. "If you ever want to talk about it again, let me know, okay? That's some powerful magic you've got going on."

"*KALISPERA*, SKELI. Nice to see you again." The speaker was a well-muscled but very round man in his sixties.

"*Efharisto*, Aristos. *Kalispera. Pos eisai.*"

"Good. Good. *Fenese poli orea apopse.*"

Wanda kissed him lightly on the cheek. "*Eisai poli evgenikos.*"

They smiled like old friends. I tried smiling, too.

The aromas of grilling lamb, garlic, cardamom, oregano, and freshly baked pita all assaulted me at once. I was overpowered.

We were seated in the garden in back. Strands of tiny beads of light offset the twilight and candles. It was early but the restaurant was already full.

"May I order? For both of us."

No woman had ever asked me that before.

"May I order the wine, at least?"

"Hmmp."

I was beginning to learn what that little sound meant—or thought I was.

"I'm entirely in your hands," I said.

She grinned and tossed her hair. A waiter appeared as though summoned telepathically.

"Do you still serve sangria here?"

"Plenty," he said.

"We'll have a pitcher."

I had not drunk sangria since a particularly bad episode in college.

"Aah," I said.

She gave that elfin laugh again. "Oh, stop. This will surprise you."

It did. Food began to arrive. Large platters filled with small dishes. Bowls of hummus and tzatziki, and a platter of warm bread. A salad. An appetizer of small grilled fish as salty as the Atlantic Ocean. Moussaka. Lamb.

"Here. You have to try this," she said, pushing a small plate of tzatziki toward me.

I could smell the garlic from across the table—my nose and palate were still adjusting to life outside.

"Not too strong on the garlic, I hope."

"Incredibly strong. And as I just had some, I would advise you to do the same. Self-defense."

She scooped up a sizable dollop with her index finger and placed it in my mouth. For a moment, my senses were so overwhelmed I thought I'd gone deaf.

"Like it?"

I enjoyed watching her eat. She was consumed with the tastes, aromas, and textures of each dish. Conversation was unnecessary—an interference. The lamb chops had been reduced to spindly ribs of bone before she spoke again.

"You are a very unusual guy, do you know that? Very few guys can just enjoy the moment at dinner. It's like they're working to impress all the time. It's a bore. But you just dig in and soak up the flavors, the smells."

"I'm sorry, I haven't eaten this well in a very long time."

"Please. Let me keep my illusions."

I couldn't let such a misperception stand. "I've been sitting here trying to come up with something to say. Something brilliant. Or at least something not completely lame. I am finding that it is very important to me that you think well of me."

She tilted her head in a look of appraisal. "I don't know what to make of you."

That didn't make me any less uncomfortable.

"Is Wanda your real name?"

"You don't believe I'm really Wanda the Wandaful?"

"Is Kelly your real name?"

"Kelly? No. Why Kelly?"

"I thought I heard the man at the door call you that."

"Aristos? We were speaking Greek."

I was no closer to having my question answered. Instead of pursuing it any further, I sipped the sangria. It was excellent.

Wanda began a soft chuckle that grew into a full-bellied laugh. "Skeli! He called me Skeli!" She smiled at me fondly. "It's an old joke of his. He says I'm like a good wine. We both have great legs."

"You speak Greek?" It was a night of revelations.

"Not really. Army brat. I can order food and ask to use the bathroom in half a dozen languages."

"I like 'Skeli.' May I call you Skeli?"

"Aristos feeds me. He's earned the right to call me Osama if he wants."

"Is that all it takes?"

"He feeds me really well."

"So is Wanda another alias?"

She gave a sly smile. "If we're trading secrets, I get to ask first."

Wanda reached over and linked our fingers. A woman's affectionate touch managed to send immediate signals to the more primitive areas of my brain. I couldn't tell if there was really a promise there, or if my deprived neurons were interpreting any signal as a sexual come-on.

"Okay, but no Deadhead questions, all right?"

"Agreed."

I braced myself for a question about Angie. The worst buzzkill I could think of.

"What did you do on Wall Street?"

If she knew I had worked on Wall Street, she probably knew the rest of the story. I wanted to take my hand back, but she tightened her fingers and gave me an intense look of interest.

"I used to manage a group of traders. Currencies. Foreign exchange. It's not very exciting to talk about." I sounded boorish, I knew. "Sometimes it was exciting doing it."

She squeezed my hand again, encouraging me to say more.

"But I made a couple of mistakes. I don't do that anymore. Right now I'm doing private consulting." I'd always thought of consulting as a joke—another way of saying you were looking for a real job. It might be as close as I was going to get.

"I've heard about the mistakes," she said.

"Oh." I did manage to retrieve my hand that time. I didn't want to talk about it. Ever. And certainly not on our first date.

"PaJohn told us. He remembered reading about it in the *Journal* a few years ago."

"It figures. He's the only one at the bar who reads anything other than the *Racing Form*."

"Don't be mean," she said, reaching for my hand again. "Nobody cares, you know. And besides, everybody reads the *Post*."

"I don't like being discussed." I sounded angry and defensive. I sounded like a jerk.

"That's what Vinny said. He told PaJohn that if you ever got around to wanting to talk about it, that was fine, but otherwise everybody should just leave it be."

I hadn't expected such sensitivity from the afternoon bar crowd. I realized that said something not so pleasant about me.

"That was nice of him."

"Yup."

"But you asked."

"Yup." She flashed me her smile again.

I took a deep breath and a leap of faith. "Okay. I spent two years away for a white-collar crime. But I didn't steal customers' money. It was an accounting shuffle. A big one. Half a billion dollars."

Her eyebrows shot up. Put that way, it was an impressive accomplishment—if not quite an achievement.

"When I got caught, I thought they went hard on me, but I'm starting to change my mind." I couldn't read her, but I kept on talking. "But if you were to ask me if I regret what I did, or if I would never do it again, I'd have to say the best I can come up with is that I don't ever want to get caught again."

It was the first time I had talked so freely to anyone about my recent past—and it surprised me how desperately I wanted to be understood. I was still trying to understand it myself. But at the same time, I left out huge chunks. Things I wasn't ready to share with anyone just yet.

The next step was hers. If she was some thrill-seeking vampire, just dating an ex-con for the turn-on of a bit of danger, I had probably blown it. And I could live with that. I just hoped she wasn't the judgmental type, waiting to shut me down, or patronize or even lecture me, as soon as she had extracted my confession.

"So, tell me. Is this a deal breaker or what?"

She put her hand on top of mine again. This time the neuron signals were crystal clear. "I just wanted to know how you went two years without getting laid."

THE DOOR TO Wanda's building was plastered with building permits, many of them more than two years old, and a large green dumpster hugged the curb out front. Antique marble lined the entranceway, yet the only light came from a bare bulb dangling from the ceiling. Plaster dust and drying paint clung to the air.

"How's your stamina, handsome?"

Before I had a chance to embarrass myself with an answer, she continued.

"It's five flights and the elevator has been under renovation since before the market collapsed."

"I'll manage."

Wanda led the way. She had no trouble. Neither did I. Prison was good for something.

She stopped at 5A, unlocked the door, and turned to me. "You made it."

"The only thing keeping me going those last two flights was the sight of your beautiful legs in front of me."

She flicked her hem upward by about an inch. "There's more."

Inside the apartment the floors needed refinishing and the fixtures were showing their age, but the space was huge. My entire apartment would have fit in her living room. There was a formal dining room, an eat-in kitchen, and a hallway leading from the foyer back to the bedrooms. Three of them.

"I'm having a Grand Marnier. Join me?" she said, leading me through to the living room.

Grand Marnier always left me with a splitting headache in the morning. "Yes, thanks."

I sat on the couch, swirling the liquor in the pony-sized snifter, while Wanda lit candles on the end table and slid a CD into the stereo. I held my breath and braced myself for Brad Paisley or Taylor Swift. It was Norah Jones. I exhaled.

"I just have to ask . . ."

"How the hell does an ex-dancer with no money," she finished my question, "and now a student with even less, get to have an apartment like this?"

"I hope there's a good story behind it."

"No such luck. My ex owns the building. I get to stay here rent-free until he changes his mind. And as long as the real estate market sucks, I'm in the clear. He also pays for my school."

"Sorry. We weren't going to talk about our exes," I said.

"Yeah, but in some neighborhoods, talking about real estate is the same as foreplay."

A second song came on. Slow and wistful. I put my glass on the table and took Wanda's hand.

"This I can dance to. Will you join me?"

There was a question in her eye—I must have answered it.

She rose off the couch in a long, fluid glide—as smooth and strong as silk. Our hips swayed, a slow and sensual dance, while I buried my face in her hair, breathing her in. It was all familiar but also new. We fit everywhere it mattered. I placed a single kiss on her bare neck and she gave a tiny shudder.

"Mmmm." It was half sigh and half growl.

Another song started up, the beat slightly faster. We almost broke apart, but she pulled me to her and we continued to sway to our own music. She pressed against me. I tried to concentrate on the batting order and stats of the Yankees starters. I was two years out of practice. I couldn't get past Jeter. Wanda giggled.

"What's that?" I said.

"If that's going to keep getting in the way, maybe we should do something about it."

I kissed her. Sweet. Grand Marnier. Wet. Strong.

I let her lead me to the bedroom.

The first time was rushed. When I came—after A-Rod, but long before Jorge—it was a two-year explosion that left me dazed. She looked up at me, pleased with herself and her effect on me.

I felt, for a moment, peace. For the briefest flicker of time, I lost all awareness of prison, an ex-wife, Stockman, the SEC, *The Science and Fiction of Autism*, the oppressive squeeze of money, and the constant awareness that everything for me seemed to have peaked some years before and all the rest was simply walking through the blocking and repeating the lines of a secondary role in my own life. For that split second, I felt like someone else. Me.

She closed her eyes. I kissed her lids and whispered, "Skeli."

"Hah! You don't get me that cheap."

I kissed her on the lips again. Still sweet, but salty now as well. Still wet. Still strong. Still hungry. I felt my body responding.

She giggled again.

I began to pull away, but she held me in place with those perfect legs. "That has to be a world-record recovery time."

I STOOD OVER the Kid, watching him sleep. I felt blessed.

I loved him no less, nor no more than a few hours before, but the anchor of onerous responsibility had been lifted—a feeling I had not had the courage to acknowledge. I still felt the responsibility, but it was now a banner streaming in the wind, a source of pride.

Sexual release. Kindness. Intimacy. The feeling of a woman's naked breasts pressed against my bare chest. The freedom of a few hours to begin to love another made me love my son more, not less.

A part of me acknowledged that I did not yet deserve such good fortune.

The Kid gave a mini-snore, something between a gasp and a snuffle, and turned his head toward the faint light reflected from the street below.

For all my sins, there was my penance, his limbs askew after kicking away the sheets, his face glowing with his mother's beauty, the picture marred only by a faint spittle of drool that hung from his lip, which, upon reflection, could have mirrored his mother under the right circumstances.

And for the few good deeds I may have done along the way, there, too, was the miracle of my reward. My salvation.

THAT FEELING, that glow, was gone by morning. That's when the bodies started piling up.

SPUD WAS HUNGOVER. Most of Wall Street—up to a certain age, which I had passed long since—was hungover. It was Friday morning and that was just part of the cultural norm.

I have heard various explanations for the Thursday-night bacchanal, most having to do with the daily and weekly migratory patterns of commuters—the Bridge and Tunnel crowd—but my favorite had a truer anthropologic ring. As colleges did away with Friday classes, students responded by adding a full third day to the weekend, a ritual they then carried on to their working lives. Whatever the reason, the public should be aware that major financial decisions are regularly made on Friday mornings by people whose brain and other nervous system functions are still suffering the effects of that last round of four-in-the-morning Jägermeister shots.

"What you got for me?" I greeted him brightly. Whenever I had been severely hungover, the thing I hated most was a bright greeting.

He looked at me with red eyes and exhaled an aroma of stale beer and tequila.

"I met up with Lowell Barrington last night."

The OTC stock trader. He was on my list for early afternoon.

"He bought me a few beers," he continued.

"And?"

"He wanted to know what you know."

"What did you say?"

"The truth. There may be something here, maybe not. Arrowhead might have something to do with it. And maybe not."

"How did he take it?"

"He switched from beer to scotch. Doubles. I think he's scared shitless."

"Anything else?"

"Something about having to talk to his father. He was getting a little wobbly by that time. I don't know what he meant."

"All right. I guess we'll find out. Meantime, anything more on the Arrowhead trades?"

"No pattern I can see."

"Keep looking. I'll be back. I've got to check in with Stockman."

GWEN GAVE ME one of her best apologetic smiles. I waited. I read all the newspapers. Just as I was about to go back and start over again, Barilla and Jack Avery arrived.

"What's this about?" Barilla asked me.

"No idea. He's kept me waiting almost an hour."

Avery sank onto the couch facing me and said nothing.

Gwen's intercom buzzed. "You may all go in now."

I wasn't comfortable giving my report for an audience. I had suspicions, but no hard facts. All I hoped to get out of the meeting was another week's work. But with a gang in there, I wasn't going to be in control.

Stockman didn't rise, but waved us all to chairs. Barilla and I took the two seats facing his desk. Avery took the couch.

"So, Jason? You have a report for us?" It sounded like a question, but it wasn't. It was my cue. I was obviously supposed to have a report prepared.

"No. What I've got is more questions. And I have some suspicions."

Avery jumped right in. "If there is nothing there, then you've found it. End of story."

Stockman barely acknowledged him. "Please, continue, Jason," he murmured, as though he had the script in hand.

"I'm pretty sure those trips to the casino have something to do with it. I need to talk with some of the junior traders. I've tried, but it's been a crazy week."

"Amen," Barilla said.

Stockman nodded agreement.

"I'm also concerned that this Arrowhead account might be involved."

Stockman looked at the other two. "Do either of you know these people?"

Avery looked blank.

"Not really," Barilla said. "I know that most of the traders don't like them. They're pickoff artists, constantly trying to catch somebody offsides. Every young guy has gotten his pants pulled down by those slimeballs once or twice—and even some of the senior guys who should know better."

"Slimy, then. But illegal?" Stockman asked.

"I have no reason to think so. I mean, I can't even *prove* they're slimy. Maybe all their inquiry is legit. Traders make mistakes, but don't like to admit it." He nodded to me.

I agreed. "It's always the client's fault. I think they teach that in Trading 101."

"So all I have is an opinion. I wouldn't bet the farm on it," Barilla finished.

Stockman turned back to me.

"So, where are we? Maybe we should just invite the SEC in right away. Brave it out."

I wanted that second week's check.

"There is one thing." I turned to Barilla. "Did you know that Sanders was doing unauthorized trades?"

His face turned to stone.

"Not illegal trades," I explained to Stockman. "Just trades that were not his normal bread and butter."

"What is this, Gene?"

Avery smelled the blood in the water. He leaned forward on the couch as though he might leap forward at any moment and slap the cuffs on Barilla.

"I don't know," Barilla said carefully. "I'd bet there's some good explanation, though. What do the senior guys in that group say?"

"They can't seem to find the time to talk with me." I turned to Stockman. "They keep putting me off."

The steam coming off Barilla could have powered a small city.

Stockman turned to Avery. "Jack? Your opinion? I'm inclined to give this another week."

Avery looked for a moment as though he were unsure how to play it. Then he became animated. "I disagree. Let's stick to the issues—this is some sideshow. Stafford and I have both been over all of Sanders' trades. There's nothing there."

Stockman nodded distractedly, as though he was only half listening. "No, there's too much at stake here. If there's anything at all irregular, I want to see it first. We can afford the few bucks we're paying Mr. Stafford. Gene? I want you to look into this business of the unauthorized trades. And tell your people to make some time for this. Now. Today. Understood?"

I didn't look at Barilla. I was afraid that if I met his eye, I'd turn to stone.

"Meantime I will have a word with the sales manager. I'll see if he has any better read on the client."

Avery broke in. "Would it help if I spoke with the account direct?"

Stockman answered very politely, as though correcting a favored, but flawed child. "A call from the head of compliance might be considered a bit over the top, Jack. It could be construed in all the wrong ways. Let's not rush ahead of ourselves."

The meeting was over. I had another good-sized check coming, but I had the feeling I was going to pay for it.

Avery brushed past us on the way out and disappeared. Barilla and I were alone facing the elevators.

"You ever pull that on me again, I will have your ass. I don't like getting blindsided on my own turf."

"I have tried to talk with those guys. They blew me off."

"Why didn't you come to me?"

He was right.

"And what the fuck is this with the 'unauthorized trades'? Where did that bullshit come from?"

"I didn't make it up. Supposedly, your senior team knew all about it."

"Fine. Then how about you, me, and the three of them all meet up in my office in ten minutes?" It was not a request.

I had an appointment to start interviewing the other junior traders. "I'll be there."

Barilla was seriously pissed, and if he was clean, he had every right to be. But the bitch of it was, a guilty man would have played it just the same way.

IN MY DAYS back at Case, the mortgage department was so huge they had their own trading floor. They had people who did nothing but work with originating banks—the small, local banks who actually made the loans and who then sold them upstream to Case,

Fannie Mae, or one of the other mega-banks. There were salesmen who serviced only a single client and yet produced millions in commissions each year. Traders specialized in ARMs, dwarfs, IOs, POs, balloons, private label, and Z-bonds. All of which were meaningless to me and to most of the employees outside the gated community of mortgage securitization.

At Weld, the mortgage department would have fit in a good-sized walk-in closet. There were six very stressed traders in one corner of the floor, huddled together like the last standing survivors at the Little Big Horn.

"I'm looking for Sudhir," I said. "Sudhir Patel?"

One of the two women traders looked up from her computer and gestured to the other side of the aisle.

Sudhir looked like a dusky-colored rabbit. He was thin, almost to the point of emaciation, and was a week or two overdue for a haircut. I judged him to be in his mid-twenties, but he looked years younger. Almost prepubescent. Except for the area around his eyes. The stress lines were those of a fifty-year-old bond trader, not the junior guy on the desk.

"Sudhir?"

He nodded, not quite meeting my eye.

"I'm Stafford. We're supposed to have an eleven-thirty, but I have to push it back. Is that a problem?"

I thought he was going to start crying.

"What is this about? I don't know if I am allowed to talk with you." He had the bravado of a scared middle-schooler. Delivered in a round, Cambridge-educated accent, it was almost funny.

"I'm going to be talking to all of Brian Sanders' friends. It's not the Inquisition."

"I barely knew the man."

This was such an obvious lie, so easily disproved, that I snapped in anger. "Enough. I'll be back in"—I checked my watch—"half an hour. Then I want to hear all about Atlantic City, Arrowhead, and the whole deal. Got it? Don't waste my fucking time."

He went pale and sweat appeared on his upper lip. I thought he might heave right there.

"Half an hour," I repeated. I turned and hurried to Barilla's office. I had the feeling that if I were even seconds late, he would gladly feed me to the sharks.

WE ALL ARRIVED together. Barilla's office got crowded quickly—there were only two chairs facing the desk. I rested a hip on the bookcase. The three honchos from the proprietary trading group were all people I recognized.

Richard Wheeler had joined a start-up hedge fund back in the mid-eighties and retired ten years later after appearing on the cover of *Fortune* magazine—twice. Weld must have offered him an incredible deal to return to the fray.

Cornelius "Neil" Wilkinson had been at Case when I was there. He still wore a bow tie and suit every day—I imagined he wore them all weekend as well—and glasses so delicate they looked as though they would disintegrate if he sneezed. In almost any gathering he would have been the smartest guy in the room. He had briefly made himself famous by marrying a Miss Venezuela runner-up with a degree from the London School of Economics. He met her while working in London. But he'd had an odd career, never quite in the right seat at the right time. He had done all right, I supposed, but he hadn't made one-tenth the money a lot of less smart guys had. Neil was the case in point for the traders' prayer: "I'd rather be lucky than smart."

Kirsten Miller also wore a suit. A men's-cut suit. She wore no makeup and her hair appeared to have been styled by a misogynist. Like most women on Wall Street, she had been screwed over and passed over any number of times—most egregiously by one of the Street's oldest, most prestigious firms. But she had fought them in court and won—collecting an eight-figure settlement. Her victory was Pyrrhic, however. She had been virtually unemployable after that. I was surprised that Weld would have taken the chance on her. But she was at least Neil's equal for pure brainpower, and she had a lust for trading anything that moved.

It was an intimidating group.

Barilla started as soon as we were settled. "This is Jason Stafford. Anybody know him?"

All three nodded. Neil smiled.

"He's here looking into this shit about Sanders. He tells me that you aren't giving him your full cooperation."

I wanted to cringe. That wasn't the way I would have expressed it. All three were staring at me coldly, any positive or even neutral feelings had been tossed aside.

Wheeler answered for them all. "It's been a busy week, Gene. We have a lot of balls in the air. I told him we would make time for him this afternoon." He looked over at me. "We still plan on that."

"He just told me—in a meeting upstairs with Bill Stockman and the compliance guy—that Sanders was doing some unauthorized trading. Which leaves me with two questions: Did you people know what he was doing? And why didn't I know?"

Neil spoke first. "Yes, we knew. And, excuse me, we didn't tell you because it just wasn't that big a deal."

"Not a big deal? I just checked his position reports from last spring. The kid was short a hundred million dollars in agency bonds and mortgages. You didn't think I needed to know that some junior trader was out there spinning the roulette wheel?"

"A hundred was his limit," Neil said. "We told him that, and he stuck to it. Really, Gene, it didn't seem a lot to us."

"You three throw around billions and we let you because, all told, you have over seventy years of experience. That's not the same as letting the new guy just whip 'em around."

Wheeler stepped in. "We monitored him closely. Kirsten checked his position three or four times a day."

Barilla made to interrupt, but Wheeler held up a hand and continued.

"Brian came to us in the beginning of the year with the trade idea. He was convinced that the mortgage mess was going to get a lot worse before it got better."

Neil took over. "I argued against it, but he persuaded me. He was right."

Wheeler continued. "We put the trade on. We sold some mortgage-backs and we bought credit default swaps and T-notes. When the trade started moving in our direction, Brian came back and asked if he could get some credit for the idea."

Kirsten spoke for the first time. "He came to me, actually. I told these guys we should let him come along for the ride. I watched him every day. He traded around the position, but basically he just rode the trade for just south of ten mil." She grinned. "He did a nice job."

"What did the three of you clear on the trade?" I asked.

"Just under a yard."

One billion dollars.

"That's not public information," Barilla said.

"Nice trade." It is one thing to call the market right—to find a strategy or a trend that will make good money. It requires a whole other skill set to put on the trade in a big enough way, and to ride it long enough, that it turns a flash of insight into that kind of money.

"Look, Gene, we just didn't think you needed to be bothered over a hundred-million-dollar position." Wheeler wasn't pleading, he sounded bored. Exasperated, maybe. "If we got your dick in the wringer with Stockman, we apologize, but, honestly, it just wasn't worth talking about."

Barilla blew out a long stream of air. "No, Rich, you're right. If you had come to me, I would have thought there was a problem. But while we're on the subject—are there any other little land mines over there I should know about?"

The three traders shared looks for a moment. Neil spoke for them. "Not a thing."

I believed him. So did Barilla.

"Satisfied?" he said to me.

It was time to mend some bridges. "I'm sorry. All of you. It looks like I set off a fire alarm when I smelled cigarette smoke." I turned to Barilla. "I'll talk to Stockman. Tell him this was all a touch of hysteria on my part."

"Screw him. He's annoying, that's all. He's got much bigger turds than this raining down on him right now. If he ever remembers to ask, I'll take care of it." He leaned forward and beat a rapid tattoo on the desk with his index fingers. "Anything else for these people?"

"I'll make it quick."

He nodded.

"Arrowhead? A small hedge fund that seems to be unusually active. Sanders did some business with them. Ring any bells?"

"Never heard of them," Wheeler said.

"Kirsten?"

"We don't do customer business. We trade direct with the Street. I know Brian dealt with the sales force—a little. But we're a proprietary desk—we trade for the firm. Legal would rather we stayed away from the clients."

Legal would not have wanted to explain how the firm made close to a billion dollars on bets they had sold to clients.

Neil had not answered.

"How about you?"

He put his head back and stared at the ceiling for a moment. "I am quite sure that I would remember." He looked over the top of his glasses. "And I don't."

I tried not to sigh. I felt like I was in hot pursuit of a wild goose down a dead-end street.

"Did you know about these casino trips? Atlantic City and so on?"

"I did," Kirsten said. "It surprised me."

"Why's that?"

"Brian did not gamble. He once said he would rather save his money and buy a casino. I suppose he went along for the camaraderie. Networking."

I was back to nowhere. Sanders had been a good kid with a great future, right on the cusp of making his mark on Wall Street. The SEC would find nothing. It was all a waste of time and talent. The only one who would benefit was me. I had another $25,000 check waiting.

"Gene, I'm sorry. Let me get out of your hair. Thanks for all your time. If I come up with anything else, do you mind if I just drop by and run it by you?"

"Not a problem," Wheeler said.

"Then we're done," Barilla said. "Back to the trenches."

We filed out. Neil Wilkinson stopped me just outside the door.

"I don't know if you remember, but we worked together at Case some years ago."

"Of course I remember." It was like asking a nuclear physicist if he remembered working with Oppenheimer. "I thought you were wasted there. They tried to squeeze you into the research department, didn't they?"

"It wasn't a good fit."

Understated as always.

"I wanted to tell you," he said. "You and your department did brilliantly with the euro conversion. You cleaned up quite nicely."

When the euro was first introduced, the EU announced how each of the various party currencies would be converted, following months of speculation. I was the youngest managing director at the firm and running the foreign exchange desk. We had cleaned up.

"I thought you had left the firm by that time," I said.

"Yes. I was with Rothkamp in London—trading sovereign debt— but we heard about your trade. You managed to nail each currency."

It had been one of my biggest coups.

"Thanks. But we missed Italy by a good margin."

"You are modest. Modesty never pays dividends. At any rate, it was good to meet you again. We should have a drink some night. Let us know if there's anything we can do. Brian Sanders was not always a pleasant person—he was young and aggressive—but I do not believe he was a crook."

He walked away, leaving me confused and conflicted. Wilkinson was not only a market genius, but a genuine human being as well. He had ignored the deficits in my past and my transparent manipula-tions with Stockman and Barilla, and had simply congratulated me on one of the greatest successes of my professional career. His decency humiliated me. I felt a sudden wave of claustrophobia. The ceilings felt too low, even the arena-sized dimensions of the trading floor seemed to be closing in on me. I needed to be outside— outdoors—with a breeze in the air and the sun on my face.

THE HEBREW NATIONAL hot dog vendor on the sidewalk outside the Weld building already had a line waiting. Wall Street eats lunch early.

I pushed past the small group of smokers and wove through the crawling traffic on Trinity Place. There was a stretch of sidewalk drenched in late-September sunshine. I leaned up against the build-ing, closed my eyes, and raised my face to the sky.

I felt my heart rate slow and my throat open up again. It was a beautiful day. How many beautiful days had I missed in my life? My two years in prison were nothing compared to the twenty years of self-imposed incarceration, sitting at a trading desk, staring at a computer monitor—or banks of them, as we had in the early years—not even aware of weather or what season it happened to be. For ten hours a day, or more, I had been able to tune out all aspects of life that did not immediately serve the needs of the great god Mammon, so that a phone call from my beautiful but often very needy wife was an annoyance, a distraction, taking me away from the obsessive clutches of the market.

I thought about taking the Kid and escaping New York once and for all. With the money from selling the apartment, we could get by for a long time in Vermont, or Idaho. I could study yoga, or become a housepainter, or buy some land and go into organic farming.

Ridiculous. The pieces of my life came sliding back into place. I could handle them. The Kid needed a very special school, and would for years to come. He needed stability, his routine. And what did I need? I was a New Yorker and therefore spoiled beyond belief. What would bagels be like in Boise? In Bennington, pastrami comes presliced in little sealed plastic packets that hang over the bacon at Food-town. I would have to mow grass and shovel snow.

But most of all, I would miss the buzz. That sense of urgency that New York imparts to all its denizens. That knowledge that, no matter the time of day, I knew where to find the best bagel, the best pastrami. And I would know it when I found it.

I was myself again. I was fine. I had no idea what was next in my life, but I had absolutely no doubt that I could handle it. I was ready to do battle once again.

I saw Sudhir come out the front door of the Weld building and head downtown toward the subway.

"Hey! Yo, Sudhir! Over here." I waved.

He turned, saw me, and ran.

———

MOST OF THE CORPORATE bond traders were busy loading up paper plates from a makeshift buffet of Chinese takeout spread across three trading desks. Carmine was already back at his station, his plate mounded high with dumplings, twice-cooked pork, a shrimp roll, chicken with black bean sauce, and a dollop of assorted vegetables in lobster sauce.

"Got a minute?" I said.

He didn't look up. "I don't have to talk to you."

"Is that the message I'm supposed to take back upstairs? The hothead junior trader doesn't want to talk to me."

There had been fear in his bravado the last time we spoke. It was gone, replaced with a seething anger. "My boss says I don't have to talk to you. You got a problem, go through channels. Now, fuck off. I'm working."

I briefly considered making a scene, getting loud, forcing a confrontation with the arrogant little prick—and discarded the idea. Let Stockman deal with it. I was being paid to conduct a polite, professional look into accounting issues. Now I had a junior trader running from me in fear and another furiously flipping me off. Life's too short for this shit, I thought.

"Hey, you got some problem here?"

A flashily dressed bantam had appeared at my elbow.

"Sorry?" I chose not to have heard both his words and the attitude.

The guy was mid-forties, fighting a widow's peak and other inevitable signs of aging, with a George Hamilton tan, a sculpted comb-over, and a few thousand dollars of Armani silk. He had the narrow-shouldered, slim-hipped build that too easily develops a basketball-shaped paunch. It was just starting to show. Twice-cooked pork and white rice weren't going to help.

"I asked you what's your problem."

"Who are you?"

"Who am I? You got some set. This is *my* department. You are bothering *my* trader. I told him, anyone bothers you, you tell him to go through channels. Well, channels is *me*!"

The scene I had hoped to avoid was unfolding for me despite my good intentions.

"I'm sorry. I don't know you."

"Well, I know you. You're the crook who got off way too easy a couple of years ago. You must have ratted a dozen of your buddies to get a deal that soft. You give up a couple of your traders? Old friends?"

We had an attentive and growing audience. They were all on his side. It was not the forum I would have chosen to discuss my past. A full retreat was in order; I just wanted to do it with a few shreds of dignity.

"I was just on my way. I'll leave you to your lunch."

Carmine grinned up at me, enjoying my defeat. I vowed that if I ever had the chance to do him harm, I would take it. No qualms.

The bantam stepped back, overplaying his moment with a bow and a sweep of his hand. I tried not to look hurried as I passed him.

He spoke to my back. "You tell Stockman if he's got a problem over here, he can come talk to me himself. Jack Avery has been all over this department and didn't come up with a thing. I run a clean operation and I take care of my own."

The traders actually applauded his speech.

THE STOCK TRADING FLOOR was just on the opposite side of the building, but judging by the change in atmosphere it could have been the other side of the planet. There was no screaming, no calling out of prices or orders, just the constant tap, tap, tap of computer keys.

Row upon row of traders sat staring into monitors, shoulders hunched, necks thrust forward. Typing. The few murmurs of conversation were hushed and monosyllabic. It looked like some Victorian clerical nightmare—only with computers rather than quill pens and green ledger books.

"Lowell Barrington?" The trader I had approached waved me away without speaking.

"Next row." A pretty assistant with a big Hello Kitty hairclip pointed the way. The traders on either side gave her brief scowls as though she had disturbed their monastic trance.

Barrington looked up as I approached. He made no pretense of disinterest. He knew who I was and what I wanted. He nodded, removed his headset, and stood up. He looked like three centuries of good breeding, wrapped in Brooks Brothers.

"Jason Stafford," I announced. "Is there somewhere we can talk privately?"

I followed him to the water fountain at the end of the row. He took a long drink before turning to face me.

"Would it be all right with you if we put this off until Monday?" He spoke in a quiet, respectful voice, as though he'd just been brought up before the headmaster.

"What's going to be different on Monday, Lowell?" I played his game. Quiet, restrained, but authoritative.

He transformed in a blink. His shoulders sagged, his face looked drawn and very tired. "There are things I want to tell you. Things I have been waiting to tell. But there will be repercussions. I need some time to prepare my family."

I had no objection—in theory. In practice, however, I could feel his need to confess. "Look, we can get help. Whatever it takes. Legal or otherwise. The sooner you come clean, the faster we can start fixing things."

He stood straighter and gave me an angry, almost insulted, look.

"I don't think you understand. I need to discuss this with my father before I speak to you. I tried to make that clear to Freddie last night."

"Before or after you started ordering doubles? You've had plenty of time to talk it over with Dad. Now's the time to fess up. Get it over with."

"Brian was my friend. I want to get all this straightened out. I will help you. But not until after the weekend."

He was adamant. But when he met my eyes, I saw a different story. They were the deeply sad eyes of a man confronting shame. I lost the willingness to push—he was already punishing himself, more than the world would ever do.

"Come find me Monday morning," I said.

"Thank you." The window behind his eyes had shut again.

"I'll be in at eight. Don't make me come find you, all right?"

His head jerked in what I took to be a nod of agreement.

I felt like a bully.

THE FRIDAY-AFTERNOON torpor had settled over the markets and the ranks began to thin. The commissioned salesmen were first to leave. The junior traders would be last. I went to check to see if Sudhir had returned.

"I'm looking for Sudhir," I announced.

The head mortgage trader looked up from his monitor. He had a little, graying mustache that made him look a decade older than his forty-or-so years. Or maybe it had just been a tough week.

"You and me both," he said.

"We were supposed to be meeting earlier today, but I saw him cutting out of the building around lunchtime."

"That makes you the last person to see him, pal."

I seemed to be having some strange effects on junior traders that day.

"Check this out," he said. "Hey, Carol. Where's the fax from the Rabbit?"

The woman I had spoken with that morning handed me a single sheet of paper. I scanned it quickly. It was a letter of resignation. No explanation. Effective immediately.

"The guy went home, typed this up, and faxed it in. Weirdest fucking move anybody's pulled on me. We're sitting here sorting through his positions. Who the hell resigns by fax?"

"He never said a word?"

"Wait. It gets better. I had Carol call him at home. She gets his roommate just as the guy is headed out for the weekend. He's pissed. The Rabbit packed a couple of suitcases and split. For the airport. He's flying home. Probably already in the air, by now."

"Home?" I was having a hard time keeping up.

"Yeah, home. As in India. North Dum Dum or whatever."

"Kolkata," Carol said.

"Same difference."

"And nobody saw this coming?" I said.

"I should be grateful," he said. "He did save me the trouble of firing his ass."

"He wasn't making it?"

He gestured for me to follow him. We walked only a few steps, then he turned and spoke quietly.

"Sudhir had a great first year. I thought he was going to be a star. Smart, cool, always focused. Then about a year ago, he started hanging out with that arrogant asshole Sanders. Excuse me speaking ill of the dead, but the guy was nasty. Sudhir turns into party guy and starts hitting the casinos every week. Then he starts getting slack. Next he's making mistakes."

"Trading mistakes."

"Nothing serious. He misprices something by a quarter point or so. I ream him out. He says it'll never happen again, and a week later it does."

"What did you do?"

"Cut him slack at first—too much, I guess. Anyway, whatever mojo he ever had went away and never came back. He practically jumped every time somebody said his name. That's when we started calling him the Rabbit. Finally, I reined in his risk limits and told him to cut back on his positions. He would have been gone by year-end."

"Did you ever think he might have been up to anything?"

"Dirty?"

I nodded.

"I had compliance go over his trades," he said. "Avery gave him a clean bill of health. It all came to nothing."

"But you weren't convinced."

"Something smelled wrong, but I've got ten other things begging for my attention every minute of my day. I let it go."

A FULL DAY of checking trade reports had done nothing to make Spud look any brighter or happier.

"You all right?"

"I'm never going to drink again."

"And a good time was had by all," I said. "Having any luck here?"

He shook his head.

"Nor me." I filled him in quickly on the scene with Carmine, Lowell's pleading for more time, and Sudhir's self-banishment.

"No kidding?" He found the Sudhir story the funniest. "He's a weird dude."

"Really? I think your buddy Lowell may have him beat. He's like a WASP zombie. Walking dead."

"Did Jack Avery find you?"

"No. I didn't know he was looking."

"He stopped by. I told him you were interviewing Brian's friends all afternoon."

It had been a long week—I didn't want another face-off with Jack Avery late on a Friday.

"I think it's safe to say these guys were up to something—but who knows what? None of them are talking. The only thing to do is wait for Monday and see if Barrington opens up after he talks with his father. Unless you have any other ideas."

"Just one." He wrote a number on a slip of paper and pushed it across the table. "Call Brian's roommate. He lives out in Brooklyn. Maybe he knows something."

It sounded like a long shot, but I was down to long shots.

I WAITED UNTIL the Kid was down for the night before calling the roommate. Eight o'clock on a Friday night and it sounded like I had woken him up.

"Jason Stafford," I repeated. "I've been hired by Weld. Brian's old firm."

"Oh. Yeah."

"So, I'd like to come over and chat about Brian for a bit."

"Okay." His voice was thin and detached and it hit me. He wasn't sleepy, he was high. "Why?"

"Like I said. I've been hired by Weld to tie up some loose ends for them."

He laughed. "That's funny."

I wondered what pharmaceutical cocktail he had ingested.

"How's that?"

"'Cause that's what the other guy said. Last week. Loose ends. That's funny."

The reason that I failed to see the humor had to be chemical in nature.

"Did this guy leave a name?"

"I don't know."

I thought about asking him to describe the man, but decided against it. For all I knew, the whole experience had been a hallucination.

"So when's good for you?" My father had arranged to take the Kid all day Sunday. "Sunday? Noon all right?"

Noon was not all right. The roomie worked nights all weekend. Late afternoon would be okay. Late.

SUNDAY MORNING.

I made pancakes while the Kid read one of his car books. I knew he couldn't read—though he could identify all his letters as long as they were in capitals—but his memory was so strong that he could look at a page that had once been read to him and repeat all the words verbatim. If he missed a word, he always missed that word—it was simply a white noise gap in his memory. And though the voice was definitely that of a five-year-old boy, the cadence and inflection were always those of whoever had first read the page to him. I could identify the ghosts of the living as the Kid turned the pages: Angie's vocal sweeps and dips, and sometimes halting pronunciation as she sounded out longer words; my father's dramatic pauses and emphasis, a skill I'd never known he possessed; Mamma's syrupy sweetness, making dual carburetors and fuel injection systems sound like magnolia blossoms and maypop berries. And there was another voice, one that I did not at first recognize. A bit flat, but confident. Both strong and unassuming. It was a nice voice. I liked it.

"Time for breakfast, Kid." Pancakes with corn syrup, a taste he had inherited from his mother, who claimed that "maple tastes weird."

"Not hungry." If I ever figured out whose voice he was imitating when he went into his "NO!" mode, I planned on waterboarding the son of a bitch.

"It doesn't matter, little one. This is when we eat."

"Not hungry." He flipped a page and began to recite the brief history of the DeLorean. The book failed to mention the CEO's arrest for trafficking in cocaine.

I let him finish. "Okay, Kid. Put it away and get up here."

His body tensed and for a moment I was sure I was about to witness a major meltdown. Then, with a tuneless whistle, like a French teapot, he came to the table and began to eat. Another minor victory for both of us.

My father arrived minutes later and I fed him, too.

"What the . . . ? What is this?"

"Corn syrup," I said.

"Tastes weird."

He ate the pancakes anyway.

After a lengthy discussion of the proper placement and use of children's car seats, and an even lengthier discussion of various possible routes, Pop bundled up the Kid and a half-dozen of his toy cars, and took him for a day trip out to a petting zoo in New Jersey.

I cleaned the apartment, shopped for essentials, read another chapter of *The Science and Fiction of Autism*, belatedly arranged for a dozen roses to be sent to Wanda with a note that avoided use of the word "love," yet did not actually preclude it, and mapped out my route to Brooklyn.

LATE THAT AFTERNOON, I rode the J train for the first time in my life—out past the projects, nearly to the border of East New York. Brian Sanders' roommate lived in one of the dozen or so brownstone buildings on the block that was not yet undergoing renovation.

It was a testimony to the insanity of the New York real estate market that a young person making $150,000 a year or more could still be forced to share a third-floor walk-up around the corner from the Lucky Seven Bar and Grill, a steadfastly ungentrified watering hole, its single window painted black and the exterior walls tagged with the red three-jeweled crown of the local Bloods chapter.

The front windows of Sanders' building were all covered in steel mesh. It would stop a brick, but not a bullet. That was probably a good sign in that neighborhood. The intercom must have worked, despite emitting a series of deafening and disheartening squawks—the door buzzed and gave way as I pushed through.

The door to the apartment was ajar, and I let myself in. The roommate was draped over a sagging armchair, which had been covered with an orange-and-blue silk batik. He was wrapped in an ankle-length Chinese silk robe with a migraine-inducing pattern in purple and silver stripes. Maybe he was color-blind.

"I'm Mitch," he said. "What's your name again?"

"Jason."

Elaborate formalities out of the way, he went back to staring, dull-eyed, at a giant, wide-screen television where a bald man with a pussy patch beard was haranguing an attractive, but somewhat matronly blond woman at a Lucite lectern. The woman was squealing and clapping her hands with all the forced enthusiasm she could muster. I waited for a commercial before speaking again—I hated to interrupt.

"I've come to talk about Brian. Can you spare a few minutes?"

He picked up the remote and hit the mute button.

"Sorry to disturb your day off." I tried to sound sincere.

"I work nights during the week. Friday and Saturday I get to play my music."

A musician. I looked around the room. No piano. No guitars. No sign of a horn or even a music stand.

"Oh? What do you play?"

"I compose." He sounded insulted, as though actually playing an instrument was beneath him.

"Modern? Classical?"

He did not sneer, but I felt it anyway. "Techno. I record street sounds and work it into a dance, pop framework. Want to hear some?"

Not a chance. "I'd like to ask you about Brian."

He let out a long sigh. "Oh, man. Can't you just take his stuff?"

"His stuff?"

"It's been forever. I want to rent the room, but I've got to get his stuff out. His parents said they'd come get it, but I don't think they meant it. I mean, why would they come all the way from Missouri for a bunch of stuff?"

I thought he made a good point.

"Do you mind if I go through it?"

"That big guy from your office already did that. He took a couple of things."

"Did the big guy have a name?" I asked. Like Jack Avery? Or Gene Barilla?

Mitch shrugged. I had the feeling that Mitch shrugged a lot.

"If you just put it out at the curb, it'll all be gone by morning."

"I'll have someone take care of it," I lied.

Mitch laughed. "See? That's just what *he* said!"

I wanted to kick myself—or him. I had given up a Yankees game and a couple of beers at P&G's to come out to Brooklyn to entertain young Mitch.

"What can you tell me about Brian? What kind of a guy was he?"

Shrug. "He was a good roommate. He worked days, I worked nights. We got along."

The definition of a good roommate in the world of youth today. At Ray Brook, a good roommate was someone who didn't insist on soaping your back in the showers.

"Did you think he was under any stress before he died? Anything at work that might have been bothering him?"

Shrug.

"Did he ever open up about anything? Did you two ever talk?"

"We talked about whose turn it was to clean the bathroom. He was my roommate, not my sister."

The commercials ended. The bald man returned. Mitch turned the sound back on. Interview over.

"Sorry. I'll just take a look around his room," I said.

Mitch didn't answer, but then, I hadn't expected that he would.

Brian's room had been searched—by someone who didn't care whether anyone knew about it or not. Drawers had been dumped and overturned. The floor of the closet was three feet deep in clothes, still attached to their hangers. It was a good-sized room, with that rarity of New York amenities, a window that looked out on something other than an airshaft—in this case, the street and a smog-throttled ginkgo tree.

I went through the mess, but if there had been anything there that would have given me a better feel for Brian Sanders, I couldn't find it. He read Neal Stephenson and Robert Heinlein and Cormac McCarthy. He bought his suits—quite sensibly, I thought—at Saint Laurie. The shirts were all Lands' End. Boxers, not briefs. He preferred ribbed condoms. But there were no letters, no bank or brokerage statements, no appointment book, address book, or diary. Like most of his peers, he had kept all that on his computer—and that was gone.

It was a wasted trip.

"I'm taking off," I said to the back of Mitch's head. "Don't get up."

He hit the mute button again. "Wait. You're not taking his stuff?"

I had his attention, even if briefly and misguided. "I don't see a laptop around. Did I miss it, or did the other guy take it?"

"It's in his gym bag."

"I didn't see a gym bag."

"Check the bottom of the front hall closet. By the door."

The closet held three seasons of windbreakers, leather jackets, overcoats, and down bubble coats. There was also a small pile of old boots, discarded running shoes, and worn-out sandals. And three cases of empty Corona bottles. And a single ski pole, a chipped clay flowerpot holding a long-dead poinsettia, and, at the bottom, a black nylon bag, scuffed and battered.

I pulled the bag out. It was heavier than it looked.

"Hey. How come the other guy didn't take this?" I called out.

Mitch waited until the commercial, touting some kind of chicken-coating mix, reached its denouement before answering.

"Nobody asked."

Maybe the roommate was smarter than he looked.

I opened the bag. Wrapped carefully in a foul-smelling towel, and buried beneath a pile of assorted, once white anklet socks, sweat-shirts, T-shirts, and nylon shorts, was a red Dell laptop. But what lay spread across the bottom of the bag was even more interesting.

I looked up at Mitch. He was again transfixed by the negotiations between the blond and the bald guy.

The bag sloshed as I moved it. Hundreds—possibly a thousand or more—of casino chips slithered across the bottom of the bag. Black, green, blue, and purple. The logos on the chips were for at least half a dozen casinos all over the tristate area. My mind was racing, trying to estimate a total value, but it was impossible. There was at the very least well over $100,000. I was looking at financial security for myself and the Kid for some time to come.

There would be complicating factors—such as what my parole officer would say if I were caught in a casino, in another state. He had the power to send me back to jail for spitting in the subway. That set one parameter—he must never know.

"I'm going to take the whole bag with me, if that's okay," I said.

"When are you coming back for the rest?" He barely turned his head.

"I'll be in touch."

The blond lady was hugging the bald guy. He didn't look happy about it.

I let myself out.

———

A SMALL GROUP of teenagers were huddled on the subway platform, just beyond the aura of the sputtering neon lights. They were all dressed in similar uniforms of dark hoodies, baggy jeans, and expensive-looking basketball shoes. They could have been on their way to gospel choir practice for all I knew, and if that were the case, I was sure they would forgive me for hugging the gym bag to my chest as I stood directly in front of the token booth attendant. The line between racial profiling and basic street survival skills is thinner in some neighborhoods than others.

When the two beefy men dressed in blue windbreakers and baseball caps and looking exactly like plainclothes cops came through the turnstile, I breathed a little easier. Until I noticed that they seemed to be paying much more attention to me than to the young men in the shadows. Or rather, working a bit too hard not to pay attention to me.

Policemen had never made me uncomfortable—before my troubles. Now they always did. But I was willing to endure a bit of discomfort for the security of an escort, as I carried my newfound treasure home through the wilds of Brooklyn.

I changed to the Number 2 train at Fulton Street. So did they. The odds of this being mere coincidence were all the way down at the far left side of the bell curve. They sat at the opposite end of the car, looking everywhere but at me. I started to sweat.

The older, grayer, and leaner of the two wore Nikes and slim-cut jeans. He seemed more reserved, contained. The younger man's head never stopped moving, his eyes darting, catching everything. I waited until the train began to roll out of the station, got up, and moved to the next car. If they followed me, I wasn't neurotic or paranoid, I was justifiably concerned. They stayed in the first car, leaving me convinced that I was neurotic, paranoid, and justifiably concerned.

The train was held at Forty-second Street, waiting for a local to arrive. I walked out and waited on the platform. I felt the younger of the two watching me whenever my back was to him.

The local arrived. I stepped in and turned to stare at the two, daring them to follow. They ignored me. The doors closed and both trains headed uptown.

By the time the local pulled into the Lincoln Center stop, I was laughing at my own paranoid fantasies. The two guys in caps had no interest in me. It was another New York City coincidence, in a city that regularly defied all odds.

But when I got to the express stop at Seventy-second, I dashed out and darted up the stairs. Then I stopped at the top to see if anyone followed me. Then I cursed myself for being an idiot and went home.

THERE WAS STILL almost an hour before the Kid was due home. I dumped everything out of Sanders' gym bag, spreading it all out on my bed, before succumbing to another attack of paranoia. I couldn't afford to have any of this mess traced to me. I needed gloves, so there would be no incriminating prints.

Serious criminals always seemed to possess a ready supply of latex gloves, the kind the guards used for cavity checks up at Ray Brook. I didn't even have a pair of rubber gloves for cleaning the bathroom. I pulled out drawers and searched through the bottom of the boxes Angie had left me, now hidden away at the back of the single closet. I found an old pair of Oleg Cassini rabbit-fur-lined leather gloves. They were not designed for delicate criminal enterprise, but they would have to do.

I packed all the dirty laundry back into the bag and tossed it by the front door. The laptop I set aside for later examination. Then I began to sort the chips into colored piles. The black pile of hundred-dollar chips was the largest. One thousand five hundred twenty. One hundred fifty-eight purple chips at five hundred apiece.

One hundred thirty-two ten-dollar blue chips. Thirty-four yellows—twenties. I did the math without thinking about it. An even two hundred thirty-three thousand dollars. 233. A prime number—an irregular prime. The twelfth integer in a standard Fibonacci series. A Markov number.

Why would Brian Sanders hang on to the chips? Why had he not converted them into cash? To avoid reporting them as winnings for tax purposes? That would only have put the problem off to another day. If he had been trying to remain inconspicuous, for any reason, he would remain so only up until he tried to cash in ten or twenty thousand dollars' worth of chips. He would have done better to have passed them in small amounts. Unless he wasn't interested in the cash, only the chips.

I scooped the chips into a plastic bag and hid them at the bottom of the kitchen garbage pail. It wasn't foolproof, but it would do until I figured out a way to cash them. Then I packed all the workout clothes, sneakers, and towels back into the gym bag and carried it down the hall to the incinerator chute.

Which is how I came to be standing in the hall on a warm September night, wearing fur-lined leather gloves, when my father and son stepped out of the elevator together.

The Kid paid me no attention. He acknowledged my presence only by stepping around me as he dashed down the hall. My father, however, stopped and gave me a questioning look.

"I was doing some cleaning," I said. "They were the only gloves I could find."

"Well, then, I know what to get you for your birthday."

"How was the Kid today?"

"The Kid had a great day. He touched a pig. And if he's anywhere near as exhausted as I am, you'll have him in bed within the hour."

"Did he eat?"

"Two hot dogs."

"How did you get him to eat a hot dog?" The Kid had a healthy aversion to food cooked by street vendors. More like a phobia.

"From across the street. Gray's Papaya. They grill 'em. Best in New York."

I could see the store from my front window. There were times when the line went out the door and down the block. Cabbies triple-parked out front in the middle of the night while they ran in and grabbed a quick dinner.

"I didn't know the Kid would eat them."

"What do I always tell you? Get to know your son when he's young."

"Right." I couldn't remember his ever having said that to me before.

"I got him a new car. The '61 Jaguar."

"Cool," I said.

He gave me a brief, awkward hug. "Take care, son."

THE JAGUAR E-TYPE *is considered by many car enthusiasts to be the most beautiful automobile ever built. It was first introduced in 1961 in the format that later came to be called the Series I, with a 3.8 liter, 6-cylinder engine, producing 265 hp. By modern standards, its 6.9 seconds zero to sixty may seem a bit sluggish, but at the time the XKE was quick enough to immediately enter the realm of legend.*

"The 1961 Corvette did zero to sixty in eight-point-four seconds. It had eight cylinders."

"I didn't know that," I said. "Shall I keep reading?"

He nodded. The Kid was wrapped up in his sheet, mummy-style. Pop had been right, he was exhausted. His head was already listing sideways.

The first 500 cars off the assembly line featured external hood latches and a non-sculpted floor, resulting in truncated leg room. These earliest models are especially prized by collectors, though subsequent models were much more comfortable to drive.

"This is a subsequent model. See? No hood latch." He held up the latest addition to his collection.

How did he know what "subsequent" meant? He could barely say the word without stumbling. But he was speaking in real sentences.

Heather was very encouraging about the Kid's fascination with cars. Of course, any interest of his, beyond the often painful limits of his own mind, was reason to be encouraged. If he had been into dino-saurs, instead of cars, he would have known how many teeth each one had, what they weighed when full-grown, and how they cared for their young. He would have been able to explain—at great length—that the Spinosaurus could never have kicked T. rex's butt because T. rex wouldn't exist for another 35 million years after ol' Spiney was dead, and besides, they lived on different continents.

"Want me to read through all the specs again?"

He didn't answer. He was gone. An inaudible click and he was out, as though the power source had been suddenly turned off. I checked to see that he was breathing. I held my breath and put my face next to his to listen. He smelled of Crest and hot dog.

I LAY AWAKE for a long time. Other than the hoard of chips, the trip to Brooklyn had been a bust. Sanders' laptop held about eighty giga-bytes of live jam band music—Galactic, The String Cheese Incident, and dozens of others, including, of course, a good bit of Phish. I also found a saved file containing the e-mail messages of a slowly deterio-rating relationship with a girl named Cherysse, who had kept asking him to "get the fuck out of Wall Street" and join her in San Francisco. The messages ended a year before he died.

But if there was a secret file, in which our man confessed to all his worldly sins, and laid out the mechanics of a great conspiracy, I had somehow missed it.

The buzz of my phone, vibrating on the glass-topped coffee table, rescued me from the clutches of the Latin Kings, who were all leer-ing in through the bars of my old cell at Ray Brook, as Jack Avery patiently explained that I was back in prison because I had stolen the pita chips. I had fallen asleep on the couch.

"Hello?" I checked my watch. It was close to midnight.

"Hey, Boo." It was Angie. I did not want to talk with her, unless she was sending money.

"How did you get my number?" "How did you get my number, bitch?" was what I meant to say.

"Mamma."

Of course. I had asked her not to give it to Angie. Unless it was an emergency.

"What's up?"

"I need to talk to my little boy." She was drunk. Not sloppy, but definitely beyond the point of operating a vehicle or attempting a delicate telephone conversation. I could hear it in the way she made two syllables out of the word "boy."

"The Kid is asleep. He's been asleep for hours. I am not going to wake him up." The Kid would have been up half the night afterward—and so would I. It would have thrown off his schedule the whole next day as well. It also felt good to tell her "No."

"It's not so late." It is always noon if you are the center of the universe.

"Angie." I softened my voice. "The Kid needs his rest. It's what? Eleven there? It's midnight here. Can we do this tomorrow? After he gets home from school? Dinnertime?"

"School? You have that boy in school?"

I wanted to reach through the phone and grab her and shake her by the nape of the neck until she started talking sense. "Angie, I don't keep him locked up. Yes, he goes to school. He goes to the park. Today he went to a petting zoo with my father and got to meet a pig."

"I've been talking with TeePaul and he says it's okay if the boy comes live with us."

TeePaul? Tee is Cajun for *petit*. Paul means "small." It was like calling someone Little Small.

"I don't think that's going to work."

"I want my boy back, Jason." She went from steel to tears in a heartbeat. *"Ma petit boug.* I want to hug him and just cover him with kisses."

The Kid would scream bloody murder.

"He is my *Tout-tout,* Boo. I know he's not right, but there is nothing a mother's love can't fix. We just need time. You know he can't be happy without his Mamma. I just want him to be happy."

Why wasn't I surprised? It wasn't going to happen. She would change her mind tomorrow or next week. I had him and I wasn't letting go.

"Angie, the Kid is going to a great school here. He's doing really well. Tell you what, you and your Mamma come visit. We'll get her tickets for *Wicked*—she'll be in heaven. Meantime you can catch the Avedon retrospective at MoMA or hit the Chelsea galleries. Or spend an afternoon being pampered at Bergdorf's. Then we'll get my Pop to meet us and take your Mamma out to Brooklyn for steaks at Luger's. Make it a vacation. You and I can even practice being civil to each other."

The pause was long enough that I thought she might actually be considering it. No such luck.

"I can't," she finally said.

"You can't . . . ?" I was tired and out of practice at making the conversational jumps, doglegs, and cutbacks that were what passed for normalcy with Angie.

"I can't come to New York," she explained, with tight-lipped patience, "because I have a hairline fracture of the radius." Implicit in her words was the evidence of my own hard-heartedness for not having already expressed my sympathy.

She did not explain how a broken arm would keep her from traveling.

"I'm sorry to hear that, Angie. Listen, it's late—"

"Mais. I got TeePaul all upset and confused. He was really sorry.

He's a sweet man, Jason, but he is not as good a driver as he thinks he is—especially when he's been drinking and gets a bit *fout-pas-mal.*"

She was drunker than I thought. Angie was perfectly capable of having a complete conversation without once slipping into Cajun patois. Usually it was an act, another from her portfolio of poses, one that she used when flirting, or being funny—or just before she fell off the barstool.

"I get scared when he drives too fast and I know I can get bitchy when I'm frightened, *mais,* when he passed this old farm truck I let him know just what I thought about that, and that made him take his eyes off the road, just as we got to that really bad curve up by Patoutville. You know the one I mean?"

If there was one thing in this world that I was dead positive on, it was that I had never been to Patoutville in my life.

"The truck was fine, I don't know why he was making such a fuss, and he gets all *boudé,* so I told him I was going to walk home if he was like that. And he got mad. Well, I know I shouldn't have said that." She burst out laughing. "*Merde, cher!* It was thirty miles back to Morgan City. I wasn't about to walk. I just got down from the truck and climbed back up the bank. *Mais,* when he gets down on his side, he sinks right up to his *coullions* in that rice field and I could not help myself, *cher.*"

I tried to establish some order in her patchwork story. "He drove off the road? Into a rice field?"

"*Ain?* That's what I said. Are you listening? I swear, you never listen to me."

She had often commented, when we were together, that one of my most endearing qualities was the way I listened to her.

"Is that how you broke your arm?"

"No, that is not how I broke my arm." Thoroughly exasperated. "If you would stop interrupting, I would tell you." She paused and waited for my apology. Not getting it, she continued, "I did something unforgivable. I laughed at him. And he is not like you, he is sensitive. You can't laugh at a sensitive man."

Mamma had often described Angie's father as a "sensitive man." In my hometown, we would have just called him a mean drunk.

"And when he's mad, he just doesn't know his own strength. You see, he was just trying to keep me from walking home, which he explained would have gotten me killed if someone had come along driving too fast and not seen me. And he took my arm, just to stop me, and you know I am delicate . . ."

Like kudzu.

". . . and it broke."

I listened. And felt nothing. Was I over Angie that completely? That quickly? One night—a few hours—with Skeli and I had managed to put seven years behind me. I felt no anger at the cowboy— that's what people like that did. I felt some disgust, revulsion at the images that came to mind, but no great outrage. I did feel some sympathy for Angie. Though she had placed herself in harm's way, she didn't deserve to be hurt. She had hurt me, robbed me, abandoned me, and was now intent on taking from me the person I loved most in the world—but I would not have laid an angry hand on her. And I also felt a buzz of irritation that I was being forced to hear it all and deal with it in the middle of the night. But mostly, I felt an undercurrent of dark fear. My son must not, under any circumstances, be allowed to be dragged down into that ugly swamp.

"Angie, listen. I am very sorry for your troubles." I tried to sound sympathetic. "I am sorry your young cowboy hurt you."

"*Ain?* I just told you! It was an accident." Outrage.

"Okay, I'm sorry you had an accident. And I'm sorry for so many things that have come between us." I let my voice harden. "But I cannot change them now. And there is no way in hell that I am going to let that son of a bitch near my son. You come see him whenever you want. But leave that asshole home."

"I told you, Jason. I want my boy here with me. I will do what I need to do." Her drunkenness had evaporated and the bayou front with it. I felt a sudden cold rush in my gut. "You think any Louisiana court is going to let some New York felon take a baby away from his mother? I've spoken to my lawyer down here, and he has promised to flay you to the bone. You will *not* get away with this."

I sat up, slammed a fist into the wall just hard enough to know I didn't want to do it twice.

"Angie, as long as our son resides in New York, it will be a New York court that hears his case, and they will hear about your drinking and how your mother kept the boy locked in a dark room, and they will hear about your abusive partner as well."

"Goddamnit, Jason! I want my son! Give me my baby."

"Over my dead body." I lost my anger as quickly as it had come. I was left with disgust for the mess of our lives—and an ugly unease.

"I will have my boy." It was a threat. She was willing to take me up on it.

"I'm saying good night, Angie. I am going to hang up now. Maybe we can talk about this again when you sober up. Good night."

She didn't respond.

I hung up.

Fuck. I would have to get hold of my lawyer first thing in the morning. Despite my brave words, I did not trust the courts. Louisiana or New York. Anything could happen there. I would take the Kid and run before I let Angie take him back to Cajun country.

MONDAY MORNING. Spud and I were back in the conference room—rumors were rampant, stocks were crashing, and everyone on the trading floor had the hollow-eyed look of earthquake survivors. Spud didn't look much better. After a few, stress-filled hours of sleep, I fit right in. Zombie central.

From the moment the Kid and I stepped out onto Seventy-fourth Street until I passed through the well-guarded front doors of Weld Securities, I was convinced that I was being tailed. The two guys from the night before seemed to materialize in my peripheral vision on street corners, in subway stations, ducking into doorways, only to transform into harmless-looking fellow New Yorkers when I looked directly at them.

The Kid had sensed my upset—a situation that had threatened to escalate into a disaster when I couldn't find him a matching pair of blue socks. I had been pleasantly surprised to find that he didn't mind mismatched socks on Monday morning, as long as they were both blue.

I needed a day off, a green tea, and a massage. I would have settled for eight hours of uninterrupted sleep.

"How'd you get his laptop?" Spud asked, for what I realized was the second time.

I kept the unedited version to myself. "The roommate let me take it."

After dropping the Kid at school, I had stopped at the post office and mailed a box filled with almost a quarter million dollars of chips to myself. It could stay in the Ansonia mailroom until I figured out how to cash them in—without going back to jail.

"Let's get started," I said.

Lowell Barrington hadn't shown up. He looked like another runner. When I called over to his desk, the bright, bubbly voice of the Hello Kitty girl informed me that he wasn't in yet. Maybe he had joined Sudhir in India. Maybe his father had grounded him.

And my lawyer had yet to return my call. Calls. So far, my day sucked.

Spud fired up the laptop.

Other than the breakup e-mails—and the music—the computer was oddly devoid of personal information. There were no drafts of letters to headhunters, no electronic checkbook, not even an address book outside of his Google account. Sanders had not been on Facebook or Myspace, he had no profile on LinkedIn, and he did not Twitter. Either he had been a unique twenty-first-century young man, or he was hiding something.

"I've got his calendar," Spud said.

"How the hell did I miss that?"

"It was sitting in his 'recycle' bin."

I burst out laughing. I had hid the chips in the garbage—the same place where Sanders kept his secrets.

But Sanders kept his secrets in code. Letters and numbers filled the squares for each date. AH2x/EH. 10K/TP. It was a meaningless jumble. I scanned for patterns. Most simple codes give up their secrets because of patterns. Short words, like articles, are used repetitively. S appears at the end of words more often than any other letter. E is next. And so on.

One pattern leaped out immediately. "Ten K? Two K? See this. They've all got to be numbers. Amounts. Are you with me?"

Spud wasn't listening. "Oh, shit," he said. "This is fucked up." He sat back, shaking his head.

"What?" I barked.

"Brian's three-way? With the two hotties from Morgan? I told you the other day."

"Okay."

"There they are." He pointed to an early-summer weekend date. !JF&!GK/Q.

"I don't get it," I said.

"Jill Felder and Grace Knudsen. In Quogue."

I saw it, but I didn't like it.

Brian Sanders had kept a diary of his sexual adventures. Less than a diary, merely a scorecard.

"HM? See here?" There were half a dozen or more. HM!/VT. *HM/VT. And so on. "Heidi Miller. I met her. Her parents have a ski house near Killington. Nice girl."

"And DH/AC?" There were another half-dozen of those in the months before his accident.

"No idea. Atlantic City?"

"Sanders was very busy."

There were easily a hundred or more different sets of initials.

"What do you think about the punctuation marks?" Spud said.

I ignored the question. I didn't want to know.

"There's two different patterns here," I said. "Look." I pointed to TNX5K/A. "Focus on the ones that look like this. Five K. Five grand. A. Arrowhead. Must be."

Spud and I stared at the screen in silence. TNX was a regular. ZNM and ZNH showed up in earlier months. We arrived at the same point by different paths.

"Those are futures contracts," I said. "M, H, U, Z. Those are the exchange codes for the delivery months. They're the same in foreign exchange. March, June, September, December."

"And ZN is the ticker symbol for the Treasury ten-year-note con-
. tract. I should have caught it right away."

"And TNX?"

"The options contract," Spud said.

We had it.

Strewn amid the coded details of Brian Sanders' sex life were the bits of evidence of his trading transgressions. Once or twice each week, there was an entry that concluded with A. Spud compared the dates and securities with the firm's records. In each case there was a corresponding trade with the Arrowhead account.

The payoff was almost as clear. I could see it, because I knew about the bagful of chips, but I might have caught the pattern anyway. The math was simple.

"Look," I said. "There are three A entries over this two-week period. Five K, seven K, twenty-two K. If we go back over his book, I know we will find the matching Arrowhead trades. All right, so that's thirty-four thousand dollars. Four days after the last trade there's this—17K/FX. That's Sanders getting his cut. Fifty percent."

"How can you know what his cut was?"

"Because it is the exact same pattern every time."

"Every time?"

"Check it out."

He did. I was right. There would be a string of two to five smaller numbers, then one substantially larger, followed sometime in the next week by a figure exactly half of the total. Every time.

"So what's FX? Or TP? Or MS?" He pointed to other weekend coded figures.

"The casinos? Foxwoods. Trump Plaza. Mohegan Sun?"

Spud gazed at the screen in awe. "No shit. It's all right there, isn't it?"

"Almost," I said. "You'd need to see all the trades from Arrowhead to be sure. But the SEC can subpoena them and wrap it all up."

"But there would be no way of tracking the payoff, right? I mean, it was at a casino. Hochstadt could just slip Brian cash each time, and who would know?"

Or chips. My brain was racing ahead—counting up the payoffs. Exactly $233,000. Whoever had the chips would know.

"**THE WHOLE PURPOSE** of your employment with Weld is the *avoidance* of scandal. Did you not understand that?"

Stockman sounded as arch and overbearing as my third-grade teacher, Mrs. Goodier.

"Allow me to educate you to one of the salient events in the history of this firm, Jason. Philip Barrington was one of the three founding partners of Weld Securities back in 1975. He is still on the board. His elder son runs our emerging markets debt trading desk in London. Lowell was his second son."

I had waited half the morning to get in to tell Stockman what Spud and I had turned up. He had listened with half an ear and then began removing the skin from my body in thin, delicately carved strips, one finely honed word at a time.

"What could you possibly have said to the boy?"

Lowell Barrington had left Weld on Friday night and taken the New Haven line as far as Stamford. There he had inexplicably exited the train, a full three stops before reaching Rowayton, where his father was waiting to meet him. According to a half-dozen conflicting witnesses, Lowell had waited on the platform until the arrival of the next fully loaded commuter train and then seemed to step out in front of it. Traffic on the New Haven line had been held up for almost an hour.

"Jack Avery tells me that he spoke to Lowell late Friday afternoon—after you interrogated him—and that the boy was severely depressed. In shock!"

Waiting patiently to get a word in for my own defense was not turning out to be a winning strategy. "Just a minute, Bill. I had a two-minute conversation with the guy. He was stressed. He was guilty about something. But I didn't do anything or say anything to push him over the edge." I was sure about that. Reasonably sure.

"Guilty! Of what? Going to Atlantic City with a customer? Is that what you are claiming?"

Standing up for myself didn't seem to be a winning strategy either.

"Those guys—the whole crew—were up to something illegal. If I found it, so will the SEC."

"Jason, there are much bigger issues involved. If what you say is true, it is all so penny-ante I will be surprised if anyone even cares! And even so, you say you have no proof other than these notes in a calendar. Notes written in some kind of *code*, which you claim to have broken. Where is your proof? Show me the money trail. Where were the payoffs?"

In the mail. I wasn't about to hand over two hundred thousand dollars just for the limited pleasure of having Stockman believe me.

"I'm not done," I said. "If the SEC goes after Arrowhead's records, they'll see both sides of all these trades. They'll be able to put it all together."

"If this is the limit of what you have found, the firm is in no danger."

That was Stockman's bottom line.

"What do you want me to do about Barrington? Talk to the father?"

He waved his hand as though chasing away a gnat. "No. Leave it. As I said, there are bigger issues and I have already devoted too much valuable time to this today."

14 "I DON'T GET IT," Roger said.

Vinny looked over at me and rolled his eyes.

"No, listen," Roger continued. "You tell me he's a crook, but I don't see who's the loser."

The three of us were huddled in Vinny's corner of the bar, talking in half-whispers. I had been trying to explain what I'd been working on—without giving up the names of any of the players.

Vinny took a turn at explaining it. "It's not that tricky. It's the same as any small-time putz stealing from the boss. Like the bartender who doesn't ring up your drink and lets you overtip instead."

Roger gave a quick, furtive look in Rollie's direction.

"It ain't like that."

I waded back in. "A trader owes his allegiance to the house. They set him up with all the tools, computers, information sources, and boatloads of cash. He gets to make bets all day long—buying and selling. He is supposed to buy low and sell high. That's it. He works for the house and takes their check."

"But these guys wanted a little bit more," Vinny added.

"So they work out a little plan," I said. "They give this hedge fund, who shall remain nameless, a guaranteed winner. Locked-in profit. And in return, the guy who runs the fund gives them a kickback."

"You still haven't told me who the loser is."

Vinny threw his hands up. "The house, Roger!"

"Every once in a while, the trader buys high and sells low," I said.

"This hedge fund books the profit from his intentional 'mistake.' The firm takes a small loss."

"And this is illegal? I thought it was all free market."

"It's fraud," I said.

"It's stealing," Vinny added.

"As long as the traders are making money for their firms, no one notices when they take a small loss on a trade—which is the beauty of the whole scam."

"How much money we talkin' here?" Roger asked.

"According to the guy's notes, most of the trades were two to ten grand," I said.

"Chump change. Right? These guys trade millions every day."

"Right."

"Roger's got a point," Vinny said. "Five grand a week on average. A quarter mil a year—maybe. Let's say there's as many as two dozen guys involved. Gross is six mil. The house takes three—before expenses. I can see why it might make sense for all the small-timers. If these guys are slick, they can keep this little machine running forever. They only get busted if they fuck up, or get greedy. But I don't see why some hedge fund would be involved. They're only clearing a mil or two a year after expenses and the first time somebody rats, they're out of business. Shut down. Don't they have better things to do than run this elaborate skim job?"

Roger turned to him. "So how come you know so much about this securities shit, huh? You been reading books?"

"Hey. It's no different than a jockey taking money to hold a horse back."

Vinny was right. I still had more questions than answers.

Roger still looked unconvinced. "And some guy steps in front of a train over this? Over a few grand? I don't buy it."

"He was about to get caught," I said. "It would've been a huge embarrassment for him and his family."

"No. He was about to come clean. That's what you said, am I right? He was doin' the right thing."

Roger was right, too. Lowell Barrington had certainly acted like a guilty man, but not a suicidal one. He had believed he was about to do something noble. But there was no point in speculation. The man was dead.

"I don't know what to say, Roger. The guy walked in front of a train."

Vinny checked his watch. "I gotta go. Am I paid up, Rollie?"

The bartender was huddled over the crossword puzzle with MaJohn. "You're good."

Vinny slipped a twenty under his glass and left. Roger waited until he was out the door before leaning over and speaking in a confiding tone. "And you still won't say who's involved here? Come on. A hint. This is good dirt."

"Not a chance," I laughed. Roger had a strong streak of noodge. "You'll know when the story hits the *Post*."

"All right, but listen, I gotta tell ya something. You sent Wanda flowers? The other day? After you two, uh, you know."

I had sent the dozen roses a few days after our date.

"Yes?"

"She don't like flowers. I'm just telling ya."

"Okay." I was decidedly uncomfortable having a conversation about my love life. Successes or failures. "I won't send her any more flowers."

"It's not you, ya see. It's her ex. Guy was a schmuck. He sent her flowers every time he fucked someone else. He'd come in late with an excuse and a bouquet, and she'd know."

"Thanks for the tip. We're having dinner again tonight. I'm bringing the Kid."

"I know. Big step."

I had been trying to convince myself that it wasn't. It was just dinner. It wasn't a test. The world wasn't going to change if it didn't go well. Then again . . .

"It's a meal."

"Ahuh." He took a long pull of cognac. "You mind if I ask you something personal?"

Offering advice on my love life wasn't personal? "Go ahead."

"You miss all that shit, don'cha?" Roger said. "I mean the trading. The action. The market. Being smart. On top of the world. The money. All that."

"Not the money. I had a lot and now I don't. Life would be easier with more, but after a certain point, the money is just a way of keeping score. It's not a business you should go into if all you care about it is the money."

"I think most people would disagree with you there, sport. Wall Street is where the money is. That's why they go there."

I laughed. "No question. If all you want to do is make money, then you gotta go where the money is."

"Amen." Roger swallowed some cognac and gasped. "That's nice."

"I'll tell you what I miss. I miss waking up and checking the markets even before I get in the shower. That feeling of plugging in. Being part of something really huge. And when you're doing it right, feeling the flows, anticipating the turns just right, it's like playing improvisational jazz while skydiving. It's a rush."

We sat in silence after that for a few minutes. I felt all my regrets crowding round, seeking my attention. Roger must have sensed them as well.

"And then you fucked it up."

"Royally."

"So, why'd ya do it?"

There had been plenty of long, uncomfortable nights, lying on my bunk, up at Ray Brook, when I had plenty of time to think of an answer to that question. But recounting the slow slide of incremental events that got me there only left me angry and frustrated.

"I don't know. You know the old line about doctors? They all *think* they're God. Well, traders know better. Traders *know* they are gods."

The truth was that I had been afraid. Afraid that I was no longer a god. That my time had passed and that my center, my core, had burned away to ashes. And everyone would know.

"I guess it's complicated," I finished lamely.

"Looks that way."

"Maybe I just never thought I'd get caught." I checked my watch. It was time to meet Skeli for dinner. With the Kid. Anything could happen.

"You know," I said, "maybe I don't miss it."

"Still, you had a nice run, ya know. Not many get there."

DINNER WAS AT a Chinese-Latin place around the corner, where they didn't mind making a grilled cheese and fries upon occasion. Skeli and I shared an avocado salad and two plates of their crackling chicken.

The place was small and the noise could get to the Kid on a crowded night, but the early-Monday dinner rush consisted of us and a pair of Spanish-speaking cabbies, fueling up for the night's work.

"What's your favorite car?" I asked her.

The Kid's antennae went up.

"A car? I don't know. I'm not that into cars, I guess."

The Kid went back to his fries.

"You never had a car that you thought was just cool beyond all others? Never?"

She gave a confused shake of her head. "No. Wait. I thought of one. My favorite cousin has an old Karmann Ghia. She keeps it in her barn and only takes it out to wax it. It's cute."

"Type 34?" My little auto encyclopedist spoke up.

"Excuse me?" Skeli said. She gave me a look for assistance.

The Kid continued. "The Type 34 has the 1500cc engine. Very few were imported into the United States. It was made up until 1969. The same factory made the Porsche 914 after that." I recognized my father's intonations.

"I don't know," she said. "Maybe it was the other one."

The Kid nodded seriously. He was used to adults who knew little about automobiles.

"The original 1200cc engine was identical to the Beetle, producing only thirty-six horsepower and a top speed of just over seventy mph, but later models generated sixty horsepower with a sportier ride. Close to half a million were sold over the twenty years of production, with only minor exterior design changes. In 1974, the Karmann Ghia was replaced in the VW fleet by the Scirocco. Ketchup!"

Skeli had been watching his flawless performance with a slightly stunned look. She gave a start at his barked order and slid the bottle of ketchup over to him.

"Wow. I didn't know all that."

The Kid was focused on his ketchup. I waited until he had a small puddle and gently traded the bottle in his hand for a large French fry.

"You must be very proud of your little genius." The compliment was for his benefit. She needn't have bothered. The Kid was intently swishing his fry through the ketchup. Once we stopped talking about cars, we lost all interest for him. He wouldn't have noticed if we both burst into green flames or sprouted wings and flew around the restaurant.

"Yes and no," I said. "He's repeating—exactly word for word—from a book my father read to him. It takes the place of relating. It's a good trick, but it's not conversation. I'm supposed to encourage him to engage and talk any chance I can, but he is a master at avoidance."

The Kid dropped the fry onto his plate and checked out. One second he was there, happily playing with his food, needing no help from a constantly fretful dad, content, with his five tiny cars lined up across the table in a perfectly spaced row. Then he wasn't there at all. His eyes were closed, his body slightly rocking, his fingers tapping out his repetitive, irregular rhythm.

"Oh my God," Skeli whispered. "What happened? Is he all right?"

"Something here is getting to him," I said. "Who the hell knows? It could be the fluorescent lights, your shampoo, or the wrong brand of ketchup."

"What do we do?"

I shook my head. "Nothing. He's trying. He wants control. Watch his fingers. That's one of his 'tricks.' He tunes out the bad by focusing on something he can control. They call it 'stimming.' He'll either pull out of it, or escalate."

I was nowhere near as calm as I made myself sound. The Kid could come out of his trance relaxed, exhausted, energized, or manic. I never knew what to expect. The whole thing left me feeling helpless—useless. Heather had the skills and the discipline to confront him. I knew I had neither. It wasn't enlightenment that allowed me to quietly observe, it was cowardice.

The Kid hummed his long single note.

"Does it help to talk to him? Should we talk about cars?"

"He doesn't know we're here."

Skeli was watching his fingers.

"Skimbleshanks," she said.

"Say what?"

"'Skimbleshanks, the Railway Cat.' It's from *Cats*. That's what he's tapping."

"I don't know that he knows that song," I said. I didn't.

"It's in thirteen/eight time."

"Wait. Are you saying there's a pattern to his tapping?" How had I never noticed?

"Of course. It's three sets of eighth-note triplets, followed by a set of four. Believe me, you don't hear that eight shows a week for two years and then just forget it."

"I don't know where he would have developed a taste for Andrew Lloyd Webber."

"Well, don't worry. It's probably not contagious."

I scooched my chair an inch or so closer to catch him if his rocking became too energetic.

"I'm supposed to watch his pupils while he does this. If they get really big, it indicates he's having waking fits. Mini-seizures. Then he'll need more testing and so on." I let out a long sigh. "Unfortunately, he closes his eyes every time."

She laughed gently. "I think he's charging his psychic batteries."

"Maybe so." I relaxed just a touch. "Do you know what some high-functioning adult autistics call us? You and me and the rest of humanity, I mean. We're 'NTs.' Neurotypicals. We suffer from an inability to conceptualize outside of a very finite set of strictures. We have problems concentrating at deep levels and we are hobbled by an obsession with emotional issues."

"Sounds serious."

"Maybe they're right. Maybe these kids are the future. Their brains are evolving, processing things in ways you and I can't. Maybe they're preparing for a digital world, a virtual world, a place where string theory and nanotechnology join up in some way that the rest of us can't even imagine. Someplace where the ability to read emotion on a human face is an annoyance—an evolutionary throwback, like an appendix."

I didn't know what had caused this sudden release. These kinds of thoughts floated through the back corridors of my mind all day long—sometimes I thought I dreamed them—but I never shared them. With anyone. Except now I had with Skeli—twice.

"Sorry." I tried to stop myself.

"No, it's okay. Go on."

"But there are all sorts of zigs, zags, false starts, and downright mistakes along the evolutionary highway. For every genius, there's scores of kids who will live out their lives in institutions."

I stopped and took a few long breaths.

"The Kid is not in that camp. Right now. But I'm scared all the time. I take him to school every morning and I see some of those other kids. And I see their parents. Some broken, some angry, some obsessed with diets, or vaccines, or chemicals in cleaning products, trying to find some reason, some explanation for why their kid is the way he is. And, yes, a few who are joyful, taking each moment or connection with their strange child as a gift. And I wonder, after another five or ten years, what kind of parent I will be."

Skeli took my hand. It helped.

"What do I know? I've been doing this for two weeks! And I'm always fighting with that Pinocchio thing in my head. You know? When will he turn into a real boy? And I know that way is madness. Evil. I have to stay focused on getting him to grow up to be himself, that's all. Just the way you would with any child. Only with him, the range of who he will be is a lot scarier."

I'd scared her off, I was sure. Too much. Too fast. Still, she kept my hand in hers. She was trying.

She looked at him again. The rocking had stopped, the eyes fluttered. He was coming around.

"He is a very lucky little boy. To have a father like you."

For a moment, I was dumb. Kindness unnerved me; I had grown used to living without it.

"Thank you," I heard myself croak. "But I think I'm the lucky one."

"Ketchup!"

Skeli jumped again, recovered quickly, and handed him the bottle.

"I'm sorry. I don't normally do this. Really. I'm actually a very reserved, quiet kind of person. I don't know why I keep dumping all my deepest thoughts and darkest secrets every time I see you."

She stifled a laugh. "I think that's one of the sweetest things anyone has ever said to me."

"Oh, shit!" I said. The Kid had produced a small lake of ketchup that was now overflowing the banks of the plate. He was focused on the slow ooze of color and had no awareness of the mess spreading across the table.

Skeli followed my eyes and without a word, or a thought, she grabbed for the now near-empty bottle.

"Oh, no . . ." she said.

"I wouldn't do—" I said.

"NNNNNRRRRGGG!" screamed the Kid. The tug-of-war for the bottle was over in an instant. Skeli lost. The bottle flew, spraying red droplets across the wall and ceiling.

I reached for the plate of fries. Too late. With a sweep of his arm, the Kid sent the doused fries off his end of the table.

"No, Kid. NO!" I wasn't getting through. His screech would have split atoms. His body was exploding—thrashing, kicking, gnashing his teeth, and scratching out at Skeli and me.

The two cabbies were staring at us, trying to figure out why these awful parents allowed their child to throw such a tantrum. The waitress was screaming something in Spanish. I didn't need it translated.

"Follow me!" I yelled at a terrified Skeli.

She heard and nodded.

I threw my arms around the Kid and pulled him to me, then I stood up and ran for the door, his legs and arms thrashing, still wailing at full volume. "He's sick! Out of my way!" I yelled.

The waitress jumped back.

I was out the door and down the block. The Kid stopped fighting me, then went limp and began moaning. I stopped and waited for Skeli to join us.

"Jesus Christ, Jason! Does this happen often?" She noticed the soft moans. "Is he all right?" She had flecks of ketchup in her hair and across her brow.

"He's fine," I muttered. "Listen." I was angry, embarrassed, and disgusted.

"'Nilla. 'Nilla," the Kid moaned.

"What is it? What is he saying?"

"He wants ice cream," I said.

"JESUSCHRIST! Ice cream? Ice cream? Are you kidding me? He wants goddamn ICE CREAM!?" She stood, hands on hips, her head jerking forward to emphasize, her words tumbling all over each other as she practically spit them at me.

She looked taller when she was angry.

"Look at this!" she yelled, showing me her bare arm. There was a little red half-circle of bite marks. "He bit me!" She suddenly found that to be funny. Hysterically funny. She doubled over laughing.

On the whole, I thought she was taking it pretty well.

"'Nilla."

"In a minute," I said, without thinking.

Skeli laughed harder.

"So, if my kid bites you, does that mean you won't see me anymore?"

She was laughing so hard, she was snorting for breath.

"Just don't tell me we can still be friends, okay?" I continued.

She inhaled sharply and held it. It worked.

"So, other than that, how was dinner?" I asked.

She smiled. "I can't remember a more romantic evening."

"Care for some ice cream?"

"Jason, you are a very sweet man. I am going home and wash this ketchup out of my hair. Then I will clean my wounds with vodka, and drink the rest."

"'Nilla."

"Quiet," I said.

"'Nilla!" he said louder.

Skeli was no longer laughing, or angry or frightened. She looked like she was making a decision. A hard one.

"Does this kind of thing happen often?"

"Define 'often,'" I said. I refrained from telling her that this had been only a minor tantrum.

"Good night, Jason." She kissed my cheek. It felt like a good-bye kiss. "I'll call you."

"Can I get you a cab?"

"Get him some ice cream." She turned and walked away.

"'Nilla," the Kid moaned.

THE CITY HIDES the darker aspects of its history.

For a hundred years or more, Five Points had been a disease-ridden slum, run by gangs like the Roach Boys and the Dead Rabbits, producing such luminaries as Meyer Lansky, Lucky Luciano, and Al Capone. There is a park there now, a few blocks from my parole officer's office, where municipal workers sit and eat their lunch on sunny days.

Lincoln Center replaced the tenements where the Jets and the Sharks murdered each other with knives, bricks, and zip guns, in an uglier, more violent world than Bernstein or Sondheim could have imagined.

Hell's Kitchen is now called Midtown West. Morgan Stanley had their offices there for a while.

And the point where Broadway crosses Amsterdam at Seventy-second Street—the view from my couch—is the gateway to New York's Upper West Side. The refurbished and expanded subway stop covers two tiny plots of land—Sherman and Verdi squares—that together were once known as Needle Park, the largest open-air drug market south of 110th Street. Forty years ago, two men in gray suits sitting on a park bench would have been an impossible sight.

I didn't even notice them.

The Kid was vastly more sensitive than I to the unseen, or barely observed. I thought I had a New Yorker's strong street sense, able to identify the mumbling schizophrenic who would attempt to extort a dollar, or scream saliva-dripping curses at me if I refused. When a well-dressed man or woman blocked the subway door for no discernible reason, I instinctively placed a hand over my wallet and looked around for the pickpocket partner. But the Kid carried a sixth sense; he had the instincts of a twice-beaten dog.

He dropped the ice cream cone in the middle of Amsterdam Avenue and began grunting and flipping his hands.

It had already been a very long night.

"Oh, God. Please, Kid, be cool. Give me five minutes to get you home."

He switched to a long, chilling whisper of a howl, too quiet to be heard across the street, but penetrating enough to stop you in your tracks.

Then he bolted.

I yelled and took off after him. Pointless. I had never seen him run. My stiff-kneed, awkward little boy whom I had seen trip over a crayon was like a fluid explosion, bursting, dodging, and bursting again, transformed into a three-foot-tall forward receiver. I was both terrified and insanely proud of him. I pushed to catch up.

Out of the corner of one eye, I saw the two men jump up from a park bench on the dark side of the park and race to cut him off. They were big, dressed in gray suits, white shirts, and ties and wore heavy black shoes. I thought they didn't have a chance of catching him.

We sped along Seventy-third toward Broadway. The light turned red. Traffic sped downtown on the single available lane. The Kid was trapped. He spun around and faced me, mouth open, still quietly howling, tears pouring down his cheeks. But he stopped. He stayed in control. He did not cross Broadway without a grown-up.

"Good going, Kid. You are the best! You rock, son." I was crying, too.

I heard the pounding feet of the two suits as they approached, and ignored them. The Kid was dancing, leaping into the air and landing on alternate feet, as though the pavement was scorchingly hot and only by remaining suspended would he not be burned to cinders.

"Hold up, Stafford." One of the two suits took my arm and pulled me around. He was definitely older and grayer than me, and had run farther, but he wasn't winded at all, and he had that ex-military look that said he welcomed the challenge to do it all over again.

"Who the fuck are you?" I tried to shake him loose. He had a strong grip. "Get your hands off of me!" How did he know my name? "What the fuck is this?"

We were beginning to draw a crowd. New Yorkers may have seen it all, but they are always ready to stop and watch it all over again.

"No more running," he said. His grip eased and I wrenched myself free.

The other suit arrived. He was younger, but huffed as he ran—he was carrying an extra twenty or thirty pounds, all around his middle, like an inflated inner tube.

"Fuck! I know you!" They were the two men who had followed me from Brooklyn the night before. "What the hell is this? What do you want?"

The light changed. Traffic stopped. The Kid had behaved himself for as long as he was capable. He took off like a shot.

"I got him," the younger one said. He reached forward and surprised both me and the Kid by snagging his arm.

The Kid's body whipped back and forth like a snake.

"Take your fucking hands off my child!" I moved to intervene, but the first suit grabbed me again. "And fuck you, too, Sarge!"

The other man pulled the Kid to him, wrapped both arms around the Kid's torso, and held him to his chest—face-to-face.

Even if I had wanted to, there was no time to warn him. The Kid is an instinctual fighter. When threatened, he runs. When trapped, he attacks. The Kid grabbed the man's nose with one hand and an ear with the other. Then he lunged with his head and sank his sharp little five-year-old teeth in the man's face.

The man screamed like a girl and dropped the Kid, who hit the ground running and darted across Broadway.

"Ah, Christ!" the older one said. His grip loosened just the tiniest bit and I was gone, too.

The Kid darted between two parked cars and kept running in the street. I lost time making the same move. Behind me I could hear the slap, slap, slap of heavy shoes as the two suits tried to catch up. I pushed myself harder and began to close on the Kid.

I almost caught him. It took me a stride and a half to make the same turn. He ran out across the street and I bellowed without even thinking, "NO! Bad Kid!" A pair of taxis were racing to make the light at West End.

"NO!" I screamed. I managed to stop myself from hurtling out in front of them.

The first cabbie saw the Kid and hit his brakes—the guy behind was completely unprepared. The squeal of rubber on road climaxed in the thud of cushioned bumpers meeting at speed.

The Kid was gone. The suits were closing on me. I ducked between two parked cars and headed for the curved driveway entrance of the Ansonia. The Kid was just ahead, headed for the doors. He would have to stop long enough to plan his navigation across the black-and-white-tiled entranceway—I'd have him.

But he surprised me again. He cut back and kept running, past the driveway and up the block toward West End. I pushed myself harder. The Kid was quick and nimble, but he still had the stamina of a five-year-old boy—a manic five-year-old boy, running in terror, but still I'd be able to catch him on a long, straight run.

The alleyway behind the Ansonia dips down to an underground parking garage, and then continues and connects with Seventy-fourth

Street on the other side. You have to know it's there or you'll miss it. The Kid found it. He barreled down the steep incline, cut to the right at the bottom, and disappeared into the garage.

I was right behind him. As I took the turn through the entryway, I looked back over my shoulder. The suits hadn't reached the alley yet. The Kid and I were gaining.

I stopped inside the door and listened. No sound. The Kid had stopped running and gone to ground. I looked around. The attendant was nowhere in sight.

"Kid!" I tried to be both quiet and heard. No answer.

Once the suits realized where we had hidden, they'd have us trapped. One to cover the entrance and one to watch the elevator. I didn't want to confront those two in that dark, solitary cul-de-sac.

I hurried through rows of expensive foreign sedans, giant SUVs, and sleek sports cars, whispering, "Kid! Kid!" in a plaintive, worried voice. At the back of the last row was a silver Rolls-Royce Phantom, guarded by a phalanx of orange rubber safety cones. And next to it, attempting to levitate high enough to see inside, was my son.

He saw me and grinned like a jack-o'-lantern. He threw both arms in the air and pleaded, "Up. Up. I pick you up."

I was afraid that if I told him "No," I would have another tantrum on my hands and the suits would be all over us.

"Okay. Okay. But we have to be very quiet. Can you do that?"

He nodded so hard I thought his head would fly off.

"All right. Sssshh." I picked him up and let him look inside. "But when Jason says to hide, we have to get down and be very quiet. Okay?"

If I made it all a game, maybe he would cooperate and I could get him to make a dash for the elevators. I watched the doorway, while he wriggled in my arms.

I heard footsteps coming down the alley. Two sets.

"Okay, bud," I whispered. "Time's up."

He squirmed in protest as I put him down, but he did it quietly. I pulled us into the shadows behind the big car.

"Come on. Now we run."

His face went blank. His fingers began to flutter.

I ducked down. Everything depended upon the Kid maintaining control. I could do nothing to help him. He was either going to come out of it quietly and we would have a chance at avoiding discovery, or he was going to start acting out again and we were screwed.

"Stafford!" It was the one I had called Sarge. He seemed to be in charge. "No more running. It's time to talk."

They were working their way down the farthest row, the chubby one darting back and forth like a bird dog.

Just out of sight, around the end of the row, the elevator doors opened. A moment later I heard another man's voice.

"Can I help you gentlemen?" It was more a challenge than an offer of assistance.

Sarge approached him. "We're looking for a man and a boy who ran in here just a minute ago."

"There ain't no one been in here, sir. I would have seen them on the closed circuit. Only ones is you and your friend there."

I peeked up over the rear end of the Rolls and watched. The garage attendant had arrived—a tall, sixtyish, stern man in a white shirt and black bow tie. The suits had their backs to me. They were double-teaming him with a barrage of questions. I couldn't hear their side of the conversation, but the man didn't seem to be at all bothered by them.

"This here is private property, sir."

They didn't like that. The older one argued.

"Well, you take that up with management, sir. I don't get paid enough to make those kind of decisions."

They made some more noise. The attendant wasn't impressed.

"Offices open at eight a.m."

There was another flurry of angry words.

"That's as may be, but you gentlemen will have to leave. Now."

I took a quick look at the Kid. He was maintaining.

The two suits gave up—begrudgingly. They walked slowly and deliberately back out to the alley and, after a momentary conference, turned right and were gone.

I took the first full, deep breath in what felt like a very long time.

"Kid," the attendant called. "You come on out now."

The Kid's eyes fluttered and he relaxed. His fingers stopped tapping. He was back.

I stood up and followed my son out into the light.

The man looked me over appraisingly. I must have passed whatever test he was running.

"You must be the boy's father," he said. "Your son is a friend."

The Kid walked up to him. "Hello, Mr. Samuels," he said in his deadpan, robot voice.

"Hello, Kid."

"That girl who minds him been bringing him down here afternoons. To see the cars. Your boy knows his cars."

Heather had found the perfect field trip for my son—an elevator ride from home.

"I owe you one," I said. "Thanks for getting rid of those two."

He held up a hand. "Like I say, the boy is a friend."

"I think they've been following us. They started chasing us when we crossed the park."

Samuels gave me a questioning look. "They never said who they were?"

I hadn't given them a chance. "Things were a little chaotic."

"They just flashed me their badges. They're FBI."

That shook me. What could I have done to draw the attention of those guys?

I didn't have a complete answer, but the image of a bagful of casino chips spread across my bed immediately came to mind.

Samuels swiped his pass key for the elevator and stepped back to let us board.

"Good night, Kid. You watch out for your dad here."

"Good night, Mr. Samuels. Thank you."

As the doors closed, I realized that may have been the longest single stream of words my son had ever uttered without mentioning cars.

I DIDN'T HAVE to read the Kid to sleep, he was out before his head hit the pillow. But each time I lay down, my body tensed and my mind raced in full-out flight mode.

The front door locks were secure—I knew because I got up and checked them three times. The third time because I had convinced myself that I had only dreamed the two prior. Each time I got up, I paced the living room, wishing I could flutter my hands and control my terrors. I gravitated to the windows overlooking Broadway and stared down at the nearly empty streets, my concentration fading as exhaustion took over. Then I dragged myself back to bed to begin the cycle all over again.

$233,000. The chips. From the moment I had looked into that black gym bag and let myself once more buy into the illusion of easy money, my world had changed. Angie was threatening lawyers and other forms of mayhem in order to reclaim the Kid. The FBI was stalking me—no, *chasing* me—through the streets. My continued freedom was contingent on my staying well clear of those kinds of people. The Kid's future, I believed with all of my soul, depended on me—my presence and my ability to keep him free of Angie. It was all in jeopardy.

But the Feds couldn't know about the chips, or they wouldn't have wasted time following me. They would simply have arrived at my door, warrant in hand. Which might still happen.

Predawn twilight took me by surprise, as it always does. I may have been dreaming, but I had still been awake—on my feet, on guard.

Having made it through the night, without having my home invaded by gray-suited, square-jawed thugs with badges, was a wonder of relief. The faint pink light, touching the top floors of the Trump high-rises along the river, soothed me.

I checked the clock, but my eyes were too tired to focus. My bed beckoned, but it was much too far away. I made it to the couch and dove into oblivion.

 **16**

A 1970 EL CAMINO drove slowly across my face, followed almost immediately by a '65 Shelby Mustang GT. The fastback. They dropped off my chin and continued down my chest and stomach before making a sharp U-turn in preparation for another run at my eyelids.

"Good morning, Kid."

"Hmmmmmm," the little engines purred.

"How about some breakfast?"

The cars halted just below my chin.

Tuesday. His red shirt. Any cold cereal in a neutral color—Cheerios. I looked out the window. The sun was high. Late for school.

The shadows of the previous few days drifted back across my mind, threatening to edge out the morning's concerns. Angie. The Feds. A young man who had stepped in front of a train rather than talk to me. And a USPS box full of casino chips that might already have been delivered to the Ansonia mailroom. I closed my eyes for a moment.

When I opened them again, two ice-blue eyes stared into mine. They were beautiful eyes, but flat, opaque, revealing nothing. Like cat's eyes.

"Breakfast," the Kid said.

"I'm on it." I rolled upright.

Food first. Chase down my lawyer. Check in with Spud. Get the Kid to school. I rubbed a hand over my cheek. Somewhere in there I would have to make time for a shower and a shave. The shadows receded, dispersed by the business of getting by. One foot in front of the other.

The lawyer finally called back while I was in the shower. I dripped water on the floor while I brought him up to date on my situation.

"She still a drunk?"

Lines of battle forming.

"Yes."

"Well, there's a blessing. Listen, Jason, your divorce contract spells it out. 'Dual legal and physical custody' and neither parent is allowed to take the child out of state without express written permission of the other. I wrote it that way, I know. Technically, she was the one who kidnapped him two years ago."

"Fuckin' A!" Having the law on my side was an unusual experience.

"However," he overrode, "I would not want this to go in front of a judge. Once you get inside Family Court, anything can happen."

"What can I do?"

"Nothing. I'm working on it. Meanwhile, try not to jeopardize your parole."

"No quick trips to Bermuda?"

"Please. Not even New Jersey."

I called Spud while I shaved. He was supercharged.

"Very big news, here. Have you seen it?"

I hadn't even looked at the morning headlines as yet.

"What's up?"

"We're the top story on CNBC. Aren't you watching?"

"I don't have a television." The Kid's doctor had ordered I get rid of it.

"Really?!?"

I flicked on the radio. Weld Securities was the lead story on Bloomberg News as well.

The firm had agreed to be acquired by a large regional bank headquartered in Nashville. The pundits raved. Weld would get cheap financing and the combined company would immediately vault into the upper realms of finance. Stockman was quoted and acknowledged as the orchestrator of the deal. The talking heads assured the world that he would play a bigger role in the merged firm.

The only thing that might screw it up, I thought, was a major trading scandal.

"This place is going nuts," Spud said.

I asked him if he had noticed anyone following him—or if anyone had questioned him about our investigation.

"Wow. You're spooking me."

I told him to lay low and we would talk later in the day.

Even Gwendolyn sounded excited—or what passed for excitement on the thirty-eighth floor.

"Oh, Mr. Stafford, thank you for calling. Mr. Stockman asked that I contact you. He is going to be tied up for the next day or two, but he would like to call you later this afternoon. I do hope that is not a problem."

"I'll be here," I said.

Alysha Carter was not as scary as two strange men chasing us down dark streets, but she may have been a close second. The receptionist at the Kid's school was six feet tall and easily outweighed the FBI men. Both of them. Combined.

"Routine, Mr. Stafford! That is the first thing we need to instill in these children. They depend on it."

"Yes, ma'am."

She gave me a pop-eyed stare for interrupting her.

"Sorry," I said.

Her desk commanded the front hallway—no one, child or adult, would have been able to get by her. She was the dragon guarding the gate. I wished I had a magic potion—or an enchanted sword.

"This business of coming in when you get around to it just will not do. You are undermining the whole school with such behavior, to say nothing of the damage you do to your own child."

The FBI had not been waiting outside the door that morning, nor had anyone followed us up to school—as far as I could tell.

"Ms. Carter . . ." I began.

"It's Mrs. I am a married woman and proud of it."

My heart went out to Mr. Carter.

"Mrs. Carter. I am a single parent doing the best I can in a difficult world. I wish I could promise you that this will never happen again. I can't. I can almost guarantee that it will. All I can say is that I will feel really badly every time. Can you sign him in now?"

I thought it was a pretty good speech, considering I was working on about two hours' sleep.

Mrs. Carter looked like she wanted to slap me. She chose to pity me instead.

"Your son is exceedingly lucky to be here, Mr. Stafford. The only reason he was accepted so late was the Yoshida family had to return to Japan."

Not the only reason. There was also the matter of my being able to write a check on the spot for the full tuition, plus a hefty contribution to the endowment fund.

"The Yoshidas were never late."

I kept my mouth shut and did my best to look contrite.

The Kid and I sniffed hands and I was on my way.

I walked back over to Broadway to catch the subway back to the Ansonia—one stop on the express train. No one lurked around the turnstiles or watched me on the platform. No one chased me.

Skeli would be in class most of the day and unreachable. I still wasn't sure if her kiss had been a good-night or a good-bye. I reminded myself *not* to send flowers.

For the next few hours, I had no one to answer to or for but myself. The sensation of freedom—brief but near total—gave me a mild jolt of anxiety. It was still too new a feeling to be enjoyed.

And again, I thought of what to do about $233,000 worth of casino chips, which might already have been delivered to the Ansonia mailroom. I had the day to research the problem.

THEY WERE WAITING for me in the lobby.

Sarge approached first, holding up a badge in a little leather folder. "Can we start over, Mr. Stafford? I'm Senior Agent Ted Maloney. FBI. This is Agent Marcus Brady."

I was trapped. Aside from the staff, there were only two other people in the lobby. None of them was going to help me. And I didn't like the idea of my neighbors watching me get braced by guys with badges.

Maloney gestured toward the elevator. "If you invite us up, we can have this conversation in private."

He was standing on a black tile. I wanted it to swallow him whole and transport him to some alternate universe where carrying a badge could get you arrested.

"Should I have a lawyer present?"

Maloney gave a tight-lipped smile. "Why would you need a lawyer?"

"Why would you follow me? Chase me? Assault my son?"

"Why would you run?" The other one sneered. He had a nasty bruise on his cheek in the shape of a horseshoe. The Kid had scored one for our side.

Maloney put his hands up for "time out." "We just want to ask some questions and then we will go away." The good cop/bad cop roles had been established.

Raoul, the doorman, was trying not to listen. He wasn't trying very hard.

"Let's go upstairs," I said.

As soon as the elevator doors closed, I turned to Maloney.

"You two scared the shit out of my son."

If they had anything to pin on me, they would already have the cuffs out. I could afford to sound off.

Maloney made calming motions. "Please. Can we tone this down? I apologize for frightening your son . . . and you. It was a mistake. It shouldn't have happened."

Brady gave me a hard stare. I gave him one back.

I could have told them to buzz off. It was the smart thing to do. But I was in the clear. Clean. I wanted to hear what they had to say. Why would the FBI be so intent on talking to me that they would have followed me all over Brooklyn and the Upper West Side?

Maloney made himself comfortable at the kitchen table. I sat facing him. Brady strolled around the living room, peeking into the bedroom, and stopping to examine random objects. He flipped through the stack of autism books on the sideboard.

"Hmm," he grunted. He held up *Autism: 20 Case Histories.* "This what's the matter with your son?"

"There is nothing the matter with my son," I said. I hated people who asked me that. "And, yes, he is autistic. Is that why you're here?"

"Sit down, Marcus," Maloney ordered. "May I begin?" He did. "We need your help, Mr. Stafford, and if you find that laughable, I can understand."

"There is a certain irony there."

"May I ask you what you were doing at Brian Sanders' old apartment Sunday night?"

It couldn't hurt me to tell them the truth. Up to a point.

"I've been hired by Weld Securities to look into their trading records. I went out to see if Sanders kept any private diary or notes at home."

"Did you find anything?"

"You saw me."

They shared a quick look. "You left with a black nylon zippered bag," Maloney said.

"With his laptop in it. Which, by the way, the roommate *let* me have. I didn't just take it."

"Where is it now?"

"Locked in a conference room at Weld. If you want it, you'll have to ask them."

"Was there anything else in the bag?"

The big question. If they knew about the chips and I lied, I was screwed. Lying to a federal agent is a crime. It could get me six to nine months. But it would also be a parole violation, which would send me back upstate for another three years. I'd lose the Kid to Angie.

"Maybe I do need a lawyer."

"Please. Mr. Stafford. We are not accusing you of theft."

"Then maybe you should tell me what this is all about. I'd feel a little better about opening up if you guys went first."

"Give me five minutes. If we're still here, I'll answer any reasonable question."

Maloney was a good negotiator.

"Done," I said. "The bag had a bunch of old clothes. I tossed it down the incinerator."

They looked disappointed.

Maloney continued. "Did you find anything on the computer?"

I held up a hand. "I work for Weld. They are paying me to look into some things for them—and to keep my mouth shut about it. If they say it's okay, I have no problem telling you. But it's their call."

"That could be viewed as obstruction." He switched to playing hard guy.

I called his bluff. "Aw, come on. And here I thought we were going to be friends."

He grinned. "You are not a lawyer, Mr. Stafford. There is no client confidentiality. If you have knowledge of criminal activity, you need to tell us."

I agreed, but I was not in the habit of giving away anything that could be bartered. I started by telling him what I was sure he already knew.

"Weld got a request for books and records from the SEC. They asked about a few different traders, but one in particular."

"Brian Sanders."

"Exactly. The people at Weld were surprised—for two reasons. One, the guy is dead. And, two, everybody swears he was as pure as Fiji water."

"What do you think?"

"I think there was something going on. But I've got to tell you, I can't see why you guys give a rat's ass about it. It's like nickel-and-dime stuff. The whole capitalist system is on the ropes and they've got a senior agent and his driver trying to nab a few junior traders? Don't you guys have something better to do?"

Maloney enjoyed my little rant. "You can assume that there was something going on. Please continue."

I was missing something. Brady looked like he was bursting to give me the news, just to show me how thickheaded I had been. I stopped talking. As my father always said, "It's hard to think with your mouth open."

It took me a minute, but I got there.

"There're bigger guys involved," I finally said.

Maloney almost patted me on the head. "Very good. So you see? We have a strong professional interest in this case."

We were buddies, sitting around and solving crimes. My inner warning system was going off like car alarms in Newark on a Saturday night.

"You need to look into a small hedge fund. It's called Arrowhead. They're a Brit outfit, with a satellite office here."

Maloney looked pleased that I was cooperating, but Brady was frustrated.

"Excuse me, but your say-so is not going to convince a federal judge to sign off on a warrant."

Sarcasm is the weapon of the small mind.

Maloney held up his hands for quiet. "What my partner means is that we already have our eyes on Arrowhead. We were hoping you could give us something more concrete."

Like a bag of casino chips? In large denominations? Not likely.

"Isn't it time you gave me a little something? Why is Sanders so important? There must be two dozen other junior guys involved. I'm sure you can find one or two live ones to lean on."

Maloney looked pained. He wasn't ready to give up anything until he heard more. "Bear with me, Mr. Stafford. When we're done, I will either answer your questions or stand up and leave. Either way, your position will be improved."

He was right. As long as I kept their interest away from the chips, I had nothing to lose.

I started with the call from Stockman, described the meetings with Barilla, the sales manager, and Avery. I described the work Spud had done on the trade reports, and ended with my trip to Brooklyn. Savoring the opportunity for taking revenge, I gave them Carmine Nardo.

"He probably thinks he has to hang tough—omerta or some such—but if you squeeze him just a little, he will squeal."

"We know of Mr. Nardo. Any other names for us?"

He showed no surprise when I named Sudhir Patel.

"Yeah, but he's in the wind."

"On his way back home," I said. Then I told him about Lowell Barrington. The words stuck in my throat. I had not yet sorted through all the debris over his death.

"That's a name we didn't have. It's a shame. A confession would have helped." Maloney didn't share my conflict. "What can you tell us about Arrowhead?"

"Or the guy who runs it?" Brady said.

"Hochstadt. Geoffrey Hochstadt. I know his name and that he lives in Darien. That's it."

"Why don't I believe you?" Brady said. "I swear you sound like a guy who's holding out. You keep telling us things we already know."

"Not true. I just gave you Lowell Barrington."

"Thank you. He's dead."

Maloney was sitting back, enjoying watching Brady get under my skin.

I told them about Sanders' calendar. About breaking the simple code he had used. About the dates and trades matching up. About the casino trips.

This time, they both looked pleased. I hated giving away what Spud and I had worked hard to earn, but it also meant I got to keep the information about the chips a bit longer.

"I'm done," I said. "It's your turn, Maloney. Either talk or leave. I've got nothing else to give."

Brady hitched up his pants and gave a nod, like he was ready to leave, but Maloney gestured for him to wait.

"We need help, Stafford. I don't like admitting it, but that's the story. Before I can get authorization to go through the records of a foreign account, I need something concrete. Something to show a judge."

"So talk to me. You think this thing is bigger than just these junior traders? I agree. Now, who are we talking about?"

Maloney shook his head, and surprised me with a curveball.

"Anybody over there talk about how Sanders died?"

"A boating accident. It was in the paper."

"Anybody mention whose boat it was?"

I remembered the article in the *Post*. I knew the answer, I just hadn't known I knew it.

Maloney let me work it out before filling in the details. "They were out in Hochstadt's sailboat, coming back from a Wednesday-night yacht club race. A squall came up and they made a run for Greenwich harbor. Hochstadt should have known better."

"He did know better," Brady threw in.

"There's about a million little islands, reefs, and needle rocks all through there. It's about the last place you'd want to head in bad weather. They hit up on a pile of rocks just inside of Great Captain Island. Boat was a total loss. Hochstadt made it ashore, banged up but alive. Sanders wasn't so lucky. His body didn't turn up for almost three weeks. Forty miles east."

Why hadn't anyone at the firm mentioned this little coincidence? Because, like the casino trips, it was all old news. Everyone knew, so it must not have been important. I'd read the story myself, and made no connection.

"The Coast Guard handled the investigation—it's their jurisdiction. They cleared it. Accidental death by drowning. They made Hochstadt take a one-day boating safety course. Case closed." Maloney leaned back and folded his hands.

"But that wasn't your take."

"No. Because we knew there was more to it."

I thought it through, adding and subtracting the bits and pieces of information that I had.

"You were already on to Sanders. You knew he was dirty."

"Almost," Maloney said. "Other way round. Sanders came to us— seven months ago—with a story. It was small-time stuff. I told him to take it to his compliance department—or the NYPD, if he felt he had to make a case out of it. But Sanders was sure there were bigger guys involved. His plan was to keep working his way up the food chain with Arrowhead until he could get us some names. We let him run with it. He reported in every week, but all he gave us was more small potatoes. We were ready to drop it."

"Until Sanders turned up dead."

"Exactly." He gave an aggravated sigh. "Sanders was a pain in the ass. He got bored with whipping around millions, so he started playing at junior G-man. But his dying in an accident with the only witness being the main suspect in our investigation was too much for me. I'm not a big fan of coincidence."

"But you couldn't get the Coast Guard to take another look?"

"No. And without that, I couldn't get a judge to listen. We went through Sanders' room, took his desktop computer, but there was nothing on it worth looking at."

"You didn't search the rest of the apartment?"

"The roommate wouldn't let us. Said Sanders only rented the one room. I think he was worried we'd find his stash of 'E.' We figured it was BS, but our hands were tied. If we found something and a judge knocked it down, we were back to square one."

"So how'd you know to follow me?"

"We leaned on Mitch. I told him to call if anybody showed up."

"Someone else went through that room," I said. "Someone who said he was from Weld."

"I know. Mitch called us. We raced out there, but we missed him."

I thought it through. "But I called in advance. So you were waiting for me."

He nodded.

"Look, I'll give you whatever else I come up with. But I'm already winding this down. I'm supposed to talk with Stockman later today—and I fully expect him to say, 'Adios.' He thinks he's seen the worst. He's got nothing to fear from an investigation. The merger goes through and he gets his shot at the top. And all this becomes nothing more than a minor embarrassment. He wants me gone."

"Stall him. Tell him you need another week or two."

I laughed. "Sorry, I already played that card. I might be able to get you a few days. The end of the week, tops."

He didn't like it.

"Get me time or get me something tangible. Something I can take to a judge. I need to link the payoffs, or show a paper trail. Something."

Something like a bag full of casino chips.

"I'm not your go-to guy, here. I've told you what I know. Now I'm done. Out of it. I want to take care of my son and look around for my next paycheck."

"You need to cooperate with me."

His insistence was beginning to annoy me. "What aren't you getting? I have cooperated! Now I'm done. If I trip over something else I think you can use, I'll pass it along."

"You're on parole, Stafford. Don't cross me or you'll find yourself on the way back upstate."

They could not know about the chips, or they would already have said something. I had nothing else to offer. Maloney knew that. The only thing that made any sense to me was that he wanted something else. Something entirely different. That shifted the game to my side of the table. I could afford to bluff.

"We're done here. Take me in. Let me make my call. I don't know what you guys think you're doing, but I'm not having any of it."

Maloney slammed his hand down on the table. It was a cheap trick, but it worked. I shut up.

"Hear me out. I've got a dead witness to what I think may be a major criminal conspiracy. Do you think I'm going to let a pissant ex-con and his gentle feelings stand in my way? From here on, you are working for me—on my terms—or you are on your way back."

A parole officer has powers once reserved for minor Greek gods. A word in his ear from the FBI, and I could be back in the system—without appeal. My next parole hearing would be in eighteen months. The Kid would go back to being locked up in Mamma's spare bedroom.

"All right. I'm listening."

Brady was watching his boss carefully, which made me think we were well off script. Maloney was fishing. He had the power to destroy my life, but only I could give him the excuse.

"First, I want you to get us that laptop. Then you meet with our techs—walk them through. I would bet there's plenty more in those files that you missed."

I wouldn't have made any such bet, but providing him the laptop would cost me nothing.

"What else?"

"Two. I'm going to get that warrant. Somehow. When I do, you come along. You show our accounting people what to look for—specific trades, dates, counterparties."

This was annoying, but nothing more. "I get paid for doing that."

"Think of it as giving something back to the community."

Again, it would cost me nothing but an hour or so of my time.

"Next?"

"You go back to Weld. But this time you wear a wire. I want all those millionaires on tape."

"Not a chance." Some of those people may have been jerks or, worse, crooks, but some were friends—or had been. They didn't deserve that kind of duplicity from me. "Sorry, but I'm just not that kind of guy. Besides, didn't your last rat get himself killed?"

"Four." Relentless. "You meet with Hochstadt. Provoke him. Threaten to blackmail him. We'll script it all out for you. Just get him on tape saying something incriminating."

It was my turn to slam a hand on the table.

"Don't you fucking get it? I'm not doing this. Call my parole officer. I can still afford a lawyer and I want to hear what a judge will have to say about you setting me up to entrap a suspected murderer. I'm a Wall Street trader, not goddamn James Bond! Out! We are done!"

Brady gave me the hard stare again. "We can run a file on you— say anything we want. How'd you like to be a registered sex offender? We can make that happen. One call to Family Services and your son is in foster care. I can have your bank account frozen. Today. By the time we're done, your own father won't want to know you."

I believed they could do it. But I did not believe they *would* do it. I fired back.

"You know what, Brady? You should stick with driving the car and the heavy lifting. Leave the brain work to your boss. The bluff only works if I fold. I want no part of your little improv group." I stood up and swung open the front door.

Maloney took his time standing up and walking over. He still looked like he held a solid two pair and wasn't too happy about leaving. But his partner had overplayed the hand and blown the dodge.

"We're not done, Mr. Stafford. You can help us. And when you get your head turned around, you'll see. It's the right thing to do."

"Right, Sarge," I shot back. "I'll be in touch. As soon as the devil starts wearing a down coat and mittens."

I closed the door firmly behind him.

**STOCKMAN DID NOT** call until the next afternoon. I had my nose buried in a book on nutrition for autistic children, and was wondering what a gluten was, and if it was possible to make a grilled cheese sandwich without one.

"Jay!" Stockman boomed in my ear. "Sorry, I'm just getting back to you. As you can imagine, I've been in one meeting after another for the past thirty-six hours."

And loving it, I thought. Stockman was the kind of guy who lived for meetings.

"Yes, yes," he continued after a pause. I realized I must have missed a cue—he had been waiting for me to offer congratulations. "Big happenings!" He went on to tell me how well he had handled the teleconference with the Secretary of the Treasury; what an extraordinary price he had negotiated for the stockholders; and, oozing modesty, casually mentioned the mid-eight-figure deal he had worked out for himself.

Only 23 percent of the firm's employees would become redundant. I thought it was a staggering figure, but he was quite proud of it. Most of them, of course, would be in "non-producing areas." In other words, clerical, oversight, and operations. The lowest-paid would take the hit.

I was sure that Stockman would not personally deliver the bad news to any employee—he would delegate.

"So, please, no bad news today. I have worked my whole life for

this moment, and want to savor it as long as I can." He laughed heart-
ily as though he had made a great joke.

I wondered how loudly he would have squealed if I told him the
FBI had been asking me questions.

"There are developments."

"Good! Good!" he boomed again, shutting me up. He really
didn't want to hear it. "Bring me your report. Write it up, will you?
I'll have Gwendolyn put you on the calendar for tomorrow—late
morning."

"I don't want you blindsided by this." I tried one last time. "Let me
give you the highlights."

"Yes. Tomorrow. I'll get Jack Avery and Eugene Barilla here as
well."

"Can we make it just the two of us? Some of this is for your ears
only." Barilla was high on my list of co-conspirators and I didn't trust
Avery, either.

"Hmm. Intriguing." A tinge of anxiety came into his voice. "All
right, we'll do it your way." He sounded, suddenly, very tired. "See
you tomorrow."

I put away my autism books and prepared to write my report.
Somehow, I had to find a way to reveal as much of the FBI's suppositions, without acknowledging their interest, or the fact that Sanders
had been working with them. I had to alert Stockman to the possibility of a murder investigation impinging on the trading scandal and
do it without sounding like a nutcase conspiracy theorist. And maybe
Stockman was the ringleader and none of it made any difference
anyway.

Three hours of staring at my laptop produced a half-page of ill-
formed sentences and a headache.

Specific trade examples would be more effective than words as a
demonstration of the way the scam had been played. For that I needed

Spud. I called the prop trading desk. Neil Wilkinson answered the phone.

"I'm sorry, Jason. It appears you have missed him." The layoffs had begun, he explained, and, at Barilla's insistence, Spud had been one of the first to go. "They seem to be cutting a very wide swath this time. It is so unpleasant when we are forced to go through these periodic cleansings—especially when so much potential talent is just tossed out. I am reminded of female polar bears who eat their young when food resources become scarce."

"Is there any way, Neil, of getting a message to him? Can I give him a call?" I could patch together something for the report without Spud's help, but I was concerned for the young man as well.

"H.R. wouldn't want us to give out personal information, but you might speak with Gwendolyn in Bill Stockman's office. She could get him a message to call you."

**18**

FALL ARRIVED that evening, with a bitter wind and a light fog, making me wish for that near-impossible New York City luxury—a working fireplace.

The cold mist didn't seem to affect the Kid at all. He was busy skipping, a previously impossible feat of coordination, which he had just mastered in school that day. I had called Skeli to brag and make sure we were still speaking after the debacle of our dinner on Monday. She was too busy with school to join us, but we talked for a few minutes. Somehow she understood the monumental importance I placed on the Kid's being able to skip. Every tiny milestone of development for any other child was for him a hurdle on an infinite obstacle course. We agreed to meet for dinner—and possibly more—the next night.

So the Kid and I celebrated alone together, with a trip to Barnes & Noble. It was late; we had taken an hour to choose our purchases—*Detroit's 50 Biggest Losers* for the Kid; *There's a Boy in Here*, another of Heather's recommendations; and something called *The Stinky Cheese Man*, which Skeli had insisted the Kid and I would both like.

Broadway was nearly empty, the early-evening crowds having dissipated with the sudden turn in the weather. Gusts of wind, funneled up the concrete canyons, had stripped the first brown leaves from the trees, and the sidewalk was a slick minefield of them. I wanted to tell the Kid to be careful, but I knew he had no concept of what the words meant.

I turned up my collar and pulled my jacket tight around my throat, like a character in a Humphrey Bogart movie, and wished I had a hat. A fedora? I didn't think I knew what a fedora was, but I was sure it would keep the rain off my face.

The Kid was a half-block ahead—his limit—but the next cross street was only a skip or two in front of him. I refrained from calling him back, and congratulated myself on acting like an indulgent, confident dad.

He reached the curb, stopped, and turned to face me. Almost immediately, he began to moan and flap his arms. His mouth formed a big O and he closed his eyes. I had no idea what was setting him off, but he was already oblivious to the traffic behind him. I cursed myself for letting him get so far ahead and ran.

But I had only traveled two steps, when a large something— someone—slammed into me from behind. My feet scurried for purchase on the bed of slick leaves and I almost recovered my balance. I turned my head to see my attacker. A mistake. I had offered him a better target. In the instant before his fist connected with my left eye, I had a quick, blurred view of a tall man with a long reach.

The back of my head bounced off the concrete wall of the Duane Reade drugstore and I slid to the sidewalk. I was still conscious when I felt the first kick to my stomach. The Kid was screaming, but there wasn't anything I could do about it.

SOMEONE KEPT YELLING my name. I wished they would shut up. It didn't hurt where I was, and if they insisted on my going where they were, I knew it was going to hurt. A lot.

"Jason Stafford!" Time twisted back on itself. First, my eyes flew open. Then I heard my name. Then I smelled the amyl nitrate. My heart raced and for a split second I had the strength of ten. Then my head started to hurt and the world started spinning again.

"Stay with me, Jason!" the annoying man yelled. He pulled at my eyelid and a blinding white light stabbed my pupil. There was a kaleidoscopic explosion of whirling pinwheels and multicolored sparks.

"Definitely concussed." The man was speaking to someone else. He probably thought he was helping, but I wished he would just fuck off.

"Can he tawk?" A second voice. Another stranger. Older.

I told him that I was quite capable of speech, but the only sound that came out was a throaty growl.

"Wha'd he say?"

The pain in my head was different from the pain in my side. Pain was no longer a universal constant—it had flavors and textures, time and place. I was returning to my own dimension. I remembered everything.

"Where's my son?" My voice sounded like a wooden spoon stuck down the garbage disposal.

"He's trying to talk." The guy with the light.

Why the hell wouldn't they just answer me?

"Is the Kid all right? Where is he? Kid! Kid! Are you there?" Only it didn't sound like that. I had to find him.

"Hold him down! Christ!"

Pain took charge. It crescendoed in a magnificent, soaring coda. Pain could bend steel, lance through cement-block walls, and grind bones to dust. I loved my pain. As long as I had it, I was alive. As long as it was there, I had no responsibilities, no duties. Then the pain started to go away. I tried to follow. I went somewhere else instead.

AN ANGRY WOMAN stood over me, wearing a white coat over a gray Yale sweatshirt. She had large, strong features, bushy eyebrows, and a big, square jaw.

"How many fingers am I holding up?" She sounded like she was already fed up with my malingering and wanted me out of her ER. STAT.

"You wouldn't believe me if I told you."

"Are you in pain?" She was speaking very loudly as though I were deaf or foreign.

I did an inventory. The back of my head throbbed. My ribs ached— they were going to hurt a lot more as soon as I moved. I tried squinting my eye. It hurt.

"Yes," I answered.

"That's to be expected," she yelled.

"Where's my son?" I yelled back.

"You've had a concussion. You were in a fight."

"It wasn't a fight," I said. I was attacked. Mugged. Assaulted. I was not *in a fight*!

She gave a brief skeptical smile.

"Where's my son?!?" I sat up. The merry-go-round started up, complete with the shower-ball lights and wailing calliope. "Aw, shit." I fell back.

AT MY NEXT awakening, a Mayan-featured woman in a green uniform was taking my blood pressure. She smiled when she saw that I was awake.

"Chubedda?" she asked.

"Yes, thanks. Much better." I was. The line dividing pain and discomfort was much easier to identify. I had a lot of discomfort.

I was still in the ER, but no longer on the stretcher. They had moved me to a full gurney and I was surrounded by beeping monitors.

"What's the verdict?" I nodded toward the blood pressure machine.

She stripped off the armband. "One-twenty over eighty. You'll live."

"I think that doctor wants me out of here. You must be short on beds."

She rolled her eyes. "Dr. Glen should've been a vet." She pushed aside the curtain to leave.

"Just a sec. Is there someone I can talk to? I think my son is missing. I need to know what's going on."

"The police. They still here, waiting to talk wichu. I send them in."

I was still wearing my watch. It was just after midnight. Almost four hours. I tried to convince myself that the Kid was fine. The police had him. He was in the waiting room, reading his new car book or fast asleep. Or they'd already taken him home. Because if they hadn't, then where the hell was he?!

A heavyset nurse came around the curtain and opened a cabinet across the room.

"Nurse? Excuse me. Nurse?"

She ripped apart a sealed plastic bag of sterilized towels and removed one. Two more fell out of the bag and landed on the floor.

"Nurse? Can you help me? I need to find out about my son."

She picked up the two towels, stuffed them back in the bag, and jammed the whole thing back in the cabinet.

"Nurse? Helloooo!"

She left with her clean towel.

"Mr. Staffud?" A tired-looking policeman appeared from around the curtain. "This a good time to tawk?" The older voice from earlier.

"Do you know where my son is?" I tried to make myself sound under control. My blood pressure was probably already up to two hundred over, and the little blinking light on the monitor for my pulse was flashing like a strobe.

"The boy is fine," he said. "He was a little scared and he ran." The cop laughed. "But, boy, you got him trained good. He wouldn't cross the street by himself, so he just kept running around the block until we got there."

I swallowed a few times, while I found my voice again. "Thank you. When can I see him?"

The cop shrugged. "Let me do my thing, awright? Then we'll see if they're gonna let you go home."

He was good, he asked all the right questions three times over. But there wasn't much I could tell him. It made no sense. I had my watch and wallet, so it wasn't a mugging. There were plenty of people who didn't like me, but precious few who would attack me on the street four blocks from Lincoln Center.

"Anything about the way he carried himself, the way he moved, maybe?"

"I barely saw him." Then I did think of something. "I don't know, maybe I imagined it, but, when he was kicking me . . ."

"Yeah?"

"It was strange. I was curled in a ball and not looking, but I think he was favoring one leg. As though he had a limp, maybe."

"Hmm." He looked unconvinced, but he made a note. "That's it?"

"Afraid so."

He put his notebook away. "You're gonna hear from the detectives at some point. Somebody'll get assigned and they'll have to ask the same questions and make a report. Sorry. That's the way we do it."

"So? My son? You guys have him? Is he here?"

"No. Sorry. His mother took him home."

"His mother?" His mother was a thousand miles away. My next thought was of Skeli. Highly unlikely.

"She showed up while we were waiting for the EMTs."

One of the monitors was emitting an annoying beep. I tore the wires off my chest and tossed the plastic clip on my index finger across the room.

"No. Impossible. Who was this? Did she give you a name? What did she look like?" I tried sitting up. It worked better than the first time—I didn't pass out.

"Take it easy." He flipped through a small notebook. "Blond. Five-eight. A looker. Here it is. Evangeline Oubre," he read. "Her license showed an address downtown. The boy knew her—went right to her."

I screamed. It's a good way to get immediate attention in an ER, but that wasn't why I did it. I screamed because I couldn't do anything else.

"OOOOhhhhhhhh, faaaack. How the fuck could you?"

The nice nurse arrived first, followed by an orderly and the butch doctor. In varying tones and volume they all gave me the same orders—lie back, try to relax, and let them help me. They couldn't help me.

"The bitch stole my Kid!"

It took another few minutes for me to explain the situation in language they could understand.

The two cops conferred and called in the detectives, which in turn led to another hour of questions, explanations, and delay. Details of my failed marriage and my recent incarceration were openly discussed as though we were on a midafternoon talk show, as hordes of the medical staff floated in and out of the room—an audience tag team that, no doubt, kept the flow of gossip running smoothly. No matter how hard I tried to spin it, I still managed to come off sounding like a schmuck. Possibly dangerous. Definitely dishonest.

Impossible. But it was Angie. No doubt. The two cops who had seen her further revealed that the woman had one arm in a cast, and that she was wearing cowboy boots—and the younger cop also offered up that she had been wearing "very tight" jeans.

The mention of cowboy boots set off another iota of memory. "The guy who was kicking me was wearing pointed boots," I said. "Probably her husband. You should be looking for a big silver pickup truck with Louisiana plates."

Depending on which route they had taken, the truck might have already been passing through Martinsburg, West Virginia, or Baltimore, Maryland.

A brown-suited detective with a Wyatt Earp mustache had taken charge. "Maybe they flew. We'll check the airlines."

He didn't know my son. Anyone who had flown with him once would much prefer to drive halfway across country and back rather than repeat the experience.

"This makes it kidnapping, right? Parental kidnapping. You can call for a whatsit—a Yellow Alert. You can stop them." I was practically jumping up and down on the gurney. "Look, I will cooperate any way I can, but if you don't start the ball rolling, they'll be back in Louisiana by Friday and that crazy bitch will have the boy locked up again, if her nutcase husband doesn't beat the crap out of both of them first."

The detective shot his cuffs, like he was getting ready for his big scene at the O.K. Corral. "I'm sorry, Jason. May I call you Jason?"

He didn't wait for me to say no.

"We seem to have gotten off on the wrong foot, here. I can see you're upset, and hurt." His voice hardened. "But I don't work for you. Right now the only witness is you, and, if you'll excuse my saying so, you are not prime material. But"—he held up a hand to stop me from interrupting—"but, I am going to investigate your claims, despite the fact that this sounds a lot like a domestic dispute that got out of hand. Maybe you want to get some rest and rethink things in the morning. Meanwhile, me and my partner will make some calls. We will get back to you. But in the meantime, we have to assume that your son is safe with his mother."

"That guy is a thug. He did this to me. He put her in the cast. He's dangerous!"

"And if he committed a crime in the City of New York, I will get a warrant and have his ass extradited back here. That includes assault. And kidnapping. Good night, Mr. Stafford."

The room felt a lot bigger without four policemen in it.

"I'm leaving," I said. It didn't sound like my voice. It sounded like someone who was borderline psychotic.

"Chuneetabe checked out." Nurse Maya tried to be both comforting and in control.

"I am checked out," I said. "I'm fine. Where are my clothes?"

I had to move—to act. The shirt and jacket were torn and bloodied, and the pants were dirty, but I wasn't on my way to a fashion show. I pulled them on, wincing and occasionally gasping as movement reactivated areas of pain.

Dr. Glen became quite solicitous when she heard that I was leaving. By the time I found myself on the corner of Amsterdam, trying to hail a cab in the rain at two in the morning, she had provided me with: prescriptions for opiate-strength pain medication, which she warned me against using because of my concussion; more liability waivers than the Feds had made me sign when leaving Otisville; and printed instructions for how to care for the stapled wound on my scalp—"(3) Some bleeding is to be expected" and "(9) Return to the ER if bleeding returns." Also "(5) Clean the wound gently with mild soap and water" and "(8) Keep the wound dry. DO NOT wash hair for _____ days."

As I stood there in the cold, light rain, with the sheaf of documents held over my head to protect my wound, I realized that I had no idea where I was going or what I was doing next.

**I WENT HOME** and called my father. He was still at work.

"Pop?"

I was sitting in my broken chair, looking down at Broadway and holding a bagful of ice to the back of my head with one hand and my cell phone with the other.

"Hey! Number One Son! What are you doing up at this hour?"

My father had been closing the bar—two on weekdays, four on Saturday and Sunday mornings—for fifty years.

"Looking for good advice," I said.

"And you called your old dad. I always knew this would happen—if I lived long enough."

"Got a minute?"

He would be sitting at the bar, sipping the single glass of Jameson he allowed himself each day, and making out an inventory list for the porter in the morning. The doors would be locked, the last customer ushered out, and the lights dimmed. During my third year of college, I had discovered it was the best time to reach him. He was never stressed or worried. Tired, but happy. Ready to joke a bit, to listen if I needed it, or just to chat about the latest Yankees blunder—their successes were expected, therefore rarely commented upon.

I brought him up to date.

He gave a groan way back in his throat. "What a fucking mess. Do you know what you're going to do?"

"I don't know. I want to get my ass down to Louisiana and get the

Kid back—and take a minute or two to get behind TeePaul with a Louisville Slugger."

"Hmm," he said.

"Yeah, I know. If I get caught down there, my parole officer will send me back—even if I don't bust that asshole's head open. Besides, I don't even know for sure if that's where they're headed."

"That's what I was thinking," he said.

"I need help."

"It takes a big man to say that. You talk to a lawyer?"

"Yes. Yesterday. He told me to sit tight."

"Good advice always hurts."

"Right." Waiting for the slow machinations of the legal system to work their fickle, black-box magic would be excruciating, but breaking parole for the sake of an ugly showdown would only work against me.

"You need allies, son. I wish I could help, but you need big guns. And the more the merrier."

He was right. I needed someone to help me protect my son— someone who might be able to talk to Angie. And, I needed Big Guns.

IT WAS LATE in Beauville—even a time zone earlier. The phone rang a long time before she answered.

"Hey, Mamma."

"Ooohh, Jason," she cooed in a sleepy voice. "Lord, it's the middle of the night. Where are you calling from?"

"Do you know where she is?"

"She won't talk to you, you know." Her voice instantly became guarded.

"Do you know what they did, Mamma? Did you know what they were planning?" I tried to bury my anger—she might be the boy's best hope.

"What happened? What are you talking about? You are scaring me." She did sound scared. Maybe she really didn't know.

"Angie and TeePaul, Mamma. They came up to New York. He jumped me and put me in the hospital. Then they took my son."

She wailed. In between long sobs, she gasped like an asthmatic in a dust storm. I stood it as long as I could.

"Mamma, I have to know. Do you have any idea where they are now? Where are they taking him? Did she call you?"

"Oh, forgive me, no. No. I am so sorry, Jason."

I believed her.

"You would be so proud of him, Mamma. He's coming out of his shell. He goes to school. He likes it. They're teaching him to be a whole person. Do you understand? I don't have to keep him locked up. He's learning to read! The Kid's got a chance at something better."

She was crying softly. I let her.

"This is my fault, Jason. I am so sorry."

There was plenty of blame to go around, I couldn't let her hog it.

"Yeah, well, I should have seen this coming. Angie called me Sunday and as much as told me she was going to try something like this."

"No!" She cut me off. "You don't know." The story started pouring out.

Angie had shown up on Monday—bruised, frightened, and hungover. TeePaul had announced that he was not going to raise "another man's son"—especially "a lil retard"—and had backed up his debating points with his fists. Angie begged Mamma to keep him away and had hidden out in her old room.

"And when that fool boy showed up on my porch—crying like a baby with a bee sting—I told him to pray for strength so that he would never hurt my little girl ever again. And he did. Right there, he dropped down on his knees and prayed."

She began sobbing again—either at the memory of TeePaul's

miraculous salvation on her front porch, or the realization of her own culpability.

Inside, I was screaming with frustration. But over the years, I had learned that you can't rush a southern woman with a story to tell.

"Oh, I am so ssss . . . so sorry, Jason." She was stuttering and hiccuping. "Forgive me, I was so touched I let him upstairs to talk to Angie. About an hour later, they came down and left in that truck she bought him."

"Mamma." The word felt like gravel in my mouth. "Please tell me. Where are they taking my son?"

"I don't know. I wish I did. I asked Angie if she was all right going with him and she told me that TeePaul was taking her to get what she wanted most in the whole world."

"Shit! How could you let her do this? Why didn't you warn me?" I was sick of her bumbling self-recriminations.

"Well, I didn't know! I thought may' he was taking her to N'Awlins for the shopping!"

She had a point.

"Mamma, you and I know what is best for the boy."

She was quieter, but still sniffling.

"He can do better, but not if he's locked up. And not if he's living with that monster she married. It's for the best, you know this."

"I know," she mumbled.

"I don't want anything from Angie but the boy. You have to help me. Help him." I was asking her to choose—her daughter or her grandson.

She didn't reply for a long time. "I know."

"Good. If she calls, let me know. I promise I will never hurt her, but you have to help me."

There were a few more sniffles before she answered. "I will."

I didn't know if I believed her, but I needed her on my side. It was a start.

———

THE CLOUDS WERE breaking up. A few stars showed. A satellite arced overhead. I called the Big Guns.

"FBI."

"I'm trying to reach Agent Maloney."

"Who's calling, sir?" He had a voice like Robert Duvall—competent, efficient, and humble all rolled into one.

"My name is Jason Stafford. He'll want to talk to me."

He put me on hold briefly and came right back. "Agent Maloney is not here. Can someone else help? Does this have to do with an ongoing investigation?"

"He's waiting to hear from me," I lied. "Tell him I'm sitting on the phone." I gave him my number and rang off.

A trickle of ice water ran down my neck, soaking the back of my shirt. It helped keep me awake. Minutes passed. The phone rang.

Maloney. "Did I miss something? I thought I wasn't going to hear from you until hell froze over."

"I need your help," I said. My mouth was dry.

"And you're willing to trade for it."

"That's what I do."

"And I figure that since it can't wait for morning, you are desperate and willing to make 'one-time-only' kinds of offers."

"I'm having a fire sale."

"All right. Talk to me."

I told him everything that had happened that night, detailed right down to the cast on Angie's arm and the Yosemite Sam mud flaps on the pickup truck. My voice cracked more than once during the telling.

"I need a Yellow Alert. That's what they call it, right?"

"I don't think so," he said. "Unless he was kidnapped by terrorists. Do you mean an Amber Alert?"

"Amber, yellow, whatever."

"I'm going to need to hear the NYPD version before I lift a finger."

"They think this is some pushing match. Domestic dispute, he called it." I started getting loud. "But this guy is dangerous. I've got two dozen staples holding my head together. He put my ex in a cast. If something sets him off, he might take it out on the Kid."

"Understood. But this is not what I do. White-collar, money-laundering, securities fraud, insider trading. I'm going to have to convince some of my peers to come on board with this."

"I'll make it worth your while."

"Yes, you will. Meantime, you're going to have to do some groundwork. Get me some documents. School records. Birth certificate. Doctor's reports. Fax them to my office."

He was engaged—in charge. I had my Big Guns. The Kid was safer already.

"I've got all that. What else can I do?"

"Sit tight. Let me make my calls."

I was on such an emotional roller coaster, I forgot I was negotiating. All I felt was a huge rush of gratitude.

"Thank you. This is great. Go ahead, make your calls. You can put me on hold."

"No. Come to my office in the morning. Late morning. Give me some time to find out if this is something the FBI will be involved in."

The panic was back. "By tomorrow morning this guy could be halfway to Louisiana!"

"Mr. Stafford, I don't know how much you know about our organization, but we actually have regional offices all over the deep South."

"That is very funny, but I need to know NOW. Can you help me or not? If you're not on board, I've got to make other plans." I had no other plans. He knew it. It was so desperate a bluff, I should have been embarrassed.

But it worked.

"Maybe we should talk about what you're offering," he said.

We were negotiating. My turf. I made a lowball bid.

"I'll pick up the laptop first thing in the morning and bring it in. I can show your guys the whole thing. The codes, the trades, the dates."

"That's a start."

I took a breath. "Put me in front of a judge. I'll get you your warrant."

"How will you do that?"

"Don't go all delicate on me. I won't perjure myself, but I will convince him. I know the players and I understand the game."

"We'll see."

"Take me with you when you hit the Arrowhead offices. I'll be able to handhold your guys through the files. I'll see connections your people will miss."

I didn't entirely believe that, but I hoped he would.

"Okay. That's smart. But you're not convincing me, Stafford. This is all nice. I appreciate it. But it's not going to get you special treatment."

Shit. I gulped air and plunged on.

"I'll wear the wire. I've got an early meeting with Stockman. I'll do the Hochstadt interview. I'll get him to talk to me."

"Tomorrow."

"Done."

"What else?"

"Are you kidding? Come on, Maloney. I'm rolling over. I'm giving you everything you asked for." I kept my voice flat. "You've got me negotiating against myself. What else?" I mimicked him. "What else? Fine. If I ever get the Kid a dog, I promise to name him Maloney. Deal?"

He didn't answer for a minute. He just let me stew. It is a very effective tool for cutting through bullshit.

"Mr. Stafford." He spoke patiently. "You might have been a great trader, stone-cold and rock-solid, but I spend my life listening to people lie to me. It gives me a one-sided view of humanity. My ex-wife didn't like it. I've got a teenage daughter who thinks I'm the devil. Only she doesn't say it that politely."

He paused again. I felt like I had talked myself into exactly where he wanted me.

"You call me in the middle of the night and want my help, but you still think you can hold out on me. Like I'm your mark. Your chump. It doesn't work like that."

I couldn't afford to squirm, so I just kept my mouth shut.

He didn't wait for me. "Every time I have asked you what else you took out of Sanders' apartment, you've given me the same con. You don't know what I'm talking about. You go all cold on me. But see, Jason, that's your tell. You're a pretty icy son of a bitch to start with, so most people probably don't notice, but when you're bluffing, you turn just a degree or two even more so. Now, if you want the full authority of the FBI to treat your pissant domestic dispute like interstate kidnapping, you better be prepared to give up everything you've got."

When it came down to it, the decision was one of the easiest I have ever made.

"I have what you need. The hard evidence for a warrant. There were chips in the gym bag. Poker chips. From a half-dozen or more casinos. That's how Hochstadt made his payoffs to all the junior traders. When you match up all the trades with Sanders' calendar, you'll see. It's all there."

"How much money are we talking?"

"It looks like Sanders milked the firm for four hundred sixty-six thousand. Based on what's there, I'd say his cut was fifty percent."

"Two hundred thirty thousand dollars?"

"Thirty-three," I said.

"Christ almighty, you are one ballsy prick, you know that? Let's put aside grand theft for the moment. Do you know what 'obstruction' means? It means three more years' room and board care of my employer."

"Screw that, Maloney. No threats. You've got it all. Just go get my son." I had played my last card.

"All right," he said. "Welcome to the team. We'll pick you up at eight. Meanwhile, you've got your Amber Alert."

MORNING WASN'T far off, but it took a long time to arrive. I lay on the Kid's bed, smelling his pillow and staring at the shadows flickering across the ceiling. My first night in prison, with the cries and evil whispers of predators and prey echoing along the concrete corridor, had been a day at the beach compared to this. I wrapped myself in a sheet and counted the minutes until first light. Eventually, it was easier to just get up and start the day.

I ignored the doctor's list of instructions and stood under the shower until long after the water stopped running red. There were aches and bruises from my knees to the top of my head. My feet didn't hurt. My stomach and ribs, which had taken the brunt of Tee-Paul's kicks, were covered with a magnificent, ugly blossom of color—reds, blues, and deep purples. Every breath ended in a short gasp as the pain hit. But the bruise under my eye was barely noticeable and by the time I had shaved, carefully combed my hair over the staples, and dressed in my loosest-fitting suit, I looked like I could pass for a member of the living.

It was only 6:30—an hour and a half to go. An hour and a half to think. To worry.

The Kid's schedule would be all turned around. The novelty of being with his mother would have sustained him for the first hour or two, but human contact meant much less to him than whether he was wearing red on a beige day. Routine. "A predictable routine will soothe many of his anxieties." That is what they had said. All the experts.

Sorry, Kid.

I called the school and braved another session with Mrs. Carter. She might have been more understanding if I had told her the truth, but I didn't chance it. Then I rang Heather and left a message. "Don't pick up the Kid from school until you hear from me again. He's staying with his mother for a few days."

Once Angie got him to Louisiana, there was no telling what she would do. She might want to play house for a while, with her little five-year-old doll, or she might just dump him on her mother again. Her unpredictability had once been part of her charm.

I went back into his room. His cars—minus the half-dozen or so he had taken to dinner—were lined up on the shelf over his bed. The spacing between the vehicles was identical. There seemed no pattern to their order—colors, makes, models were all mixed together—but I was sure the Kid would have immediately noticed any change. One car out of place could bring on one of his tantrums. A screaming fit.

A great gasp of a sob forced its way up and out of me, leaving a great void in its wake. I needed my weird little boy.

I gathered the necessary documents—his birth certificate, the acceptance letter from the school, copies of his doctors' bills—and told myself, again, that my best shot at getting him back was to cooperate with the Feds and let them work their magic. I didn't like it, but what I wanted wasn't all that important.

Brady met me in the lobby and walked me out to the car.

"Any word on my son?" I said.

"Not yet," he said. "We should know more soon. All the East Coast offices have been told to report in by eight."

I stopped in the middle of the sidewalk. "That sounds like a brush-off." I was tired, angry, and worried—I was also paranoid and feeling aggressive. "Are you sure your people are holding up their end of this?"

Brady looked me over, as though I were a necessary evil. "Actually, Mr. Stafford, the search for your son is a full Amber Alert. That means that not only is the FBI on the lookout, but every state and local police department, every news agency, every airport, train or bus station, and every single highway toll taker between here and Atlanta has been notified. Let's see you hold up your end as well. Do you have the chips?"

"They're safe. When my son is safe, you get your proof."

He tried staring me down. I shrugged and walked past him to the car.

Maloney waved me into the backseat. "Where's the chips?"

"Where's my son?"

Impasse. Brady drove. Traffic was terrible.

"What's in the envelopes?" Maloney asked.

I handed him the first. "Documents for the Kid. Birth certificate. Letters from doctors, from his school."

He grunted. "Good. That'll help." He took the envelope. "And that one?"

"My report to Stockman." I passed it to him.

Three pages of facts, projections, and suppositions.

Maloney scanned it quickly. "I don't want him to see all this."

"Why not? If he's guilty, he knows it all already. And if he's innocent, what do you care if he reads it? Besides, that's what he paid me for. It's my job."

He handed me back the report.

"Working with you is going to be a pain in the ass."

We finally agreed on something.

WELD SECURITIES looked no different—they may have merged, but they hadn't yet changed the name over the door. I asked Gwendolyn to get a message to Spud.

"Nothing pressing. Just have him call me. I heard he was let go. I just want to know he's okay."

She said she would get right on it. Then she showed me in, which threw me. I had expected to sit on the couch for at least half an hour.

I walked in with Sanders' computer in one hand and a file folder full of trade reports in the other. Stockman needed convincing.

He stood up and stepped smoothly down off the small platform around his desk. "Jay, thank you for coming in."

We sat on the couch. He poured coffee for both of us with as much formality as a Japanese tea ceremony. It was red carpet treatment.

While he fiddled with cream and sugar, I checked the transmitter in my pocket. A cute little item disguised as a pre-BlackBerry cell phone. Maloney had assured me it would pick up every sound in the room and broadcast it directly to his monitoring equipment out in the car.

The coffee was good. And strong. I needed it.

"How's the coffee?"

"Excellent," I said.

The computer monitor on his desk began an insistent beeping.

"One moment," he said. He went over, tapped a few keys, and then gave me a poker-faced stare. He tapped again and returned to the couch.

"So, what do you have for me?"

I handed him the report and tried to order my thoughts. My mind wasn't blank, just muddy.

"Most of it is in here," I began. "This is Brian Sanders' laptop. When you're done going over the report, I'll give you the show-and-tell version."

He held up a hand to silence me—it was an order, not blatantly rude, but quite definite—and took the three typed pages out of the manila envelope. He read quickly. He grimaced twice and looked pained as he scanned the last few paragraphs, where I had speculated on the likelihood that there were more senior traders involved in the scam. His face paled. He was in shock.

He stared out the window. It was a gray day, with a strong wind throwing up whitecaps all across the harbor. Lady Liberty looked cold.

"Has anyone else seen this?" His voice was flat. Numb.

The man was hurting—I couldn't lie to him.

"The Feds know about it," I said. I could feel Maloney listening to every word.

Stockman nodded. "I understand." He stood up and crossed the room, where he fed the report into a document shredder. Paper snowflakes fell into the trash can.

"Jason," he said, turning to me. "I appreciate what you have done. Do you have any idea on timing?"

I shook my head.

"The whole world economic system is threatened, Jason, This merger is important. A demonstration of confidence, not just in this firm, but in the capitalist system itself. Billions in equity will be saved. It is imperative that nothing derail, or even hinder, this. We are on the brink of the abyss, Jason, and we must all do our part to hold off catastrophe."

It may have been the most self-serving, self-aggrandizing pile of horseshit I had ever witnessed. And what did I know? Maybe he was right.

"I want you to continue your investigation. Would another two weeks be sufficient? In the meantime, I would prefer the record show we never had this meeting."

He thought he was buying me. The cell phone in my pocket felt suddenly very heavy.

"I don't know that I can do this," I said.

He shook his head stiffly. "Please, do not misunderstand. I am not asking you to bury anything. I want a full inquiry. I welcome it. I encourage you to take any necessary steps to uncover the full extent of this . . ." He paused, searching for the precise word.

"It's embezzlement," I said.

". . . situation." He ignored my interruption. "And when you have explored this from every angle, come back to me. Say, later this month?" He walked to the door and opened it. The meeting was over. "I'll have Gwendolyn take care of getting you a check."

Stockman was a master. His survival skills would have made a cockroach proud. He was a mediocre accountant, without honor or balls, but he possessed a breathtaking talent for finding, in the midst of chaos, the sole path that served him best.

"Meantime, I'll try and stay out of your hair," I said. I stood up, taking the laptop and trade blotters.

I stopped at the door.

"Good luck, Bill." I meant it.

"HE'S INNOCENT."

Stockman had surprised me. He was a shape-shifting little gnome, good for not much more than self-promotion, but he was innocent. He really hadn't known what had been going on right in front of him. But there had to be a conspiracy of senior executives running the scam—giving cover, and sharing the take. Avery was a likely candidate—as senior compliance officer he had the power to investigate and sign off on every trade the firm did. But the fact that I would have been ecstatic to find that Iron Man Jack was one of the big bad guys was reason enough to be skeptical. Barilla was another possibility. His self-righteousness could be nothing but cover. Who else?

Carmine's boss? The Armani-clad peacock? A couple of years upstate without manicures and hair dye and he'd come out looking like his own grandfather.

"Innocent, my ass." Maloney, his anger, and me made a tight fit in the backseat of the Town Car. I would have been glad to be somewhere else. Anywhere else. "What in hell do you base that on?" he continued. "His honest smile? Stockman knew you were transmitting the minute you walked in."

"What are you talking about?" I said.

"That beeping you heard? That was his computer telling him that the security system had picked up the transmitter in the phone."

"And how the hell do you know that?"

"Because a few seconds later, the whole thing cut out. He turned on a blocker. I've got nothing but white noise on the recorder."

I played back the scene in my head. He was right.

"Okay, he knew about the toy in my pocket. But you had to see him when he read that report. The guy was blown away."

"He played you, Stafford. What'd he say? Did he thank you for bringing all this to his attention? Keep up the good work? He was playing you, for Christ's sake."

Maloney had some of it right, but not all.

"No," I said. "You weren't there. You didn't see the look on his face. Stockman may be a weasel, but he's not a crook. The guy is too wrapped up in his own legend to have any part in this crap. He honestly believes he was sent down to this planet to complete this merger. And he's not going to let anything—even a combined SEC-FBI operation—get in the way."

"What did he do with the report?"

"Shredded it. As soon as the merger closes, he gets control of the information flow again. He'll find a way to come out of this looking like the hero."

"So we got nothing out of this." Maloney moping was even harder to take than Maloney angry. "A waste. Only now he's tipped off. He won't talk to you again."

"It doesn't matter. He doesn't know anything." I handed him the laptop. "This is what you need."

"I need those chips," he said. It sounded like a threat.

"Where's my son?"

"Goddamnit! We're working on it."

Work harder, I thought.

BY MIDAFTERNOON I FELT as useful as week-old French bread. Someone should have ground me into bread crumbs and fed me to the pigeons.

We were sitting on a long bench outside the Federal District Attorney's office, waiting for an assistant to make time for us. There was still no word on the Kid.

My head hurt, my staples itched, my eyes were burning with stress and exhaustion, and I was too worried to eat. Coffee was my only friend.

"You all right?" Brady said.

My head whipped back. I had fallen asleep upright on the bench. "I'm okay."

Maloney leaned into me. "Listen to me, Stafford. I don't think you understand. Without something tangible—like those chips—no ADA will put this in front of a judge. And once he hears that you are holding out, he will have you thrown in jail until you cooperate. Talk to me. I'm willing to work with you."

Maloney wanted us to be friends. He was only looking out for my best interests. And Attila was really only sightseeing.

"Where's my son, Maloney?" The chips were my only bargaining tool.

"Ah, Christ!" He sat back.

The SEC lawyers and forensic accountants had slavered over the trade records and the coded diary. For most of the day, I had walked them through trade after trade. They all saw the pattern. They all agreed it was great stuff. They just needed to see Arrowhead's books and records to make their case. If only they had something to put in front of a judge to get the warrant.

"Call again," Maloney ordered.

Brady had been making calls to check on the Amber Alert all day. So far, the silver pickup was invisible. They'd been gone for eighteen hours. If they'd driven straight through, that would put them in Alabama or Mississippi. But Angie would have made them stop somewhere. She was a hothouse flower and too long on the road tended to make her wilt. If they were smart, they would have driven most of the night and holed up in a motel somewhere, sleeping through the day. The Kid's schedule would be turned upside down. He'd be living on the edge of a meltdown every minute.

"Wake up," Maloney said.

"I'm not asleep."

"Then take your chin off your chest and stop snoring."

I pulled my head up.

"Where's Brady?"

"He went to find you some coffee."

A round-faced paralegal stuck her head out the door. "The meeting is just breaking up. Someone will be available to see you guys in just a few minutes."

Maloney practically jumped me. "Smarten up, will you? Once we are in there, I'm no longer in control. There is nothing I can do for you. Some thirty-year-old ADA trying to make his bones will walk all over you. He will crush you and go home and laugh about it over dinner. Give me those chips and I can protect you—I can keep up the search for your son."

He was starting to make sense to me, and I didn't like it. Maloney had his own axe to grind. But maybe that didn't matter.

"Do you have kids?" I said.

"Two boys and a girl."

"So, what would you do? In my shoes? Two crazy alcoholics took my child and are running around somewhere between New York and New Orleans. The mighty FBI can't find any sign of them. And the only hold I have on you guys is those chips. So, what do I do, Agent Maloney?"

I watched his eyes. If he heard me and understood, I might be able to trust him. But if the little wheels were whirring away, he'd just tell me what he thought I needed to hear.

He looked away. "I'd figure I had to trust someone. And it might as well be proper authorities."

Now it was his turn to play me.

"Thanks," I said. "Then I should give the chips to my father."

The paralegal popped her head out again. "If you're ready now, Mr. Ramirez will see you."

We stood up. Maloney stepped in front of me.

"Last chance, Stafford. What's it gonna be?"

I stared him down. "Where's my son?"

"STAUNTON, VIRGINIA. A Paul Martin used a credit card there when they checked into a motel early this morning. Nobody caught it until this morning."

Brady was filling us in as we drove uptown. I had agreed to turn over the chips as soon as he walked up and announced that the Kid was safe.

"We dispatched a team from the Richmond office and heard back from the Augusta County Sheriff's Office. Staunton City Family Services has the boy and the two adults are in custody."

"When can I talk with him?"

"Our people should be there anytime."

"Who found them?" Maloney jumped in.

Brady chuckled. "A social worker on her lunch break. She recognized them from the Amber and called her kid brother, who just happens to be a deputy with the sheriff's department."

"So they'll be claiming jurisdiction?" Maloney said.

"Who cares? I don't!" I threw up my hands. "You guys are all so credit-hungry you make me sick. Give the deputy a medal if that's what he wants. Just get my son back home."

Maloney spoke through gritted teeth. "It is not a question of who gets credit, Mr. Stafford, but who has control. If your son was in the hands of the Virginia State Police, we could request that he be turned over to our people, and you would be able to tuck him into his own bed tonight. Right now, your son is in the hands of the child welfare bureaucracy. Will local police back them up or will they listen to us? Will they want to do their own investigation before handing him over? Will there be a hearing? Jurisdiction in such cases can get complicated quickly."

I thought it over. "Sorry," I said. "I'm a little stressed. I don't know much about this kind of thing."

"I keep telling you. We're working on it."

So why didn't I believe him?

WE WERE BACK downtown, sitting outside the federal courthouse. Maloney had taken the box of chips into his meeting with Assistant District Attorney Ramirez. I kept falling asleep, only to jerk myself awake each time, retreating from my stress-filled dreams. Each time, the Kid was in danger and I was stuck somehow, unable to get to him. Each time the setting was different—sometimes surreal, sometimes mundane—but the situation was always the same. Sleeping was more exhausting than staying awake.

Brady's phone buzzed and he spoke quietly for a moment and rang off.

"That was Maloney. The lawyers say they'll have a warrant in the morning—maybe late tonight."

"I'm thrilled." Wit was beyond me. I was reduced to sarcasm.

"He'll be out in a minute."

"The world awaits."

Brady chuckled. It wasn't that funny. Maybe he was trying to be nice. I felt myself nodding out again and prepared for another scene of mental torture.

The buzzing of his phone saved me. He answered, and a moment later, handed me the phone. "They're with your son, now."

"This is Senior Agent O'Connell. Who am I speaking to?" He had the jarring, flat vowel sounds of South Boston. They must have been loving him in Staunton, Virginia.

"My name is Jason Stafford. I understand you have my son."

"We are *with* your son, sir. He is currently being cared for by local social services."

Legal niceties. "Can I speak with him?"

"He's not saying much."

I fought for control. "Would you please put him on the phone?"

There was a long silence and then I heard a shallow, light breath on the other end.

"Kid? Kid, it's Jason. Your father. Are you okay?"

He moaned slightly.

"Kid, those people are policemen and they are going to bring you home. They will bring you here to me. Do you understand?"

No answer. Damn. What would Heather do? I had no idea. Panic began to strangle me. What would my father say? I was all alone. I opened my mouth and let out whatever sounds were able to scrape their way to the surface.

"I'm sitting in a Town Car," I said.

"Hmmmm," he hummed loudly. I stopped talking and waited.

"The Lincoln Town Car?"

"Yes, Kid. A Lincoln."

"Hmmmm. Signature or Signature L?"

He was okay.

"I don't know. Listen, Kid. I want to come and bring you home, but I can't. These men will bring you here."

"Glade—the welcoming scent of home."

Less than a day with his mother and he had already slipped back into quoting taglines.

"Yes, Kid. Home to the Ansonia. We'll go for ice cream."

"'Nilla?"

"Of course. Now be cool. Listen to the men, okay? Do what they say."

The silence went on so long I checked the face of the phone to see if we were still connected.

Finally. "'Kay."

"Very good, Kid. Very good. You are a very brave boy and I am proud of you. Do you understand?"

Another long silence, then, "'Kay."

That was the best I was going to get—and as much as I could have hoped for.

"Let me talk to the man again. Give him the phone again, will you?"

The Boston voice came back on.

"Are you still there, Mr. Stafford?"

"Yes, thank you." Relief was overwhelming. At that moment, I would have promised that anonymous voice anything he would have asked for. "Can you tell me what happens next?"

"That will be up to a judge. There will probably be a hearing in Family Court here in the morning."

I felt an explosion coming on. "But, wait! They kidnapped him!"

"Sir, the New York office has instructed us to stay on the scene, and act as your son's advocate until further notice. We will do our utmost to get this resolved first thing. Your son should be on his way home by noon tomorrow."

Another whole day. I wanted to scream. His routine. The schedules that let him order his world. All were upside down.

"Wait! Listen. What's he wearing?"

"Sir? Uh, a red shirt and jeans."

"Good." Angie must have done something right. "And tomorrow's Friday, right?"

"Yes, sir. Tomorrow is Friday." The Fed sounded like he was talking a psycho into dropping the chain saw.

"Black. Pants and shirt. Don't worry about the socks so long as they're clean. Make sure they know. It's important."

"Yes, sir. Black. Don't worry, sir, we will take care of it." He rang off.

I gave Brady back his phone. Brady was my new best friend. He was such a great friend. An FBI friend. He had made it so I could talk to the Kid.

**22**

"**RIGHT TURN.** Fifty feet." The voice of the GPS jolted me awake again. She sounded like a BBC announcer crossed with a third-grade teacher.

I had slept through the drive up to Darien and I felt almost human—Maloney had made me eat something before we started out. Then he had tried to prep me for confronting Hochstadt, but I kept nodding out while he was talking. Then I nodded out while I was talking. Maloney left me alone after that.

We were deep down a meandering boulevard, drifting through an arboretum of huge spreading oaks and impenetrable ten-foot-tall rhododendron forests. Every so often we passed an entryway, sometimes marked with a pair of stone gateposts. Far back from the road, lights twinkled through the leaves, giving the only evidence that the area was currently inhabited.

"Pull over," Maloney said.

He checked the cell phone/transmitter—again. "Just stick to the script and you'll do fine. No tricks. No improv. Let him take the bait. Don't push it."

I tried to remember the script.

"I still say we should have called him first. I just show up at his door? He's going to be totally panicked."

"Panicked is good. He'll start making mistakes. Just don't make any yourself."

"Don't worry about me. I'll be fine."

A second car pulled up beside us—two more FBI agents.

"We'll be out here. Seconds away. If anything starts to go wrong, sing out. We'll be all over it."

I didn't want to think about what he meant by things going wrong.

"Let's get this over with," I said.

Maloney got out and walked to the other car. Brady pulled forward.

A miniature lighthouse doubled as a mailbox. We pulled around it and entered a long straightaway, bordered on one side by a long line of those pine trees you always see bordering fields in pictures of Tuscany. A wide lawn on the other side sloped up a long hill to a grove of three spreading oaks that blocked the front of the house. Brady drove up slowly and stopped the car just past the trees.

"Not the castle I expected," I said.

The house was a two-story colonial with a built-in two-car garage. It wasn't small, but neither was it one of the vast mansions we had passed after pulling off the highway.

"It's got to be the smallest house on the block," he said.

"Or the county."

Brady's phone buzzed. He answered and listened.

"That was my boss, asking why you haven't gone in yet."

"Tell him I'm gone." I got out and followed a wide brick walkway to the front door. I rang the bell. If it was working, I couldn't hear it. I waited a minute longer and used the heavy brass knocker shaped like a ship's anchor. The door boomed. Still nothing. I turned back to look at Brady and shrugged my shoulders. He shrugged back.

"There's no one home." I spoke loud enough for the transmitter to relay my disgust to Maloney. "Can you take me home, now?"

Just as I started back toward the car, the door swung open. "You must be in a big hurry," a smoky female voice warned.

The woman must have come straight from the shower. Her hair was turbaned in a mauve towel and the rest of her was wrapped in an ankle-length matching robe. She had the frame of a large woman, but the proportions to carry it off.

"Mrs. Hochstadt?"

"Sorry about all this." She let her hand flutter over the V in the robe. If she was trying to be demure, it wasn't working. "I didn't expect you until eight. I just got in. Come in." She turned and walked inside, leaving the door ajar behind her. I followed.

"I'll be back in just a minute. Please go ahead and look around down here." She disappeared behind a wall and I heard her climbing the stairs.

"Mrs. Hochstadt? Is your husband here?" I called after her.

"No." She turned it into a laugh. "We don't need him, do we? You go ahead and get started."

Whoever I was supposed to be, it wasn't getting me any closer to interviewing her husband. I decided to wait for her return and then make a quick exit.

The living room had the pristine, unlived-in look of having been prepped for sale. There were no stacks of magazines, no clutter along the top of the waist-high bookshelves, not even a hint of ash in the fireplace. A thick book of Jill Krementz portraits lay on the coffee table as though it had been placed there by a real estate agent. A few low-numbered washed-out prints by artists I had never heard of hung on the wall over the bookcase. Otherwise, the walls were neutral and featureless, save for a big, empty rectangular space over the fireplace, outlined in a faint, grayish smoke residue. It didn't look like the palace of a hedge fund king; it looked like the pleasant but characterless abode of a moderately successful CPA.

The furnishings were all good quality, but straight out of the showroom. There was not one favorite chair, or funny lamp, or antique end table that said anything about the people who lived there. The space felt as cold as an oncologist's waiting room.

The lady came clacking down the stairs in a pair of backless, low-heeled shoes, black toreador pants, and a scoop-necked fuchsia sweater. Suddenly, the décor made sense. Whenever she was in the room, all eyes would be on her.

"Please, sit. Make yourself comfortable." She directed me to a surprisingly comfortable swivel chair facing the couch. "I just need to find my glasses." Her hip brushed my shoulder as she swept past to a closet by the front door. She rummaged through a large handbag. "I am blind without them and hopeless with contacts," she said as she eased down onto the couch. For a woman with such obvious assets, she was touchingly shy as she turned her head away to put on the glasses. Then she turned to me and her face registered sudden shock.

"Jesus Christ! Jason Stafford? What the hell are you doing here? You are Jason Stafford, aren't you?"

"I am. I'm sorry to frighten you. I'm here hoping to talk with your husband."

"The Worm? What would you want with that son of a bitch?"

Did I know this woman? How would I have forgotten her? "Uh," I stammered. "It's about work."

"Of course." She tossed her hair back and looked down her nose at me. "He's always looking for people with your talents."

Whatever those talents were, she clearly didn't like them.

"Look, I'm sorry to trouble you." I started to rise. "If your husband isn't here, I should just leave."

"Oh, shit," she said. "Sit down."

I sat and waited for her to make the next move.

She looked flustered. "I thought you were the appraiser," she said, with an embarrassed laugh. "I'm selling the house."

"Ah." I nodded as though I now understood.

"You don't remember me," she said. It was less an accusation than a statement.

"No," I admitted. "Though I can't imagine how I would have forgotten."

She acknowledged my awkward compliment with the kind of look that hinted more than promised, but was still guaranteed to make most men sit up and bark, or roll over and beg for their belly to be rubbed. But it wasn't a friendly look.

"About ten years ago. You were visiting Case's London office. I was assigned to be your factotum."

"I must have been seriously jet-lagged," I said. And then a face came to mind. A much different face—and body. Lank hair, roseate complexion, a much bigger, wider woman, but with the same green eyes behind oversized glasses. She had efficiently organized two weeks of client meetings, prepping me, guiding me, and even chauffeuring me when necessary. "Wait. I'm sorry. Diane . . . ?"

She nodded. "Havell. I still used my maiden name then."

"It was good to have a fellow Yank to translate for me." More memories came back. "And keep me from getting run over every time I stepped off a curb."

"And find you someplace that served cold beer."

"But you were . . ." I paused, fumbling for words that would not offend.

"Pregnant," she said. "Six months."

"Ah," I said. I hadn't suspected.

"I didn't use the name Hochstadt until our daughter started school. It was just much easier."

"Ah," I said again, trying to arrange all the clues into a coherent picture. "I'm flattered you remember me."

"You were famous."

Not yet infamous.

"And your daughter? Where is she now?" There was no sign that a child had ever walked into that barren living room.

"She is in school. In Switzerland. I plan to join her as soon as all this"—she waggled her fingers expressively—"is done with."

"And your husband?"

"Soon to be ex-husband," she corrected. "The Worm is living in Greenwich. I asked him to move out this spring. He was surprisingly gracious about it. What is it you want with him?"

"I have to ask him some questions."

"I'm sure," she said, drawing out the word dismissively. "About Arrowhead, no doubt. All your old crowd."

I was losing her. We were past pleasant memories and easy rapport.

"I never heard the name until last week," I said. "You may think you know all about me, but you're wrong." Maloney would be champing at the bit, but I thought there was a chance to get some information, if I could keep her talking.

She looked away. "Talk to my husband." She rattled off his address.

I didn't bother to write it down—Brady would already be plotting it on the GPS. "Diane, you helped me once. Please, you can help me again. It's important. Who's the 'old crowd' you're talking about?"

"Are you asking me to trust you, Jason?"

It was time for cards on the table. Maloney was going to have a conniption. "I've been hired by Weld Securities to look into Arrowhead. And what I've found so far is going to take a lot of people down. But I need help. Give me names, Diane, please."

She looked up and glared at me. "I lost my marriage to them. That ex–Case crowd. I was married to a nice guy. A little nebbishy, but he treated me like a queen. He ran back-office operations for a small hedge fund—moving money around the world to avoid the tax collectors. He was good at it. Then he got hired by Arrowhead. They convinced him he was a trader and turned him into the nastiest little bundle of raw nerves you ever saw."

"The business chews people up," I said. "Trading's not for everyone."

She snorted. "He was no trader. He came home with these stories of crossing big trades between major players, as though he knew the markets better than Rothkamp or Dresden Bank. It was absurd."

"Names?"

She shook her head. "And he was still moving funds around. All over. Hundreds of accounts. Then they relocated us here. Three years ago. I never knew why. But they bought the house for us. Paid for Alana's school."

"Sweet deal."

Her nostrils flared slightly as though she smelled something rank. "They treat the help well."

I kept digging. "I imagine there's a lot of money to go around."

"I don't know how the money works. Geoffrey had a big expense account—they never questioned it. They paid for the boat to be brought over from England. The summer rental on Nantucket and the vacations at the Bitter End on Virgin Gorda. And he got paid more than he ever would have made as an ops guy. But nothing like what a trader gets who was supposedly clearing a couple of hundred mil a year."

Two hundred a year. I must have looked stunned.

"That's what he said." She sighed. "Of course, that was before he started lying to me. About everything."

"You never met any of the Arrowhead directors?"

"No. I went along on some of the client outings, but Geoffrey never bothered to introduce me to his bosses."

"The client outings? The casino trips?"

She looked away before she answered. "Once or twice."

There it was. She was holding something back, but she wasn't going to give it up easily.

"Well, if that's it, I will be going. Thanks for your time. And I sympathize. I'm divorced myself."

She visibly relaxed.

"My, you are in a hurry. No time for a drink?" She shifted one leg a fraction of an inch and instantly changed from someone's angry ex to a hungry predator. The glasses came off. My body was having a very primitive response.

"Can I get a rain check?" I stood up, reluctantly.

She made a moue of disappointment. "Rain or shine. But you better hurry. I plan on spending Christmas with my daughter. In Gstaad."

As she rose off the couch, she managed to lean forward just enough for me to see she must have made a habit of sunbathing topless.

We were face-to-face across the coffee table. The room felt very warm. I fought my way through the fog of pheromones. Pieces shifted and suddenly fit. Sanders' diary. His scorecard. DH/AC. Diane Hochstadt—Atlantic City.

"Just one more thing." I looked directly into her eyes. "How well did you know Brian Sanders?"

For a split second, her guard came down and she looked as though she'd been slapped. She wrapped her arms around her elbows and glared back at me.

"I can't see how this is any of your business."

"People tell me he wasn't a gambler. So what was he doing while his buddies were hitting the tables? What were you doing? You were there, weren't you?"

"You should leave now."

"You know you're in his diary. You and a lot of other women."

"Brian Sanders was a pleasant diversion. He was energetic, experienced, and endowed. But he was not a nice person."

"But dying on your husband's boat must have been an odd coincidence. I wondered if you thought so, too."

She looked angry, afraid, and vulnerable. "Please. Go."

I took my time moving toward the door. "I mean, they were the only two on board and your husband manages to swim to safety and a kid twenty years younger doesn't make it. You see? It keeps bugging me."

"Good-bye, Jason," she said, swinging open the front door. "Please don't come back."

My rain check was canceled. I put my hands up in mock surrender. "Sorry to have disturbed you. I'm gone."

I was almost down the steps before she spoke again.

"Ask Geoffrey about that night."

I stopped and turned back to her. Her hair was brushed back by the breeze and the aura from the porch light backlit her body, emphasizing each curve. I saw what had attracted a player a decade or more her junior.

"Diane, I'm sorry. I hope things work out for you."

"Yes, well, I hope things work out for you, too. These are not good people. Watch your back."

"I'll try."

"There was a third person on board that night. Ask Geoffrey about that, too." She closed the door and turned off the light. The night air felt a lot colder than when I had gone in.

I SPOKE INTO the phone as I walked to the car.

"Everybody listening? Are we all here? Tape rolling? You guys have got to be the biggest bunch of fuckups I ever had the bad luck to meet up with. How did you not know that Hochstadt doesn't even live here anymore?"

I wrenched open the door of the Town Car and threw myself into the backseat.

"How's my son, Senior Agent? Has anyone checked on him lately?"

Brady turned to me and handed me his two-way radio.

"Easy," Maloney said. "It wasn't a wasted trip. And you rattled her nicely at the end there. She knows more. We'll go back and lean on her again. Nice work. We learned a few things. Now we go to Greenwich and pin the husband. Pick me up out front. I'll ride with you."

I leaned back into the soft leather seat. "Let's get this over with."

As I handed the radio back to Brady, I heard Maloney's last words. "And this time, try to stay on script."

HOCHSTADT LIVED in a little condo community down by the water. It looked like middle-aged-divorced-guy headquarters. Every apartment was a duplex with a water view from the top floor, a small balcony on the first, and a carport underneath. And every carport held a recent-model middle-aged-guy's fantasy of a chickmobile—a Jaguar XK convertible, a Porsche Boxster, a BMW 650. The Boxster shared the space with a big Harley. The spot under Hochstadt's apartment had a bright yellow Hummer. It practically screamed issues of inadequacy and compensation.

Each balcony had an almost identical pair of plastic chairs and table and small hibachi grill. I could just imagine the wild Saturday nights with a line of balding, lonely men grilling up their rib eyes, popping the top on another tallboy, and wishing there was someone sitting in the other chair.

"I could become suicidal living here," I said.

"Save it and get going," Maloney said.

"*Morituri te salutant,*" I said quietly.

"What's that?" Brady asked.

"The gladiators' motto. It works for traders as well." I got out of the car and hurried over to the front door. The intercom buzzer appeared to work.

"Who is it?" His voice was fluty with a hint of an affected British accent. Already I didn't like him.

"Geoffrey Hochstadt?"

"Who is this?" He sounded like someone born to grievance.

"My name is Jason Stafford. I'm an investigator for Weld Securities. I need to talk to you."

There was a long pause.

"I can't help you. Good night."

I hit the buzzer again.

"You can talk to me or talk to the cops. Your choice, Mr. Hochstadt."

"I know who you are." He tried to make it sound like a threat.

I gave him the frat house whine. Traders use it on each other all the time. It is surprising how often it works.

"Come on, Geoffrey. Don't be a pussy. I just want to talk. I'm not going to hurt you. Come on, let me in, it's getting fucking cold out here."

The door buzzed. I pushed through.

Geoffrey Hochstadt was a tall, thin man with big hands and an Adam's apple that made him look like he was having trouble swallowing a brick. His thick glasses magnified his dark eyes, giving him a look of constant surprise. I couldn't imagine him at the helm of a big sailboat—he looked like he would blow away in the first stiff breeze.

He stood back from the door and watched carefully as I entered the apartment. The place was almost bare. A white card table and two folding chairs sat in the middle of the dining area. One of the chairs was strategically placed to face the single piece of furniture in the living room—a huge flat-screen TV, perched on top of the box it had come in. On the far wall was the missing artwork from the house in Darien—a four-foot-tall portrait of Geoffrey himself, looking almost elegant in a white windbreaker and captain's hat, standing at the helm of a heeling sailboat, foam swirling up along its side. A crew of strong young men, who seemed to have been selected from a Ralph Lauren catalog, pulled on ropes or cranked winch handles. *Serenity*. It was the boat from the *New York Post* article. The one that had smashed up in Greenwich harbor. You could probably see the rocks from an upstairs window. It was the only decoration on the walls.

"Nice painting." I smiled. "Anyone we know?"

Hochstadt pulled himself up, unintentionally mimicking the pose. "I had it commissioned when I ran the London office."

I nodded. "And now you run the New York office."

"The U.S. subsidiary. What is it you want with me?" The accent became more pronounced when he tried to sound in control.

I pulled out one of the chairs and sat down.

"Maybe we could do this over a beer?"

"I don't drink," he said.

"Anything? How about coffee? Tea? Water?"

He tried to stare me down—for maybe a full second. Then his shoulder fell and he dug out glasses and poured water from a Brita pitcher. He was holding himself together so tightly he practically vibrated a high C. He sat facing me.

"What is it you want?" he asked again.

"I spoke to your wife this evening. She told me where to find you."

He took a sip of water, hiding behind the glass.

"She mentioned that we have some mutual acquaintances. Who would that be? Old friends? New ones? Not many of my old friends want to know me these days."

His eyes blinked once.

"All right," I said. "I will get to the point. I'm conducting an investigation into a possible trading scandal at Weld Securities. But you probably know that."

He put the glass down and examined the blank table.

"When I started, I really didn't think they wanted me to find anything. Or rather, they wanted me to find nothing. They can't afford to be anything but squeaky clean in front of this merger."

Hochstadt tried to lift the glass again, but looked like he didn't have the strength.

"But I found something. I found a very clear pattern of skimming by a group of traders."

He made an attempt to brave it out. "I don't see what this has to do with me. I think you should leave." It was sad. He wasn't a fighter.

"Hear me out. Please. When I'm done, if you still think there's nothing to talk about, I will just get up and go home."

He turned his head and stared at the windows. It was a dark night, there was nothing to see but our reflections.

"Come on, Geoffrey. If I give them everything I've got, they'll have to give it to the regulators. I'm just trying to see what works best for everybody."

He looked at me and smiled skeptically.

"All right," I said. "Best for me."

He gave a slight nod.

"They wanted me to look into one trader only at the beginning. Brian Sanders."

He nodded again.

"Only that led to more. The trips to Atlantic City. Foxwoods. I followed the whole trail. A whole group of junior traders."

He gave a dismissive little laugh. "All the little shits."

"But there's more. Lots more. Hundreds of millions. Am I right?"

He shrugged. "You tell me."

I laughed. "You can't bullshit a bullshitter. Another day or two and I'll be ready to name names. And when I do, it all gets rolled up. It will be too late for you and your partners."

"And what do you get, Mr. Stafford? Job satisfaction? Give me a proposal and I will pass it on. These people are businessmen—they're used to cutting deals."

"Sorry. I thought I was talking to a decision-maker. If you're not the guy, tell me who is."

He smiled. "Do you think you can provoke me? Petty little jabs insinuating that I am insignificant? I know what I am. I know what I've already given up. What I've lost."

I wasn't shaking any revelations out of him. He was becoming more comfortable, not less. I wanted him back on the ropes.

"Nothing like what Sanders lost."

His eyes went flat. "An accident."

"When did you find out he was screwing your wife?"

There was a brief flash of anger, before his eyes clouded again. "My wife is a good person, no matter what you've heard. Brian Sanders was not."

I wasn't getting to him. He was too depressed to be rattled.

"Tell me who I'm dealing with. The old Case crowd. Your partners. Who's pulling the strings, here?"

He shook his head—a lot more times than was necessary. "Do you have a proposal? I think I want this conversation to be over."

I leaned into him. "Two mil. And I want to meet with them. Him. Whoever. Set it up."

"I assume you'll want the money offshore somewhere?"

"That's what you do, right?"

"I'm one of the best," he said. "I'm surprised. Considering the scale of all this, I would have expected you to be more aggressive. Or acquisitive. I doubt the money will be a problem. As for the meeting? We'll see."

"That's not negotiable," I said.

He handed me his card. "Call me tomorrow morning. Use the cell-phone number." He stood up and walked me to the door.

I had nothing for Maloney but a vague possibility. If I didn't pry something out of Hochstadt, I was doomed to have the FBI in my life for days to come. I stopped just outside the door. A small cloud of moths fluttered around the big floodlight, taking turns immolating themselves on its surface.

"One last thing, Geoffrey."

He stepped back as though I had swung at him.

"I know there was someone else on board that night. I know who it was. When I can prove it, I'm going to want more. A lot more."

It was completely off script. And it got a reaction.

Hochstadt darted his head out the door, as though he expected someone to be hiding behind the boxwood hedge. His voice was a hissing whisper, equal parts anger and fear. "Are you out of your mind? You can't threaten him. He doesn't make deals. He cleans up problems. He'll find a way to get to you."

He slammed the door, locked it, and turned off the light, leaving me and the moths in the dark.

I PULLED MY jacket closed. The temperature was still dropping. We could have the first frost of the season if it got much colder. I hustled over to the car.

Who was this "he" Hochstadt had threatened me with? This was something beyond a conspiracy of traders, skimming a little extra for their own pockets. Hochstadt was scared. Terrified.

"What the hell was that?" Maloney was fuming when I got in the car. "Where did that come from? Christ! I gave you a simple enough game plan. Push him a little. Then tease him with the blackmail. Get him talking."

"Well, he wasn't talking, was he? He was more afraid of me *before* I started talking. The only time he lost it was at the end there. Look, if he gets me the meeting with one of the head honchos, you guys will have what you need."

"Who was he talking about? Who's this fixer?"

"The other man on the boat? No idea. And I'm not looking forward to finding out."

The lights in Hochstadt's apartment went out and a moment later he appeared briefly in the doorway.

"What is he up to now?" Maloney said.

Neither Brady nor I had an answer. The yellow HMV pulled out with a screech of tires and swung by us. Hochstadt was at the wheel.

"He never even looked our way," Brady said.

"Give the other car a heads-up," Maloney said. "Have them stay on him. We'll follow."

Minutes later, we were hurtling south on I-95, with Hochstadt and the yellow Hummer boxed. The agents in the other car were slightly ahead of the big vehicle, we were fifty yards back. Brady kept to the middle lane where most of the limo drivers avoided speed traps, and did his best to keep up without blowing his cover.

Hochstadt was a terrible driver—all over the road. He sped up until he was practically riding the bumper of the car in front of him, and then slowed back down as soon as the highway immediately in front of him was empty. He changed lanes—without signaling—to gain any advantage, even just a few feet. And he was a two-footed driver, his brake lights lit even as he accelerated up behind a smaller vehicle.

"Christ, he's worse than my ex," Maloney said.

Just past the big green sign for Exit 18A, the highway opened up in front of us and the Hummer took off. For a moment, Brady hung back.

"Goddamnit, don't lose him!" Maloney yelled.

Brady sped up. Suddenly, Hochstadt veered from the far left lane all the way to the far right, into the exit lane and down the ramp. Brady cursed and tried to follow, but the Town Car was hemmed in by a row of road warriors jockeying for supremacy in the right lane.

He hit the brakes and spun the wheel. The Town Car slewed sideways down the center lane while horns blared at us from all directions. I was too scared to speak. A pair of headlights seemed to be aimed right at me, approaching at seventy miles an hour. In that moment of desperate panic as my brain prepared for death, I remembered that I wasn't even supposed to be there. I was two hours late to meet Skeli for dinner at Danny Meyer's Shake Shack on Columbus. My obit would read: "He died while helping the FBI with an investigation." What a fucking waste.

Brady hit the gas and the car pulled out of the slide and shot across the right lane, narrowly avoiding an SUV full of screaming teenage girls. We were past the exit ramp, but Brady kept going. We hit the curb and the front end flew up into the air. The seat belt threatened to cut me in two. The rear wheels found traction and we slalomed down the grassy slope, while the GPS lady kept repeating the word "NO!" as though reprimanding a particularly stupid golden retriever. We left behind a screen of flying grass and dirt and two long divots. Then we bounced back onto the roadway, heading the right way down the exit ramp.

There was no one in front of us. Hochstadt had already made the turn at the bottom of the ramp. We had lost him.

"GODDAMNIT, BRADY. Where is he? How in hell did you lose him?" Maloney had another victim.

"Shut up!" I yelled. "It's not his fault. Hochstadt set us up—he knew he was being followed."

Maloney looked as though he was about to start in on me. I didn't give him the chance.

"He put on that lousy-driver act and cut out as soon as he saw we were easing up on him. I didn't think he had it in him—and neither did you, so leave off!"

The engine hummed. The traffic light changed to yellow, then red. Nobody said anything. The road stretched into darkness in either direction.

Maloney spoke first. "You're right. He made us. So, where would he go? Thoughts?" It was an open question. No one ventured an opinion.

"Where's the rest of the team?" I said.

Maloney nodded and spoke to Brady. "Call them. Have them circle back around. Wake up local law enforcement as well. Where the fuck are we anyway?"

Outside it was dark and we were surrounded by trees. It was a long way from Seventy-second Street.

"New York," Brady answered. "Somewhere between Rye and New Rochelle."

"Left or right?" Maloney said. "We're not going to find him sitting here."

"Hold up," I said. "Let me call his wife." I pulled out my own phone and dialed.

"What are you thinking?" Maloney said.

I held up one finger as the phone rang.

She answered in a low, tired voice. "Yes?"

"Diane? It's Jason again. Things are swinging out of control. I need your help—and I think Geoffrey does as well." Whatever he was up to, I knew he was frightened.

"I want nothing to do with this. I thought I made that clear."

"I'm happy to keep you out of it. But I'm worried."

She must have heard something in my voice. "What do you want?"

"Tell me. Did he buy himself another boat?"

Maloney's eyes bulged.

"Why?" Now she sounded frightened.

"I thought you wanted to stay out of this."

She paused. "Yes. It's another big sailboat. A racing boat. He keeps it in a slip at Mamaroneck."

"Mamaroneck?" I asked, giving Brady a look.

He nodded and gave a thumbs-up.

"Yes. Is he all right?" The concern in her voice surprised me. Maybe it surprised her.

"I hope so."

I didn't know what else to say. I couldn't tell whether she was afraid for herself, or him, or merely sick of all of us. Little shits, big shits, crooks, pretenders, and me. She hung up before I thought of the words.

Brady was already tapping away at the GPS.

"Left turn," the computer lady ordered.

MAIN STREET MAMARONECK gave way to an open park facing the harbor and Long Island Sound. Aluminum masts stood out brightly against the black water. A stiff breeze had the lines rattling in a clack-clack arrhythmic staccato. A cold mist wisped by in patches that left the windshield bedewed with tiny raindrops that sparkled golden in the overhead lights.

A wide concrete walkway led down to the floating docks. Save for the single yellow HMV in the parking lot, the place seemed to be deserted.

"A great place to have a conversation you didn't want anyone else to hear," Maloney said as we made our way out along the dock.

The two agents didn't make a fuss about creeping along, but they managed to make very little noise. The slap of the lines on the masts drowned out footsteps.

Toward the end of the dock, one boat emitted a glow from the cabin lights.

"You think that's his boat?" Brady said.

I had no clue. "Sailboats have the big stick on top, right?"

We crept closer. *Serenity II* was written in an italic kind of font along the back end of the hull.

"That's it," I said.

"So we wait to see who comes down to join him?" Brady said.

Maloney shook his head. "We go in now. We'll wait on board." He pulled himself over the rail and the boom creaked as the boat swayed under his weight, announcing our arrival as effectively as a siren.

"Mr. Hochstadt?" Maloney called out. There was no answer.

We must all have caught the same wave of apprehension simultaneously. Maloney took out a gun. Brady pulled himself on board and moved around to the far side of the open hatchway.

"Geoffrey Hochstadt? We are FBI agents. We're here to talk to you."

The lines kept slapping against the mast. The wind hummed through the rigging.

Brady ducked his head and went down the cabin steps. Maloney followed.

I stood alone on the deck, feeling the cold mist work its way through my clothes. Maybe I shivered.

"We're too late," Maloney called up.

I looked down the short stairway. The space below held two long, built-in couches, a small desk surrounded by navigation equipment, and a miniature kitchen. Splatters of blood covered most of it.

Geoffrey Hochstadt was sitting upright, leaning back slightly on the couch. His mouth hung open and his eyes bulged. He looked like he was doing a bad Jim Carrey impersonation. I had to crane my head to the side to see the blackened hole in his temple. The exit wound was in shadow, but the arc of blood and other matter across the walls and ceiling was easy to read.

The sight of death—violent death—affected me much less than I would have expected. I felt no revulsion at the blood and brains spewed across the cabin, just a cold stab of loneliness. I wanted my son. I wanted to be home in my apartment, tucking my child into bed, and reading to him from *The History of the Muscle Car: When Detroit Ruled the World.*

"That him?" Brady spoke softly.

I nodded.

"Bet he looked better before." Cop humor can be as inane and infantile as Wall Street humor—and as dark.

"Can you close his eyes?" I said.

There was a handgun of some kind lying on the cushion next to his open hand. I had seen enough cop shows to know it was an automatic, not a revolver. I decided that two experienced FBI agents would not need me to point this out. Though he couldn't have been dead for more than ten minutes, there was already a faint smell of decay mixed with the odors of mildew, gunpowder, and fresh urine.

"I guess he kept the gun here," I said. They both looked at me quizzically. "On board. He came here to get the gun."

"So you think this is suicide?" Maloney asked.

"Don't you?" I said.

"Not likely," Brady said. "The guy's left-handed. Nobody shoots himself with his off hand. It is the one time where you really don't want to have to take a second shot."

I stared at the body. "How do you know he's left-handed?" I finally said.

"The watch."

Maloney nodded. The dead man was wearing a gold Rolex—on his right wrist. "They teach you to look for things like that on the Discovery Channel."

Brady snorted a laugh as he rifled through the drawers and cabinets.

"I thought you're not supposed to touch anything. At a crime scene, I mean."

Brady ignored me.

"Maybe you should wait outside," Maloney said.

I thought about waiting in the dark, wet chill where a murderer might still be hanging around.

"How about I stay here and keep my mouth shut," I said.

"That works, too."

It took them just minutes to discover that there was nothing to find. The drawers held some charts, an engine manual, and a booklet of the most recent sailboat racing rules. Otherwise, the boat was bare.

"He came here to meet someone," Maloney said. "Someone who killed him almost as soon as he arrived. And then immediately cut out."

"So what do we do now?"

Maloney looked around. "Get our guys in here to coordinate the locals. Meantime, we go after records." He turned to me. "And the first place you should look is back at Hochstadt's apartment. Did you see a computer there? An office?"

"No. But I never looked in the bedrooms. I suppose . . ."

"Then go. I'll move on the offices downtown."

I reached for a rail to pull myself up the stairway.

"And don't touch anything," Maloney said.

MALONEY HAD local law enforcement dancing in two states. New York and Mamaroneck shared the murder scene, while NYPD joined the FBI at the Arrowhead offices back in the city. Brady and I went back to Connecticut, where the most polite police officers I had ever encountered met us and opened up Hochstadt's apartment. It paid to be polite in a town where a major crime consisted of a maid stealing the silverware. White-collar crimes, perpetuated daily by the hedge fund kings, mortgage bankers, and derivatives traders who populate the town, are never investigated by the town police. They are its lifeblood.

Hochstadt's home office was a corner of the master bedroom. A flat-screen monitor and keyboard were the only items on the small desk. A pair of plastic file drawers and a wheeled, ergonomic knee chair completed the ensemble.

"What is this?" Brady asked. "It looks like one of those walking trainers for toddlers."

"It's a chair," I said. "You kneel on it. It's good for a bad back, they say."

"It would give me a bad back," Brady said. "If I didn't already have one." He dragged the desk over and sat on the edge of the bed.

I tackled the file drawers. Tax returns, a file from an attorney in Hartford about the terms of the divorce, and a folder full of hard copies of e-mails from his daughter. No secrets. However, there was a cigar box full of four-gigabyte flash drives.

"Having any luck?" I asked.

Brady made a face. "Nada. Nothing's password-protected—but so what? Every file folder is empty."

"How about the trash folder?"

"Checked it."

"Try one of these," I said. I pulled the chair around and knelt next to him as he plugged in the first flash drive and opened the folder.

A spreadsheet blossomed before us. Dates. Trades. Securities. Amounts. Prices in various currencies. And counterparties. Brady scrolled down. The data flew by. The flash held trades for a six-month period back in 2004. There were dozens, scores, sometimes hundreds of trades each day. Even when he was in London, Geoffrey Hochstadt had been a very busy man.

"I've got to call Maloney," Brady said.

"Go ahead. I'll keep going through these." He stood up and I wrestled the monitor around. I plugged in another flash. The last four months in 2007. Another. And another. The only incriminating pieces of information not on file were the names of the traders at the various firms. Every major bank was involved at one time or another. I saw that over a two-year period the bulk of the trading had migrated from London to New York, though there were regular players involved in Singapore, Chicago, Zurich, Los Angeles, Frankfurt, and Hong Kong. I searched for patterns. There was too much data—it was overwhelming.

"There's months of work here," I said. "Somebody has to go through and check every trade."

And then they would have to identify every trader, many of whom would have changed jobs, changed firms, or changed what they traded over the years.

"There could be a couple of hundred traders involved in this thing," I continued. "You guys will be chasing this down for the next decade."

"And we're very good at doing just that," Brady said. "Job security."

I searched through until I had all the flash drives in chronological order. The earliest was almost a decade old, the most recent included trades for the previous week. There was one that I did not understand. It was wrapped in a piece of well-worn silver duct tape. The files held nothing but columns of numbers and letters. I set it aside.

Patterns. They emerged slowly at first, but then they began to cascade down into place. Trades with one counterparty were often offset with the same bank later in the day or week. Or trades with two different counterparties were revealed to be mirror offsets. It was not coincidence, it was collusion. Every time Hochstadt had executed a trade with the high-grade corporate bond desk at Rothkamp in Amsterdam, he made a profit of $1,000 per million. Every time. Without fail. Over three years. Impossible. But the more I stared, the more it became apparent—Hochstadt had not lied to his wife. Two hundred million dollars a year was a very conservative estimate. The total would top two billion.

Who had been the beneficiaries? I would need to find the money trail. That kind of money hadn't been paid in casino chips.

I went back to the most recent files. There were the Sanders trades. Increasing in size and profitability over time, but still Lilliputian in comparison with others. I found Sudhir's trades—sporadic, almost tentative. And Carmine's—a consistent flow of three or four a week, though all small in size. And Lowell Barrington's. Four trades. That was it. The young man's ambivalence and guilt were glaring. Arrowhead had barely cleared two grand combined on the four small trades. Lowell had stepped in front of a train for less money than his broker might spend at Sparks on a typical Thursday night.

It was depressing. I wanted to sleep.

"Brady? Did you get hold of your boss yet? Tell him this thing is huge. A hundred traders in the States, that many again around the world. Tell him when he takes this down, he'll be famous. They'll put him on the Discovery Channel. What am I saying? They'll give him his own show!"

I looked around. I was alone.

I walked out to the top of the stairs. The two Greenwich cops were sitting at the card table watching a *Law & Order* rerun on the big television.

"Hey. What happened to my FBI guy? Agent Brady?"

"He went out, sir."

"Weird. Did he say where?"

"No, sir. He asked that we stay with you."

"Did he say he was coming back?"

They looked like a matched pair of purebred guard dogs.

"Not to us, sir."

I walked back and sat on the bed. I checked my watch. It was well past midnight. I couldn't remember the last time I had slept. In the past thirty hours I had been assaulted, had my child kidnapped, and seen my first murdered corpse. I had been dragged from one crazy scene to another by the FBI, who had now, seemingly, abandoned me. And all I wanted was to hear my little robot-voiced boy tell me, "Good night, Jason."

I lay back and tried to stop the flow of flickering images of death. Sleep approached cautiously. Just as the curtains began to close another memory floated to the surface. Skeli.

"Shit!" I sat up. I flipped open my phone and found her number. Then I stopped. What did I have to say? Sorry. Unavoidable. I should have called. Could I have explained all that had happened? Not in my condition. I closed the phone and lay back down again. Caution or cowardice? Tomorrow would be soon enough.

I AWOKE FRIDAY morning with the sickening feeling of having spent the night in a dead man's bed. It was coming up on nine o'clock. I did a quick survey of my aches and pains. A night's sleep had helped. I felt better.

There was a quiet bustle from downstairs and the aroma of fresh-brewed coffee snuck up the stairs and found me. I splashed water on my face and went out to face the world.

The two Greenwich cops were sitting at the card table, drinking coffee and sharing a bag of donuts. They looked as clean-shaven, ironed, and polite as they had the night before.

"Good morning," I called. "Is there another cup?"

"Yes, sir," they answered together.

They shared the donuts, too. I had a blueberry. For the anti-oxidants.

"Have you heard anything? Any instructions?" I asked.

"Just to stay with you until further notice, sir."

"You've been here all night?" Up close, I could see the hint of beard, the tired eyes.

"We don't get much chance for overtime."

"Or to work on a murder case," the other added.

"What's it like so far?" I was almost embarrassed for them. They wanted to be action heroes, not babysitters. "I'll make some calls and try to find out where I'm supposed to be."

I went back upstairs and called Maloney's office. He was "un-available."

"Let me talk to his partner. Give me Brady. Tell him it's Stafford."

I didn't have much of a hand to play. Outrage wasn't going to get me very far.

"Agent Brady is unavailable," said the voice of Don Corleone's consigliere.

"What! That . . ." I discarded a number of names that came to mind. "I'm sorry. Would you just deliver a message for me?"

"Certainly."

"Tell Agent Brady that I am making a pile of all the evidence we found up here in Greenwich and if he doesn't come to the phone in the next thirty seconds, I am setting a match to it and walking out the door."

"Would you like to hold?"

"As long as I don't have to listen to canned music."

It wasn't canned music—it was a continuous loop advertisement for a career in law enforcement. The two cops downstairs would have enjoyed it.

"Brady here."

"Will you explain to me what the hell is going on? Right now I feel like the 'I' in team."

"Something came up."

"Something came up!? Are you shitting me? You duck out and leave me here with the Aryan Twins? You know what? I am going to set this shit on fire."

"Don't bother. Maloney has it all. Those files are duplicates. We got the originals off the computer in the Arrowhead office."

"So you just leave me up here? I don't get it."

"As I said, something came up. I can't talk about it."

"Fucking brilliant! This is a murder investigation now and you don't give a shit?"

"Local and state police are capable of handling that."

"And I bet you can't talk about that, either. Well, what can you talk about? How about . . . Where's my son?"

"I think the hearing is scheduled for late this morning. I'll tell our people down there to call you as soon as they know anything."

"Can I talk to him? Have them call me now."

"Look, I've got to go. I'm sorry about this, but there's nothing I could do."

"Tell me, Brady. You guys owe me. What the hell is going on?"

He paused. "We got pulled. Not just us. Every white-collar agent east of St. Louis has been called in. Maloney's pissed, but he's got no choice. We're on hold until this gets taken care of. I can't say anything, but believe me, it is big."

"Are you kidding? We've got a couple of hundred traders involved. Two billion or more! What trumps this?"

"I can't say anything." He paused. "Watch the news. There's a press conference called for eleven-thirty. I gotta go." He hung up.

AS IT WAS the police who had brought me up to Connecticut, I figured the system at least owed me a ride home. I stuffed my jacket pockets full with the flash drives and went back down to the Doberman twins.

"The FBI says you two are supposed to see I get back to New York safe and sound. Are you ready for a ride into Manhattan?"

If they'd had tails, they would have wagged them. More overtime.

I let them drop me on the corner of Amsterdam, so they wouldn't have to go all the way to West End to head back uptown. Then I gave them alternate sets of directions for how to get back to I-95 North, until I heard myself starting to get manic.

"You'll find it," I finished.

"You'll be all right here, sir?"

They may have been warriors, keepers of the peace, hyper-fit and ready for action, but they still had the suburban distrust of New York City.

"I live right across the street." I waved. The Ansonia was still there.

So was P&G.

I wavered. Then I went home.

THE DOOR WAS unlocked. I walked in, took one look, and called the front desk and told them to get the police. Then I called Brady again.

"Somebody broke into my apartment. Totally trashed the place. They searched everything. Everything! They dumped the Kid's cereal on the floor. They took the toilet apart!"

My laptop was open—someone had gone through my files. The stack of autism books was now an archipelago reaching across the floor, surrounded by a sea of pasta, cereal, tea bags, and the solitary jar of peanut butter. At Ray Brook, the guards held periodic searches, working their way down one side of a cellblock, hitting some cells, skipping others in a seemingly random process, the main purpose of which seemed to be to remind us all that prisoners were powerless, unable to protect even their own minuscule space from violation.

I felt dirty. And frightened. It occurred to me that that was exactly how someone wanted me to feel.

"What's missing?"

"Nothing. I think." I was flipping between bouts of overwhelming anxiety and crystal-cool vision, at one moment terrified, the next, unconcerned and able to focus on detail. "They left a laptop and a thousand dollars' worth of brand-new Bose audio equipment. But they dumped a few thousand CDs out of their cases. They're all over the floor."

"What's on the laptop?"

"My report to Stockman."

"Your notes? Any of the evidence?"

"No."

"That's why he left it. Listen, don't stay there."

I remembered my last sight of Hochstadt, bloody eyes bulging at me.

"You think they'll come back?"

"He didn't find what he's looking for. Last night, before Maloney got to the Arrowhead offices, somebody else tried to get in. The security guard told him to get lost. That's why I left the two Greenwich cops with you."

"All right, I'm convinced. I'm out of here. There's a place across the street where they know me."

"I'll have the NYPD put a man on the floor. Until they find the killer. I wish I could do more."

"Any word on the Kid?"

"Way too early. Call me later."

I DIDN'T SEE anyone watching me as I crossed the park. No one was following me. No eyes darted away as I looked in their direction. It was a cool, fall day, with high, white wispy clouds and a pale blue sky. Two nannies with sleeping toddlers in strollers looked at me suspiciously as I passed. A handsome old man with a mane of swept-back silver hair was tossing bread crumbs for the pigeons and squirrels to fight over. The rats would show up after dark for what morsels remained.

It was all so normal. I felt like I was walking through a movie set—something light where people might suddenly break out in song. And I could plod safely through, in dim-witted comfort, immune to danger. Exempt from feeling.

Vinny was studying the *Racing Form* and making notes. Rollie was busy restocking the back bar. I slid onto a stool and asked for a beer.

"You don't look so good," Vinny said. "Maybe you want to start with a cuppa coffee."

"I've felt better," I said.

"Give him a coffee."

The coffee was hot and black. It had no taste. My body kept humming with too much energy, while my brain sputtered and gapped.

"I think I'm in shock," I said.

"Bad day?" Vinny said.

"Bad week." Couple of years. Bad decade. The surface of the coffee was covered with tiny ripples. My hand was shaking. I wanted to explain—I wanted someone to understand—but I couldn't decide what event of the past few days to start with. "My ex took the Kid." That hurt the most, but compared to getting attacked, or having my apartment ransacked by a murderer, it sounded weak. "I've had some other problems," I finished.

"Better give him a cognac with that," Vinny said.

The cognac burned and soothed, but I couldn't taste it either.

I checked my watch. It was almost 11:30.

"Would it be all right if we watched the news for a bit?"

Rollie raised a questioning eyebrow and Vinny gave a nod. Everyone was being nice to me. He put on CNN.

"You know that investigation I was working on?" I said.

Vinny nodded.

"Well, it has snowballed. And somebody is killing people to protect it. Last night I had my own private security force and today I've got zip. Not quite zip. Brady's taking my calls."

Vinny nodded like he knew what I was talking about.

A red banner replaced the ticker tape running across the bottom of the television screens. Breaking news. Stay tuned. I wasn't going anywhere.

The talking heads were replaced by a street scene somewhere downtown. A group of gray-suited men stood in front of the glass doors of a gray building. One of them stepped forward and spoke to the cameras.

"Turn it up, Rollie."

It was still hard to hear every word, but the story was simple. A combined task force of the FBI and the SEC had just arrested the renowned, but reclusive, head of a major hedge fund, who had owned up to running a $50 billion Ponzi scheme over the past twenty years. One of the largest in history. I saw Brady and other lower-level agents carry box after box of files out of the building. Maloney was among the senior agents who stood and watched, all with serious, concerned frowns plastered in place. The U.S. Attorney spoke as though someone had just given him the briefing two minutes before the cameras rolled. He looked like he wasn't having as much fun as he had anticipated.

They gave the perp his walk of shame, but he refused to play the part. He came out the glass doors smiling, looking relieved rather than guilty. He didn't quite wave to the cameras, but he made sure they shot his good side. For him, it was over. The fear of being discovered a fraud always outweighs the guilt.

I had felt that relief once.

I didn't want to identify with him. This guy, the pundits told us, had destroyed the lives of hundreds of investors. People he had looked in the eye, taken their money in exchange for his trust, and never invested a penny of it. He was a predator. A vampire.

But a part of me cringed. The world saw us as the same. I knew why people like Barilla hated me. I knew why friends had not returned my calls, and I wondered if those who did harbored some pathetic sympathy for me because of some weakness of their own.

"Rollie," I said, pushing away the coffee cup and the empty snifter. "Could you fix me a cocktail? Vodka on the rocks. Ketel One. With a twist."

It didn't matter if I couldn't taste it.

**BOTH NEW YORK** baseball teams were lame ducks for the playoffs and Vinny was content to watch horse racing on only two television screens, so Rollie kept the third tuned to the news. The collapse of the big Ponzi scheme was the day's story. The networks were milking it like it was the fall of Baghdad.

"This that thing you was working on?" Vinny said.

"No. This is some other thing."

I kept reaching into my jacket pocket and feeling through the dozen or so flash drives I had taken from Hochstadt's apartment, searching for the one wrapped in duct tape. Each time I found it, I rewarded myself with another soothing sip of vodka. I was getting hammered, but I still didn't want to go home and wait alone.

I dialed the FBI's number again.

Robert Duvall's voice answered again. "Senior Agent Maloney's line."

"I thought you were amazing in *The Apostle*."

"Excuse me, sir?"

"This is Jason Stafford calling. Agents Maloney and Brady know me. Please ask one of them to come to the phone." If I spoke very carefully the words all came out in the right order.

"Senior Agent Maloney is in conference, sir."

No, he wasn't. He was on television again. Standing to the right of the DA with a handful of other serious-looking men. No. I had seen this earlier. It was a replay from the morning's press briefing outside the office building downtown. Maloney must be cold, I thought. They all looked cold.

"Sir?"

"Never mind. Let me talk to Brady."

"One moment."

He put me on hold. This time there was no message exhorting me to join the most elite police force in the world. They didn't really want me anyway.

"Stafford? You there?" It was Brady. "NYPD went through your place. They left two men. One in the lobby. One on your floor."

So I could go home again.

"I can't tell you how sorry I am about this," he continued.

I was instantly sober. He couldn't be that upset about a break-in.

"What are you sorry about, Brady?"

"Maloney hasn't called you?"

"No."

"That son of a bitch."

"Tell me what the hell is going on." I wasn't quite as sober as I had thought. Anger came too easily.

"Christ! We heard from our people in Richmond. Two hours ago. Your son was released to his mother and stepfather. Maloney was supposed to have called to tell you."

It was the word "stepfather" that lit my fuse. I understood the other words and knew they mattered much more, but vodka has a way of twisting truth and shifting emotional priorities. It's what makes Russia a nation of paranoids.

Brady let me rage. Between my bouts of screaming curses, useless threats, and demands for instant action, he gave me the story. My lawyer had warned me, a Family Court judge has powers Idi Amin would have envied. This one had listened to Angie's side of the story and made an instant, absolute, and irrevocable decision. The fact that the United States government had sent two FBI agents and a Justice Department lawyer to speak for me and my son only seemed to convince the tyrant he was in the right.

"There are things we can do," Brady continued.

"I depended on you guys. I did everything you asked. I should have been there."

"Jason, from what they tell me, it wouldn't have helped. But we can make this right. Not today. Everybody's too backed up. But I promise you, Monday morning I will get our people on this."

"Monday? Fuck you, Brady. Fuck you and your promises."

"Please. Don't do anything stupid. We'll pull out all the stops for you. You have my word."

"Have a nice weekend," I said, and hung up.

BY THE END of the day, I had already told Tommy that the Dead sucked without Garcia and that the rest of the band had morphed into a nostalgia act, working just enough to keep their loser roadies from going on welfare, and it was time for the band, the fans, the roadies, and the whole goddamn bunch of hangers-on to give it a rest. Fucking tie-dyed Trekkies! Move on!

It was unforgivable.

PaJohn had the bad luck to ask me where my son was. I told him both that the Kid was on his way to Louisiana with his drunken bitch of a mother and that it was none of his fucking business. The double *s* in "business" gave me a hard time.

I looked around for my next victim.

Roger came in the door with Skeli right behind—she held the door for him. For a brief moment, I felt a swelling of euphoria at the sight of her, dashed immediately by the realization that I had stood her up the night before and that I was now far too drunk to finesse the situation. Not that any of it mattered.

She saw me, and relief, annoyance, and joy swept over her face in a hectic triple bill.

"I haven't been stood up since I was married," she said, grinning enough to let me know that I still had a chance to pull a rabbit out of a hat, turn water to wine, and redeem myself in her eyes. All somehow miraculous, but attainable.

I wasn't up to the task.

"I had some things I had to take care of," I muttered, earning me a sidewise glance of incredulity from Roger as he sidled onto a stool.

"So? What? You can't call? Lost your charger?" Once mounted, he sagged over the chair back as though his spine had suddenly melted. "Rollie! Gasoline! And whatever for the broad."

"I'm buying," I said—with a lot more vehemence than was warranted.

"Well, fuck me for a frog. Your boyfriend's pissed, Wanda. Never thought I'd see the day."

I threw a few twenties on the bar and tried to remember why I was so mad at Roger. Maybe I wasn't.

Skeli was looking at me as though I had grown a second head.

"Are you okay? You don't look so okay."

Where to begin? "I'm fine."

"The ex showed up," Vinny explained. "She took the Kid." The condensed version left a lot of room for misinterpretation.

"Oh my God! And you just let her take him?"

The injustice of this was not her fault—I recognized that. I just couldn't do anything about it. It was like watching myself step off a cliff.

I wanted to tell her how bad I felt. For the Kid. For standing her up. For myself. For Diane Havell, mourning a man, or at least a marriage. For Lowell and Sudhir. For all the "little shits" whose lives were ruined—or ended—because of greed. If I could just tell her the whole story, I was sure she would understand. She would forgive me and hold me and fix me. I wanted her to fix me. I wanted to feel something other than despair. But I did not want sympathy. Sympathy would just curdle whatever was left of my sanity. Sympathy meant somebody cared and wanted me to care as well, and right then, at that single moment in time, I was trying very hard to *not* care.

"Can we talk about something else? Anything else." I avoided her eyes.

"Jason! Are you out of your mind? Get your ass out of here. You can't just let this happen."

Every guy there looked someplace else, the way men do when a woman is telling one of them the truth.

"Wanda, my life is very fucked up right now. Way too complicated. I've got a boatload of shit to deal with. You don't know. Just trust me on this. You will be much better off without having to worry about my sorry ass. Do us both a favor and just walk away."

It got through. Part of the way.

"You are drunk. And full of shit."

"Fuck this," I said, pushing by her. "I gotta take a leak."

Somehow, I found the bathroom. My piss ran clear—not the barest tint of yellow. All the health guides say that's a good thing. It shows you're hydrated. I was beyond hydrated. I was liquefied.

It was cool in the tiny bathroom. It smelled awful, but it was a nice place to be. No one wanted me to do anything. Or say anything. Or be anything. I could be nothing and get away with it.

"Fuck!" I yelled. No one heard me.

I remembered to zip up before stepping back into the bar. The place had become packed with the Friday-night happy-hour crowd. A young man with short, spiky, heavily gelled hair jostled me. Was he the one who had broken into my apartment? Unlikely. He was too well dressed. I pushed him back. He fell.

One of his friends stepped in between us and pushed me back. I swung. He dodged it easily, but tripped over his buddy's leg and went down. I heard myself giggle.

People started making a lot of noise—girls screaming, guys yelling—none of which was helping to restore order. The first guy was back up and in my face, managing to land punches on my bruised ribs that hurt like fire. It felt like there were two or even three people hammering on me and maybe there were. I was past caring. Other hands reached in and pulled at me. Stretched out to protect me. I saw Vinny and Roger. Roger's too old for this shit, I thought. So was I.

Then I was outside and Vinny and Roger were yelling at me and Tommy was laughing—which pissed off Skeli. She took a swipe at him and called him an asshole before walking off alone into the night. God, I wanted her to stay. But I was caught in a timeless eddy, circling endlessly between pain and limbo, and I could no longer speak. Or cry.

THE FRONT DOOR slammed. I hoped it wasn't someone who wanted to hurt me, because I couldn't move.

Early-morning sun was streaming in the front windows. I tried turning my head to get the light away from my eyes. Pain forced me back to immobility.

But it was only hangover pain. Righteous. Earned. My ribs hurt, but the rest of my physical wounds were healing. My soul was another matter. The previous day's events came back to me in ugly little vignettes.

The intruder had not yet come over and stabbed me in my bed. In fact, judging by the sounds and smells, he was laying out breakfast in the kitchen. I smelled coffee.

"Hello," I croaked.

"Good morning, Sunshine."

It was Roger. I remembered. I had seen him curled on the couch when I got up to piss in the middle of the night.

I swung myself into a sitting position and waited for the pain to localize. Not much more than a headache. A gargantuan headache. I was still wearing my suit pants and shirt, though someone had kindly removed my jacket and shoes.

"Thanks for getting me home."

"Yeah, not a problem. I brought coffee. You ready for it?"

He had also brought an egg sandwich—on a roll, with ham, cheese, and home fries. Salt, pepper, and hot sauce. Washed down with sixteen ounces of hot black coffee and about a quart of water out of the tap, the sandwich swelled up in my stomach into a lump the size of a melon—but I felt better for it.

I looked around. The floors were clean, the CDs swept up into a box, drawers back in their proper places, shelves realigned, my books stacked neatly again.

"Shit. Did you do this?"

"Ah-huh. Place looked like it got tossed." His sipped his coffee and nibbled on a minuscule morsel of the corn muffin he had brought for himself.

"It was. Thank you for cleaning up. I don't know if I could face it just yet."

We drank coffee in silence for a minute.

"So. You gonna tell me about this shit, or what?"

I told him. He didn't interrupt, but he did let out with a "Holy shit" when I got to the part about finding Hochstadt dead. And when I finished with Brady's call about the Kid and the results of the hearing in Virginia, he summed it up in one word. "Fuck."

"Amen."

"What can you do?"

"Right now, not much. If I chase after Angie, she can have me back in jail with one call. I need to find a way to get my parole officer on board."

"I meant what can you do now. Today. This morning."

"I've got a few calls to make first. Apologies."

"Ah-huh. That's how drunks start the day."

"I can't imagine you starting the day that way."

"Yeah, well. I'm not a drunk. I'm an alcoholic. There's a difference."

The distinction escaped me and my head was starting to hurt again. "Enlighten me."

"I may down most of a bottle of cognac every day—I been doing it for forty years—but I don't ever get drunk. I don't like the feeling of being out of control."

"I see."

"I don't think you got it in you. Drunks, especially mean ones like you, give alcoholics a bad name."

Some remaining element of self-respect floated to the surface. "I don't normally do that kind of thing."

He laughed. "Or you'd be dead."

"I've had some . . . setbacks."

Roger laughed again. "Okay. So you got a one-day pass to act like an asshole. Day's over, sport. Whaddya goin' do now?"

"I don't know."

"Screw that! You wasted one day feeling sorry for yourself. Hiding. Pulling a liquid blanket over your head. One day. That's all ya get. Do you know what set you off? Why you had to do that to yourself?"

"Yes."

"Good. Then you're in better shape than ninety percent of the drunks in this world. So, go take care of your shit."

"Roger, I can't—"

"Right. Right. You can't fly off to Louisiana, like the fucking cavalry in the last reel. I got that. But you can fix some shit, right? Start with something easy. How about a shower? Shave? There's a start. Then pick one of those things you can do something about and just fuckin' do it. Just one. You get that under your belt and you'll be on your way back to the human race. Then—if you really need to—you can make some apologies."

"Like to Wanda."

"Well, yeah. That'd be top of my list. But if you go grovelin', she will disrespect you forever. You have to go strong. And whatever you do . . ."

"I know. No flowers."

Monday I could start to deal with the parole officer. He would have to let me go to find my son. I could get Brady to help if I had something to trade. At some point, he and Maloney were going to come back to the Arrowhead investigation, and I had what they needed.

"Just a sec," I said. I grabbed my jacket off the closet door and went through the pockets. The flash drives from Hochstadt's apartment were all there, including the one with the silver duct tape.

"Roger, you are a friend. Thank you. Right here I have something that I can finish. If this has the information I think it docs, I can nail these guys."

"There you go. Now you got somethin' to look forward to. All you need in life. Something to do. Someone to love. And something to look forward to. You're good to go." He pulled himself up, tossed the barely touched muffin in the trash, and headed for the door. "My work here is done. Now I gotta meet Wanda and go entertain a bunch of five-year-olds. I got nothin' to look forward to."

"Thanks again. Hey, and tell Skeli . . . I mean Wanda . . ." There were too many things I needed to say to her. "You know what? Don't tell her anything."

"Yeah, I think that's best." He was halfway out the door when he turned. "Fuck me and my white horse. I forgot. There's two city cops making nuisances of themselves out by the elevator. One downstairs and the other right here on the floor."

"That's comforting."

"Yeah, but how long are your neighbors going to put up with that shit? Best of luck with that, sport."

I was a New Yorker, I barely knew my neighbors to nod to in the lobby. "Thanks, but that problem is not top of my list."

I locked up after him and headed for the shower.

WHEN THE MARKET is doing its best to teach a hard and painful lesson, when every brain cell is shrieking for safety, comfort, security, and when every well-thought-out strategy based on value, historical relationships, and statistical analysis has become a dog's breakfast of toxic securities floating in a stinking pond of hedged derivatives, there is one trading skill that cannot be taught: the ability to act coldly, rationally, in the midst of chaos. A trader looks for the next opportunity. If he cannot do that, he may still have a career on Wall Street—in sales or research—but he will not be a trader.

I had allowed chaos—personal and professional—to rule me for too long. It was time to put away my pain, fears, and anxieties and go to work.

Once again I searched for patterns. Every trader leaves a trail, a mark upon the market, sometimes unique, more often banal. As prices ebb and flow in a random dance, accelerated by electronics to an impossible pace, traders take various approaches to managing their risk.

Position traders are all about guts and muscle; they take the long view. They will hold a position for hours, days, or even weeks. They set parameters for themselves and review the facts, trends, or rumors that influenced their decisions, but they tend to trade rarely, looking for the great sea changes, rather than trying to catch a single wave. When they are right, they hit home runs. They are often wrong.

They make money by following the adage "Take your losses early, and let your profits run."

Then there are the spread traders. They rely on brains, agility, and computational skills. They rarely care whether the general market is heading up or down, they look for anomalies between markets and pounce, buying one security while simultaneously selling a different one. Profit on any one trade tends to be relatively small, but more predictable. A good spread trader is nimble and quick, hitting singles and stealing second, rather than smoking homers over the fence.

Day traders play the game by scalping. They tend to rely on a combination of luck and an ability to read the psychology of the market moment to moment. When is fear exhausted and it is time to buy? When is greed overdone and it is time to sell? They dash in and out, taking their profits and moving on. They may ride a trend, but only for a heartbeat. If they are disciplined, they almost never make a killing on one trade, but they can eke out small gains on hundreds of others. They hope for a streak, where they're hot and can do no wrong, and when they're cold they sit on their hands.

The Arrowhead trades fit none of these patterns—or all of them. Geoffrey Hochstadt never had a losing trade. He hit singles and doubles every time. Unless one were to accept the proposition that a trader with no research, little capital, and no access to extraordinary information could consistently outsmart scores of traders from all the top shops, then the only other possible interpretation of the facts was that a widespread scam was being perpetuated, with Hochstadt pulling the strings.

I loaded the duct-taped flash drive—the one that seemed to be in code—and imported the data into the same spreadsheet. The rows immediately rearranged themselves. A new pattern emerged. I had found the money trail. I just couldn't read it.

The first column that revealed its secrets to me was an embarrassment. It was a list of dates, written in European format with the day of the month first and the year truncated. I should have recognized what it was right away; instead I had wasted half an hour comparing the figures to the other columns.

My next success was a bit more satisfying. The column showing the profit per trade matched up quite clearly with one of the newer columns. Identically. And after an hour or so of playing with a calculator, I was able to see that the next column was always a percentage of that profit, though the share differed from one trader to another. Some of the smaller, less active traders were getting a 60 percent cut, others got 70 or even 80 percent. The bigger the fish, the larger the share.

The other columns were still a mystery of seemingly random letters and numbers.

Some days, our good deeds, hard work, and good intentions do come back to reward us. Often enough to keep me believing in luck. My phone rang.

"Hey! Mr. Stafford." It was young Spud.

"Mr. Krebs. It is very good to hear from you. How are you? I tried to reach you the other day, and heard that you had left the firm."

He laughed easily. "They jettisoned me out the airlock. One of the first. Barilla had me on my way before I had a chance to order lunch. I didn't know he even knew who I was."

"I gather Gwendolyn got a message through to you."

"Yeah. I'm up visiting my folks in Vermont. I took off the day after the debacle. I really appreciate you getting in touch, though."

"Any ideas on what's next? Anything I can do? I could make some calls for you—not everyone takes my calls these days, but I do still have some friends."

"Wow. Thank you. Let me think on it, okay? I don't mean to be coy, I'm just rethinking things, know what I mean? I don't know if Wall Street is the best place for me."

If he was thinking along those lines, then it probably wasn't.

"You'll let me know. Meantime, I was wondering if you had any time to help me finish up our investigation. I'd make it worth your while."

"Sure. I'm planning on being back in the city sometime this week. How's Wednesday?"

"How's today?"

"Dude! I'm in Vermont!"

"I'll have a car pick you up. You can be here for a late dinner. We'll work straight through."

"No, really. I'm at my folks'."

"Sure, sure. I'll pay you two hundred an hour. Minimum a thousand dollars. It's a puzzle. You'll love it."

He took a minute to think about it. "I like the money. What do you need me to do?"

I described the files, what I had been able to come up with, and the problem.

"I don't need to come to New York. E-mail me the files. We can work it over the phone."

Simplicity itself. I zipped the files and sent them. Then I made a pot of coffee while Spud looked them over.

"What do you think?" I said.

"Does the minimum still hold?" he said.

"Is it that easy?"

"Yes and no. I see what you were saying about the dates and the dollar amounts. I agree, all that makes sense."

"And?"

"Okay, the next column over? Letters and numbers? Those are SWIFT numbers. International bank ID codes for wire transfers. If they were domestic, they'd all be ABA numbers."

A clerk would have caught it—not a trader.

"Show me."

He did. Within a week of any trade, a wire transfer went out. The banks were all in countries that had a greater reverence for client privacy than the U.S.—and lax or nonexistent tax regulations. The Cayman Islands and the Bahamas led the pack, though some of the accounts were held in the old standbys of Switzerland, Luxembourg, Liechtenstein, and others. One enterprising soul was using a facility in the Cook Islands in the South Pacific.

"I'm thinking that the numbers in the last column are individual accounts at those banks. And, just a guess, but the second column, right after the date? That's gotta be Arrowhead's internal code for each trader."

It made sense.

Spud continued. "He used the last three digits of the bank's code in his own coding, you see? That way he couldn't really screw up and transfer money to the wrong account."

"It still doesn't tell me who the traders are."

"I don't get it. Look at row twelve. Whoever that guy is moved twenty-four million over in three years. His firm didn't miss it? Is that possible?"

"A guy like that might make thirty or forty a year for his firm. How much are they going to question him if he only makes twenty or thirty? They may cut his bonus, have a sit-down, and so on. But unless he screws up, no one is going to start investigating him. He's still a big earner."

"This could have gone on forever, then?" Spud sounded half disgusted, and half in awe.

"Hiding in plain sight."

"So, do I get the thousand dollars?"

"Absolutely. Ready for the bonus question? See if you can find me a key somewhere for the account names," I said.

"I think you've already got it. But the files came over as read-only. You need to connect the flash again."

I plugged it in and opened the file in a new window.

"Now click on one of the bank account numbers. Any one," he said.

A drop-down window appeared. *FBO Mrs. Karen Nunn and family.* I knew Karen Nunn. I had been there when she married Gerald Nunn, who had been trading Yankee bonds at Case when I was starting out. We had lost touch when he moved to London.

"Anything there?" Spud said.

"Just a second," I said. I clicked on the other column. *Gerald Nunn, Finsbury & Wallace, Ltd.* "Holy shit."

"It worked?"

"Mr. Krebs, you just earned the bonus."

I clicked on the next row. Another ex–Case employee, now trading for another large American bank here in New York.

"This is the goddamn Death Star. I could smash planets with this file."

No wonder someone had searched my apartment. They must have known this file was out there somewhere. Anyone on the list had a very big incentive to find the file and destroy it. And destroy anyone who might have seen it.

"Listen, Spud, if anyone contacts you—anyone at all—and wants to know if we talked, I want you to deny everything. We never spoke."

"You're scaring me, Mr. Stafford."

"Good. And call me Jason. There are at least two people who died because of this—maybe others. Stay up in Vermont until you hear from me. And stay around people you know."

I CHECKED THE LOCKS on the door—again. I kept working.

I saw why Diane Hochstadt had referred to the "old crowd." Case Securities was well represented. But like a virus, the scam had leaped oceans and raced over continents, spreading its infection through almost every major investment bank.

My neck was stiff and my eyes ached before I discovered the three non-trading accounts.

The first was a recent addition—less than a year old. There was a single payment of $1 million to a bank in the Caymans, followed by monthly payments of $100,000 each. When I clicked on the bank account number, a name came up. I wasn't surprised.

The other two accounts dated back to the beginning. The amounts varied each month and it took me some time to figure out the system. A week after closing out business for any given month—and after having made payments to all of the active traders—these two accounts split whatever remained after expenses. The smaller share—about 10 percent of the net—went to a numbered account in Switzerland. I scanned down quickly, estimating, truncating, adding. It came to over ton million. I clicked on the name. It wasn't exactly what I expected. *FBO Diane Hochstadt*. Geoffrey had put all his tax-free profits in his wife's name. When he lost her, he had lost it all. I knew how that felt.

The last account was a puzzle. When I clicked on the account numbers, nothing happened. No drop-down window revealing the name of the mastermind. Hochstadt would not need a reminder of who had first envisioned the whole operation. The man who had recruited him and all of the major producers. The driving force behind it all who kept it running with tact and diplomacy, hidden behind a mannered veil of secrecy. Not a greedy man, either. His cut was modest—though it came to well over a hundred million, but only because the scope of the fraud had been so large, and had gone on successfully for so many years.

But years ago, when the system was first put in place, the man had traded with Arrowhead. Probably testing the system, I thought.

Once it was running, he had stopped. Why shouldn't he? Why take the risk, when he was getting a cut of every trade that went through anyway?

I searched through the files for the earliest trades and lined up all those I thought were his. The trades all took place in London over a six-month period. I stared at them until the pattern emerged. A picture of the man shaped itself in my mind. I knew who it was. I just couldn't prove it. Yet.

"I TOLD YOU there's nothing I can do until Monday." Brady sounded beyond exhausted.

"You're still tied up?" He wasn't the ideal candidate for what I had in mind, but he was all I had.

"This is going to take months."

"Could you get away for a couple of hours?" I said.

"Not a chance. They've got me checking bank transfers. In eight different time zones. It's a twenty-four-hour operation."

"How about on a Sunday morning? Before the Far East opens."

"I was hoping to get three or four hours' sleep sometime tonight."

"I can hand you the killer. Gift-wrapped."

"I don't handle violent crime, remember? I push paper. Now, let me get back to it."

"No! You owe me. You know it." I took a breath and tried to calm down. "I'm not crawling or begging, Brady. I've got something to trade. Something good. I'll set it up. You show up with a posse and nab this guy and you're a hero. Maybe they even transfer you out of pushing paper and give you a real job."

The clicking of gears into place as he thought it through was almost audible. I was only taking the physical risk—he was risking his career.

"And what do you get out of this?"

I had him. "You make one call for me. I have to go to Louisiana for a day or so. You clear it with my P.O."

"That's it?"

"And don't let this guy kill me, if you can help it."

"All right. I'm listening."

I STOOD AT the window, watching a soft rain turning the street-lights on Broadway into a mirrored kaleidoscope. I wasn't savoring the end of the chase—I was afraid and not ashamed to admit it. I couldn't afford a mistake. From the moment he answered the phone and heard my voice, I was all in. No hedged bets. No chance to deal again. I had to play my hand against a wary, intelligent killer. And I had to win.

I found his card in my wallet and dialed.

"We need to talk," I said. "I've got what you've been looking for."

I MADE THE KID'S bed before I left. I used the SpongeBob sheets. As far as I knew, he had never watched the show, but he loved the sheets. Just one of his million mysteries.

Roger had left all the little die-cast cars on the bureau, wrapped in a towel. He had rescued them from the four corners of the room where they had been scattered by the intruder. None were broken or chipped. The Kid might miss a car if it disappeared, but he would have had a major meltdown if it were damaged.

One by one, I inspected them and placed them carefully on the shelf by his bed. Halfway through, I stopped to stare at the line of cars. Then, without giving it any more thought than where I would place the fork when setting a table, I moved the London taxi and placed it behind the Mustang. The rest of the cars followed. For twenty minutes, I stood there, placing them all in perfect order. Time well spent.

When I stepped out on the street, I was glad I had dressed for a fall run—long-sleeved sweatshirt and pants. The air was crisp. The FBI's cell phone/transmitter was in my pocket, along with a set of keys. I carried a manila envelope containing most of the flash drives.

Brady had said they would be watching for me on Broadway. "Take your time. Let him see you. We want him comfortable. Let him follow you down to the park. Don't worry. We'll have him boxed."

I was going to worry, no matter what he said.

The Sunday-morning crowds were just beginning to fill in. The used-book vendors were all out, lining the sidewalk in front of Loehmann's. A handful of early Fairway shoppers were waiting at the bus stop, plastic bags surrounding their feet.

I looked for undercover policemen, masquerading as street vendors, or young mothers with strollers—packing heat and wearing odd-shaped earphones. Improbably, I identified dozens of them. For the past two years, the man in uniform was the enemy—as dangerous, unpredictable, and unreliable as any convict. Now he was my ally.

At Seventy-third I turned right, toward the river, and began an easy jog, just enough to loosen up, and not much faster than a brisk walk.

The light was against me at West End and I fought the urge to look over my shoulder. Somewhere back there, I was sure, was a murderer and right behind him—I hoped—was a crowd of armed cops.

A dog walker with five or six leashed animals was blocking the sidewalk as I approached Riverside. I slowed to a walk. When we reached the corner, the dogs all stopped to sniff the fire hydrant. I jogged on by.

Once inside the park, I cut down past the dog runs and sped up through the tunnel under the West Side Highway—I always thought it would be a great place to stage a murder. Then I held up for a minute on the overlook on the far side. There was a long, sloping trail to my right, leading down through a stand of trees. Too hidden. Too isolated. I jogged down the steep staircase instead, heading for the esplanade along the river.

Two pairs of screeching ravens were fighting for dominance over the crab apple tree at the end of the path, though none of the big birds, nor any of the sparrows or other smaller birds that flitted about, seemed interested in eating any of the fruit. Brown and ruby-colored apples were being knocked to the ground as the huge birds jumped from branch to branch, their neck ruffles open like those spiked collars on pit bulls and Goths. Their beaks were as thick and sharp as hunting knives. I gave the tree a wide berth.

The walkway was busy with weekend traffic—spandex-clad, helmeted bicyclists, runners from plodders to sprinters, speed walkers exaggerating the roll of their hips as they moved, like mimes doing a forward moonwalk, and couples, singles, and families, strolling in the bright morning sun. I welcomed the safety of being in a crowd.

The Kid loved to stand at the railing and watch the river flow around the rocks below, though the barely revealed remains of the old wooden docks, jagged black spikes peeking above the surface at low tide, caused him to groan and grunt with discomfort. Like the rest of us—he was frightened most by the unseen.

When I reached the railing, I stopped and turned back to face the long steps. I waited.

A tiny apple hit the pavement and bounced up almost waist high before dropping and rolling down to stop between my feet. When I looked back up again, he was standing at the balustrade outside the tunnel—looking for me. Our eyes met.

Here was the test. Would he smell the trap and bolt, or would he follow me down to the river? How desperate was he? Fear and greed—that's what drives markets.

He believed he had to kill me—but I didn't think he would do it in front of all these people. I needed him hungry, not in a panic. He had to think he was controlling the scene. Then he would be comfortable enough to make a mistake.

Brady had almost pulled the plug when I got to this part. He didn't trust the odds. Another dead civilian wasn't going to win him a promotion.

The man scanned the crowd, scenting the air. He had no reason to think I had called in the police, but he was still cautious. He believed I was capable of duplicity—he depended on it—but he thought I was just like him. Greed won out. He started down the steps.

The benches were adorned with plaques, dedicated to the New Yorkers who gave to make the park possible. Not the Trumps or Rockefellers who need skyscrapers to frame their legacy, nor the Cantors or Sacklers who make do with a wing at the Metropolitan Museum of Art. The benches there were dedicated to everyday New Yorkers. People who ride the subway. I sat down on the one that salutes "Mike on his 50th. Box Seats—riv vu." I tried to enjoy his river view as I waited.

I didn't have to wait long. Iron Man Jack Avery dropped down on the bench beside me. The last two weeks had aged him. His hair was noticeably thinner and there was a red line of anger—or madness—bordering his eyes. He was still an imposing presence, but his face sagged and his shoulders slumped. He didn't look like the man who had crossed the triathlon finish line, grinning, with victory in his eyes; he looked like a man running from defeat.

But that didn't make him any less dangerous.

"This is a gun." He was carrying a copy of the *Post* doubled over his right hand. He moved it aside and gave me the merest glimpse of the weapon.

"You won't need it. I'm only here to talk business."

Was the runner by the water fountain adjusting his iPod? Or was he part of the surveillance team, adjusting an earpiece? The lady with the baby carriage might have looked my way.

He had come; he was hooked. I took a slow breath and began to reel him in.

"That was you who tossed my apartment, am I right? You left quite a mess. Find what you were looking for?"

"You know I didn't."

I held up the manila envelope. "Not to worry. It's all here. You just had to ask."

I was too flippant. It spooked him. "Pull up your shirt."

"Why? You think I'm wired?" I stood up, pulled the sweatshirt up and did a slow turn. No one even glanced our way. "Happy?"

"Hold it." He patted me down. "What's in the pocket?"

"Cell phone. Keys."

"Give me the phone."

I handed it to him. "Don't turn it off, okay? I have an autistic son. I need to keep it on in case his shadow needs to reach me."

He looked it over and handed it back.

"Give me the files."

"As soon as we have a deal. Did Hochstadt tell you what I'm looking for?"

The ravens took that moment to escalate their confrontation with impossibly louder shrieks, drowning out thoughts as well as speech, until one pair spread wings and flew down to the next crab apple tree, twenty feet away. They're supposed to be very smart birds. So why didn't they think of that solution earlier?

"Say again?" Avery said.

I repeated the question and angled the phone in his direction. I wanted his response to be quite clear.

"He said you want two million." He was clear.

"Only now I have the files."

"I knew you were going to be trouble."

"I'm not trouble, Jack. I'm your best friend. I just want value for the goods I'm offering."

He glared at me. I didn't melt. He shrugged.

"I'm authorized to go to three. You want more? I don't think it'll fly, but I'll deliver the message."

"It's worth a lot more, if I go to the cops."

He sneered. "Oh, yeah? What are they paying? Look, a word of advice?" He put a hand on my shoulder. We were pals. "Don't get greedy. This whole thing works—and keeps working—only if every-body involved behaves themselves. That's the hard thing for the young turks to understand. Sometimes, I've got to manage their expectations."

"Is that what happened with Sanders? You were just managing expectations?"

"What do you think you know?" An unpleasant growl came into his voice. "Whatever it is, don't think it. Life is too short, as it is. Understood?" The gun waved in my direction again.

"Sanders is what brought me into this. He's why I was hired." I needed him comfortable and talking.

Avery thought for a moment. He must have decided we were still pals. "The guy was a head case. He thought he was a whistleblower. The SEC came to me right after he started talking to them." He gave a laugh that sounded like a garbage truck starting up on a winter morning. "They ratted out the rat."

And the SEC killed Sanders. Not according to any law, of course, but that didn't make him any less dead. Ham-handed bureaucracy set him up. Avery just did the heavy lifting.

"No one ever questioned you?"

"You gotta love this laissez-faire approach to regulation. Let Wall Street regulate itself, right? These guys think they're living in some Ayn Rand novel. Let the market rule! It's a fuckin' joke."

"But you were already on to the whole thing, weren't you? You saw it right off." It was like petting a lion.

His ego was as outsized as his chest. "My first month on the job. I had my secretary run trade pair-offs for the whole firm. I was just sniffing around, not sure what I would come up with. You met that jerk who runs corporates, right? He gets sloppy sometimes—his trades stood out. I grilled him and he almost started crying. Telling me about his two daughters in college and all this, like I give a shit."

"But you got the names of the guys running things."

"There's only one man who makes the decisions."

"When do I meet him?"

"When he says." Like any flunky, he was jealous of his access to power. "Don't rush things. You get impatient and you make people nervous."

Now he was too comfortable. I was learning nothing.

"Did I make Hochstadt nervous?"

The eyes flared again and the gun swung back in my direction. "You are starting to piss me off, Stafford. No more questions. Keep your mouth shut, hand over the files, and you'll get paid. Why make it hard?"

"It was you he called the other night. After I left." I wasn't asking anymore. I just hoped Brady and his team were listening and ready to move.

"Enough. Stand up." He gestured with the gun.

"And you were on the boat with Sanders that night, too. Did you help him over the side?" I wanted him angry enough to give me one precise admission of guilt. But I wasn't getting it.

"Get up. We're done here. I don't think things are going to work out for you, Stafford. You are just too stupid to know when to shut the fuck up."

"It would have been an easy swim to shore for you, right? Even with the wind kicking up, Iron Man Jack Avery would have had no problem."

He jammed the gun into my stomach. "Time's up, asshole." He grabbed the front of my sweatshirt with his free hand and stood up, taking me with him, as easily as if I were a child. "Nobody knows who was on board that night."

"Nobody living, you mean? But Hochstadt told his wife and she told me and here we are. You can't kill everybody, Jack. It's time to fold your hand, take your winnings, and move on."

He slapped me with the barrel of the gun, snapping my neck around. Where the hell was Brady? Things were suddenly moving too fast. I swallowed the vomit that was burning the back of my throat.

"You think I won't kill you, too? I'd be happy to add you to the list, asshole. Now give me those files." He let go of my shirt and reached for the envelope.

Over his shoulder, I saw Brady closing in—finally. Four other armed plainclothes cops were with him, weapons drawn, shields held forward like magic talismans.

I should have realized—Avery was watching me. The moment I lost my poker face, he moved.

A lot of things happened at once.

"Drop the weapon! FBI!" The baby-carriage lady and the jogger with the iPod came on, their guns seemingly pointed right at me.

Avery swung me around, gripped my throat in one hand, and jammed the barrel of his gun into my temple. "Stand the fuck down or this citizen is meat!"

I tried to pull away, but he ground the gun into my head. I felt a rivulet of blood run down my cheek. I stopped moving.

The police fanned out around us. A Texas standoff.

"Drop the weapon, Mr. Avery." Brady tried to sound relaxed and in control. "We don't want anyone to get hurt."

"He dies first," the Iron Man yelled. The manila envelope slipped from his fingers and split open as it hit the ground. The dozen or so flash drives skittered across the sidewalk in every direction.

My son was trapped in Louisiana—probably already locked in a darkened room. If I died, there would be no one to ever lead him out of that room.

Brady stepped forward. "Let him go, Mr. Avery. You know the drill. Ex-cop. The only way this ends with you still standing is if you drop the weapon. Now. After that, we sort things out. Things are never as bad as they look right now."

Even I didn't believe him.

"Stop there!" Avery pulled me back until he was up against the railing. Some idiot on a mountain bike steered around the whole group of policemen and continued his morning exercise, oblivious to, or unconcerned by, the drama unfolding. Just another Sunday morning in the big city. He was probably running late for his brunch date.

Brady stopped and let his gun point at the ground. "Come on, Avery. We've all got loved ones we want to see later today." He sounded strong and sincere. In control. "Let's just talk about this."

I could feel Avery wavering. The pressure of the gun eased just a touch. I let my knees drop and sagged forward against the arm around my neck. It almost worked.

Iron Man was too strong. As I fell, he made a last snatch and caught my throat in a hand the size of a baseball glove. He lifted me off the ground and slammed the gun against my head again.

"Back off!" he screamed. There was both fear and rage in his voice.

Everyone froze. Control was back in Avery's court.

"No one is taking me," he said.

Brady began lifting his gun again. I was about to become collateral damage. I closed my eyes.

Avery threw me. He tossed me, one-handed, like a sack of recycling. Brady threw up a hand to ward me off and I rolled to the side and landed on my back. I watched Avery place one hand on the railing and perform a perfect vault, landing on the edge of the jutting parapet, facing the river.

The police rushed forward, reaching for him. "Stop! Don't move!"

I saw Avery's pistol arch out over their heads and sink beneath the water. Then he launched himself into the river. He went in a flat racing dive, his body arched, his chin tucked, hands extended in a V to cut the water as he entered. Perfect form. For a flicker of a second, I thought he might make it.

He landed with a horrible thud, not a splash. The ancient, broken piling, lying just below the surface, had speared him in the center of his chest, lancing through and out his back. His face and hands were hidden underwater, and if he screamed, no one heard it. The water around him turned red and dark. Torn flesh and bits of white bone gleamed around the spike of blackened wood sticking up from his back. The current took his arms and they waved a lethargic farewell. One of the cops vomited into a latticed trash container.

"Holy Christ!" Brady said. "What the hell was he thinking?"

I shook my head. "Iron Man. He thought he was going to swim to Jersey City."

**ONCE AGAIN,** I woke up much earlier than necessary. In that brief, twilight moment before I was fully awake, I imagined I heard the Kid's gentle breathing from his bedroom and I did an automatic mental inventory of his clean clothes. Monday. Blue jeans. The dark blue long-sleeved shirt. Did he have clean socks?

Full consciousness brought the return of depression. The Kid was still in Louisiana.

One fucking step at a time, I thought. I got out of bed.

The day was going to be a long one—long and painful. I was not looking forward to it. Careers would be destroyed by what I had to say—and not all of those who would fall would be guilty. And it was just as likely that not all of those who were guilty would fall.

I put in a call to London for a final confirmation of what I already knew. Then I left for downtown.

GWENDOLYN SHOWED me right in.

"I'm surprised to see you again so soon, Jason. I thought we agreed you were going to need another couple of weeks at least to finish things up." Stockman looked both older and smaller—like Frodo after carrying the ring for too long.

"I haven't done a very good job of containing things for you. Events have a way of unfolding at their own pace." I told him about Hochstadt's murder, and the files that implicated a dozen or more traders at Weld and scores more all over the Street. Then I told him about Avery—and the FBI. "They'll want to talk to you," I said.

"I wish you had come to me first with all of this. You have put me in a difficult position."

I had shown him the whitecaps forming on the waters the last time I had been in his office and now he was bitching I hadn't told him about the hurricane. But I felt for him. When there had been any chance left for denial, he had maintained like a marine. Now, he was shrunken in upon himself—smaller. He looked like somebody you should be saying prayers for.

"They kept it off the front page for today, but that's not going to last. As soon as some reporter Googles Jack Avery, they'll be all over this place. Meantime, though, you have a window—a week, maybe only a few days—before the FBI and the SEC come knocking. They're tied up now with that other matter, but they'll be back."

He stood up and turned to the window. The harbor was covered with low, gray clouds, the Verrazano Bridge nothing but a dim blur. A lone ferry plowed its way through the dark water to Staten Island.

"Jack Avery was a worker, not a leader. Obviously a violent man, but essentially a plodder, not a thinker. Not a creator. Do you agree?"

"Okay." I thought I knew where he was taking this, but I let him do it at his own pace.

"Nor did he have the requisite people skills to put together something like this." He smiled sadly. "So who did, Jason? Do you know? You must."

I didn't answer the question. "The Feds don't know at this point." That was the truth. "They'll figure it out eventually."

He picked up a photo of his family and examined it closely. For a moment, I thought he might cry.

"What would you recommend? How should I approach this? Any thoughts?"

"Go public." I handed him a handwritten list. "Fire every trader here. Put a hold on their in-house accounts. Tell them you're going after all their other assets. Announce to the press that an ongoing internal investigation revealed a Street-wide problem and Weld has provided information to the authorities that will identify all those involved. The regulators will have to play along. The press will love it."

Stockman's basic survival skills would see him through. He would come out the far end looking like a leader. He already looked taller.

And I could upgrade my reputation from a criminal to a whistle-blower.

"You'll have to sacrifice a couple of other people. The salesman? The Brit, Jones? If he didn't know what was going on, he's an idiot. Either way, he's history."

Stockman nodded. "And I'm afraid the sales manager will have to go as well."

"Right," I said. "The SEC will expect some heads to roll, you may as well do the choosing. Give them all hefty severance packages, so they don't sue, and promise them legal support if the regulators try to go after them."

He straightened his perfectly straight tie. "I can bury the costs in the merger packages."

He was already thinking like an accountant again. He'd be fine.

"There are one or two other people I want to talk with before you go public. Can you give me, say, an hour?"

He was back on top. He granted the hour magnanimously.

Stockman's secretary, Gwen, was waiting to come in as I walked out. An odd bit of flotsam surfaced in my mind.

"Just one last thing, Bill," I said, turning back. "Avery mentioned a secretary yesterday. But I've been to his office. He had to be the only lawyer on the floor who didn't have a secretary."

Gwen looked away. Stockman looked uncomfortable.

"Yes," he said. "Very tragic. A troubled woman. It happened some time ago. She jumped off the roof garden. We have had to restrict access to it after that."

"Out of respect?" I said, making my voice as neutral as possible.

He cleared his throat. "Liability."

"Ah."

"It was ruled a suicide."

"Really? I don't think so."

I DIDN'T HAVE to meet with Eugene Barilla. Stockman would quickly realize that the head of global trading couldn't outlive a scandal covering twenty-some of his traders. It would have been easier to let Stockman deliver his own bad news, but I liked Barilla. I admired him. I even liked the fact that he didn't like me.

"What have you got?" He didn't ask me to sit.

"This may take a minute," I said. We were practically face-to-face across his desk.

"You looked like bad news the first time you walked in here."

"I'm just the messenger," I said.

He backed off. "All right. Sit down."

We sat.

He didn't interrupt, but halfway through he picked up a pencil and began bouncing the eraser on the desk blotter.

I described the scam and Sanders' role. I listed the traders involved, and told him how the money had been funneled back. I told him about Avery. And I told him about the murders.

"People died over this." His face had gone pale.

"Three—at least." I thought someone should also take a hard look at Lowell Barrington's suicide-by-train and Avery's secretary's swan dive off the building. Avery looked good for both in my book. It might be too late for justice, but their families would care.

Barilla took the pencil in both hands as though about to break it in two. Then he stopped, slid open the drawer, and carefully put the pencil away.

"What will Stockman do?" he asked.

"He's sharpening his axe."

He pushed back from the desk. "You must be enjoying this, Stafford. The chance to bring down some of the people you missed first time around."

"No. People make their own mistakes." There was no thrill in it, other than the feeling of a job well done.

"Failure to supervise. That's what the regulators will say about me."

"No argument," I said.

He made a growling noise that could have been a laugh. "And they're right. I trusted the compliance guy instead of doing my own looking. Complacent. Lazy. Stupid!"

He wouldn't go to jail. He wouldn't even be forced to pay a fine. He would just be barred from ever again working in the securities industry.

"What'll you do?" I said.

"You ever miss the biz?"

"Every day."

He laughed out loud. "I won't. I promise you that. I will never again play a round of golf with someone I don't like. How's that for a fresh start? God almighty, I can't tell you the number of perfect days in my life that have been ruined because I had to listen to some hotshot whine at me about an eighth of a thirty-second on some two-year-note trade while I have to pretend not to notice every time he kicks his ball back out of the rough or clears his throat while somebody else is trying to putt."

He looked happier than I had ever known him.

"First thing I do, I go upstairs and twist that little prick's nuts until he promises me a severance package big enough to choke an anaconda."

"There you go."

"Little fucker will give it to me, too, as long as I promise to go quietly. He can be a mean little backstabbing cunt, but he's never been afraid to spend someone else's money to solve a problem."

If it was all a front, it was a really good one.

"What's next?"

"Christ, Stafford, get the fuck out of here before I start thinking I have something to thank you for."

THE TRADING FLOOR had lost whatever shreds of community it had ever possessed. Merger mania had set in. Whole departments would be saved—others swept away. It was no longer a team of highly paid athletes working together to make it to their version of the Super Bowl; it was a mob comprised of passengers and crew from the *Titanic*, some huddled in their life vests waiting for orders, others already elbowing their way onto the lifeboats. No one was sailing the ship.

I threaded my way through aisles full of traders and salespeople— some angry, some confused, some happy, others just smug—until I got to the arbitrage group. Rich Wheeler and Neil Wilkinson were on the phones. Kirsten Miller noticed me first. She stood up and put out a hand.

"Good working with you again, Jason. I suppose you've heard all the news?"

"You're leaving?" I said.

"The new management team is not comfortable with the levels of risk we are accustomed to taking. So, we have agreed to part ways. Amicably." She laughed. Amicably must have meant a very large severance package.

"I'm sure you'll land somewhere."

She winked. "Already in the works. But I can't say a word."

"Understood."

Rich gave a short wave, but his attention was on his phone conversation. He was going over the details of a big trade.

"We're winding down," Kirsten explained.

Neil hadn't yet looked up at me. I tried staring at him. It didn't work.

Kirsten couldn't help but notice. "I guess Neil's a little backed up. I'm sure he'll want to say good-bye. Can I have him look you up a little later?"

"Please. When he gets off the phone. I'll be in the little conference room I've been using. You might mention to him that I've had a long conversation with Jack Avery."

I knew it sounded cryptic. It would get his attention.

Kirsten covered her confusion well. "Will do. Thanks for stopping by."

I waited in the small, cold conference room. Someone had "fixed" the AC vent, reversing whatever Spud had done to it. This time it didn't bother me. The gray walls didn't frighten me anymore either—they kept their distance. Two weeks ago, the room had felt like a cell. Now it was just a small, shabby room with a scuffed round table and four cheap swivel chairs.

I didn't have to wait long.

Cornelius Wilkinson had the brains and the experience to set up the whole trading scam. He was familiar with a wide range of securities; he would have known just how much a trader was able to skim without setting off alarm bells. He had been in London during the years Hochstadt had first begun working for Arrowhead. And he was possessed of enough tact, charm, and nerve to sell the idea to scores of other traders.

And he had the motive.

Anyone on Wall Street who had seen traders, less bright, less diligent, less ethical, make millions through dumb luck, superior ass-kissing, market manipulation, lying, cheating, or outright theft might have had the motive. Few of them would have been able to carry it off so successfully, for so long, or to such an extent. But even fewer would have attempted it, either out of innate honesty or fear of being caught.

The markets survive on trust. That trust is assailed every day. Opportunities for violating that trust are rampant. But how do you find and train a trader to be a cutthroat, loot-gathering pirate, willing to take gut-wrenching risks that 99.9 percent of humanity would shy from, and still expect him to be the kind of guy who, when he finds a wallet on the sidewalk, returns it to its owner without even counting the cash? Suppose it's a grand in the wallet? Suppose it's a mil?

Neil knocked on the open door and came in. He never showed stress—if he even felt it. His bow tie and suspenders matched, complementing the pale-striped shirt. His hair, probably worn in the exact same cut since he went off to prep school, was perfectly parted, every strand a testament to order, discipline, good breeding, and the constant attention to the details of living well.

"I received your message," he said. His movements were casual, but practiced. Grace and style almost hid the fact that he was as taut as a bowstring. He spun the seat on the chair facing me until it reached the height he desired. Then he lowered himself, elegantly.

I waited until he finished his entrance.

"Jack Avery and I had a long talk yesterday."

"Oh?" The eyebrows went up. Innocent. Oblivious.

"There's not much I don't know at this point."

He nodded politely.

I needed to rattle him.

"Did you know he was going to kill Hochstadt? He implied it was an executive decision."

"Why are you asking me?" He meant, "What do you know?"

"I knew Hochstadt was in a panic when I left him. But why would he run to Avery? Avery scared him. Shit, Iron Man Jack scared everybody. So, he must have been going to meet someone else. Someone he trusted. That would be you, Neil."

He pursed his lips. "Jack is not a manager. Geoffrey could have been managed. He'd had episodes before, driven by guilt or fear of discovery. He did not need to be killed. I sent Jack to deliver a message. That was my mistake. He can be impulsive."

"It sounds like he doesn't like your style, Neil. Why bring him in on the scam anyway? Besides muscle, what does he bring to the table?"

"Jack was not invited. He insinuated himself. After his secretary ran an audit on all of the firm's trades with Arrowhead, she went to Jack with her suspicions. Jack saw an opportunity. He came to me with a set of demands. They seemed reasonable. I would have agreed to much more."

"And the secretary?" Avery would have had to get her out of the way.

His eyes flicked up to the ceiling. "I understand she had personal issues."

"Is that what Jack said?"

He locked eyes with me. "The subject never came up."

Avery had killed her, I was sure of it. But had Neil known? Or had he willed himself not to know? I decided to let the woman rest in peace.

"Jack's dead," I said.

For a moment, his mannered reserve almost abandoned him. But he recovered.

"I had not heard that."

"The police are sitting on it. They'll get here."

"How did it happen?" he asked.

"He went for a swim."

"An accident, then," he said, as though he could not have been less interested. He leaned forward and for the first time appeared to become fully engaged in our conversation. "What do you need, Jason? Is there a problem that money can solve? I am willing to make some sacrifices."

"I just gave Stockman a list of all the traders at this firm who did regular business with Arrowhead. I told him how the whole thing works. From the casinos to the offshore accounts."

He didn't blink.

"The FBI has the same information," I continued. "But it may take them a little time to get to it. They're a little backed up this week."

"I thought we were negotiating," he said.

"We are." I held up the duct-taped flash drive—the one that contained the names, the bank accounts—the one I had kept hidden from Avery. The one I had held back from the FBI. "This is Hochstadt's copy of all the offshore accounts—all the money transfers. Including yours. The original is probably on his office computer, but I would bet it's either encrypted or well hidden."

He smiled. "Bravo. I thought Geoffrey had done a very good job of hiding my involvement."

"He did. He was very good at moving money around. It's a shame he got involved with you."

The smile faded. "You said we are still negotiating. It is time to make your offer."

"You and I are so similar in some ways. We look for mathematical patterns everywhere. Repetitive movements in numbers perhaps, or mathematical relationships between one market and another. It is what we are trained for, but we were adepts first. You probably learned to multiply by thirteens the first time you saw a pack of cards. When you were in grade school, you memorized the value of pi out to one hundred digits."

"A hundred and twenty."

"Patterns. My son has shown me that people have patterns as well. He is autistic, so his patterns of behavior are more visible, though sometimes confusing. They can be much more convoluted—at least on the surface—than ours. When he's fighting off a panic attack—which can arise from virtually anywhere—he relies on little patterns to hold himself together. He does a circuit of our living room—three times. Each lap has the exact same number of steps. If he needs to do it again, he does another three full circuits."

"They call it stimming, I believe."

I nodded. "When he is frightened or angry and fighting for control, he does this drumming thing with his fingers. I thought it was completely random, chaotic, until a friend pointed it out to me. It's an intricate meter in thirteen/eight time. Three sets of triplets followed by a set of four. His fingers fly, over and over, at a thrash metal pace. Blindingly fast."

Neil gave a too-polite smile of feigned interest.

"I'm sorry," I said. "I seem to be taking the very long way round."

"No, please," he said. "Continue. I hang upon every word."

"For the past two weeks, I've stared at trading reports. Lists and lists of anonymous buys and sells in a whole array of products. And I've learned something I always suspected. Every trader has a mark, a signature, a pattern. Once I knew to look for it, it was easy to find yours."

"But I never traded with Arrowhead."

"Almost true. But Hochstadt was a pack rat. He kept everything. Including the trades you ran when you were first testing the system. When you first created Arrowhead. You were trading for Rothkamp. For six months or so, you did a handful of trades a week. Once you knew it worked and that other traders would line up in droves to be part of it, you stepped into the background. You took your cut of the profits and let others take the risk."

"Patterns? Something you intuit? Like tea leaves? You can't prove my involvement." He seemed most concerned that he had been somehow predictable.

I help up the flash drive again. "You forget. Hochstadt threw nothing away. But just for grins, I called an old friend at Rothkamp in London this morning. I had him check to see who was trading Dutch mortgage-backed securities back then. It was a small market."

He took off the glasses and pinched the bridge of his nose. "And what now?" He sounded irritated. Not angry or even annoyed. This was all nothing more troubling than a headache. Two aspirin and a liter of bottled water would set the world right again.

"Your wife is Venezuelan?"

He looked amazed at the abrupt change of subject, until he thought it through. He chuckled. "And you think this might be an appropriate time for me and my family to emigrate?" He was no longer irritated, he was intrigued.

"They have a non-extradition policy. A man can live quite well there on the kind of money you've salted away."

"I would have to act quickly, I assume."

"One week. Next Monday I will go through the pockets of the jacket I was wearing the other night and I will find this missing flash drive. I will, of course, immediately turn it over to the authorities." Unless I found a better use for it.

"What will this cost me?"

I took a Post-it pad and quickly made some notes. "By close of business today, you will transfer five million dollars into each of these two offshore accounts."

"Ten million? It seems excessive."

"It's less than ten percent of what you've taken out of this. A finder's fee."

"You misunderstand. I only meant that it was excessive in terms of what I gain. A week. Why not a month?"

I shook my head. "The Feds aren't going to wait. Soon they will take another look at Geoffrey's computer files. They'll find you, just as I did. And Neil? Take it from one who knows, you won't do well in prison."

He leaned back and pulled at the corner of his mouth with his eyeglasses, à la William Buckley. "There's no point in negotiating your fee, is there? No. Ah well, there is something almost sensuous about shrugging off the difference between ninety and a hundred million dollars."

He put the glasses back on and read the note. "Nassau? Not a problem. The funds will be there in a matter of hours. What are the names on the accounts?"

"They're numbered. No names necessary."

"For my own edification, then."

"The first is the Jason Stafford, Junior, Irrevocable Trust. For my son. I'll be the executor."

"Why not ask for more? You have me by the short hairs. Why not a third? Half?"

The little fund I had set up for the Kid might last another year or two at the rate we were burning through it. School, doctors, and Heather came to more than one hundred and fifty thousand a year. Five million invested in a mix of high-grade bonds would generate that much with a small cushion. Enough to keep the wolves at bay.

"It's all he needs," I said.

"And the second account?"

I grinned. "That's for me."

He stood up and brushed imaginary dust off of his perfectly creased trousers. I had just blackmailed him and turned his life upside down and not a bead of sweat was showing.

"Forgive me if I don't shake your hand," he said.

I stood as well. "If the money is not there, Neil—"

He cut me off. "Jason, no matter what my other qualities, I am a man of my word. The money will be there. Excuse me, but I must run. This will all take some explaining when I get home."

After he left, I turned off the mini-recorder in my pocket. A little insurance policy.

**29**

I WALKED OUT the front doors of Weld Securities for the last time and hailed a cab to La Guardia. My mind was racing ahead of me. I tried to keep Roger's advice in mind—one step at a time.

I had nothing to check and my only carry-on was a briefcase with a fresh shirt and underwear, toothbrush, and razor. And the Matchbox car I had found the previous afternoon. No matter how things turned out, I didn't plan on staying in Louisiana any longer than necessary.

There was just enough time before the flight for one long-overdue phone call.

"Wanda?" I didn't have the guts to call her Skeli—yet. "It's Jason."

"Believe it or not, I recognized your voice." She managed to sound both amused and disinterested.

"I've been meaning to call. There were some things I had to take care of. There still are, but . . ." I trailed off. All the speeches I had practiced in my head over the previous twenty-four hours were fighting for primacy, leaving me with nothing to say.

She didn't hang up. I took that as encouragement.

I cleared my throat.

"Sorry." I did not want to be misunderstood. "I mean, I'm sorry for coughing in your ear." Which pretty much guaranteed that I would be misunderstood. "I'm sorry about the other night. Too." I felt like the guy who avoided hitting the squirrel by driving off the bridge. "Especially."

Damn. Every man in the bar the other night—including the one I had slugged—would have said something by this time. "Hey, don't worry about it." Or, "Enough said. Let's move on." I would have bought a round and it would be over. Almost forgotten. The subject of a painful joke six months down the road and nothing more.

She gave me silence.

"I'm on my way down to Louisiana. I'd like to see you when I get back." There it was—a simple, straightforward declaration. She couldn't avoid responding to it.

"You're going down to see Jason?"

"To bring him back. I hope."

The Saint Paddy's Day parade could have passed by in the time it took her to answer.

"Well," she finally said. "Good luck."

I almost thought she said, "Good-bye."

"Listen, I'm sorry. I would love to undo that whole day if I could. Please, Skeli. Let me call you."

"Why?"

There it was. She was asking me for something. Not exactly commitment, but intent. The ball was in my court. Where I wanted it.

"I'm different without my son. I didn't know that. Now I do. I need him. Loving him makes me a better person. Or at least I'm a much worse person without him." I had no idea whether I was getting through or not. "When I brought him up here a few weeks ago, I had no idea what I was doing. I figured I was going to be a hero and save him from a life locked in the attic. But a part of me wanted to hurt Angie, too. I wanted to hurt a lot of people."

"You'd lost two years of your life. That would leave most people angry."

Maybe I was getting through. At least she hadn't slammed down the phone.

"But I'm learning something from him. Something about starting again. I know I'm better for him right now than his mother or his grandmother or anyone else in the world and it's right that he should be here with me. Even if he barely acknowledges my existence. Because I also know he's right for me as well."

There was another long silence. I still hadn't managed to say the most important things.

"And I think you're right for me, too. I like myself a lot better when we're together. I want a chance to be right for you."

The Macy's Thanksgiving Day Parade went by.

"All right. Call me when you're back."

Another link in the steel chain around my chest dropped away. Breathing was easier. My heart stopped trying to force its way out of my chest.

"Thank you, Skeli."

"For what?"

"A second chance."

"Yeah, well, try not to get in any more fistfights between now and then, okay?"

NOLA EXOTIC CAR RENTALS met me at the baggage area. The young black man was wearing a three-button suit, starched white shirt, and black tie. He could have passed for an undertaker.

The BMW Z4 was sitting in the curb lane out front—it matched the new blue Matchbox in my pocket. Finding the new toy and lining up the rental had taken an hour's worth of phone calls the day before.

The stern-faced young man checked me out on the car, demonstrating the controls, the shift, the music system, the environmental controls, the retractable hardtop.

"Show me how the car seat works," I said.

He smiled. Then he opened the small trunk and returned with a block of molded plastic. It looked like the booster seat at a Denny's.

"That's it? My son is kind of on the small side."

"You don't want a baby seat," he answered.

I didn't argue. I hoped the Kid was tall enough to see out the window.

I slid into the driver's seat. It felt like it had been sculpted for me. There was a half-liter of designer water, a tiny gold box holding a single Godiva truffle, and a box of tissues in a mirrored container. I felt like I was checking into a four-star hotel.

The car was a dream. It handled exactly the same at ninety-five as it did at forty-five. There was no sensation of speed, just an almost liquid feeling of flow.

A magnificent, dust-in-the-air sunset was getting started as I drove down Main Street. Dark purple jellyfish clouds were backlit with pink and pale-orange, each cloud hanging in an iridescent sky like Lando Calrissian's Cloud City. I was in an alien world. All the rules were different.

I made the turn onto Hoptree and pulled into the driveway.

The house looked deserted. The curtains were all drawn and not a light on anywhere. Angie and the Kid could be hiding anywhere. Mamma could be up in Lafayette with Tino. TeePaul's family were all down in Morgan City. I could spend a month driving around southwestern Louisiana looking for my son. But I had to start somewhere, and the first place Angie would run would be home.

I knocked and called for Angie, then Mamma. I rattled the knob. No one locks their door in Beauville, Louisiana, if they're at home. Half the time they don't lock up if they're out. The door was locked.

I thought through my options. Back up to Lafayette? To Tino's? I could be there in half an hour. Forty minutes, if I kept to the speed limit.

I knocked once more. Still no answer. I turned and started down the wide, wooden steps. Out of the corner of my eye, I saw it—a curtain flickered.

This time I banged on the door. I hammered it with both fists. "Mamma? Open the damn door! Open it or I'll kick it in."

I counted to ten—slowly. Then I kicked the door. It always looks easy on the cop shows. The door didn't budge. My foot hurt.

But it was enough. Mamma started howling.

"Don't you kick my house, young man! I told you if you was to come around here again, I'd be calling Sheriff Thibodeaux on you. Now you git! I got my phone. I am calling."

"Mamma!" Who did she think she was talking to? "Mamma! It's Jason. Open the goddamn door!"

"I know your family, TeePaul. You can't come around here scaring an old woman. You get yourself gone, boy, or I am getting the law on you."

I did not want her calling the police—even to report a case of mistaken identity. The police would only slow things down and muddy the waters. I turned around and noisily clumped down the front steps. When I reached the bottom, I stopped and sat down. And waited. It took only a few minutes.

I heard the bolt turn, and a moment later the door cracked open.

"Jason?" The door opened wider. "Is that you? What in the Lord's name are you doing sitting on my front steps?"

I stood up. "Where's Angie, Mamma? Where's my boy?"

I thought I spoke quietly, but the anger escaped anyway. She took a defensive step back.

"Oh, you don't know, Jason. Things are not good for my little baby girl right now. That man is pure evil. You know my feelings on divorce—I never divorced my husband, no matter what that man did. It was the way I was raised."

I wanted to shake it out of her.

"But I can tell you, I am so glad she is rid of him. He comes storming around looking for her and I just send him on his way. She will have nothing to do with you, I tell him. But does he listen?"

"Mamma, where's the boy? Where's Jason?"

She backed up again—guarding the door.

"He's here, isn't he?" I charged up the steps.

Mamma backed through into her parlor and made a less-than-earnest effort at keeping me out. "I will surely tell Angie you were by to see her when she gets back. She is visiting with her brother up to Lafayette."

I brushed past her and started for the stairs. She was still talking.

"Angie always goes to her brother when she's feeling blue. He finds some way to make her smile. It touches me that they are so good for each other. I wouldn't go up there, Jason."

I was already up there and headed for the front room. The latch was down. I wanted very badly to punch someone. At that point, almost anyone would do.

The door rattled when I knocked. There was no answer.

"Kid? It's Jason. It's time to go home, son."

I unlocked the door and pushed it open. The Kid was sitting in the middle of the floor. Three Matchbox cars were lined up in front of him. He was humming softly.

"Kid?" I dropped down to my haunches. I still towered over him. "Kid?"

I dreaded the possible—or probable—explosion if I touched him.

The hum was a single note, waning and waxing, but never changing pitch, almost meditative, but with an edge. Like trying to chant "Om" when you're really pissed off about something. A sound like a wasps' nest in the wall.

"Kid. I got you a new car." No reaction. I set the miniature BMW down on the rug.

The Kid growled. "Nnnnnrrrgggghhh." Then he settled back into the hum again.

I waited. Some perverse part of my brain was begging me to check my watch, but I knew time didn't matter. I refused to move first.

Finally. The Kid reached over, picked up the car, and set it down at the end of the line of other cars.

It looked right there.

I waited some more.

"Kid? It's time to go. Mrs. Carter says I have to get you back to school. I got us a special car today. The same as your new car there. The BMW Z4. Blue." I didn't bother to mention that it cost—with taxes, fees, mileage, and gasoline—about a thousand dollars a day. But if it worked, it was worth it. Besides, we could afford it.

The humming stopped.

I held the back of my hand out to him. He bent forward and sniffed.

An eternity later, he held out his hand to me. I sniffed it. His arm dropped and he began to collect his cars one by one and put them in the pockets of his blue shorts. He stood up, his knees as stiff as my father's on a February morning, but his hips so loose as to seem double-jointed. His fingers curled and he began tapping the thirteen-beat progression. He was stressed—severely stressed—but he was fighting for control. I let him take his time. He grunted loudly and turned to me.

Across his left cheek, hidden from me until then by the angle of his head and the dimness of the light, was the unmistakable bruised print of an open hand.

The man who'd just been released from prison would have lost it. He would have jumped up and gone looking for someone to hurt.

"Your Grand-mamma get you your cereal this morning?" I made my voice light.

He grunted in three syllables.

"You were Crunchatized?" I forced a smile. It didn't matter, he never responded to a smile. He didn't know what it meant.

"Good. Then we are out of here, bud. We'll get you something to eat on the road."

He gave a disgusted look.

"No," I said. "We'll stop at a diner."

I let him walk out first. I still didn't trust him above me on a flight of stairs.

Mamma had stopped talking. She was yelling. The sound was punctuated with repeated thumps on the front door. I ran down the stairs and cut in front of the Kid just as the door slammed back and bounced against the wall. There was a spray of wood splinters and brass fittings. Mamma had stopped yelling. She was screaming.

TeePaul pushed the broken door and walked in. He ignored Mamma and her unintelligible shrill squawks. He looked at me briefly and dismissively. He spoke to the Kid.

"Hey, Boo. You come with me now, boy. We're going to see your Mamma. I hear she's up at Lafayette with her sissy brother."

The Kid began to moan, his eyes unfocused, and his neck and shoulders began to twist and turn as though his whole upper body ached in one huge cramp.

"You're not taking my son anywhere," I said. "And from what Mamma tells me, Angie doesn't want you around."

"Oh, she'll see me. If I got that boy with me, she'll see me." He grinned at me, making it a challenge.

I wanted to hit him. Beat him into dust. I didn't know that I could do it, but I wanted to try. The old Jason wanted to try.

Mamma was sobbing into a lacy handkerchief.

"This would be a good time to call the sheriff, Mamma," I said.

She looked amazed, then ran for the phone.

TeePaul and I locked eyes, each waiting for the other to make the next move.

Mamma dialed. TeePaul's jaw clenched.

"That's enough of that, old woman."

She spoke into the phone. "This here is Mrs. Oubre over on Hoptree. There is an intruder in my house. Yes. I'm very frightened."

TeePaul snickered.

She hung up.

We all stood in an awkward tableau; the only sound was the Kid's soft moan.

TeePaul licked his lips—a tell—and tried one last bluff.

"Hey there, Mr. Wall Street Man. Always doing deals, right? I got a deal for you. You leave and I don't hurt you. The boy stays. That's the best offer you gonna get."

I wanted to throw that first punch. To try to take him down before he had a chance. Then I realized that was exactly what he wanted me to do.

I thought of leaving with my son. Our life in New York. I thought of Skeli. I relaxed and called the bluff.

"I'm leaving now, TeePaul. Jason is coming with me. You will not try to stop us. If you try, I will kill you. You will not touch him. If you try, I will kill you."

I thought of Angie—the catalyst of her own destruction, forever running to leap over the nearest cliff. Still, she deserved better than this man.

"And if you ever lay a hand on Angie again, I will know. I will hear of it and I will find you. And I will kill you. Have I made myself clear?"

"You think I'm afraid of you? You threaten me and I'm supposed to jump? That right?"

"I'm not threatening you, TeePaul. I'm just telling you how it's going to be."

He tried the stare again, but he didn't have the hand. A siren sounded a few blocks away.

"You'd best go," I said.

He turned and stomped out the door, the shreds of his cowboy dignity keeping him from running until he hit the bottom step.

I waited until the big pickup was roaring down Hoptree.

"Mamma, the boy and I are going. You come visit sometime, all right?"

She nodded and looked away.

The Kid was amazing. His fingers were flying, tapping out his odd rhythm, his eyes were blank, focused on some point beyond the horizon, and deep in the back of his throat there was the sound of an almost silent growl. But he was maintaining. He was holding himself together.

"You're doing great, son. We're all safe now. It's time for us to go. Say good-bye to your Grand-mamma, Kid."

His body gave one last shake. Then he turned and very politely said, "Good-bye, Grand-mamma."

He stepped out the door and I followed. He rocked slightly as he walked, side to side, like a toddler. I walked past him and held open the door of the Z4. The kid's eyes were gleaming.

"Climb in. Hop onto that seat."

He looked at the booster seat and shook his head.

If I had to pick him up, I risked a bite.

"Listen, I got you this seat special. Special! I told the man that my son needed to see out the window like a big person. He didn't want to give it to me! They don't give them to just anybody. You have to be special. Christ, Kid, I don't know anyone more special than you. I told him you wouldn't ride in the car without it."

The Kid sighed as though the whole responsibility for our continued relationship rested on his shoulders and humoring me in this was only one of the dozens of ways he sought to accommodate his idiot of a father. Then he climbed up onto the seat and flopped back, arms spread wide, ready for the crucifixion of the seat belt.

"Have I ever mentioned that you seem to have inherited some of your mother's more dramatic ways of expressing herself?" I snapped him in and closed the door.

He took the toy out of his pocket and held it in both hands. "The Z4 350 has a straight six with Twin Turbo and direct High Precision fuel injection with a maximum output of 300 hp at 5,800 rpms. . . ."

For the first half-hour, the Kid babbled happily about his new car. The booster gave him just enough lift to see over the door, but he ignored the view. The toy was more real to him than the rental; the world inside his head more interesting than the sights along the way.

I thought about having to face a long trek through the airport with him—again. The last time we had barely known each other. He must have been terrified. In hindsight, it was a small miracle that it had gone as smoothly as it did. We would certainly be able to do better this time around.

The closer we got, the less sure I became.

"So, Kid. I was thinking maybe you might want to drive all the way home. Take our time. Enjoy seeing a little of the country."

I took his silence for acquiescence.

I made a quick call.

"Skeli?"

"Jason! How's it going? How's Jason?"

"We're both doing much better. In the car and on our way."

"Already? You'll be back tonight?"

"Well, no, actually. We've decided to drive. It'll take us a few days."

"Hmm. Any problems?"

"No. The Kid's not a great flier."

"I meant, any problems getting him?"

"Ah. No," I said proudly. "I didn't hit anyone."

"Well done." Her voice became as sultry as a Louisiana night. "Get back here soon."

"I'll call tonight. From wherever." I rang off.

The last blood-red aura of the setting sun filled the rearview mirror. Already, the road ahead of us was fully dark.

"How about we pick up 59 to Chattanooga and then cut over and drive up through the Smoky Mountains? We'll get on Skyline Drive and take it all the way up to 66?"

The Kid looked over at me as though I had suddenly started barking or speaking in Urdu.

"It's faster up 81. I've got a pretty girl waiting for me, but all you've got is Heather, so I'll leave it up to you. It's your day. You decide."

He turned his head away and watched the flickering reflections of headlights in the side-view mirror.

"Fair enough," I said. "We take the scenic route, but if we get bored we cut over and pick up the highway."

His head rested on the seat—his eyes closed.

"There's this bakery I've got to take you to. In College Point—by Pop's place. The best black-and-white cookies in New York. You won't believe how good they are."

He was asleep.

"I know, I know. You don't like chocolate. No problem. That's the cool thing about sharing black-and-white cookies. You get the white half. I'll take the black."

He might have smiled. It was hard to tell in the light from the dash.